SUGARMILK FALLS

Ilona van Mil was born in the Netherlands, grew up in Canada and now lives in the UK where she teaches law at the University of Essex. *Sugarmilk Falls* is her first novel and was awarded the Crime Writers' Association Debut Dagger in 2002.

ILONA VAN MIL

SUGARMILK FALLS

PICADOR

First published 2005 by Picador

First published in paperback 2006 by Picador
an imprint of Pan Macmillan Ltd
Pan Macmillan, 20 New Wharf Road, London N1 9RR
Basingstoke and Oxford
Associated companies throughout the world
www.panmacmillan.com

ISBN-13: 978-0330-41939-0
ISBN-10: 0-330-41939-0

1 3 5 7 9 8 6 4 2

A CIP catalogue record for this book is available from
the British Library.

Typeset by IntypeLibra, London
Printed and bound in Great Britain by
Mackays of Chatham plc, Chatham, Kent

To John Dunning
B.Sc., M.B., Ch.B., F.R.C.S. (C/Th.) Ed.

PROLOGUE

Sugarmilk Falls, le 13 février 1993

Tonight I am invited to the Armand place, the warm wooden house with all its rambling comforts built at the foot of the vast maple hills. Lucien Armand is insistent. Despite the heavy snow quite a few are expected, he says. They'll be open with me, share with me their recollections about what happened here, though the priest and one or two others have refused to go – generally they all avoid remembering that terrible time. Then he raises his eyebrow at me and makes a point of saying that it's give and take round here when it comes to story telling.

The people are friendly enough, though I suspect they watch me. Do they mistrust my motives? Or is it just that the memories are painful? Of course memory distorts the truth. Like witness statements in the police files I have read, it shifts and shapes the facts to suit the circumstances in which they are remembered. The facts themselves become elusive.

*

When I first arrived I went over to see the Armands. I tasted Lucien's maple syrup, Claudine's maple-flavoured baking, before choosing my own maple trees. The old sugar-maker and his wife are hospitable and welcoming, perhaps a little anxious. But I am a stranger here.

'More than likely the talking will continue the whole night through to dawn,' he warns me now. 'The way these things go isn't always straightforward and a lot of water's gone over the falls since everything happened. Once we get started it's impossible to say where it will end.'

They are uneasy about my interest, though they seem to want me to understand. Can the facts be sifted from the disorder of their memories? Or will there be just versions of the truth moulded to take account of my particular probing at this particular time? And what will I do with the information? Does anyone even know the whole truth?

I'm ready to listen for as long as it takes, I tell him.

'A bientôt,' and he smiles.

PART ONE

I

Écoutez, Lucien said to the stranger. Listen. You can hear the snowflakes brushing against the windows. Outside the north wind is shifting softly in the branches. Some of us here still call him Keewatin. Maybe you noticed too how the dreamed ones enter and settle down in the corners of the room? They think it will all be out in the open at last.

Come closer. He touched her arm with his bony hand. Sit among us – here, in this chair by the fire. Take this knife, these small pieces of wood, and work with us while we talk. Just watch how I do it – it's easy – you'll soon get the idea. Eh bien. Tonight we will speak about the things that happened in this place, it must be twenty years ago now. I expect you know already – you say you've read the police files. Anyway, it was in all the newspapers at the time. But they'd only interviewed those who said it all began when Grand'mère Osweken, the worse for moonshine, lost the prime rock-maple forest in a crap game. I guess they had their reasons for not telling the whole story. Don't get me wrong, now – it happened like they said, but there is a lot more to it.

How that old Indian came to own the sugar bush is

still argued about these winter nights as we whittle sap spiles – they only cost a nickel at the store but here we don't buy anything we can make. In her youth, it's true, she'd struck lucky in the Chibougamau gold find, far to the north of the Sugarmilk country. Unusual for a woman to know about prospecting, but then she was a shaman. Some say her menfolk used to disappear at regular intervals to work her stake. According to Sergeant Martello they were regularly put in jail. Me? I reckon the vein gave out long ago. The only gold I ever saw her with came in a bottle. But she always was one hell of a crap shooter, that Grand'mère, and the general view is she won or bought or was handed down the maple woods long before anyone can remember. Of course the Indians say the bush has always been theirs, part of their ancestral lands. And I guess you've heard about the Sugarmilk land claims that are still going on. All that came later and nobody will know for sure who owns what until they're settled. But the way we saw it back then, and that's what matters, was that most all the Sugarmilk country was owned by a sodden Ojibwa squaw.

It's the kind of story that doesn't need fancy touches, so I'll just tell it how it was. Then you can make up your own mind about what really happened here. And maybe you'll agree that after all this time it's better not to mess with what's been buried.

*

It isn't often mentioned now that it all goes back to Miss Marina Grochowska. She was the new schoolteacher hereabouts at the time and she failed little Bobby Osweken in an arithmetic test – though his answers were right enough. A small thing to make such big sparks. Anyway, she got upset by something he'd done and soon she was making her way to the clearing beside the river above the falls. We've all gone up there along the old portage and thought we were alone, though Zack Guillem somehow always seemed to know. Zack told me plenty before he disappeared that time.

No one knows where Zachariah Guillem came from, only that it was back from the war. I knew him in the war. He was the one who got us out when we were shot down that winter in the mountains of France. Only three of us made it, Zack and Joe and me. How we did it, what we did, has not been talked about since and we split up as soon as we could. Then a few years later he just turned up here with his bundles of pelts, one of the crowd of trappers that took over the town each spring. Those days the fur was everywhere, beaver piled high on the rooming-house verandas, mink, marten, raccoon, fox, cascading down the clapboard walls. Mostly these men just made their deals at the Hudson's Bay store, got drunk for a week and went back to their traplines that always seemed farther north than they'd remembered.

That year the sap-running winds, rowdy with homecoming Canada geese, blew soft and steady. The wooded hillsides thrummed with the strong spring pulse. Sunlight sparked off a million droplets trembling like diamonds on the tips of a million spiles, sometimes as many as ten to a tree, filling bucket after bucket after bucket with clear sweet water. The honeycombed snow refracted rainbows. Makeshift camps jangled with horses, laughter, conversation. Under blackened cauldrons the fires burned like rubies, and pearly steam, heady with the boiling sap, coiled through the web of branches. Zack Guillem was caught up by the long sweetening and he just stayed on. With the wood smoke sting in his eyes and the harsh sweet maple taste in his mouth, his pockets fat with new green dollars, he was seduced by the great glacial valley of the Sugarmilk River, dressed up as she was like a rich widow in all her springtime furs and jewels. He worked where he could, guiding city-bred deer-hunters through her quaking muskeg swamps or fire-ranging along the water trails that linked her three hundred and eighty named lakes.

And for a long time he was content, until Miss Grochowska arrived with her old-world sophistication and something he could not put into words, an uneasiness that evoked best-forgotten things – his Métis friend, Joe Naiscoot, whose traps along the Wanapitei failed, who took to stealing for a living and died in prison, of a heart attack they said. And Rachelle Osweken, coming up fifteen, raped, they said by a lumber gang. And the war. Sometimes Zack would look at Grand'mère and the same feeling came over him. Her eyes were beaver dark. Her face was creased and lined like the intricate river routes on an old prospectors' map. He'd remember that when he first came to the Sugarmilk country, wolves sang under the northern lights.

*

But these things happened long ago. There are no trappers now, in the spring. The sugaring is a tourist attraction, like the colours of the leaves in the fall. When the land claims are finally settled and the chainsaws close in, these too will be gone. Rachelle later took up with a car factory worker and moved south. No one hears from her anymore. As for

Miss Grochowska, well, you've seen the photographs. You've read the files, you say. There are stories that she went out west but they can't be true after what happened here.

That's good. You're really getting the hang of it. It's staghorn sumac – don't confuse it with the poison kind – much better than cedar for making spiles. It's a pretty wood – hard, with a large pithy middle. We carve away all winter but come the sweet-water weather there are never enough. Our collecting buckets too are made of wood. None of that tin or plastic for us. You can always tell if the sap's been handled carefully. We sugar out in the open, over wood fires. Feux d'enfer we call them, the fires of hell. You won't find any of those newfangled evaporators round here. Some maple stands nowadays are nothing but a tangle of tubes, from the trees straight into the machinery. But here we'll have nothing to do with suction pumping or reverse osmosis, whatever they say about increased yields. That technological stuff is okay for the hotshot sucreries of Beauce County. Sugarmilk syrup might be harder to turn out, but the maple connoisseurs all agree it sets the standard to judge the others by.

Time was we all went round on snowshoes tapping each tree by hand, real back-twisting work. I can remember when the Indians used hatchets – such skill they had to make those perfect cuts. We use power drills now. We let our trees mature at least forty years before they're worked. We don't suck them dry. The Ojibwa believe the sap is the blood of the forest Manitou, his gift to them. No such thing as owning a maple lot. In the old days they sugared off with hot stones thrown into buckets made from hollowed-out logs. The world must have turned more slowly then. It takes near fifty gallons of sap and a stack of wood as big as a man to make just one gallon of good maple syrup.

You begin to think winter is going to last forever but then you come across fresh raccoon tracks in the snow. The first crow gabbles in the branches. We see to our pails and Father Souris blesses the maple groves. Maybe you've already talked with Father Souris? No? He'll give the usual version of what happened here, though he knows the facts well enough. Him and Sergeant Martello both. They're thick as thieves. I've heard tell that Sergeant Martello brews the communion wine from the grapes he has sent up from Niagara. It's probably true. Between freeze-up and snow-melt, when bush plane is the only way in or out of the valley, those two are the law hereabouts, temporal and divine. And that's how it was twenty years ago when it happened.

Lucien paused a moment to watch the stranger whittle spiles. She looked up at him and smiled. Then he settled deep into his chair and began . . .

2

Mathieu Souris felt again the tickle of pleasure when the new doors of his garage opened automatically to receive his car. It was an agreeably sinful tickle, too. They'd been expensive, the first of their kind in the entire region. He smiled the prayer of gratitude at the plastic Virgin mounted on the dashboard by means of a rubber suction cup – a pretty Virgin, he thought, in her white dress and blue veil and with her uncanny resemblance to Marina Grochowska.

All day he had been round the sugar camps to bless the spring harvest. All week the party lines had hummed, 'Sap's running . . . Sap's running strong . . .' whenever he'd lifted the telephone receiver to make a call. He prayed daily that he might be vouchsafed a private number. Sugarmilk phone conversations were very public affairs. But he did his own share of listening in on the party line. That's how he kept his sermons topical. That's how he first found out about the schoolteacher and that bushwhacker Guillem.

'I just don't know what to think,' the telephone cackled one summer morning. 'There they were. Well. I guess she's no better than she should be. What's she doing here, anyway? Damned commie DP. Send them all back where they belong.' Other voices joined in the censure and arrived, by a convoluted route that included the declining moral standards of the valley, at a general condemnation of foreigners, half breeds and Indians, 'those filthy Oswekens' in particular, about whom something had to be done and fast.

Father Souris had a private word with Miss Grochowska. 'Why, Mathieu,' she replied, 'have you been listening in to the gossip?'

He blushed. 'We are all sinners, Marina.'

'I appreciate your concern,' she said frostily.

Senior Constable Martello too made a point of greeting the schoolteacher on Main Street. 'If anyone's been bothering you, ma'am, we can deal with him. That's what we're here for.'

'There is only one of you, Frank.'

*

Oui, the party lines continued their insinuations throughout that summer and fall. Father Souris preached at length about tolerance and the casting of stones. Miss Grochowska tested her first-graders' understanding of arithmetic. The priest and the schoolteacher met, as they had since the sap run, in the clearing by the waterfall.

*

Beside them the Sugarmilk River cascaded into the forest. Ochre leaves flurried into the glittering eddies. Flinty branches swayed across the cobalt sky and the cold wind hissed through twisted jack pines, primeval as malachite.

Miss Grochowska shivered as Father Souris placed his arm around her shoulder.

'Marina?' he prompted gently.

Her hand churned in the white water surging over the rocks, shattering in their faces like splinters of ice. 'It was a stupid and unforgivable thing to do, Matt.' Brittle emotion laboured in her voice as she explained. Bobby Osweken's six-year-old brain had encompassed the concept of numbers and understood precisely the quantities of objects indicated by the symbols. He had complied with her instructions; she could not fault his grasp of the principles. 'Draw whatever you want,' she had encouraged her class. Miss Grochowska considered it essential to first construct the intellectual trellis around which sprouting imaginations would twine. She was careful not to inhibit either, at this early vulnerable stage, by confining the expanding universe of mathematics between dusty clichés such as fruit and domestic animals. To tell the truth, she said with a humourless laugh, the sheaf of test papers included far more pictures of dogs and apples than she'd hoped to see. She had needed to remind herself that six-year-old minds approach everything with the same profound wonder.

Father Souris smiled, but Miss Grochowska blinked back tears. At the end of the allotted time Bobby handed in his childish military drawings: one bomb, two helmets, three machine guns, four tanks, five submarines and so on. Each armament was decorated with black and red swastikas. He had drawn nine rifles aimed at ten stick people wearing bright yellow stars. Technically his answers were correct, but for his innocent chafing of old deep wounds she deducted marks. Bobby Osweken's eager face crumpled with incomprehension and Miss Grochowska bled.

'He doesn't mean anything,' Father Souris told her, 'it's just those war comic books the kids buy at the store. You shouldn't let it bother you.'

Marina Grochowska shook the water from her hand and blew on icicle fingers. On the inside of her arm, above the wrist, the tattooed numbers flashed darkly. 'You were over there, Matt. You saw. How can you say that to me?'

*

After Toussaint Mass the presbytery telephone rang three times – the call was for Father Souris. 'Can you come over, please, Matt?' Miss Grochowska sounded distressed. Sugarmilk ears were suddenly alert and Sugarmilk tongues clicked. He drove the short distance across town and parked in front of her trim little house. Crude red swastikas had been daubed on the white clapboard walls and blue front door.

'A Halloween trick, Matt?'

'Do you know who might have done it?'

'I haven't seen Bobby since he failed the test, but you know what these Oswekens are like, always off to set traps or bait fishing lines, or do whatever they feel like doing.'

Senior Constable Martello investigated. 'Has Bobby Osweken been to school this week? Have you seen Zack Guillem around this week? Or Grand'mère?'

Winter hardened and the incidents continued. Snowfalls brought fresh swastikas marked out on Miss Grochowska's lawn. Yellow stars were chalked on the blackboard when she arrived in her classroom in the morning.

In February, at the beginning of Lent, all the incidents stopped. There seemed to be no explanation. The policeman scratched his ears. Father Souris's garage opened and closed its doors. The dashboard Virgin trembled on her rubber mount and the party lines continued to shriek, 'Disgrace! That DP woman! That no-good Guillem! Those vile Oswekens! Something's gotta be done to clean up the valley!'

*

Lucien hesitated. His eyes searched the faces in the room and settled again on the stranger.

3

'Can't you shut that Lucien Armand up, Frank? Arrest him for something – verbal squits – before he goes too far?' Mathieu Souris could feel the tightness of his smile. Lately he'd begun to feel that his old friend the sergeant could see right through him. He hoped he did not sound anxious now, though the palms of his hands were moist as he transferred the telephone to his other ear.

'You know they'll all be round at his place tonight, including that snake in the grass who's been snooping everywhere since fall . . .' Damn it, he thought, he shouldn't have let that slip out. His chewed fingernails drummed on the desk and he could feel one leg quiver as he listened.

He'd been sitting there a long time, he realized, wondering whether or not to do something, and if he did, what it ought to be. Next Sunday's sermon lay unfinished in front of him, no longer legible in the vanishing light. The afternoon had passed before he finally picked up the telephone – thank God he no longer had to endure the party line – to have what was going to be just a light-hearted talk with Frank Martello, mostly about other things. The corners of the room were now in deep shadow. The snow had eased. Cold blue moonbeams flitted across the bare floorboards nearly to his desk. Outside the bare window, the half-buried pedestal of the garden sundial cast intermittent shadows in the moonlight, measuring the time-gaps between the clouds.

'It must be more than twenty years since I last saw them, Frank. I'm not even sure where they are, or whether I ever had them . . . I'll have to call you back – give me an hour.' He put down the telephone and leaned back in the chair, chewing his lower lip. The call had not gone as he'd hoped. He'd wanted a casual noncommittal conversation about things in general, one which would put his mind to rest without him having to say specifically what was worrying him. Instead the wily old policeman had homed in on the problem straight away. Mathieu Souris sighed deeply. He was going to be on his own, he realized. The phone call had confirmed this much. No one could help him decide what he should do next. Fortunately he'd tried to sound amused by the whole thing, a little bored rather than concerned. And he hadn't been entirely honest with Sergeant Martello. He knew exactly where the papers were.

Father Souris switched on his desk lamp, checked the time on his wristwatch, then on his new clock. It sat on his desk, next to the half-written sermon, where he could look at it often – a black plastic case, a circle of black numbers on a round white face and the usual hands pointing out the passing of time. The bright red second hand, however, instead of measuring out the minutes by a series of regular beats, moved seamlessly. The new clock was atomic. It was said to be accurate to one second in a million years. He altered the time on his watch to read the true time; he did this once every day.

Atomic time. The idea suddenly lit up in his brain, gold this time, but it might just as easily have been red or blue or green. It could do this, switch itself on from out of nowhere with a nearly audible click, and glow for a while, neon-bright, before fading into the general hum in his head. He always found the experience exhilarating. Time, comfortingly, even tediously, familiar coupled with atomic, ultra-modern, ultra-dangerous, but still measurable. It was a mind-bending union that made him feel a lot more at home in the universe.

Mathieu Souris tried hard to be a modern parish priest who could look scientific advances squarely in the eye, internalize them, include them in the vision of the divine purpose he expounded to his congregation. He'd never been one to say he thought only God could do things like that, or let a bit of inconvenient dogma get in the way of the latest discovery. 'The world is moving on,' he once said to Marina Grochowska, 'I'll be around in the third millennium.'

She had looked levelly at him. 'You'll never get promotion, Matt. They'll leave you here in charge of St Augustine's for the rest of your life.'

He had not scoffed, and she had been right. The millennium was fast approaching now and he was still the solitary incumbent of this most far-flung of parishes. Advancement not only never came his way but he'd been called more than once to make the long, difficult journey to explain himself to the Archbishop. Though not recently. And back then, in the heady days after Vatican Two, there had been plenty of others in the same mould, the city priests who celebrated the newly vernacular sacrament with loaves of Christie's white sliced bread, still in its wrapper, and bottles of Bright's red table wine. Or, more worryingly, the politicized ones who joined the New Left. Some of them had gotten out altogether, married, raised families . . .

Not Father Souris, however. Though life on the outside sometimes beckoned, almost irresistibly once, he'd gone no further publicly than to try the loaf-and-bottle approach at High Mass. It had not been a success here in remote, traditional Sugarmilk Falls. The bread, an aromatic, crusty loaf specially baked by his housekeeper, and the wine, one of Frank Martello's best, had looked out of place on the altar, turned around to face the congregation. 'Holy! Holy! Holy!' the choir sang while he struggled with the corkscrew. The sniggering altar boys rang the Sanctus bells until the cork finally popped out, and the congregation muttered with displeasure. He'd brazened it out and continued to play the progressive, informed, in-control clergyman fit for the modern age. But somewhere along the way sin had ceased to matter much. It was a gentle scouring, like grains of sand on the wind, that had gone unnoticed while his mind tackled more interesting, more novel concepts such as pulsating atoms.

He'd been intrigued when he read in a popular science magazine about time synchronized with an atomic signal, and bought himself an electric clock radio. It had seemed a good substitute; atomic time was going to be broadcast over the airwaves. He'd tried imagining the soft silvery caesium atoms whose vibrations told the most accurate time in the world, and wondered about the spaces between the pulses. Is this where time stood still? Is this where life could change direction? Now the clock radio looked old-fashioned with its pale green electric-filament numbers, some of which no longer worked. It still stood on the middle shelf of the bookcase, next to the volumes on gestalt psychology, where Marina had moved it, nearly thrown it, from the table beside the bed.

'Oh, you and your infernal gadgets!' she had whispered, her face white. She did not like to be shocked from her sleep by disembodied voices. He should have realized that.

Marina. He tried not to think of her nowadays and usually didn't. It had not been so easy in the beginning, especially right after it happened. Tonight, however, he saw her in his mind more clearly than for years, sitting in the chair in the corner of the room just like she used to, away from the window, in the shadows just beyond the reach of the moonlight. He closed his eyes and rubbed his forehead with his fists. 'Damn that Lucien,' he thought. 'Why can't he leave things alone!'

Mathieu's attention returned to the chair. She used to sit there when she came to see him, cross her legs and light a cigarette. Sometimes she wore trousers, or, more often, a skirt that was far too short for a woman of her age, in her position. Okay maybe in the city but certainly not here in Sugarmilk Falls. Sunlight or firelight would gleam in her dark eyes and on long, dark hair falling about her shoulders.

'It was short, Mathieu. Have you forgotten?'

It had been a wide-open, starry night, he remembered. They were gazing at the heavens, into layer upon sparkling, nebulous layer of the galaxy. For him, the new thrill of looking at time itself, as if from the outside, as if you could turn it over like a star in your hand, had a touch of omnipotence. What happened, he had wondered out loud, where one pulsating atom of time collided with the next? Was there a spark, a moment, when time might suddenly change direction?

Marina was already familiar with the relationship between atomic pulses and mathematical precision. 'Sparks of time,' she had said.

'Sparks of time?'

'*Scintilla temporis*. A spark of time. Lawyers sometimes talk about it. It's not a new idea at all.' Even during moments of closest intimacy she could come over all schoolteachery. He'd liked that, and the Latin certainly gave an extra buzz to the science, like a prayer or a magic spell.

She brought him back to earth. 'It's a contradiction, of course. The idea confuses time and the beginning of time. Big-bang theory with its explosions, sparks, and the continuum of time without breaks.'

Atoms of time in a continuum, strung tightly together like the amber beads of the necklace she sometimes wore and then left behind. He remembered holding it up to the light and discovering the uniqueness of each red-gold bead. Some contained specks of matter, or minute winged insects caught in liquid resin a million years ago. Particles of time between wingbeats preserved in amber. He glanced at his new clock again and the old question repeated itself. Is there ever a moment between the atomic pulses when time stands imperceptibly still? A space where sin could hide?

'*What sin, Matt?*'

She had kept him standing on her doorstep. He remembered staring past her at the Viennese wall clock in her hallway, its slow brass pendulum swinging back and forth, back and forth, as the final harsh words were spoken, its silvery chimes lingering on the silence. He looked towards the corner again. Where was she now?

*

Mathieu Souris opened the top drawer of his desk and reached for the letter opener. Moving across the empty room to where the snow-bright moonlight streamed steadily through the window, he counted the floorboards from the wall and folded back the braided rag rug. He found the joins, about two feet apart, in the seventh board, and turned the blade of the letter opener in the groove of first one screw, then a second further down. They came out easily. He lifted the section out of the way and reached into the cavity. There was the old tin box, and not so very dusty. He easily opened it, looked at the contents and smiled. Everything was there, in its place, the old pair of dice, the folded documents, some a little charred, some tied with faded ribbon, the fragile string of animal teeth and claws, the bundle of bones and feathers knotted together, the braided sweetgrass. He rolled the dice in his hand, trying again to discover if they were loaded. He looked through the documents and shook his head slightly. He picked up the necklace and held it in front of his face, moving it through his fingers like prayer beads. It felt warm and light. The moon glowed on the red-gold amber flecked with the debris and flies of a million years ago.

4

Matt seemed awful edgy tonight, thought Frank Martello as he put down the telephone. But maybe he was right to be. That old sugar-maker Lucien Armand needed to have his head examined. Surely he knew that things could still turn out real bad for a lot of people, even after the trouble they'd gone to way back then. But it had all happened such a long time ago now that nobody would remember what had really taken place. And anyway there wasn't any evidence left when they'd finished. The policeman himself would be in the clear, of course. He'd made sure of that. No flies on him. When the snow melted, he hoped, double fingers crossed, the new replacement constable would arrive at last. He and Elviana could leave this godforsaken place. They'd pay off that swindler Arnie Anstalt for the reconditioned Winnebago and drive down to a long care-free retirement in Florida, thaw the ice out of their bones forever, tan themselves to leather in the sun. He'd be well out of the way, he hoped, if there were going to be any repercussions. And that, he supposed, all depended on what turned up. If anything. Maybe they'd want to talk about something else. Pretty unlikely, but you never knew.

Sergeant Martello leaned back and rubbed his large belly. Not much out of the ordinary had occurred during his time as the Sugarmilk country's law-enforcement officer. He'd come here with Elviana when he was a young constable and he was retiring as sergeant. Not a bad career, he supposed. He'd dealt with the brawls, the road accidents, the break-ins, the stealing, a fire now and again, men beating up their wives, a couple of suicides, the usual sort of thing. A lot of drunks had experienced the hospitality of his cell, there'd been a few rapes and shootings, and, of course, some trouble with the Indians, that vindictive old crow Grand'mère in particular. It was pretty much as you'd expect in a northern outpost like this. You could almost go as far as to say it was a law-abiding kind of place. Dull, even. Of course everything is relative. The trappers with their seasonal ruckus had long gone. And fortunately Sugarmilk Falls had never yet been the centre of a mining boom. Just high spirits from the lumber gangs now and again, though they'd thinned out when the cautions were put on the land.

There hadn't been many corpses in suspicious circumstances either and those that did turn up were easy enough to sort out. A couple of stiffs at the bottom of the falls. Some unexplained disappearances, but what did you expect in this rough country with its wolves, bears and fast water, its deep lakes and hidden muskegs and not many real roads to speak of? It had been a quiet life on the whole. Nothing too out of the ordinary, nothing that couldn't be quickly wrapped up, except one incident about twenty years ago that had really grabbed everybody's attention for a while. City newspapermen had turned up. Radio reporters. Even a TV news crew. And that's what they'd no doubt be chewing over tonight at the Armand place. Better to just wait and see and deal with whatever came out, which is just what he'd been trying to explain to Mathieu Souris, without much success it seemed. In the meantime . . .

Sergeant Martello reached into the drawer of his desk for a key and heaved his bulk out of the chair. He took a glass jug out of the filing cabinet, the place where movie policemen always kept their drink, and walked towards a low wooden door. He unlocked it, opened it and switched on the light. The warm rush of air filled with the heady smell of wood and grapes hit him, engulfing him as he descended the stairs. In the dim light of a single bare bulb, he surveyed the wooden barrels lying on their sides along one wall of a low, small room of the basement. A second wall was lined waist high with racks of bottles. The rest of the room was stacked to the ceiling with chopped wood, two or three layers deep. The wood-furnace rumbled next door.

He walked with difficulty around the press and the filters piled out of the way in the middle of the room. Holding the jug beneath the tap of one of the barrels he filled it with dark pungent wine. Even in the dim light it glowed a rich ruby. He raised the jug to his nose and inhaled deeply, making himself a little dizzy. He closed his eyes and tried, as usual, to picture Elviana's suggestion of black cherries or redcurrants, or as someone else had proposed once he began sharing a bottle or two, dried figs in oak. But he saw only grapes. He took a large mouthful, swished it around his teeth, and swallowed. Great, he thought. It was going to be one of the best yet. And full of . . . grapes. That's what he recognized in the taste and the smell, the dusty bushels of dark purple, almost black, bunches, their skins wrinkling, splitting and oozing juice after the nonstop drive in the back of the pickup. He could almost feel the weight of them in the taste and smell, see the juicy plumpness squirting and squelching as the press got to work. In the early days he had pressed them in the old way, removing his trousers and washing his feet before treading them to a pulp. Matt, sworn to secrecy, sometimes joined in and the two of them, a little drunk on the ends of last year's vintage, danced in the big old enamel bathtub he had adapted for the purpose, squeezing the cold pulp and skins and pips and juice between their toes. Sometimes they'd play old 78s on the wind-up gramophone, 'Sweet viiiii-olets, sweeter than all the roses . . .'

Come October he'd scan the skyline for signs of early snow. Blocked roads meant no grape delivery. It was a long way to Sugarmilk Falls from Niagara. He'd gone there once, he and Elviana, to see the miles upon miles of rectilinear vineyards stretching as far as you could see into the flat horizon. They'd made a detour to visit the falls, one of the wonders of the world he'd been told. He had gone right up close, leaning over the sturdy iron railing next to where the water plunges over the edge. Magnificent, he thought, but it was all a little tame, despite the world-famous thunder, the drenching mists, the ever-present rainbow, the tales of daring in barrels and on tightropes and of Indian maidens in canoes. Elviana admired the magnolia trees, but there was too much of the resort about Niagara Falls, with its tourist traffic, motels, souvenir stores, and rock candy. The falls on the Sugarmilk River were a whole lot smaller, but seemed to him much wilder, more savage. Until, that is, you looked up the famous Horseshoe instead of down.

He and Elviana had bought tickets for a ride on the little steamer that went as near as you could safely get to the bottom of the falls, and that had seemed dangerous enough. As they stood on the reeling deck in their black and yellow oilskins, holding tightly to the handrail, he saw, as he peered through the spray at the rocks and the cataclysmic wall of water, a branch, or could it really have been an arm, briefly circle in the foaming, swirling rapids before it disappeared, sucked down again. Suddenly, he felt queasy and was glad that Elviana was looking the other way.

Constable Martello had reminded himself he was on vacation and that he'd felt seasick enough to hallucinate. Nevertheless, he casually mentioned what he'd seen to the barman when he went out later for a beer. Yes, he was told, there were sometimes a few floaters – suicides, or accidents, or even murders – often you couldn't be sure. They'd be pretty well unrecognizable when they were fished out near the whirlpool a few miles downstream, even when they were still in one piece. Running the rapids alone could tear them to pieces, and it was thought more than likely a few got stuck in the turbulence of the undertow at the base of the falls. There's no way of telling just how deep it is down there, the barman said, and you could just go round and round until the water and rocks ground you up into meatballs.

*

Sergeant Martello sipped his homemade wine and smiled to himself. Funny he should think of that tonight. He'd forgotten all about it for years. Of course, it wouldn't happen here in Sugarmilk Falls. As far as he was concerned, anyone going over the falls could count on being recovered sometime, either dead or alive.

5

Now Claudine turned to the stranger. You say you have an interest here? she asked. More than just turning over a lot of old stones? More than just renting a few of our trees at thirty dollars a throw? That scheme was my idea, and quite a good one too for just a sugar-maker's wife, eh, Lucien? Earning a living is not so easy with cautions placed on the land. We rent out Mother Nature in the meantime. Every tree tenant gets a copy of a hundred-year-old leasing deed and, when the sugaring is done, a personalized gallon can of maple syrup. No hard work required. Of course, some want to get involved – like you, perhaps? – and it has brought a few more visitors to our summer maple festival. Each one wants to touch his own tree. It's something different, a bit special, and what can be nicer than eating my famous doughnuts, as you do now, with syrup made from the sap of your own Sugarmilk tree? Maybe owning the whole sugar bush, eh? You smile, my friend.

These winter nights we get together and remember old times, but not much is said about what has been in our minds for so many years. All of us – maybe you also –

have things we hesitate to say. You have looked more than most at what went on here. You stay in this town and ask uncomfortable questions. Perhaps too much time has passed for straight answers but we've decided to give you a few of our stories. Then maybe you'll tell us why you have really come here.

*

I guess you realize by now that, however you look at it, it wasn't the usual kind of thing. Nobody knows it all except maybe Zack Guillem but he disappeared soon after it happened. And old Grand'mère, of course. She always knew everything. You might say we should have handled things better. We had the best reasons to do what we did, but now we need to look at the truth, if that can still be found. Even though it happened so many years ago it's right behind us, every day. We look over our shoulders, are nervous to speak of it even to each other, just in case – of what? We don't know. And if it turns out we were wrong, it's better to know that than to keep on as we are. Perhaps it goes back even farther than we think. It's always difficult to decide just what moment in time to point at and say that's when it started, that's whose fault it is.

It has always been too easy here to just blame the Oswekens. I can remember when the trappers used to come to town, there was sometimes trouble then. The boys would get into fights with them if Grand'mère won too much at cards or watered down the whiskey. The Indians have always been here, usually just passing through, but sometime long ago, perhaps with the coming of the Hudson's Bay post, the Oswekens settled down in

Sugarmilk Falls. Lucien's great-great-grandpère traded for furs with an Osweken chief. There have never been reserves round here so I guess they weren't what you might expect. But they were not like us. Their children didn't always go to school, except Rachelle. With one or two of them, especially young Bobby, you wouldn't know they were Indian, unless you looked real close.

They didn't seem to belong to any particular Ojibwa band, though Grand'mère was an elder and there are some Oswekens at Crowberry River beyond the haute terre, the height of land. Travellers from as far away as Algoma came to see her for a cure for one or other ailment or to put a troubled mind to rest. There were many stories that she cast spells. A few in the town used her remedies or just wanted advice. She was wise. You know she was, don't shake your head so, Lucien. I asked her about my rheumatism once. She made me something which seemed to help and afterwards I visited her now and again. Once she got to know you old Grand'mère liked to talk and sometimes we'd laugh together like girls. She could see the future in the colours of the flames inside her open stove. We would read each other's tea leaves for a joke. Grand'mère would tell me how when she was a child they'd go off all the way to Manitoba in the fall, to the midewiwin where Ojibwa from all around gathered together. For a while it was Oswekens who had the Braemar Lodge up on Roseau Lake. I guess maybe one of them, Henri most like, got lucky, or else Grand'mère bought it with her gold – she didn't say.

But they never fitted in, no one wanted that. Mostly they kept their distance, and we kept ours. They did things their own way, and mon Dieu! they could gamble. That left a bitter taste in many mouths. And then there was that business about Bobby and the stones. That is also something to be pointed at. A small thing that ended in disaster.

Claudine closed her eyes. My friend, she said, I will tell you about the Oswekens, about Rachelle, and Bobby, and how the schoolteacher angered Grand'mère who was not one to stand by. Then Claudine softly cleared her throat and began.

6

Maybe you know the Ojibwa name this bitter heart of winter the Moon of the Windigo, after their most ancient fear, the crazed cannibal giant who swoops down from the north bringing madness and destruction. Each breath of pale frozen air catches in the throat and nostrils. The hard packed snow creaks loudly underfoot. At night you hear the tamarack trees crack like gunfire in the iron cold. Constellations glitter wildly and the northern lights shimmer across the sky.

You could say it began like this, with the windigo moon bright on the snow and Grand'mère, snowbound in her cabin on the edge of the muskeg, staring into the flames of her round black stove. She drank from a bottle of moonshine whiskey and the past became the present . . .

*

Rachelle has taken to hanging around the store with the older girls after school. They sip cherry soda and giggle through their hair at the loggers who also stop by at this time. They want movie magazines, strawberry bubblegum, grape-flavoured lipstick, and the lumber men, enchanted by the schoolgirl laughter, pay.

Rachelle does not come home as usual. For three long days and nights she is missing. Even Grand'mère, who knows all the places, can find no trace. Zack discovers her on the fourth day, abandoned in a sugar shack, a bruised, distraught, unspeaking girl, gripping tightly the coat he wraps her in. Little by little Grand'mère pieces together all that has been done to Rachelle. She tells no one. Eventually the ones she concludes are responsible wander into the muskeg and long before Bobby is born they are all lost in the cold, shifting, bottomless mire. Constable Martello questions the Oswekens about the disappearances. He looks long and hard through narrow eyes at Grand'mère. But there is no evidence. Others have vanished this way. No one ever knows for certain, not Zack Guillem, not Father Souris, not even Rachelle.

Bobby is born in the Moon of the Windigo; he is a bright and difficult child. Grand'mère cares for him as she has cared for all her large family. But Rachelle will have nothing to do with the boy. She quits school and finds live-in work at a holiday lodge on Medicine Chant Lake. She paints her face and chain-smokes. Zack sometimes calls by but she pretends not to know him. Soon the resort manager tells him to stop coming round. Later he learns she has gone to the city, where the money is better. It is Grand'mère who tells him this. She speaks without emotion, but hopelessness gathers like a freezing mist. 'There is Bobby,' she says flatly, 'with a child it is always springtime.'

Bobby plays on her soft, shining moosehide rugs. He bangs her cooking pots and beats her drum. Sometimes she holds him up to sit astride her dogs. Bobby watches her prepare the herbs she uses in her medicine. He holds her hand when they go out to pick the tawny leaves, the mosses and lichens, the cherry bark and cedar for making steaming broths to drink or splash on red-hot stones, the forked and hairy one she calls root of a thousand roots. On winter days he takes her collection of mineral samples out of the grey canvas bags and arranges them in rows. He smells spices, the cinnamon, cloves and nutmeg, and sneaks the raisins when she bakes. She makes deerskin mittens, decorates them with coloured beads. He echoes her chants and sees inside her medicine pouch, the necklaces of animal claws and teeth, bones and strips of fur. Sometimes, not often, they go to Mass. In the evenings he sits close to her. He holds her long grey braid in his hand and they eat popcorn.

Bobby watches the men, Louis and Ovide, prepare the traps and fishing lines. Later he goes into the bush with them, far beyond the maple groves, and learns to take the skins from animals and cut up the meat for food. Once he helps to build a shelter in a sudden snowstorm. He listens to the fireside talk and story telling on long winter nights, about ancestors and spirits in the magic Ojibwa world. He hears there can be persons in all things, even animals and trees, who sometimes visit in a dream. He learns some people may not be as they appear and wonders if Father Souris is one of these. Miss Grochowska also comes, this time in nightmares. He wakes up screaming. They are very powerful, these dream visitors. He must not make them angry, for if they are offended they will surely pay him back. He must not tell anyone these things lest telling it should make them stronger still.

Grand'mère and Bobby hunt for crayfish in the river. They bend in the shallows and turn over stones where they know the crayfish like to hide. It is Indian summer, warm and still, and mosquitoes swarm in the sunlight. Bobby stands up abruptly. 'Are all the stones alive, Grand'mère?' he asks.

She hesitates. 'No, Bobby, but some are.'

'Which ones?'

Grand'mère thinks for a moment. 'Only those stones that look alive. You'll know when you see one.'

'I saw a stone that moved,' Bobby says excitedly, 'all by itself.'

'Maybe,' says Grand'mère. 'Things aren't always what they seem. Maybe it isn't a stone at all.'

'It looked like one. I think it was one.'

'You'll have to ask it next time what it really is.'

Bobby tells Miss Grochowska what he saw in the river. 'Stones are never alive, Bobby. That's impossible. They are inanimate objects,' she says. 'You'd know that if you came to school every day like you're supposed to.'

'But I saw one move.'

'Don't be ridiculous.'

'It was alive. I asked it, just like Grand'mère said.'

On his way home, Bobby sees Zack Guillem. 'I saw a stone that moved, Zack. All by itself.'

'That's great, Bobby. Better keep it to yourself. You don't want those powerful stones to get mad 'cause you told about them too soon.'

Miss Grochowska talks to Father Souris. 'Heaven knows what else she's telling him, Matt. She tells Bobby things aren't what they seem, that stones are alive. I confronted her. "Yes, Mamselle," she says, "some maybe." I told her I won't allow the boy to be confused by all that native nonsense. "Try telling that to the stones," she says. Matt, something must be done.'

Bobby is taken from her. It is the fault of that school-teacher woman, the possessed one, who has so turned Zack Guillem's head he no longer thinks straight. She blames Bobby for the symbols on her house and on her lawn. He is placed with Catholic foster-parents in far away Penetanguishene. It is either this or he'll end up in reform school after what he's done, Father Souris insists. They, he assures her, will provide the stable and structured family environment he needs. They will make sure he goes to school every day. Bobby attacks them with a skinning knife. He sets fire to their car and runs away. A police patrol picks up the little boy hitching unerringly back to Sugarmilk Falls. And now Bobby is in jail.

*

Grand'mère gazed deep into the embers flickering like seams of gold in hard black ore. The hiss and flare tormented her. Slowly, unsteadily she rose to her feet. The time for patience, for wisdom, was over. She loaded bullets into her .22 calibre rifle. Drifting snow dust tinkled against the window. The windigo moaned.

7

No! That isn't how it was, a voice said at the back of the room. Of course the Oswekens came into it, Claudine, but there's something you and Lucien are forgetting. I know you're all looking at me now and thinking it's only old Arnie Anstalt singing the same old hymn, but the big thing on everyone's mind back then was whether to vote yes or vote no. It was the most hot-button question ever decided here – should the sale of alcohol be legalized in Sugarmilk Falls? It split the town right down the middle, No Committee on one side, Yes Committee on the other, and things have never been the same. If your so-called friend here is going to get a proper understanding about what happened, it has to be taken into consideration.

You all know I don't hold with this talkathon kind of thing but as it's been decided I guess I'll go along with it. Not to mention the chance of sampling a few of Claudine's maple-syrup specials. The way I see it is this: the vote was the cause of all the trouble. If there'd been no vote, things would've worked out different and Sugarmilk Falls would be a better town. Oh, I know we pride ourselves on our model northern community, and I'd be the first to shout about it, but we know that's just all pretence. Just below the surface there's infection and it's spread everywhere, and not just because of those damned land claims.

You might think it was started by Hugo Jansen over there, when he first wanted to open up a bar in the Falls Hotel. But it was the likes of that Zack Guillem brought things to a head, with their bootleg beer and their moose milk and any hooch they could squeeze out of an illegal still. Zack always denied it, of course. On Sunday mornings we'd walk to church and there'd be empties all over certain front yards and often as not some drunk sleeping it off down a ditch. It upset the women and wasn't something the children ought to be walking through in a public place. Oh yes, Zack Guillem could keep you supplied, him and that sidekick of his – Henri Osweken, wasn't it? – the one who had the Braemar Lodge that burned down. You have to remember it was a hell of a way in those days to the nearest liquor store, almost quicker to cross over into Québec and much less hassle there about buying the stuff so long as you weren't an Indian.

Last thing we wanted in this town was a public bar. It was bad enough here already on a Saturday night, with the North Star dance hall down on the lakeside and the lumber gangs cruising around in their trucks and cars looking for a bit of fun. Frank Martello – wasn't he made a senior constable round about that time? – mostly turned a blind eye and it was usually Indians who got themselves booked. Grand'mère herself got pulled up pretty regular when she was on one of her binges. She'd fight and be hauled off to court and fined. One time, middle of winter it was, she was staggering up Main Street shooting off her rifle in every direction. Put out a couple of windows and holed a few tyres, but did no other damage as I recall. Lucky she didn't kill someone. You all remember how that one ended. Did she end up in jail? No! Some fool of a magistrate put her on probation and sent her off to get counselling for her alcohol problem. Some hope!

And what about her granddaughter or whatever she was, that pretty little Rachelle, who got herself pregnant and was never the same again. Frank Martello did his usual not too much about that. She split town not long after, with some city guy. Then there was quite a spell of those lumber men disappearing, probably got themselves trapped in the muskeg – easily done if you're too drunk to care where you're putting down your feet.

Bobby too took to drinking and gasoline-sniffing but that was later, after he ran away from reform school. A bad one he turned out, though Grand'mère always thought the world of him when he was little. He used to sneak into houses and take money and liquor or break open car fuel tanks for the gasoline. Sergeant Martello did take a hand there one night. He heard someone trying to break into his house and decided the burglar was about to pull a gun on him. So he shot him. Turned out it was Bobby. And then Father Souris got involved.

Damn it, drink has a hell of a lot to answer for in this town. But there were plenty of otherwise-thinking folk who felt that the properly regulated sale of alcoholic beverages in a licensed bar would put the lid on the illegal supply.

You could say the law should've done its job better

about Rachelle but you have to give Frank Martello his due. He's a good policeman. These Indian girls are usually pretty easy and Rachelle turned out to be just like the rest. That bushwhacker Guillem tried to get him to look into the matter more but he couldn't come up with any good enough reason why he should. After those guys from the lumber camp disappeared Frank talked to a few folks and that was the end of it. The official line was they lost their footing somewhere in the muskeg.

But it sure was different when that schoolteacher went missing twenty or more years back, round about the time of the vote. He searched high and low, taking statements from everyone and his mother, even flying in that detective to give him a hand. A body was discovered. It was so badly burned I don't think they were ever really able to work out exactly who it was. Not for definite. But they could do arithmetic so they put two and two together and just hoped it added up to four. The Oswekens were on hand to take the blame and before you could blink an eye, that was that. And good riddance, too. That's what I'd still say if you were to ask me what I think.

The town's been a lot quieter since then, except on Saturday nights when the remaining lumber crews come in. The North Star still has its weekly dances. I make no bones about it, alcohol has a lot to answer for. You just need to look at what's happened. The illegal stills are going strong and bootleg is regularly trucked in. Everybody drinks more, but in a secret sort of way. Somehow the town's more subdued after what happened here, drowning its sorrows I guess. But I've been saying for a long time that the lid'll blow off one of these days and we'll surely need our wits about us when it does. What we needed most back then were clear and sober heads. What we had were poisoned minds.

*

Arnie Anstalt paused abruptly. He looked the stranger up and down, and then began to tell his story.

8

The boy stood waiting in the Anstalts' hallway, his hands outside his pockets, his face absorbed in the old-fashioned hall stand with its pocked mirror and row of brass coat hooks.

'So, young man,' Arnie tried to sound friendly, businessman to businessman, 'you've got the job of delivering all these Vote No letters.'

'Yes, sir.'

Sir. The boy has manners. 'What's your name?'

'Ricky, sir.'

'So you're Ricky Shaw. Your father's got the sawmill.' The boy nodded and smiled back. 'How old are you, Ricky?'

'Twelve, sir.'

'Well now, Ricky Shaw, about these letters. There's enough here for every house in town. You know what you have to do?' The boy nodded. 'Put one in each mail box or inside the screen door. Knock on the door if you have to. Don't miss anyone out and go all the way down to the end of every street. It's a very important letter. Understand?'

The boy nodded again. Arnie lifted Arnie Jr.'s old newspaper delivery bag containing the folded letters and placed it around Ricky's shoulder. 'When you're done, come round to the car lot and you'll get paid. Two dollars and fifty cents.'

Ricky Shaw looked straight up at him, unblinking, 'It's three dollars fifty, sir,' he said firmly. 'That's what you told my dad.'

Arnie smiled broadly, showing his yellow teeth. A chip off the old block if there ever was one! He could do with a kid like this to help out on Saturday mornings. 'Just joshing, Ricky. You'll get your three fifty. Maybe a bit extra if you've earned it.'

Arnie Anstalt showed the boy out of the front door and watched from the veranda as he proceeded down the street delivering the letters. He was a big boy for twelve, nearly as tall as his own son, who was two years older. Nice manners too, and not afraid to stand his ground. So different from Arnie Jr., who was shifty and couldn't be trusted with either newspapers or the letters or helping out on Saturday mornings, but was nevertheless, for some unexplainable reason, the apple of his mother's eye. Arnie stepped back inside to pick up his topcoat. The days were getting colder now. He walked along the sidewalk which began at his elegant white clapboard house, in his opinion the finest house in Sugarmilk Falls, and down Park Road. Yellow leaves were beginning to fall from the maple trees that lined the street. He inhaled deeply. The chilly air, the hint of wood fires, the tinge of dry leaves brought unconnected thoughts as he walked, hunting trips with his father, high-school football games, the homecoming dance with the lovely cheerleader he had to marry, the pretty grade-school teacher, Marina Grochowska, the school board had hired a couple of years back. He'd liked the look of her, the erect way she sat, the way she looked them all straight in the eye without defiance. They'd all been impressed, but as the interview progressed he'd become increasingly uneasy and in the end argued against taking her on. She was an outsider in the worst sense, a displaced person, which probably meant she had a lot of personal problems. Her qualifications were just a little too good. Her English was just a little too correct. Her French too perfect. And why wasn't she married, at her age? She showed just a little too much vocation for a town like Sugarmilk Falls.

'You mean she's too pretty and too smart for you, Arnie. She makes you feel inferior. Hell, she makes us all feel inferior.' Ed Perriault, head of the school board and just about everything else, had laughed out loud, dismissing his arguments. The others nodded in agreement. 'She's just what we need here,' Ed added, 'a challenge.'

But Arnie had been right. Marina Grochowska was an unsettling presence in Sugarmilk Falls. He couldn't put his finger on why, exactly. She somehow brought in a chill from the outside world and got him thinking that maybe, just maybe, the town, the people, he himself didn't come up to scratch. A vague notion, nothing more exact than that. And now there was talk about something going on with her and that fire ranger Zack Guillem. It was all a bit worrying.

Arnie Anstalt reached the intersection of Park Road with Main Street and paused. He could see his destination, his haven, a little way off, and he began to relax. He could almost smell the oily rags, the gasoline, the antifreeze. Anstalt Motors, with its second-hand car lot taking up a big frontage. Near the side of the road stood the last gasoline pump for a hundred and fifty miles. In the middle of the lot, surrounded by parked cars, was the sales office, a low wooden building with oil company advertising posters nailed to the walls. Outside the door he could see the battered Coca-Cola cooler. In his mind he saw the large window displaying the dusty engine, partly dismantled to show the shattered pistons. Above it was pinned a surprisingly neat handmade warning, 'Don't let this happen to you. Book your service now'. There was a small indoor showroom occupied by a new blue and white snowmobile and several red and yellow chainsaws. Behind the counter the cans of oil, boxes of filters, head gaskets, fuel lines – almost any spare part you would ever need – were stacked high on the shelves. Pinned to the wall, next to a calendar of motor-trade nudes were two faded photographs of properties, no more than shacks, for rent or to buy and advertised as ideal summer or hunting locations. Arnie once had high hopes for a real-estate side to the business but it never took off. A doorway led to the repair shop lit by a single fluorescent tube, with its racks of tools, oily repair pit, cars and trucks with their hoods up and Charlie in his grimy overalls, his face smudged with grease, his cigarette drooping from the side of his mouth, Charlie his brother and partner, leaning over an engine, popping his head out from under the hood to wink at him or to snarl. Charlie with his flamboyant ideas and little sense.

The Anstalt Brothers – For All Your Motoring Needs. The motto that hung above the door was printed at the top of all their stationery. Here at Anstalt Motors everything was predictable. Given just the right amount of turn on an adjusting screw, clean oil and a new spark plug pretty well anything could be made to hum. Here Arnie could put out of his mind the problems he couldn't solve – Arnie Jr.'s school reports, his wife Irene's extravagance with the mail-order catalogues, his own responsibility as one of the first citizens of Sugarmilk Falls, and lay preacher at that. And now this unholy business of the vote.

He'd felt obliged to take the lead in the opposition campaign and called a meeting at his house of like-minded townspeople. Reverend Byers and his wife from the Presbyterian church had come, and Angela Norton from the nursing station. The Tronquets, Phil and Sophie, who had the store, and Freddy and Lily Chen from the Chinese restaurant also came, as well as Sammy Dutoit, who'd opened the North Star dance hall a few years back. That one surprised him. 'I got enough trouble there already,' Sammy told the gathering. Irene was excited by the attention she and Arnie began to attract and decided to host a bring-and-buy. That raised a bit of money and Arnie ran off some posters on the office mimeograph. These were tacked to telephone poles or taped inside windows around the town. No Committee flyers were regularly distributed. He'd given a couple of talks. And now he had written a letter, one for every household in Sugarmilk Falls, a strong warning about the dangers of voting yes, which were being delivered at this very moment by that nice kid Ricky Shaw.

Arnie Anstalt turned the corner and walked up Main Street. There were no maples trees just here, only bare poles supporting the telephone wires and the No posters. The buildings, mainly wood with clapboard walls, lined each side of the road which was metalled at the central crossroads but soon dissolved into gravel. There were three churches, one with a small steeple, the store, the Falls Hotel, and the newly opened Chinese restaurant – he couldn't see that lasting long. In every direction the town disappeared into maple woods, sloping steeply towards Michton Lake, named after the Indian word for maple, and rising in the direction of the falls. The trees were already beginning to turn. There were touches of yellow, red and brown in the rolling green-black hills, all under the cloudless blue sky. Arnie caught his breath. He told himself it was the chilly wind that made his eyes water suddenly, though he had to admit the world around him was almost too pretty to look at on a day like this.

Across the street the hotel was newly painted, white walls with green windows and doors. The entrance stood wide open and Arnie smelled the coffee and the bacon. It was tempting, but he hadn't been inside since the first days of the campaign. Walking past the hotel one day back in the early spring he'd decided it would be a courtesy to have a word with the Jansens. He'd crossed the road, rung the doorbell and walked in.

'Hello, Arnie, you old grease monkey.' Birgit Jansen rested her elbows on the counter and leaned forward, her pink cleavage framed by rows of tight white ruffles. Fluffy wisps of blonde hair were held in place with black hair-grips. She winked heavy blue lashes at him and smiled a wide red smile. 'What can I do for you?'

'I'd like a word with Hugo if he's around,' he said brusquely.

'Well now,' she replied, 'why don't you tell me what it's about and maybe I'll go see if he's here.'

Arnie sighed impatiently but he would have to play along. 'Birgit, it's something I don't really like to bother a sweet lady like yourself with. A little bit of a disagreement, that's all.'

She looked at him, smiling broadly. 'If it's about this here,' she pointed to an official-looking paper on the hotel noticeboard, 'you can tell me. I can take it.' She wrinkled her nose coyly. 'It was me talked Hugo into it.'

Arnie had thought as much. 'In that case, Birgit, you might as well know a lot of good people don't think it's such a good idea and we mean to make ourselves heard. I just wanted to give you that information out of politeness and if you want my advice for what it's worth, I think it would be best for everyone – you take my meaning – if you changed your mind about getting up that petition.'

Birgit hesitated, weighing up what he had just said. 'I can't say we didn't reckon on that being the case, what with the town having been dry for so long. I can't even say Hugo and me didn't reckon on you being of that opinion. What I didn't reckon on, Arnie, is you turning out to be a threatening kind of guy. What do you mean, it would be best for everyone?'

'No, I meant no threats, Birgit. Nothing in particular. But you know how it is when people get upset round here. You've only got to think about the Braemar Lodge.'

Birgit's smile did not falter. 'Are you suggesting, Arnie, that was no accident?'

'No, Birgit, of course I'm not suggesting that. But you have to admit it was a mighty coincidence that it burned down when it did.'

*

Arnie frowned at the recollection and hurried on past the open doors of the Falls Hotel.

9

A few months earlier Arnie Anstalt had been astonished to see the item regarding the Falls Hotel on the agenda for the spring council meeting. Like many others he'd thought the Jansens' application would never see the light of day. The municipality was dry. It had been dry a long time. That was tradition. True, he'd been surprised that some people seemed inclined to sign a petition, but what was that, after all? Just names on a piece of paper, not much to upend the long-established status quo with, and he thought no more about it.

At the start of the hunting season, Hugo had put up notices in all the rooms of the hotel. These asked the guests and diners a simple question: 'Wouldn't you like to be able to relax with a drink in our bar? At the present time, as you've probably noticed, there is no bar here and alcohol can't be sold in the dining room. But you can help make all this happen by signing our petition before you leave. Thank you for your support and we hope to see you here again.' Many of the visitors had signed.

Ed Perriault read one of these notices and had a quiet word with the Jansens. 'It's no good getting together a list of a lot of outsiders who've stayed in the hotel,' he told them, 'if you're serious about this you need people who live around here to sign or it won't get you anywhere. You need a long list of names of people who are eligible to vote.'

The Jansens stepped up their efforts. But for several weeks the petition remained unsupported by the residents of Sugarmilk Falls, although its existence was common knowledge. Hugo thought about abandoning the idea. Then, not long before Christmas, Charlie Anstalt, moved by seasonal spirit of one sort or another, told the owner of an old Pontiac he was respraying that he thought he might sign it himself only he didn't want to be the only one. Soon a name appeared, quickly followed by another and before long quite a list was growing. Early in the new year the municipality council was advised that a significant number of eligible people seemed not averse to the idea of a bar opening up in the Jansens' hotel. But before the Jansens' application could even be considered, there would have to be a vote in favour of changing the dry status quo.

The meeting would be held, as usual, in the old schoolhouse, a single-roomed log building going right back to the early days of Sugarmilk Falls, which had been kept on as a general-purpose community hall when the new school was built. Arnie liked taking part in discussions there, inside the rough mellow walls, sitting next to the ornate cast-iron stove where he'd once aimed spit balls with his ruler when the teacher wasn't looking and learned his three Rs when she was. He felt it gave their opinions an air of pioneering enterprise. Even the most reactionary views, and he had to admit there could be plenty of those at times, seemed to have an eye out for progress. As for this screw-brained idea of the Jansens, it would never happen, not here, and not just because Sugarmilk Falls was dry by tradition. It was because that tradition had the future squarely in its grip. No amount of names on paper could alter that, he was sure. If only the Jansens had taken account of the so obvious thisness and thatness of the place, they would have known better than to pitch this particular screwball and saved everyone a lot of bother.

It was not yet dark when Arnie set off after supper for the old schoolhouse. The sap-run had finished, the snow was thawing rapidly. Rivulets of meltwater trickled along the sidewalk, the street and into the ditches. Gurgling, rippling sounds filled his ears as he walked. He'd seen the first robin of the year a couple of days ago and in Irene's flower bed, the only real flower bed in Sugarmilk Falls as far as he was concerned, the daffodils were already beginning to peep above the ground. Inside, the old school room was dim and warm. The front of the stove had been left open and firelight flickered over the faces and the thick plaid shirts of the men sitting around the table. The talk was of the sugar-making, by all accounts it was expected to be another prize-winning year. Arnie removed his coat and took his place, just as Sammy Dutoit lit the kerosene lamp and hung it from a roof beam, illuminating them all with its sulphurous glare.

'Hi, Arnie. We're all here now.' As usual Ed Perriault, the reeve, began the meeting. 'Hugo sends his apologies – he thought it best to keep away and anyway he's gone to bed with a cold. So I guess you'll be taking the minutes tonight, Jerry. Since I haven't had my supper yet I'll come straight to the point. About this business at the Falls

Hotel, in the ordinary way of things we'd just give it a quick once-over and file it under "waste paper". But the Jansens have gone and got themselves a proper petition, quite a big one too. Took me by surprise. Only it's not big enough.'

'Then what's the problem, Ed?' asked Reverend Byers. 'If there aren't enough names that's the end of it.'

'Normally that would be the case, Roy. But it's only one more name they need.'

'Then there aren't enough. And that's all there is to it.'

'That occurred to me too, and it might be that nothing more'll come of it. But since the Jansens are nearly there I thought we ought to at least discuss it. I haven't signed myself, but I never got as far as deciding I wouldn't sign. I might even still do it. So as it's such a close-run thing, I've raised it for tonight's meeting. What do you all think we should do about it?'

'Forget it,' said Reverend Byers, 'there aren't enough names.'

For a while no one spoke. Then Lucien Armand cleared his throat. 'I think we're right to consider it, Ed. And I think maybe it isn't such a bad idea. To be able to have a drink in a properly run bar – it's progress. Might bring a few more visitors to the town. Maybe we ought to let it go to a vote. Let everyone have their say.'

'Bring more visitors to the hotel, you mean,' said Arnie sullenly. 'And if you allow one licence where do you stop? Soon there'll be bars everywhere. We've always got along fine without it. We don't need it.' There were murmurs of agreement.

'Hold on a moment,' interjected Phil Tronquet, 'I'm not saying I'm in favour of it, but I don't think we can just ride roughshod over this petition. A lot of people, in fact nearly enough people, think it's a good enough idea to at least have it go to a vote. We can't just ignore that.'

There was another pause as the men looked uncomfortably at one another.

'I signed it myself,' said Charlie Anstalt.

'You what?' asked Arnie in disbelief.

'I signed it. I'd like to go for a nice cold beer and a chinwag at the end of a hot summer day. Excepting the Reverend here we all of us have a drink now and then, even you, Arnie. I don't see why that shouldn't be in Hugo and Birgit's bar.'

'Might I remind the meeting,' Reverend Byers put the tips of his fingers together and looked into the roof timbers, 'this has been a dry municipality ever since the Temperance Act. There are sound reasons for that, namely law and order. When there used to be a lot of fur-buying here the townsfolk didn't want things to get out of hand, so in their wisdom they decided Sugarmilk Falls would be dry.'

'There hasn't been a trapper here for more than fifteen years, unless you count Zack Guillem as one,' interrupted Charlie.

'But now there are all these forestry boys,' continued the Reverend, 'and they can get pretty rowdy. It would be a big mistake to open up a bar here. This place needs to stay alcohol-free.'

'Alcohol-free! You should come to town on Saturday nights!' shouted Sammy. 'You should see my parking lot on Sunday mornings! More empties than a bottle factory!'

Ed Perriault looked at his watch. 'It's not up to this meeting to decide whether Hugo and Birgit can open up a bar. All we can do is say maybe this petition is enough to hold a public vote. That will decide whether or not we stay dry. Then it'll be up to the liquor authorities to say whether the Falls Hotel is or isn't a suitable place.' He paused, choosing his words and scratching his ear. 'We can go round and round in circles on this till the cows come home, and there aren't many cows round these parts far as I know. As there's such a variety of opinions here, maybe it's time someone proposed a motion to the meeting.'

There was a hush in the room. Reverend Byers began to open his mouth but he was too late.

'I propose we have a public vote on staying dry.' Phil Tronquet spoke formally. 'There's a lot of people in favour of changing that. It seems change is in the air. This is a big thing for Sugarmilk Falls. The size of this petition shows that maybe it's time to let everybody decide.'

There was another long pause. Arnie and Reverend Byers looked threateningly from man to man.

'I'll second that.' Dave Shaw put up his hand. 'I'm not for it myself but I think there's enough indication that this is something everyone ought to be able to have their say on.'

'Then we'll vote on Phil's proposal,' Ed said with a grin. 'How many in favour of letting this petition go as evidence that there should be a public vote on whether to stay dry?'

Phil was the first to raise his hand, followed by Dave. Then slowly Lucien Armand's arm went up, then another as Charlie Anstalt with a sheepish grin raised his. 'Right,' said Ed, 'that makes four in favour. Now, how many are against the proposal?'

Reverend Byers and Arnie raised their hands quickly. 'Come on, Sammy,' urged Arnie, 'you're not for this, are you?' Sammy shook his head and raised his hand.

Arnie turned to the man at the end of the table who was writing with concentration. 'What about you, Jerry?'

'I don't see the point,' he replied, 'this town has always been dry. It'll stay dry, you'll see. No point at all in having a vote.'

'So you're against it too,' said Ed. 'I make that four in favour and four against. I guess that means it's down to me.' He sighed, looked at each man in turn, cleared his throat and grinned. 'Hell, we're all grownups here,' he said with a laugh. 'Let the people decide for themselves whether or not they want to stay dry. They've got the whole summer to make their minds up. A heck of a lot of them are going to have to vote in favour to change anything. And just to make sure there are no awkward questions asked about the number of names on the petition, I'll put my name down on it. Now, if there's no other business I'd like to go home and get my supper.'

*

After the meeting, Roy Byers walked part of the way home with the Anstalt brothers. 'It's all very worrying, Arnie,' he said as they parted. 'The devil is at work among us here. We'll have to pull together to fight these powers of darkness. We'll talk about it soon. I can feel one of my sick headaches coming on.'

When the Reverend had gone Arnie turned to his brother. 'You're a damned nuisance, Charlie. How am I supposed to keep up my position with you monkey-wrenching it whenever you see a chance?'

'Oh, come on. Your position looks just fine to me.' Charlie drew deeply on his cigarette and exhaled slowly. Their feet splashed in the puddles as they walked. 'Look at this,' he said, 'it's gone dark and it's not freezing.'

'So what?'

'At this rate the waterways will open up soon and we'll be able to go take a look at it.'

'Take a look at what? What are you talking about?'

'The Beaver.'

'You're nuts, Charlie. There's no Beaver. Everything was taken care of. There's nothing out there.'

'So you say. But I know better. I know where it is. Suzanne told me.'

'She's more nuts than you are.'

'Anyway, I'm going for it as soon as I can. You coming?'

'No. This is just another one of your wild goose chases through the bush.'

'It could be worth a mint, Arnie.'

'There's nothing out there. Anyway I'm going to have way too much to do about this damned vote. You know as well as I do it's got to be stopped. And you'd better be careful. We don't want to be attracting any attention round here.'

*

Henri Osweken raised his eyebrows when he saw the front page of the *Sugarmilk Gazette*. Well, well, he thought, so the Jansens have made it as far as getting a vote organized. That's a whole lot farther than he reckoned they'd get. In the unlikely event that enough of the municipality voted yes, it could make quite a difference up at the Braemar. He'd quit drinking soon and start rebuilding. It'd have a bar, maybe a casino in the back. More tourists in the summer, in the winter too, and more hunters in the fall. He'd show that Sammy Dutoit with his two-bit lakeside shindig joint what a class operation looked like. And Hugo Jansen. And those goddamned Anstalts. When the Braemar Lodge was up and running again, it would be like that year-round place near Ottawa he'd worked the dog-sledding for a long time ago. Before the war, wasn't it? Before he found Flora? Things got mixed up in his head a lot of the time. There'd be sleigh rides and skiing and snowmobiling in the winter, canoeing and sailing and fishing and hiking in the summer, and, of course, hunting in the fall. You name it, the Braemar would have it. Even his dear dead Flora would be impressed. They'd come up in droves from New York, maybe even all the way from Florida, with their wads of US dollars, to a place like that. It was time those bastards who'd torched the old lodge at the end of that big drought summer choked on their own vomit. He'd see to that.

10

The red-gold amber reflected the moonlight as Father Souris slid the necklace through his fingers above the black tin box. A soft 'vous avez choisi' whispered in his mind. You have chosen. The words were faint and dim at first but grew until they glowed green in his brain. The years dissolved and old memories came suddenly to life . . .

*

Captain Mathieu Souris was on leave, out walking again, determined to see everything there was to see, to make the most of this experience of a lifetime. War can have its advantages and its surprises as well; how else would a young man from Trois Rivières, dressed in a British army uniform, come to be sashaying on this blissful spring morning down the length of the Champs-Elysées, the finest avenue in what must surely be the finest city in the world? A hero in a hero's paradise, he wandered, whenever he could, the streets and boulevards, cramming it all into his memory. He couldn't believe his luck. To be breathing the same air as Hemingway breathed. To walk the streets Abélard once walked – well, maybe one or two remained. To actually be attached to SHAEF, Supreme Headquarters Allied Expeditionary Force, and stationed here in Paris, which as everybody knew was just about the most heavenly place on earth!

Earlier, he'd stepped out from under the colonnade of the Hôtel Meurice, adjusted his cap and taken the métro to Étoile. He sauntered around the Arc de Triomphe, pausing by the flame over the tomb of the Unknown Soldier, reading the lists of names inscribed on the monument, the names of battles he thought he recognized from high-school history lessons, Austerlitz, Smolensk, the Pyramids. He climbed the steps to the top and looked along the avenues splayed out in all directions like a grand compass. From the summit he could see the budding Bois de Boulogne on the right, Sacré-Cœur brilliant as champagne bottles on the left, and the Egyptian obelisk in the Place de la Concorde ahead. Triumph, concord, and Elysian Fields, he thought. What a grand finale to his years of warring with the enemy, what a suitable ending to his life as a man who had choices.

Then the overweening edifice of the arch was behind him as he strolled on, past the bustling sidewalk cafés under the plane trees just coming into leaf, past the pavilions in the parks. In the Place de la Concorde he looked again at the shattered pillars of the Hôtel de Crillon, where Proust had sometimes stayed. He traversed the square, and rounding the Tuileries Gardens crossed the river. A brisk wind funnelled between the buildings along the avenues and boulevards, scattering flurries of petals from the chestnut trees into the gutters. Opalescent clouds scudded across the bright blue sky. Sharp bursts of silvery rain glittered in the sunlight, glistened on the trees, the cobbles, the iron railings. The streets were narrow now. He was hungry, he was getting wet. Another sharp shower and he took shelter in a small café. Shaking the rain from his overcoat, he nodded to the proprietor and sat down in a wicker chair at a small round table in the corner, near the window, where he could continue to observe life at the centre of the world.

In the haze of cigarette smoke turbulent conversation engaged the drinkers leaning on the zinc bar, an intense discussion between two or three, interrupted by gesticulation and noisy agreement or disagreement – he couldn't be sure – from several others, a contribution from the proprietor, a passing waiter's opinion on the matter, a throwing-up of hands, a shaking of heads, a crescendo of laughter. At the tables chattering diners crammed elbow to elbow tucked enthusiastically into their plats du jour. Waiters hurried to and fro, laden trays held high, or clearing up, quickly resetting the places and rearranging the chairs just so, or asking new arrivals 'Vous avez choisi?' and after a detailed discussion of the simple menu shouting the order through to the kitchen. As for the food, it had quickly become apparent to Mathieu Souris that despite the restrictions, despite the shortages which were nearly as severe as they had been right after the liberation, even rutabagas coming out of a Paris café kitchen were heaven itself compared to army rations. He drew deeply on his cigarette.

'Vous avez choisi?' A soft voice penetrated his attention. Someone was speaking to him. He looked up to see a thin girl with large dark eyes and short dark hair, and a smile that was just for him.

'Pardon?'

'Vous avez choisi, monsieur.' A statement rather than a question. She was wearing a necklace of red-gold translucent beads and there were holes in her sweater.

'What have you got?'

'It's all on the board, over there.' She pointed to the blackboard next to the bar. 'The plat du jour is not bad.'

She spoke with such simple authority that he was instantly persuaded. If she said the plat du jour was not bad it must be excellent. How could he possibly not have what was obviously going to be the best dish of the day he'd ever eaten.

The chaotic euphoria that engulfed Paris immediately after the liberation had calmed into an air of determined optimism. He was no longer kissed and embraced by almost every passer-by simply because of his uniform. Just below the surface, however, layers of bitterness heaved, disbelief and grief at what had been done and who had been lost. Life was brittle. Freedom was unsteady. Disillusion already peeped over the horizon. Mathieu Souris, smart in his officer's uniform, looking up at the girl in her worn black sweater and heavy amber necklace, was sensitive to this. All the same, here he was experiencing a once in a lifetime opportunity – a chance to take a good look at the world, smashed up though it might be – and he intended to make the most of it while he could.

*

He had wandered the devastated streets of cities he passed through, cities with names he'd read in history books, and it had been like seeing them without their clothes on. They were venerable, certainly, though he'd wondered how the notion that this was civilization ever saw the light of day. But Paris was different. It had been spared most of the wrecking. It glowed, golden and intact, on the banks of the brown River Seine, bright with promise and hardly an audible sigh of shame or regret. Walking along, admiring the prospect, he noticed only occasionally the bullet holes in the sunlit stone, or maybe here and there a few flowers wedged between the railings, sometimes with a handwritten note, sometimes not, marking another place of execution or just bad luck. Here on the city streets with their shops and bistros, pedestrians, bicycles and army jeeps, everyone, everything engaged in getting on with the imperatives of daily life, that ultimate courage of those recent heroes also seemed mundane. But Mathieu Souris, who had seen far worse horrors on his way across the plains of northern France and in the city's secret places, was nevertheless moved. Here he was, strolling out on a spring morning, the tricolores snapping in the breeze, the sun sparkling on the elegant tiers of windows in the grand Parisian design flaunting its grandiose monuments to past wars and glories, and his feet would step on the place, the very place, where this one or that one, not long ago, had been hustled against the wall and shot. Just like that. Sometimes a red or a white carnation would intrude into the periphery of his admiring gaze and hold him a moment, a moment between footsteps, on the exact spot where someone had fallen. The realization stabbed like a knife wound, but he barely altered his pace.

After his first foray into the Luxembourg Gardens, he avoided the parks, the Bois de Boulogne, Versailles, for what he might come across in the pale green light under the regimented lime trees. He did not like those rows of trees, pruned square, nature kept firmly in her place even as war raged. This vain compulsion to keep the spirit of life under control showed him the kind of place it really was, the kind of place where terrible things happened. He had seen the execution posts in the cellars beneath the ostentatious apartments on tree-lined Avenue Foche. He had overheard a conversation in the courtyard, how during the Occupation sleep was often disturbed by screams coming from those cellars. He thought how much better the innocence and exuberance of the untouched trees around Trois Rivières. Soon he would go home and put all this behind him. Probably he would never come here again. He needed to talk, long and deep, with Abbé Galinée, so many questions were swirling in his brain after all he had seen, all he had done. Will He forgive these things? Is it really me He wants? Do I have a true vocation?

And then the sudden burst of sunlit rain, the silver-rimmed clouds scudding above the golden avenues, a fleeting rainbow, and shelter in this small café. Another burst of laughter from the bar and, somewhat impatiently, 'Monsieur, vous avez choisi?'

'I'll have the dish of the day.'

He watched her walk serenely to the bar and shout his order to the kitchen. Gosh, she was a pretty girl. By the time she leaned over him to place the steaming plate of food on the small round table, smiling all the while just for him, he was head over heels in love.

Her name was Marina, she said in reply to his question. She sat down opposite him at his mild insistence, for no one yet refused an Allied soldier anything. No, she was not from Paris, but came here as a child from

Warsaw. Her father had dealt in antiquities before the war. She now lived nearby, alone, not in the looted apartment that had been her family's home. Yes, everything, everyone was gone. She spoke as if it was about someone else, her serenity like a frozen lake. But what about him? Where was he from, in his British uniform but so French? Not British, he told her, pointing to his Canada shoulder flash, but from Québec, and he talked about Trois Rivières, so small, so dull compared with this, so safe. He told her how he had joined the Fusiliers, been loaned to the British army when it was short of officers and now was here, on General Redman's staff, because of his excellent Québécois French. They laughed. Yes, she would finish work soon, she said. Yes, she would come out with him. To a restaurant or a show, whatever he wanted to do.

And later, after the wine, the singing and dancing and all the talking – although he did not tell her about the exquisite pleasure of his revenge for the time he lay face down in the shingle on Dieppe beach, scared shitless – they walked in the dawn along the empty streets and watched the sun rise over the river. In the silvery morning light they passed the Palais de Justice, and soon arrived at the door to the courtyard of her apartment building in a narrow street off the Boulevard St-Michel. He would be back later that day, he said. Would she see him again? Of course, she replied, and he kissed her. Walking under the chestnut trees along the river, he felt as though his world was turning on its axis. He needed to think and to pray. Across the square the grinning gargoyles of Notre-Dame leaned out towards him, like fingers urging him in. Inside the cathedral he knelt for a long time trying to beseech the tall medieval Virgin for guidance. But she had eyes only for the Child in her arms, and the cold black stoniness of the thick pillars stifled his prayers.

He decided to say his confession. 'I think I am called to go to the seminary,' he whispered in the close darkness, 'but I have killed and felt justified. I have no regrets. And now I love a woman. I want her to marry me.' Why had he said that? The words had a life of their own, slipping out before he knew he wanted to say them. There was a long silence.

'These are unusual times,' whispered the voice behind the grille. 'It is easy to lose one's way. You have sinned and must repent of your sins. The agents of Satan will try to come between you and your true vocation. She is such a temptation. Forgiveness will only come if you follow your true path.'

He knelt again trying to pray, to say his penance, but the sun made colourful patterns on the stone where it shone through the stained glass, and the heavy columns were richly carved. He got up and strolled around the ancient building, more tourist than penitent, inspecting the tombs, pausing at the side chapels, each one dedicated to a different saint, the likelihood of whose successful intercedence was indicated by the number of candles flickering in front of their image. He stopped by the statue of St Rita, a nun holding a large cross and a rose. A wide rank of candles burned to her and row upon row of votives and thank yous were pinned to the walls. He had never before felt inclined to seek the aid of this patroness of desperate causes. Lighting another candle he crossed himself and thought of St Augustine, who as a young man went to study in Carthage, the hub of civilization those centuries ago, and was troubled by what he called its cauldron of unholy loves. He'd always liked that description of temptation. And, like the saint, Mathieu Souris prayed for chastity and self-control, but not yet.

*

Vous avez choisi? It was the first thing she said to him, just the patter of the cafés and bistros, the cellar bars and restaurants. Have you chosen? A question, or was it a statement – you have chosen – the rising inflection doubting the choice already made. And the choice had been made, nearly made, years ago, before he enlisted, when he sat before Abbé Galinée and together they mapped out the route his life would take, the seminary, the university, career priesthood, with his gifts and talents all put to do God's work, eventually archbishop maybe, or even more. Together they knelt and prayed and Abbé Galinée had been generous with his blessing. He walked home in the comfort of important decisions made, the warm glow of the knowledge that he, Mathieu Souris, from Trois Rivières, a one-horse town in southern Québec, had actually caught the Almighty's eye. His mother wept tears of joy and his father beamed. Three glasses were quickly wiped and filled with wine.

'To Mathieu,' said Papa with satisfaction. 'We are very proud of you.'

'My son, the priest,' said Maman, wiping her eyes.

Oppressed, suffocating under the certainties of hard decisions taken, difficult choices made, he enlisted one day in the Fusiliers Mont-Royal. That had been easy by comparison. It seemed so obvious that the only thing to do in 1940 was join up for the war. It required hardly any soul-searching, almost no thought at all. In this present emergency, the rest of life could safely be put on hold. And once the regiment took over mapping the route of his life, Mathieu Souris stretched out his arms and breathed a deep, deep sigh which he recognized immediately to be one of intense relief. Maybe this was one of Satan's cunning strategies for deflecting him from his true vocation, he wondered briefly, but the thought did not occur again until recently when it passed unexpectedly through his head as he lay face down in the white sand of the Normandy beach. Amid the shelling, the mayhem, the screams, with death again looking him in the face, he was amused to think he had once asked himself if this was temptation. He was reminded of it in the confessional in Notre-Dame. Why had he been drawn there immediately after seeing Marina home? He told the priest he wanted her to marry him. The words tumbled out by themselves, but once he said them he knew it was exactly what he wanted. It had been so easy the following day or the next when he put the question to Marina. She nodded – maybe she thought it was a joke – and he felt the same release of pressure, the same intense relief as when he joined the Fusiliers.

'Marry me,' he said again, just to be sure. 'Save me,' he wanted to cry.

'Of course,' she replied. 'Why not.'

'I was going to be a priest before the war.'

'And do you still want to?'

'I don't know. I haven't thought about it for a long time,' he lied.

*

Have you chosen, sir? Father Souris smiled again at the recollection. The amber felt warm and light sliding through his fingers. After a lifetime he knew he had not yet really made up his mind.

He remembered when, years later, he saw the necklace again. On his first brief encounter with the formidable new schoolteacher Miss Grochowska there had been something, a resonance, a tremor of acquaintance, but it dispersed before he located it in his memory. But one day he passed her in the street and as he was saying, 'Good morning. A lovely day,' he saw amber gleaming in the sunlight. With a sharp intake of breath he searched her face. In the sun's glare the years dissolved and he was shocked by sudden recognition. 'Marina? Marina Serac.'

'Mathieu,' she replied with a smile. 'I was beginning to think you'd forgotten all about me.'

An aftershock shook him as he realized that she had known him all along. He opened his mouth to speak but no words would come. Had she come to Sugarmilk Falls to look him up? His mind reeled this way and that, struggling in a flood of screaming questions. Why has she come? What does she want? Who will find out? What will happen to me? And with the questions came the tidal wave of emotions: pleasure, frustration, anger, guilt, fear. She has no business here. She has to go, now, today. It was all a mistake, a big mistake that he thought had been obliterated long ago. Surely she was dead, has been dead these twenty years. Surely she has not deliberately come here to seek me out. It was a coincidence, a horrible coincidence that must be taken care of with the greatest possible speed. His entire barricade of certainties, so carefully erected over the years, collapsed into dust.

Yes, it really was Marina, and looking good despite the years. If only . . . if only what? If only he could go back in time and live those years again. If only the earth would swallow him up immediately . . . if only . . . oblivion. He sighed.

'What are you doing here, Marina?'

'Teaching. As you well know.'

'You can do that anywhere. Why have you come here?'

She looked as though she was about to explain, to tell him something important, but all she said was, 'Oh, Mathieu. Is it so difficult for you?' She shook her head sadly and continued on her way.

*

The white sun seared into Father Souris's eyes as he walked quickly back to the presbytery. He closed the blinds, shutting out the light and the world and poured himself a large glass of whiskey. He drank it rapidly, and sat with his face in his hands, his fingers pressed hard into his forehead. Vous avez choisi, she had said, but she was wrong; he had been called. In the dim glow of the shaded sunlight and the whiskey he knew there was a life he might have chosen if only he'd dared; indeed he almost had.

II

I saw it all, you know, clear as daylight. Everything. Sergeant Martello – he was only a constable back then – and that detective all the way from Wawa wrote down what I said. They asked me where I was at the time. They asked everybody. I told the truth, told them all about what I'd seen and it wasn't pretty, I can tell you.

Then they shook their heads and warned me about wasting police time. 'If you were a man, Suzanne Armand, we'd lock you up for this!' I can hear that pig Martello now. He was really mad.

I'd been home for the summer, working over at the Jansens' place to pay off my student loan and think about getting a job but really to be near Charlie Anstalt. That was pretty dumb, I know. We got married but it didn't last. He was always over at the garage or down in the basement, making love to some damned engine instead of me.

No kidding, clear as daylight, I saw it all. But what I told them won't be in any newspaper reports or police files. They tore it all up when I said I saw it in a dream, even though it was like I was right there, watching.

'You're supposed to be collecting all the evidence,' I said to Frank and that detective, 'I had this amazing dream. I was right there and saw it all. If that's not evidence I don't know what is.'

'You weren't there. You were asleep in bed,' says Frank. 'What did they teach you at that university, Suzanne? That dreams are real?'

Frank can be such a pleb. 'It was a real experience,' I told him, 'I thought experience is what counts.'

I talked it over with Matt Souris. He's supposed to be interested in psychology and stuff, but he was nearly as bad. 'Dreams can have meaning,' he says. I thought this was a good start. 'But they aren't reliable. They're not real. The mind can play tricks.'

He talked to me as though I was still a little kid. Hell, I'd gotten a degree. 'It was a real important dream, Matt. Like the one about the flight into Egypt. If that hadn't been taken seriously where'd you be today?'

'It's not the same at all,' he says. 'An angel was sent by God in a dream . . .'

'That's exactly my point, Father.' And I left.

I told Charlie about my interview with the police. He hit me. He was very sorry afterwards, really sorry, said he didn't know what'd gotten into him, said he'd never do it again, and like an idiot I believed him. You live and you learn. He's with the others, in the corner over there, shaking his fist at me. You can't keep me quiet any more, Charlie. You might as well be dead.

*

Lucien shook his head. Suzanne. Ferme-la. We don't want to hear about your problems with Charlie. Our friend has come to find out what really happened here so let's stick to the story.

Listen. I will tell you how it all began. You might say it goes back before the old schoolhouse was built, even before the Indian treaties when there was nothing much here at all except the Hudson's Bay post. Over the years loyalists and war veterans and those with connections might sometimes receive or be allowed to buy Sugarmilk land, big portions too, but the script and deeds and letters patent usually ended up in Osweken hands. Not this place though, where we meet tonight. Even the first Armands knew better than to gamble against Ojibwa magic. But people stayed here anyway and nobody asked questions about entitlement. Maybe they felt cheated, or foolish. Maybe they just decided that's what they'd do. So what if they'd lost their documents in a game of cards with an Indian, they told themselves. Nothing to stop them staying on in so-called Indian country with hardly any Indians in it. Indians didn't count for much, they thought. And pieces of paper didn't count for anything out here in this faraway wilderness when you didn't read too well but could fire a gun all right. Those papers most likely were destroyed long ago. But now, with these land claims going on, it sure would help us to have them. Somebody called Macleod is claiming ownership, and a few Oswekens from beyond the haute terre. We've wondered if you are involved too, mon amie. You shake your head and look at us like an innocent.

D'accord. A government geological surveyor passed through about a hundred years ago. He found the Sugarmilk country by chance, the story goes, and it's not certain if he even made a survey. Now and then a prospector would turn up with a copy of a hand-drawn map. But nothing much ever came from their efforts, except more rumours. It's been over fifteen years now since the cautions were recorded on the Land Register. That simple bit of legal formality has put the land to sleep. Nothing can be done with it, no selling, no licences for prospecting or lumbering. The land is trapped in time. We have the sugaring, it's true, and the hunting and fishing. Tourist attractions, but they're not enough. Many say it's lumbering and mines that really bring these northern parts to life; without them they die. But I look at our unravaged wilderness and wonder if that's really true. And when the cautions are lifted the staking rush and the land grab will begin. That's what's happened elsewhere.

But this is just to help you see the picture, like Claudine's story about the Oswekens and Arnie's talk of the vote. What you want to know about began before the schoolteacher came to Sugarmilk Falls, long before land claims were even thought of. Years before.

*

Écoutez. I remember it like yesterday, the hell-hot summer of 1961 that broke the records for heat and drought. We were all on edge like tinder. With fingers crossed we turned on the TV, not for the latest news, but to watch the weather reports. We stared into the white-hot sky hoping to see thunder clouds. Praying for a sign of change we even paid Grand'mère to cast spells. But the rain just would not come. Leaves were curling up and falling from the trees. Anytime, we thought, any moment, the bushfires will start, and that will be the end of everything. Zack was busy fire-watching, not his way of doing it, travelling the water trails by motor boat or canoe. All day long he perched high above the treetops leaning out from a wooden lookout tower miles into the bush. It was sheer boredom at best, sheer agony when the wind blew. I know, I have done it myself.

When Zack first climbed the ladder, his heart was in his mouth. Ever since our plane was hit over France he disliked high places. He did not dare look down or up, with his legs trembling all the while and his back aching by the time he reached the top. But what a view from way up there! The Sugarmilk country was stretched out below, the blue-grey hills, rolling like waves into the horizon, sprinkled with blue and black lakes, the winding courses of the waterways, the great twisted ribbon of the Sugarmilk River snaking through the forest, and the falls surging, foaming, over jagged black rocks and crashing into the chasm below. He was shocked to see so many wide, bare ugly drifts cut by the logging crews. But he looked away at the softness of the colours shimmering in the heat haze, the black-green and grey-green trees edged with gold in the distance, the white and yellow rapids, the pink and turquoise falls, the deeper blue of some of the lakes, the red-brown rocks, the blue and green and yellow sky, the setting sun turned blood red from the smoke of forest fires hundreds of miles away.

The inactivity made him restless, edgy, as he repeated his little circuits of the lookout tower day after day, gazing across the undulating treetops into the unchanging sky. For a while he passed the time by trying to pick out landmarks he recognized, certain lakes and hills by their shape, a house, a road, a hamlet, the sawmill, the town in the distance, or a particular river route. But all too soon he would find his bearings. He tried to work out new routes along the water trails but would end up wishing he was down there, on the move, dipping his paddle, the canoe swishing through the cold, clear water. He felt trapped. So what if he had a two-way radio. What was he supposed to do when the fire that was certainly going to happen somewhere if it didn't rain soon happened close by? The steel supporting structure would glow red hot. This rickety lookout tower was kindling if there ever was and it would all be burned to cinders before he got even halfway down the ladder. And he hated going down. Mon Dieu, that was a scorching summer. There's not been one like it since.

But there was something else too. Zack heard the faint drone of an airplane engine on the hot, dry breeze. He lifted his binoculars and searched the sky. But he couldn't see anything and the sound disappeared. Probably just another delivery for the lumber camp to the north. They seemed to be needing a lot of supplies up there just lately. Another morning, as he made the first circuit of the lookout tower, he thought he saw a wisp of smoke far in the distance, rising through the trees. Again, by the time he trained his binoculars onto the spot it had disappeared. No such thing as smoke without a fire, he thought, glad to have something real to do for once. He looked in the direction where he thought he'd first seen the smoke but there wasn't anything to cause alarm, and he saw nothing more. Maybe after all he'd just imagined it. He knew being stuck up here day after day would affect his brain sooner or later, though he thought he might take a closer look sometime. On the remaining days of his shift in the lookout tower he saw and heard nothing else of interest.

*

Shortly after dawn on a fine summer morning he set off in the pickup and drove along the lumber tracks as far into the bush as he could get. By the time he launched the canoe it was already hot. There was hardly a sound but the singing of the ovenbirds and the swish of his boat through the water. He preferred to paddle the canoe, not use that noisy outboard. It was so still he could hear the waterfalls whispering in the distance. A mist hung over the river and the lake, and the treetops appeared above the mist. The sun was hazy on the water and on the solid greenness of the shore. There seemed no obvious place to land. He paddled on, kneeling in the back of the canoe, thrusting the paddle forward at the end of every stroke to keep a straight course. Everything, everywhere was the same: dense, green, mostly maple trees, a few spruce, here and there a cluster of jack pines on a rocky outcrop, a stand of birches by the shore. And all the time the calling of the birds. Sometimes, resting for a moment, drifting with the current of a river, he saw the scarlet flash of a cardinal, or a red-winged blackbird, a golden oriole, a blue jay, but mostly they stayed hidden in the trees, their song heavy in the heat. At dusk the squabbling of the ducks and the troubled calling of the loons bounced across the mirror of a lake.

The next day, when the sun was nearly overhead, when the mists had long vanished, he turned the canoe towards the shore. The bottom scraped on the stone and gravel and he got out, pulled it onto the bank and turned it upside down. Zack headed into the thicket. The ground was overgrown with scrub where the trees did not cut out the light. It was cool in the woods. There was occasional scurrying nearby and somewhere in the undergrowth ahead grouse thumped. He moved easily through the trees with his unnatural sense of direction. You can lose all idea of where you are in such places, become lost, disappear and never be found. It would not have been easy for me or you to find the path back to the canoe if we had to. But Zack was always able to find the way, even back in the war, in France.

Where the woods thinned out, the tough low shrubs, a few pink flowers still remaining, grew more densely. They were heavy here with blueberries, busy with ptarmigan and grouse, and Zack was aware of a faint, odd smell. By a small clearing near a stand of pines he paused. This would be good hunting country, he thought. Maybe he'd bring a party up this way in the fall. But it was all as he had expected, just miles of undisturbed wilderness. There was a sudden scuttling in the undergrowth behind him. Zack turned quickly. He saw nothing – more than likely it was only another bird – and it was then that he noticed the thin dust coating the leathery leaves and purple berries. Looking around he saw in one or two places the dust was thicker. Crouching down to take a closer look where it was heaviest, grey, almost white on the bark of the trees, he rubbed a finger over it. He didn't recall ever coming across anything like this before and wondered what it might be. Some kind of fungus? Something to do with the lack of rain? He dipped a moistened finger into the powdery coating and tasted it, gingerly moving his tongue over his teeth. He recognized it and tasted it again, more this time, and saw that everything around him was dusted with the fine film. He tasted it a third time, just to be sure, and stood up, looking everywhere, unable to find any sign of what he now knew he was looking for.

*

Some time later he mentioned what he'd found to Henri Osweken and asked him whether he'd noticed anything odd up in that direction during the summer. By then the long heatwave had broken and the powdery film would have been all washed away by the cloudbursts.

'Nothing out of the ordinary,' he replied, 'just too damned dry.'

'You ever come across flour in the bush lately?'

'Flour! Here? You gotta be kidding?'

Zack looked at him quizzically and shook his head. Of course Henri knew why there might be flour in the bush. It had been dropped from an airplane to mark a likely place for prospecting.

12

Henri Osweken smiled with satisfaction as he surveyed his splendid Braemar Lodge between the trees on the shoreline. He was sitting by the outboard motor at the back of the boat in the middle of the lake, the float on his fishing line bobbing lightly in the water. The muskies were not biting. The glare of the midday sun ricocheted off the glassy surface. It was very hot, even for that hell-hot summer. But Henri was content gazing at his hotel, something he liked to do whenever he could. He knew Flora's brochure off by heart and he often made little mental alterations to reflect the particular moment of a silent recitation. He did so now.

'The Braemar Lodge occupies a clearing on the rising eastern shore of Roseau Lake where after midmorning it shimmers under the full force of the August sun. It is a mellow plank building with a couple of newer plank cabins on either side. When the afternoons have run their course and the fish begin to snap at the flies hovering over the water, the double spectacle of the sunset sky mirrored in the lake can be enjoyed from the lawn or the veranda or the dining room. Next to the dining room, with its wagon-wheel chandelier, there is a comfortable den with wide windows looking out into the trees, antlers and a moose head on the walls, braided rugs scattered about, and blue and green tartan armchairs ranged around the red granite fireplace. The hotel shines with new paint and polish, it smells of beeswax and freshly baked bread . . .'

It had not been like this at all when he first brought Flora there. He'd seen her face drop and felt her heart sink when he pushed open the blistered front door with a single shove of his foot and carried her inside.

'I thought you said it was a hotel, Henri,' she said at last in her lilting Scottish accent, her arms tight around his neck.

'It is,' he replied. 'Maybe I forgot to mention it was a bit run-down.'

'A bit run-down! And it's not near the road. Who's going to come here?'

'Come hunting season the place will be buzzing. You'll see.'

Henri put Flora down on her own feet. She looked around, at the dirty windows, the stained and curled wallpaper, the threadbare furniture, the dust, spiders' webs and dead flies. It did seem a great deal worse than he remembered, but he'd been faraway fighting a long time.

Flora shook her head. 'Henri,' she said, trying to sound severe, 'I can't believe I've come all the way from my clean and respectable home in the Highlands for this.'

'Of course not,' he replied with a grin. 'You left all that behind for me. The hotel is a bonus.'

Flora tried not to smile back at him. 'There isn't even a sign. Does it have a name, our hotel?'

He thought for a moment. 'I never asked, just "Hotel" I guess.'

'You never asked,' she repeated, sighing with exasperation. Then she looked at him sternly. 'Henri, if I'm going to put up with this as well as you, it must have a name. A respectable name, too, because this will be a respectable establishment. We'll call it the Braemar Lodge, just so I don't get wistful and go home straight away.' Henri did not argue.

*

Flora began by cleaning everything thoroughly, inside and out. She ordered him to paint the doors and window-frames, put up new wallpaper and repair the veranda and the roof. The curtains were taken down and washed and those that survived, ironed and rehung. A large bonfire dealt with the unrepairable furniture and the repaired was waxed until it gleamed. Rugs were taken outside and beaten until they changed back to something resembling their original colour. The bedsteads were polished and new mattresses and linen arrived. Finally a sign was put up and then Flora began to advertise. It was not too long before Henri needed to think about building a couple of extra cabins and by the time Rachelle was born all the debts owed to Phil Tronquet at the store had been settled. Soon the Braemar was in profit.

Grand'mère, he knew, observed the whirlwind stirred up by his little Scottish war bride with some trepidation. Sitting in front of the big wood stove in the hotel kitchen while the breakfast rolls rose in their tins, a cup of coffee in front of her and baby Rachelle on her knee, she wondered if Flora was aware how the Braemar and all the land around came to be theirs. She's never asked about it much, Henri told Grand'mère. He'd mentioned Indian lands in a vague sort of way and that had been enough. She wondered too if Flora had any idea about what went on in the room behind the den. She must know, Grand'mère said to Henri. She's what they call a canny Scot. Besides it could get noisy in there at times. He'd never been asked to explain, he told her. If Flora knew, she didn't let on, and a good thing too. Even in an out-of-the-way place like this you had to be careful. The smallest hint and that eagle-eyed new Constable Martello would be over like a shot to arrest them all.

*

The boat rocked gently on the water. Henri pulled the peak of his cap lower down his forehead and closed his eyes. The sun burned on his arms and back, glowed red through his eyelids. In the still air he could hear the rush of the distant rapids, calmer than usual from the lack of rain. Flies buzzed softly around his bare feet. A loon call rippled across the lake.

He woke gradually to the sound of an engine, very faint at first, materializing, intruding into his reverie. As it became louder he realized it was not part of the dream and opened his eyes. Squinting at the yellow lake and the white sky, he saw an airplane some way off heading towards him. In itself this was not strange. Occasionally a bush plane flew over, delivering supplies to the lumber camp or rich sportsmen to some remote back-country fishing locations. But just recently, during the long hot days, he was aware the flights had been more frequent.

From what he could see now, the airplane seemed not

to be heading in any familiar direction. It approached from the north, flying unusually low, just above the treetops, not following the water route as they normally did but moving in a straight line and then disappearing behind the hills and out of earshot. He was surprised when it returned after a while, from the south this time, and he noticed that it flew along a line parallel to the previous one. It disappeared beyond the trees, and when he'd begun to think no more about it, the plane came back a third time. Henri watched the red and white Beaver go back and forth, then back and forth again, the traverses roughly the same distances apart. The flight path struck him as too regular, too deliberate, too grid-like. He decided this pilot was systematically looking for something rather than going anywhere. It flew so low over the lake that Henri could see the man's dark glasses. If it doesn't climb soon, he thought, he'll clip the tops of the trees.

'I think we're being surveyed again,' he said to Grand'mère later.

'They won't find anything. They didn't find anything before,' she replied.

'That was a long time ago. They use these big Geiger counters on planes nowadays.'

Grand'mère hesitated. 'How many are there?'

'Maybe it's just one.'

'I hope so.'

*

One afternoon in August a stranger walked into the Braemar Lodge and asked Flora for a room. He was wearing shorts and a chequered shirt and carried a smart leather suitcase and a briefcase. 'A nice, quiet room,' he said, brazenly looking her up and down. 'It'll be for a few days.'

Flora was used to those stares. 'I'll see what I can do,' she replied and gave him the key to a small bedroom at the end of the upstairs hall. 'I'm afraid it's all we've got. It's peaceful back there, once everyone goes to bed.'

'It'll be fine. Thanks.'

Flora gave him the hotel register to sign. 'Are you here on vacation?' she enquired pleasantly.

'Sort of just passing through,' he said.

She showed him to the room, pointing out where the bathroom was on the way. The man put the suitcase down on the floor and lifted the briefcase onto the bed. It seemed to be rather heavy. He thanked her once more and pointedly waited for her to leave.

Downstairs, Flora looked again at the register. Now why would Mr James Levine with a city address and a bulky briefcase say he was passing through here in August, she wondered. 'Henri, are you setting up another one of your wee sessions in the back room?' she asked.

'Wee sessions?'

'You know what I mean. Are you expecting anyone?'

'No. Why?'

'It's probably nothing. This person,' she showed him the register, 'this James Levine has arrived with a briefcase. He says he's just passing through.'

'Maybe he is.'

'The Braemar Lodge is not on the way to anywhere.'

'I guess he'll find out soon enough when he's had a look round.'

Their new guest did not spend much time looking

around. He lazed about in a deckchair on the lawn or sat in the shade on the veranda, yawning and staring into space, or reading the *Gazette* and dog-eared paperbacks borrowed from the bookcase in the den, sometimes chatting with the little girl. Rachelle seemed very taken with him. Occasionally in the afternoons he dived off the jetty and swam briefly in the lake. He was not unfriendly but he did not seek out other hotel guests for company. He did not use the telephone, and only once drove into town.

Flora was intrigued. 'I'd say he is waiting for something or someone,' she said to Henri after a few days. 'Or maybe he's hiding out here. Rachelle calls him Jim. She's drawn a picture of him. And she says she owes him a quarter. Unfortunately her entry in the toad race wasn't placed.'

*

One morning Jim Levine asked, 'I suppose I could hire a boat? Maybe I could have a look around the lake?'

'No problem. I'll leave one by the jetty, ready to go with some spare gas,' replied Henri.

James Levine began to take the motor boat out regularly, always setting off in the same direction. He would be gone most of the day and return after supper, the wide V of the boat's wake rippling the silvery twilight water. Increasingly, he enjoyed these trips, his first real experience of what he liked to think of as the virgin wilderness; well, virgin for the time being, anyway. Under the clear sky, Roseau Lake zigzagged deep turquoise blue between the bright green hills. It was wide in places and over twenty miles from end to end, with a scattering of small densely wooded islands. The broad Sugarmilk River flowed into it from Sugarmilk Lake to the north, and out again at the southern end, gaining speed as it swirled and tumbled between miles of jutting rocks and cascaded over the sheer seventy-foot drop of the waterfalls.

According to a rare geological survey of the region mapped out at least fifty years ago, areas around these northern lakes showed the purplish cobalt bloom and copper green and other coloured stains which were so enormously interesting to mining types but meant nothing to him. Like so many explorations at that time, it was probably based on no more than tip-offs from fur trappers or Indians, or else followed up one or other wild rumour about lumps of gold or silver the size of cannon balls lying around on the ground. People seemed to lose all sense of reason when they heard these stories, thought James Levine. Like his client had, old Benjamin Rabinowicz the small-time mining promoter. He'd somehow gotten hold of one such forgotten, unreliable map and was determined to spend all his money investigating it. He couldn't afford to back an all-out Algoma-type onslaught and didn't want to risk causing another staking stampede if it did turn up trumps. So he'd planned this small, very hush-hush operation, just a claim-staker, a geologist and a lawyer, which no one would know about until all the potential there might possibly be in the area was safely recorded in his own name. Then all hell could be let loose to do as it pleased, as it inevitably did in these situations. You only had to remember the uproar in Algoma. And although the uranium boom had fizzled out for the time being, he was taking advantage of the lull, betting almost everything he owned on there being another surge in the market soon.

James Levine was heading north to meet up again with the prospector and the geologist at a prearranged location. He would assign the claims they'd staked out the previous few days to his client on the spot, and when the staking work was complete, or the money ran out, he would drop the whole bundle of assignments in a single job lot on the nearest mining recorder's desk.

*

'He takes his briefcase,' Flora said to Henri, 'I tidied his room myself. It was gone.'

*

'A letter came for him,' Flora said, 'from South Porcupine.'

'Who from?' asked Henri. She shrugged her shoulders. 'Why didn't you steam it open, read what it says?'

'Henri! This is a respectable establishment!'

*

'I saw papers in his room,' Flora told Henri. 'They were legal papers, I think.'

*

Henri decided to see whether he could engage the man in conversation. He sauntered casually out onto the lawn holding two chilled bottles of beer by their necks. 'You want one?' he asked the guest, sitting down beside him on the grass.

'Yeah, thanks.' He took a bottle.

'There's a fishing trip out to the end of the lake tomorrow, back by suppertime,' said Henri after a while. 'You interested?'

James Levine shook his head vaguely and drank a large gulp.

Henri sipped his beer slowly. 'What line of work you in?' he asked at last.

The man did not reply immediately. 'Oh, a bit of this and that. Whatever.'

'Hmm. You're not some kind of inspector, are you?' Henri raised his bottle. 'Liquor board? We don't sell it here.'

'No, no. Nothing like that at all,' replied Mr Levine with a laugh. He paused, then added, 'But since you ask, it's sort of book-keeping.'

'Book-keeping?'

'That kind of thing.'

Henri was silent again and gazed across the lake. He absently took a pair of dice from his pocket and rolled them around in his hand. There was no sound but the sighing of the hot dry wind in the trees and the soft uneven clacking of the dice.

Mr Levine was watching Henri's hand. 'Which end of the lake are you going to?' he asked after a while.

'Bottom end. The fish bite better.'

'How many do you think you'll land?'

'We usually catch a few down there. Say maybe between five and eight each.'

'What odds that you get more than ten?'

Henri chuckled and thought for a moment. 'Two to one seems about right.'

'You take the odds for twenty bucks?'

'Bet.'

*

'The guy from the city is a betting man. Could be a high player too,' Henri said to Grand'mère. She nodded once.

*

Grand'mère took to playing solitaire in conspicuous places around the hotel. Whenever James Levine passed, on his way out to the lake or back from it, she was there, engrossed in a game. He would pause and observe for a while, sometimes offering advice, sometimes having a small bet with her on which card would come up next. One day he watched her expertly shuffle the deck. 'Do you play anything else?' he asked.

'A little poker sometimes,' she replied, 'and blackjack.'

'For good odds?'

'Hmm.'

'I'll play you?'

'Sure.'

'He's a gambling man, all right,' Grand'mère told Henri. 'Better get a couple of the boys round.'

*

When James Levine woke up, the afternoon sun streamed through the open curtains of his room. The bed spun and he had great difficulty opening his eyes. His head felt about to split itself in two, that's if he didn't turn himself inside out throwing up first. His mouth was as dry and his tongue as thick as he could remember. What was that stuff he'd been drinking? Moose milk, someone told him. Tasted not bad, either. Pure poison. He tried to get up but lay down again immediately, groaning. He groaned again as he recalled what had happened the previous night.

It began as a light-hearted little poker game, just himself, Henri and his mother or whatever she was, with easy stakes of fifty bucks. Then that guy Charlie and some other fellows turned up, one called Louis, another Ovide or something. They joined in and it all got a bit serious, a bit hazy, a bit out of hand. They were good too, damned good for an outpost like this, especially the old woman. He was losing. He was handing over money at first and then it was his Rolex. His Rolex! Through the alcoholic haze he saw the old lady's face as she looked over the deeds of assignment. Where had they come from? He must have brought them out in order to stay in the game. He couldn't recall.

'Well now, Mr Levine,' she said, 'this really is something worth playing for.'

When it was all over the old lady reached out her thin brown arms, grasped the deeds and pulled them across the table towards her. It made him shudder to remember. Henri told him that changing the names would settle up everything he owed. He could even have some of his money back, or his watch. He felt his wrist. Damn! He must have opted for the cash. 'Cross out this here Benjamin Rabinowicz,' Henri said, 'put in Marguerite Osweken. Easy.'

James Levine recalled he had tried protesting, maybe even refused at first, but that Henri was a big fellow and in the end he must have done as he was told. He vaguely remembered wondering why all his clients had names that were so damned difficult to spell. 'You look after them real careful, Henri,' the old lady said when he'd finished. He now consoled himself with the thought that those deeds were probably worthless anyway. The market had crashed a year or two back and, he told himself, it would never recover. Nevertheless Mr Rabinowicz would be none too pleased when he found out there were no claim assignments to record. No, his client would not be happy at all. Oh well. As for himself, he'd be back in the city in a day or two and he could rely on his knack for coming up with any number of foolproof explanations whenever he put his mind to it. He was a lawyer, after all. Anyway, he hadn't met up with the prospector and the geologist for several days. Surprising. They'd been pretty reliable. He hadn't seen the plane either. Maybe they'd given up and gone back to South Porcupine.

*

'I've had a call from the South Porcupine police,' Constable Martello said to Zack Guillem. 'They're looking for a DHC-2 Beaver they think might have headed over this way a while back. Did you see anything while you were on the fire-watch?'

'There was a plane flying low. Passed over once or twice. Thought it was something for the lumber camp.'

'Nothing else?'

'No.'

*

'See anything during the summer, Charlie? A Beaver, red and white?'

'Nope.'

'Arnie?'

'No, sorry.'

*

'See anything out of the ordinary up your way, Henri? South Porcupine police are trying to trace a Beaver that's gone missing. They think it was headed somewhere over this way.'

'What kind of beaver?'

'An airplane, of course. Red and white.'

'Can't say that I have, Frank. What would it be doing way over here?'

'No idea. Probably just some fishermen.'

*

'Has anyone stayed here who knows anything about a Beaver, Hugo?'

'What on earth are you talking about, Frank?'

'The South Porcupine police are trying to find a missing plane. They think it might have headed this way.'

'How the hell would I know?'

'Okay, okay! Just doing my job.'

*

'Grand'mère, have you seen an airplane at all this summer, a red and white airplane?'

'Yes, they sometimes go to the lumber camp, or fishing.'

'Nothing out of the ordinary?'

'There was one flying over the lake up by Henri's place. Happens sometimes. That's all.'

*

'Lucien, have you seen anything unusual in the airplane department recently?'

'Pardon?'

'A red and white Beaver. South Porcupine police say one's gone missing, maybe somewhere round here.'

'Can't help you there, Frank.'

*

'Sammy?'

'Sorry.'

*

Phil Tronquet shook his head. Ed Perriault wondered if any of those geologist guys had been seen in the area lately. Father Souris said a Mass for the airplane's safe return home.

13

When Charlie Anstalt sang the blues those within range usually stopped what they were doing or saying, just to listen. This was fortunate because once Charlie sat down to strum his guitar he quickly disconnected from his surroundings. He would not respond when spoken to. Sometimes he missed meals. It was as though his spirit was interested only in the chords emanating from the instrument and resonated alongside them in the air, in the ears and brains of his audience until he finished playing and the music died away. Only when the last note had faded and the air was still again would he take up a conversation exactly where he left it or answer a question he'd been asked before he began to play.

During that dry, hot as hell summer 'Saint James Infirmary' featured prominently in Charlie's small repertoire. He practised the piece whenever he had a spare moment, in the house or at the garage during lunchtime. When he felt he'd gotten far enough with it, he entered the North Star talent show, wailing out the pain of the song in his surprisingly accomplished voice. He didn't win – his blues style didn't suit Sammy and the other judges – but he made a big impression. His favourite place to work on the piece, however, was outside the store. He would swagger down Main Street in his cowboy boots, the guitar slung over his shoulder, a red handkerchief tied around his uncut hair, and get himself a Coke from the cooler. He'd sit down in the chair or on the steps, drink without stopping until the carbonation nearly paralysed his throat, and play until Phil put his head out and shouted at him to go learn something else. Then Charlie would light up a cigarette and saunter back to the garage, taking no notice at all of the profound admiration unconditionally offered by the group of teenaged girls.

Suzanne Armand had never heard anything like his rendering of the twelve-bar blues. When Charlie twanged the strings and sang in his gravelly voice, her throat tightened up and her eyes blurred. By the time he got to 'I felt so broken-hearted . . . She used to be my own . . . She was all I had to live for . . .' her breathing was rapid and she felt warm and weak. This happened not just the first time she listened but every time. She began to seek him out, at first loitering among the second-hand cars lined up outside Anstalt Motors, hoping to see him pass by. After a while she began to lean in the doorway to the repair shop, silently gazing at him while he de-coked a cylinder head or stripped down a gearbox. Sometimes he would momentarily catch her eye and grin a little with one side of his mouth while he lit a cigarette. They did not speak.

'Are you all right, Suzanne?' Claudine asked her more and more frequently. She was concerned. Her daughter mooned about the house, when she was there, that is, sighing or humming the same awful tune over and over. She spent hours in the bathroom. She stopped eating. The other night Claudine heard her cry herself to sleep. And she smelled of cigarette smoke.

'What on earth is the matter with you?' Claudine insisted. Suzanne burst into tears.

Claudine began to find little scribbled notes, folded over and over into small packages and secreted in Suzanne's pockets, or inside her shoes, or tucked away in the drawer among her underwear. The handwriting was Suzanne's. Claudine's heart softened when she read them.

'Our little girl is desperately in love,' she informed Lucien.

He was amused. 'Who's the lucky guy?'

'Charlie Anstalt.'

Lucien was shocked. 'She's only fourteen, for God's sake! If that crotte de chien . . .'

'No, it's not like that. He probably doesn't even realize it. But we have to be careful. We have a very grand passion on our hands. And she has begun to smoke.'

'What? Cigarettes?'

'Not a pipe, Lucien.'

'What do you want me to do?'

'I don't know. Nothing. I'll try to talk to her.'

Charlie, however, was far from oblivious. Not only did he realize, but he thought it was great. To be the object of such adoration, well, he must be very talented and good-looking. That classy kid, Suzanne Armand, too. Wow. A bit young, younger than she looked, but, hey, look at Elvis and Priscilla. They'd have to wait a few years, of course. Give her time to grow up a little more, give Lucien and Claudine time to get to like him. Suzanne Anstalt. That'd show big brother Arnie and his tight-assed wife once and for all. When it came to who really counted round here, the Armands were right up there. Beside them the Anstalts were still working their way in. Armands were trapping and trading and making their way in these parts long before these parts became distinct from the rest. There'd always been Indians, of course, those Oswekens in particular who seemed to think they owned all the land, but they were just Indians. Even if they were right one more little treaty would've been all it needed to put an end to that. Or maybe just another poker game.

The knowledge that he was the object of such deep devotion added a whole new dimension to Charlie's playing. He introduced more complex guitar chords and spent longer on improvisations. When he came to the final lines of the song his voice took on just enough falsetto to make him seem vulnerable, but at the same time, daring and dangerous.

Suzanne listened. She noticed the changes.

'"When I die I want you to put me in straight-lace shoes . . ."' sobbed Charlie, looking into her eyes. The guitar throbbed. The hot wind ruffled his hair. '"Box-back coat and a Stetson hat . . ."'

Suzanne felt as though she was going to faint.

*

'Fill her up.' The stranger grinned at Arnie from the car pulled up alongside the gasoline pump. 'Have you got a phone I could use?'

'In there.' Arnie gestured in the direction of the showroom.

'Sure is hot,' the stranger said pleasantly, getting out of the car. 'It's a long-distance call I want to make. I'll reverse the charges.'

'Go ahead.' Arnie placed the gas nozzle into the filler and watched the stranger walk into the building.

The doors of the showroom and through to the workshop were wide open, as were the doors into the yard. A hot breeze drifted through, stirring the papers on Arnie's desk, the price tag dangling from the new snowmobile, the corners of the red-lipped calendar nude pinned up on the wall. The stranger looked around carefully before making the call. He did not see the boots on the ends of a pair of oily overalls protruding from under the far side of the two-tone convertible with one corner propped up on a jack.

When Charlie heard the tinkle of the telephone and the unfamiliar voice, he stopped turning the wrench on the nut directly above his face and tried to listen. The stranger was being very polite. 'No, not yet, sir,' he said several times, 'I haven't made contact yet . . . I don't think they've started staking out . . . It'll be another few days at least . . . No . . . No . . . Okay . . . I won't phone again unless there's a problem . . . Goodbye, sir.' He hung up and went outside.

Staking out! The words blazed in Charlie's mind. Who was this guy? Where was he from? Where was he staying? Why would he be telephoning here and being so polite unless he knew Anstalt Motors had about the only private line around? And using words like 'staking out' as well? He hoped Arnie would be his usual nosy self and ask the man a few well-aimed innocent questions before he let him leave with his change.

'Who was that?' Charlie asked Arnie after the man had gone.

'Some guy staying up at the Braemar.'

'Why didn't he use their phone?'

'I didn't like to ask him.'

'Arnie, that guy was talking to somebody important about staking out something or other.'

'Are you sure? Staking out? He used those words?'

'Yeah.'

'Damn. Did you get his name?'

'No. Le-something, I think.'

Arnie paused, biting his lower lip. 'Charlie, you remember that old survey map of Grandpa's we used to play buried treasure with when we were kids. Have we still got it?'

'I don't know. Doubt it. We were always trying to find the lost Indian gold, weren't we? I'll ask Mom to have a look for it.'

*

Claudine had persuaded Suzanne to help her bake maple-sugar pies for the money-raising bingo supper in St Augustine's Church basement. The heat in the kitchen was volcanic. They talked about this and that – the new school year that was not far off, the continuing drought, Grand'mère's spells on the weather. Neither mentioned what was in the forefront of both their minds. When the still bubbling pies stood to cool on racks on the kitchen counter, filling the stale summer air with the fresh smell of early spring, after all the things of far less interest had been discussed and they sat at the table drinking lemonade, Suzanne looked up at Claudine. 'Ma?' she asked.

'Yes, Suzanne.'

'What's a box-back coat?'

'I'm not sure. Where did you hear that?'

'It's in Charlie's song.'

Here was the opening Claudine had been looking for. But she was at a loss. She didn't know how to continue the conversation, how to set about having the heart to heart she so desperately wanted, how to guide her daughter away from this looming disaster, Charlie Anstalt, without losing her confidence and love. So many questions clashed with so much advice in her head. Feeling feeble and disappointed with herself she could only ask, much too casually, 'You like Charlie, don't you?'

'Yes,' replied Suzanne, too innocently.

*

Arnie leaned his elbows on his desk and held the telephone away from his ear to hear the clicks as other users on Ed's line replaced their receivers. He always waited a moment before hanging up. It gave him an unpleasant kind of satisfaction. There wasn't a whole lot of use here in having a private number, he thought, not for the first time. With almost everybody in Sugarmilk Falls on a party line, it was only useful when you were phoning long distance. That Le-something person staying at the Braemar must have realized the situation. He obviously didn't want to be overheard. Arnie's own local calls had taken on an almost code-like brevity. Anyone listening in to this one would know only that Arnold Anstalt of Anstalt Motors was going to stop by Edouard Perriault's place on his way home. Nothing unusual there, but he knew that even as little as that, one local big wheel calling on the reeve, could be enough to set the most absurd rumours going.

He drove out of town bumping along the narrow

gravel road, his elbow jutting through the open window, the tyres churning up a wake of the fine dust that already covered the nearby trees. On one side of him tall dense maples rose steeply up the hillside, on the other they descended towards the river. Arnie saw an opening in the grey-green wall of foliage. He turned in and followed the rough track. Gradually the trees thinned until he came to a clearing and Ed's long log house by the shore of a small blue lake sparkling in the sunshine. Ed would hoot with laughter whenever he was asked what the lake was called. 'We've always called it Lac Perriault,' he'd say, 'Do you realize what that means? It means the Sugarmilk country has three hundred and eighty-ONE named lakes!' And he'd laugh and laugh, as though this was just about the funniest thing he'd ever thought of.

Ed came out of the house to meet him and together they walked to the water's edge. The lake was deep by the shore and so clear that Arnie could see the rainbow flashes of sunfish darting through the grassy weed.

'Could be something and nothing, Ed,' Arnie began. 'There's this guy staying all by himself at the Braemar Lodge. He filled up with gas and asked to use the office phone. It was a long-distance call and Charlie listened in.'

Ed Perriault laughed. 'Should put up warning signs round here: private telephone calls not possible in the Sugarmilk. What did he say?'

'Not much. It seemed to be hush-hush. But he used the words "staking out". And he was being very polite, like he was talking to his boss, Charlie says.'

'Oh dear.'

'If it means what I think it means it could be pretty serious.'

Ed paused rubbing his chin. 'You're right there, Arnie.' They looked across to the green lakeshore opposite. Blue jays scrapped in the trees. A raucous convoy of ducks made its way across the water.

'Have you been over to Algoma lately?' Ed continued. 'Used to be such beautiful country before the boom came. Suddenly thousands of people turned up. Big new towns, big new mines. In places now it's beginning to look like an atomic bomb's been dropped. In a way I suppose it has. And it could all happen here. It's too easy to get hold of a prospecting licence these days. We'd be swamped.' He looked away from the lake and turned to Arnie. 'But we might be jumping to completely the wrong conclusions. We don't know for sure whether there's been any claim-staking round here, though I think we can guess what they'd be looking for if they have come looking. We have to find out. See if we can stop it if there has. But we have to be careful. We don't want to cause any unnecessary alarm. Or another damned staking rush.' Ed paused again. 'On the other hand, if it turns out there's a big strike and it can't be stopped we want to be part of it. Don't want these big mining corporations having it all to themselves and leaving us here with nothing but the mess. It's a difficult one, Arnie. I'll see what I can find out on the quiet. You too.'

Sylvie Perriault joined them and for a few moments they all silently gazed at the landscape. 'Would you like to join us for a cup of tea, Arnie?' she asked him, 'There's nothing quite as refreshing on a hot day as a cup of China tea by the lake.'

Arnie smiled and thanked her. Irene would be interested in that cultivated notion, he thought. He tried it out in his mind: there is nothing so refreshing on a hot day as a cup of China tea by the lake.

*

Ed Perriault had a quiet word with Lucien Armand. 'No, Ed. I haven't heard or seen anything. But Zack mentioned he'd seen a plane. He thought it was making for the lumber camp.'

'Keep it to yourself, Lucien. We don't want people to get excited.'

*

Zack suppressed a grin when Ed Perriault made a point of bumping into him by chance. Yes, he'd seen a plane a couple of times. Probably making for the lumber camp. Thought he'd seen a bit of smoke in the distance one morning but he couldn't be sure. Thought he might take a closer look sometime.

'Nothing else?' asked Ed. 'No sign of any prospecting or claim-staking?'

'No sure sign, but that doesn't mean there isn't any,' said Zack. 'In country like this it could be going on right under your nose and you wouldn't know. Like happened over Algoma way a while back. Nobody knew a thing until all hell broke loose.' Zack shook his head. Yes, he'd keep his eyes open and his mouth shut.

*

'See anything up this way, Henri? Anything that might suggest there was any claim-staking going on?'

'Can't say that I have, Ed.'

'Is that lone fellow still here?'

'He is. How'd you hear about him?'

'Can't keep anything quiet for long in Sugarmilk Falls, Henri. Any idea why he's come?'

'He's just on vacation, Ed. He's come here for the peace and quiet. These city types really appreciate that.'

'Well, if you hear of anything, will you let me know?'

'Sounds like you'd know about it anyway. See you around, Ed.'

*

Ed Perriault's car pulled into Anstalt Motors, ostensibly to buy gasoline. 'I think we're right to be worried, Arnie,' he said. 'I can't find out anything specific, but Henri Osweken is being cagey. Could be he's in on it. After all it's mostly Ojibwa land round here.'

'Maybe, but Indians don't control mining rights far as I know. What do we do now?'

'Keep our eyes and ears open. It's all we can do for the time being.'

*

Charlie sat slumped in a chair in the garage showroom. 'You look terrible,' Arnie said. 'All your own damned fault.'

'There was one hell of a poker game up at the Braemar last night,' groaned Charlie. 'Played with that guy who used our phone. Turns out he's a lawyer, name of Jim Levine. Couldn't handle the moose milk. You'll never guess what happened.'

'You can handle it, I suppose,' Arnie sneered. 'What happened?'

'He lost everything, dough, watch, and you'll never guess what else.'

'What, Charlie?'

'Claims.'

'Claims?'

'From what I saw a lot of claims have been staked out up north, beyond the Sugarmilk. You'll never guess who has them all now?'

'Who?'

'The Oswekens. That guy had to sign them over to cover what he lost.'

'You mean it's already been staked out and now the Oswekens have the claims?'

'You got it, Arnie.'

'Damn it, Charlie, that can't happen.'

'It already has.'

'Somehow we've got to stop it. Does anyone else know about this?'

'Only the Osweken boys. They all had a lot of moose milk too.'

Arnie's face dropped but Charlie didn't appear to notice. 'Jesus, Arnie,' he sighed, 'I wish I played poker like that Grand'mère.'

*

Summer's shadows lengthened across the dust-dry land and still it did not rain. The waterways shrank and the roar of the waterfalls dulled almost to a whisper. Suzanne haunted the garage and Charlie worked on cars or trucks or his song. On a still, oppressive afternoon, when even the feeble breeze through the repair shop failed, a great crash of thunder exploded out of nowhere. It shook the buildings and rattled the windows. People looked up in surprise, at the black, turbulent clouds gathering so suddenly over the town. A long fierce zigzag of lightning hissed to the ground immediately followed by another ear-splitting clash of thunder. Another, and another, each one so closely following on behind it seemed like one continuous rumble. As suddenly the rain began, first a few great drops splattering heavily on the road and sidewalk, then drumming tensely on the tin roofs of the cars and the repair shop, then the deluge. Great sheets of rain and hailstones descended, beating against the windows, piling up in the gutters, in the ditches. The wind screamed and soon rivers of slushy water rushed down the road. Ditches and gutters overflowed. The repair-shop ceiling dripped in several places.

Charlie looked up from the work bench. Suzanne stood in the doorway watching him, silhouetted by flashes of blue lightning. Water overflowed the gutter above her. 'You'd better come in, kid,' he pointed to a chair, 'before you get completely soaked.'

She came inside and sat down. 'Thanks, Charlie,' she said.

'When it eases off I'll drive you home.' He carried on working. Suzanne watched and waited. The storm growled and roared.

'You're not afraid, are you?' he asked her after a while.

'Sort of,' she admitted.

'You know, you shouldn't hang around here like this,' he said eventually. 'I don't think your mom would like it if she knew.'

'No, she wouldn't.'

'Why do you do it?'

Suzanne looked confused for a moment. She swallowed hard and shrugged her shoulders. 'I guess I just like to hear you sing.'

He smiled broadly at her. 'Well, thank you. That's really nice to hear.' Rain drummed on the roof and clap after clap of thunder shook the building. The repair shop was very dark one moment, lit blue by lightning flashes the next. Charlie switched on the light. 'How about staying away from here so as not to worry your mom.'

Suzanne did not reply. She looked up at him, her eyes shining. 'Charlie,' she said at last, her voice trembling a little, 'there's something I have to know.'

'What's that?'

She hesitated so long he thought he wasn't going to find out after all. 'Have you got a girlfriend?' she asked suddenly.

He was amused and looked at her. 'No, Suzanne,' he said conversationally, 'I can honestly tell you that there is no girlfriend at the present time.'

There was another long pause. 'I'm nearly fifteen. Would you consider me?'

What a strange forthright kid, thought Charlie. 'Maybe . . . one day . . .' he joked but stopped when he saw her strained face. 'Look, Suzanne, it's like this. You bet I would, but not yet. You've got to admit you're still very young. There's a whole six years between you and me. It'd make Lucien and Claudine fly right off the handle if they knew and you can't really blame them, can you?' She sighed and tearfully shook her head. 'But strictly between ourselves, I've been noticing you a lot, Suzanne, and I like what I see. Give it a while and I reckon we just might get together properly. In the meantime, I promise

I'll let you know if the situation changes and maybe you'd do me the honour of agreeing you'll do the same if you change your mind? Is that a deal?'

'I'll never change my mind, Charlie.'

'Never say never, Suzanne. Do we have a deal?

'Okay.' Suzanne smiled.

Charlie continued to work and she watched him, waiting for the storm to subside. 'Charlie,' she asked after a time, 'what's a box-back coat?'

'I don't know. Something to do with coffins, maybe.' He turned to her with a grin. 'You won't tell anyone, will you?'

14

The wall of flames subsides into the autumn night. Henri floats near the edge of wakefulness towards the gentle beating of the drum. Grand'mère chants softly. The crackling of the wood fire wreathes around her calm low voice and the light rhythmic colliding of the seeds in her tortoise-shell rattle. From the sounds he knows that help will come. It is near. She is powerful. For a moment he is comforted, and drifts once more.

Grand'mère's chant fades into Flora's cries. 'Henri . . . Henri! What will become of us!' The flames surge again. 'The deeds! We must not leave the deeds behind!'

'Damn the deeds!' he sees himself shout. 'We've got to get out of here fast!' Again he fights his fear as the fire rages. Again he feels the scorching heat, the searing pain, his utter helplessness. Somewhere in the distance he hears Grand'mère's soothing chant, 'I, the wind in the forest . . . I am the sound . . .'

Deep inside the flames Flora cries, 'The money, Henri! We'll need to start all over again!' She turns to try to rescue it, beseeching him to follow her. 'We can't leave the money behind!' Flames explode all around her.

He starts awake and sees the feathers move near his face. Grand'mère shakes the rattle, steadily, rhythmically. Her eyes are wide and far away. She is in her trance. Sweet-smelling vapour hisses from the embers. 'I, the wind in the forest,' she chants, almost whispers, 'I am the sound . . .' Help is near.

Flames burst around Henri. 'Rachelle!' sobs Flora from their midst. 'Where is Rachelle?'

The drum beats in his chest. The seeds collide in his brain like tinkling crystals. Grand'mère's soft voice caresses him. 'I, the deer . . . I, the wolf . . . the mighty one comes with the sound . . .' Help is almost here.

The flames subside again. 'Rachelle is safe,' Henri sighs. 'She is with Grand'mère!'

How could he know that?

He struggles to focus his eyes. In the dim flickering light of the wood fire Grand'mère sits on the deer-hide rug. An arm rests on her knee. She stares wide-eyed, unblinking, and shakes the rattle of seeds. With the feathers she sprinkles liquid from a bowl into the flames, onto him. 'I, the river . . . I, the rock . . .' The words come from her trance. Her hair hangs in damp, limp coils. Sweat glistens on her ridged ochre skin. The animal teeth and claws wreathed round her neck rise with each short breath. 'The sky will echo when I come . . .' Steam spits and hisses from the red-hot stones surrounding the flames. The air is hot and moist with bitter roots and sweet herbs.

'Rachelle?' gasps Henri.

The throbbing drum, the rattling seeds, the rippling chant stop suddenly. There is stillness now, only the softly crackling, flickering fire. 'Rachelle's with me,' says

Grand'mère after a time. 'Here, drink some of this.' She gives him a cup of bittersweet broth.

'Flora? I see her in the flames.'

'Yes.'

'She was looking for the deeds.'

'They're here too.'

'She went back for the cash.'

'I know.'

Henri drifts far away. Once more flames engulf him. Once more he feels the searing pain. Flora stretches her arms towards him. 'Henri!' she screams in terror. Again he cannot reach her. Again the burning roof crashes down . . .

*

'Can he talk?' It is Constable Martello. What does he want?

'No, not yet. He's still sedated.' Who is that? Angela Norton? What is she doing here? Is he still at the nursing station? Is he dreaming again? 'He's got some burns and he's inhaled a lot of smoke.'

'I need to ask him a few questions,' says the policeman.

'I couldn't get out,' Henri tries to explain to him, 'I put Rachelle through the window and went back for Flora . . .' The words will not form.

'Don't upset him, Frank,' says Angela, 'Come back in a day or two, after the doc's given the okay. Even better, wait till he's gone home to Grand'mère's place.'

'Awful, awful shame about Flora,' he hears Frank Martello say. 'I've had a good look round. Couldn't see any sign of anything suspicious. Thank God the season's over and the place was empty. Damned good thing too there's been so much rain at last or we could have had a real disaster on our hands.'

Faraway Grand'mère whispers, 'I, the deer . . . I, the wolf . . .'

'The door wouldn't open,' Henri tries to say, 'Jesus, Frank, I couldn't get her out . . . I . . . I . . .'

'That's enough, Frank! Leave it for now.' Angela says firmly.

'Henri!' cries Flora. 'The deeds! Don't leave the deeds!'

'Damn the deeds!' he shouts. 'Someone's jammed the door!'

Henri looks down. Below him the Braemar is in flames, lighting up the surrounding trees, reddening the surface of the lake. Red sparks and burning debris rise into the starry sky. The fire explodes. The roof collapses to the ground. Flora? The flames die down. In the grey dawn light he sees the blackened granite chimney inside the glowing skeleton of the hotel. Flora? He sees a movement in the shadows. There it is. There.

Another cloud of sharp sweet steam hisses from the fire. The wooden drum throbs steadily. Feathers brush his face, seeds jangle in his ears. The broth soothes and cools. Grand'mère stares into the flames. In the darkness of the corners the dreamed ones watch and wait. He sleeps.

*

Henri lay awake for a long time, watching bright sunlight lance the beads of condensation thawing on the window. The fire had gone cold. The air, still bittersweet, was chilly. On the bunk on the other side of the small room Grand'mère slept. She lay on her back, very still, barely breathing, gaunt and timeless as the Sugarmilk hills in winter. His head was clear now, she had seen to that. He could breathe more easily. The pain from his burns had eased as well. He felt numb. No, it was more than numbness. He was drained of all feeling, as empty as the frosty air.

Flora was dead. He repeated the thought in his head, trying to understand it. He would never see her again, or hear her, or speak to her, or smell her, or touch her. For one bleak moment he considered what that meant for him, weighing up the loss, calculating its worth, inspecting his own feelings as though he was inspecting an animal caught in one of his traps or a fresh kill of game. It was a brief moment only. He hurriedly brushed the thought aside and the wave of grief overwhelmed him. Melting fingers of frost trickled down the glass, forming rills and rainbows, making pools on the ledge.

*

'I hear her calling me.' Henri spoke with deep sadness. He sat by the fire staring at nothing, as he did most days. It was the first time he'd mentioned Flora. 'It's time for her spirit to move on,' he said.

'I'll go with you tonight. I will help her,' Grand'mère replied.

'No. It would worry her. She was not like us. She never really understood. I'll have to go alone and do my best.'

Grand'mère looked at him with deep concern. 'It's not a good idea to be by yourself at such a time. The powerful ones can be tricky.' She paused. 'Maybe Zack will go with you. He knows our ways.'

'They're not Flora's ways, Grand'mère. Besides, she

thought Zack was a bad influence.' Henri smiled at the memory. 'She wouldn't want him there.'

'What about Reverend Byers? She went to his church.'

'Would he come? I don't think so.'

'Matt Souris? He seems to understand these things. There is something there. I think maybe he's known loss himself.'

'Flora used to say if it wasn't for all that popish nonsense he'd be a good Presbyterian.'

'Okay, I'll ask him,' said Grand'mère. 'And I'll make payment to persuade the powerful ones.'

*

Henri dressed in the soft deerskin shirt, beaded at the throat and on the chest with spiralling flower buds and berries, and at the cuffs bands of intertwined leaves. Red and blue, green and white and purple beaded garlands, blue and gold ribboned borders, a special shirt. The sun went down behind the trees. He crouched on the jetty, tossing pebbles into the silver lake and mist formed over the spreading rings of ripples.

Father Souris sat down next to him. 'Grand'mère has asked me to be with you tonight while you ask for the repose of the soul of Flora,' he said to Henri. 'I'll be nearby,' he added, crossing himself.

'Thanks, Matt.'

Grand'mère was right. Father Souris seemed to understand the delicate position. Henri hoped Flora would not see the purple stole he wore underneath his coat. He'd brought his crucifix as well, and his pockets were probably stuffed with rosaries. She wouldn't approve of that at all.

Evening darkened and still Henri stayed by the side of the lake, looking back at what had been the Braemar Lodge, remembering. The charred timbers took on weird shapes in the dying light. The granite chimney rose tall from the pile of ashes. Behind him the mirror-black lake shimmered with starlight. Above him the black layers of sky blazed with galaxies. All around, the dark, breathing forest, silent and cold. Flora was everywhere, inconsolable at being so suddenly parted from him. He felt her silent anguish as she wandered through the ruins of their home. He felt her reaching out to him, time after time, entreating him to follow her, to stay with her forever. Would this never cease, he wondered, this reaching across the threshold where she clung so desperately, so near, almost, almost touching, but not quite touching, never, never touching again? Henri sat still and silent as the lake, his tears as many as the stars glittering on its surface. Would there ever be enough?

The owls finished calling and the moon crossed over the lake. The sky began to pale in the east. Henri began his chant, slowly, hesitantly, just a word, like the first snowflake, then another, then a tremulous phrase, then a flurry of renewed sorrow.

He raised his head and began again. 'You are ready to leave me now, my Flora,' he said into the silence. 'It is time for you to depart.' Once more he faltered, unable to speak.

The darkness faded and light from the rising sun reddened the treetops. He braced himself. A third time he spoke, slowly, sparsely, gathering strength, like tentacles of ice forming at the shoreline. 'Do not look back as you go, my dearest. Your glance draws me with you. Look straight ahead of you, as you always did in life.'

He paused again. 'We live in the world for as long as we are meant to. Don't wish me to hurry up and join you. You will find all your forefathers where you are going. You will be happy. You will not be alone. Every day that passes I will think of you. Rachelle will not forget you. Whoever did this to you will pay, I promise. So do not long for us who must stay behind. Do not trouble us by lingering here.'

The sky grew red, then gold and green. The hoar frost began to thaw. In the rosy light the maple forest shone, ochre and vermilion. Wet leaves dropped like coloured stones and diamonds of ice criss-crossed at the water's edge. Henri sighed deeply and his breath turned to mist. The bitter smell of cold wet ash tainted the clear sharp air. He looked around, at the turquoise sky, the indigo lake, the painted trees, the black stone chimney standing in the ruins. Seeds of anger lodged in his heart.

Suddenly he felt bone-weary. The chant was finished. Flora was gone. The bright land was cold and empty. He was alone.

15

The amber beads fell with a clatter into the black tin box, disturbing the fragments and dust that lay in the bottom. Father Souris frowned as the picture flared in his brain. The tobacco odour was still there. Over the years the dried leaves had frittered away but the mellow acrid smell clung to the yellowed, charred documents, the necklace of animal claws and teeth, the bundle of bones and feathers, the intact braid of sweet-grass. From the moment he became aware of it, she was there again, vivid as life, Grand'mère, the shaman, with her all-seeing black eyes and unearthly power of persuasion. He'd always regarded himself as a modern man of religion with his feet firmly planted in the late-twentieth-century world of science and progress. Yet oh how easily had he been ensnared.

The snow was falling again, tapping softly on the window. The logs hissed and crackled in the fireplace. He held the papers in his hand. Why not throw them all into the flames and have done with them, he thought. Tell Frank Martello they were gone. They were meant to be burned. If they'd gone up in smoke when the Braemar burned down it would all have been so, so different.

The claims were worthless now anyway, time-expired long ago. The rest . . . ? He should have done it years before. Cleared the air once and for all. What, who was holding him back this time? Still that old medicine woman? Marina? His own accursed indecisiveness? He looked through the documents and shook his head. It was papers that had brought Marina here. Everything had happened because of this bundle of papers. And everything now was as pointless and as useless as the tobacco dust.

But what could he have done? Could he have prevented it? Had there been a time when he should have acted? The time will come, Grand'mère had told him, when he would know what to do. Had he ignored the signs? Or somehow missed them altogether? Was he unable to choose among the alternatives? Or simply incapable of seeing what should have been obvious? Was it all his fault?

Of course it was all his fault. He should never have come here to Sugarmilk Falls. He should never have taken vows. He should have married Marina Serac. No, that much at least was not his fault. She had put an end to that. But he should have married somebody, gone to live in the city, got himself a regular job as a translator or something, anything but spend his life alone out here in this vast glittering wilderness of ice and snow and dark malevolent forests. Most of all he should have shown Grand'mère the door that day all those years ago, certainly not have acceded to her request. That much at least should have been plain as his nose. She knew he was being compromised. The wily old witch had even said so, but that was only to put him off the scent. He should have realized.

Come to think of it he did, but no, he had to play the hero. Fool!

*

'This isn't a social call, Matt,' Grand'mère had said, 'I have a request.'

He hadn't heard her come into the presbytery. He was reading the *Gazette*, he recalled, an interview with Frank Martello about the recent fire at the Braemar, and he looked up when he felt the rush of sharp autumn air that entered with her. She was standing directly in front of him, so close he saw the vein throbbing in her temple. Her voice was low, a little fey. 'I have a request.' He was taken by surprise; that's always been the devil's way. Did he still believe in the devil? Maybe. Most of the time he regarded Grand'mère as simply someone moving on different but occasionally approaching tangents who briefly touched his own orbit before continuing on her way. She'd proved to be as confounding as a bad dream and he had plenty of those.

Father Souris was intrigued. Grand'mère did not make social calls on him in any event. He did not speak with her much at all. At Easter she came to Mass, but that was about it and he was oddly reluctant to press her to attend more regularly. She was a familiar figure but a baffling one, much more so than the other Indians he knew. It was a remote familiarity born of time and diffidence and his acquaintance with Henri Osweken, who'd been a soldier too.

The cold smell of decaying leaves filled the room. The old woman sat down on the edge of his couch and leaned towards him, holding a leather pouch. She accepted his condolence with a single nod, refused his coffee with a brief shake of her head. He was able to study her closely for the first time. She seemed tired and very old, but she was old when he first came to Sugarmilk Falls. She sat opposite him now with her ankles crossed, wiry, straight-backed, leaning forward slightly, her hooded eyes dark, intelligent, penetrating. There was something else too. Shyness? Cunning? He couldn't be sure, and was finding it difficult to be charitable. Her demeanour emanated such authority, such an aura of apartness, that he began to feel uncomfortable and at the same time resentful. Here he was in his own presbytery where, if anywhere, he should be able to rely on the certainties he'd accumulated, indeed take them for granted, but instead they were letting him down. They seemed to have hurried away to hide behind his chair, peeping nervously over his shoulder now and again to see if she was still sitting there. The empty space between himself and this old medicine woman who dealt on a daily basis in arcane phenomena he hardly dared even to imagine was disconcertingly neutral. He felt threatened, strangely excited. He was apprehensive. He felt as if he was about to be challenged, but what could she possibly want from him?

'Ask away, Grand'mère,' he replied airily, on his guard.

'Before I do, you need to know it is something not really in your usual line of work. If you think it is too compromising for you, I would understand. I hope you won't be embarrassed to refuse.'

Who did she think she was talking to? Telling him his job! Father Souris was used to being addressed with a bit of deference but he tried not to show his irritation at her presumption. 'Has this something to do with Flora?' he asked benignly.

Grand'mère looked levelly at him. He felt a strange sense of connection. 'Yes, but it's more to do with Henri,' she replied. 'And Rachelle, of course, though she is still small.'

The silence was like a presence while she chose her words. 'Flora is distraught and it preys on Henri. He worries she may become vengeful. It is time she went to the southern lands, as we say. I would deal with this myself but Henri is concerned for her. She was not Ojibwa and he fears she would be frightened and offended. We don't want to antagonize her spirit.'

Grand'mère paused, suspending her words in the space between them. They were unholy words, primal, compelling, the dangerous words of a shaman. Father Souris resisted strongly, but his certainties crept farther away. He could feel her scrutinizing him, looking for his reaction. 'Go on,' he said, feeling himself forced into accepting the challenge.

'Henri has decided he must go alone to speak with her. This is not wise. It is not an easy journey that she has to make and he doesn't have my medicine knowledge. But then, Flora was not one of us but Presbyterian. Roy Byers has done what he must do. Her body is buried, so that side of things is complete. He did it well, although his understanding is limited.'

She paused again, searching his face. Father Souris suppressed his affront at her startling arrogance and waited for her to continue.

'Flora's spirit still troubles us. Henri feels he must find a way to help her depart. It means addressing the powerful ones. Their presence is always risky. Henri needs assistance, but he says it must be someone who will not frighten her or offend them. They would respect your attendance.' She paused a third time. 'Will you think about this, Matt?'

He hesitated, considering the request, hoping to find a plausible excuse. 'You are asking me to go with Henri to the Braemar Lodge, to pray for the repose of the soul of Flora?'

'Henri will do this in his own way. But in your terms, yes.'

It was simple enough. A straightforward request, in fact. Why had he felt so intimidated? Now he even sensed a small tingle of pleasure that her spirit world approved of him. She spoke with such apparent candour. How could he say no? Even if he came to regret it later, in her presence he could think of no reason to refuse. 'I understand,' he said. 'It's a delicate situation.'

'It could take all night.'

Matt sighed with resignation. 'I'll go with him, Grand'mère. Do you want me to do anything special?'

He was surprised by the look of relief on her face, 'No. It's up to you.' She held out the leather pouch.

'What's this?' Father Souris asked.

'The payment,' she replied. 'We too make payment for ceremonies. Like the collection in your church.'

'What do I do with this payment?'

'Keep it. You'll know what to do when the time comes.'

'The time for what?'

Grand'mère shrugged. 'It will be clear when it comes.'

'When will that be?'

'Who knows?'

He took the payment from her. 'May I look?' She gave another nod. Inside were some twists of tobacco wrapped in a beaded cloth, and a thick brown envelope. He opened the envelope and pulled out a bundle of papers. They were documents, some were charred at the edges.

'Papers were important to Flora,' Grand'mère explained. 'We have them but now she is gone.'

'Your name is on this one,' said Matt looking through them. 'And this one, on all of them. They're mining claims.'

'The land is Ojibwa land. It was never surrendered.'

'Yes, I've heard that story. Surely you could record the claims yourself. Lease the rights. Make a fortune.' He looked at her. 'I can't take these, Maggie.'

Grand'mère did not reply immediately. 'When claims like this are recorded the news gets out. Next thing there is a staking rush. Before you know it the mining companies have moved in.' She paused. 'I am an Ojibwa healer. In the summer people travel far to see me, sometimes from Algoma where land is dying and water is poisoned from uranium mines. None are rich. They are sick, some are very sick, and I do what I can. But not your medicine or mine is strong enough for this sickness.'

'Uranium? Here? How do you know?'

'I was a prospector before Geiger counters, Matt. There's all kinds of stuff round here, including lots of uranium.'

He returned the documents to the envelope. 'I think you should keep these, Maggie. There could be more exploration some time. You never know when you might need them.'

'No. I must make payment for Henri.' Neither spoke. Then Grand'mère sighed. 'This is what we'll do, Matt. We'll be wise like Solomon. Half each.'

Father Souris removed half the documents. He put the envelope inside the leather pouch, and handed it back to Grand'mère. He placed the rest with the tobacco into a black tin box he took from a shelf of his bookcase. 'I'll keep these here for the time being, but you must tell me if you need them back.' His equilibrium had been restored. 'Did you ever find gold like they say?' he asked.

There was a sly look on her face and she laughed. 'It depends on what they say, but yes, I did.'

*

There. That's when she snared him, and he never noticed until much, much later, and by then he'd pulled the wire so tight it cut off the blood supply to his will. Where did she get such power?

'Don't be ridiculous, Matt,' Marina used to say, 'she's just a pre-logical tribal witch doctor who's seen better days.'

He'd tried several times to explain Grand'mère to her. 'Maybe she's seen better days, Marina, but in her day she was really quite something.'

'What did she give you?' Marina once asked him. 'Have you still got it?'

He pointed to the black tin box standing on its side in his bookcase between works by Jung and Freud. 'There isn't a key. It's unlocked.'

Marina opened the box and removed the contents. 'Tobacco!' she said with surprise but did not wait for him to speak. She opened out the documents and began to read. He could almost sense the ice forming in the air while Marina silently perused each one. 'I don't think you realize what these are, Matt,' she said eventually, 'but there's no reason why you should.'

'They're expired staking claims.'

Marina's face was white. Her eyes glittered. There was a long pause before she spoke. Her voice was cold. 'They're my staking claims,' she said.

Mathieu was taken aback. 'No, they're not. How can they be? They are in my safekeeping for the time being. They all belong to Grand'mère.'

Marina composed herself. 'I thought she gave them to you . . . Is this all of them?'

'There were some more.'

'Do you know how she got them? There's a name crossed out.'

'She didn't say.' He was surprised at how defensive and evasive he had become.

*

Grand'mère may not have explained to him how she came to have them, but he knew. After the Braemar fire the story of how the old woman had outwitted the city lawyer at cards into signing over thousands of acres of mining claims became common knowledge, another Osweken tall tale. With each retelling the story evolved, until the claims became the deeds to gold mines and silver mines in secret places, and they'd all gone up in the flames. For years afterwards school kids bicycled up from the town during the summer vacation. They picked over the ruins of the hotel, hoping to come across buried treasure maps somehow miraculously preserved in the ashes, until one day Henri Osweken loaded up his rifle and scared them off. After the fire he lived with Grand'mère but after a while he moved into a cabin beside the burned-out old Lodge. He lived alone; Rachelle stayed with Grand'mère. He was silent and sullen and drank more and more. He spent long periods alone in the forest. His only companion, now and then, was Zack.

Zachariah Guillem. That damned bushwhacker who tricked Father Souris and took Marina away. That was something else he hadn't noticed until it was too late. He first heard about it listening in to the gossip on the party line. Was there a time when he should have acted there? Was there anything at all he should have done? Could have done?

He did confront her, several times. The last time she kept him standing on her doorstep, and her Viennese wall clock chimed the hours. Her eyes glittered angrily. 'What on earth do you expect of me? Look at you! Look at what you've become! What can you possibly be to me except an episode in the past?'

She was angrier than he had seen her, and it made him equally angry. 'It would have been a hell of a lot different if I hadn't dropped the gun in the Seine!' he blurted out, jealous and unreasonable.

There was a long silence. 'You did that? I didn't know. I always wondered what happened.'

His anger collapsed. 'I was sent home. I thought you were dead. All those years I thought you were dead.'

'You could have taken the trouble to find out.'

'I did, Marina. I wrote to Emile. For a long time I got

no answer and then a letter came. It was from Thérèse. She said you were not with them anymore.'

Marina looked at him, nodding slightly. 'Yes. I told her to say that.'

He couldn't believe her words. Did she have any idea at all about the terrible anguish he had suffered? 'Why?' he gasped.

For a moment he thought she was going to explain, to make amends, to make everything all right again, but she shook her head and her words were cold. 'Because you left me, of course. I don't owe you anything, Matt. You are the one who walked away, remember.' She took a deep breath, as though about to fire a tirade of accusations and consequences, but she only said, 'Anyway, it's far too late now.'

Marina stopped, her mouth quivering. Was it just emotion, he wondered? Or was it from the effort of holding back her words? What had she almost said? But then she continued, as if to deliberately make matters worse, 'Besides, he's nice. I've never known anyone so completely self-contained. It is liberating, uncomplicated. I'm tired of being secretive and I'm tired of being alone, Matt.'

'You're not alone. I love you. I only ever wanted the best for you. He's not nice at all.'

'What gives you the right to decide either?' she'd sneered coldly. 'When did you decide anything, Father Souris?'

*

After all the intervening years her voice still burned in his brain. He compared the time on his watch with the atomic clock. He put the documents back inside the tin box with the amber beads, the sweet-grass, the fragile necklace of animal claws and teeth, the bones and feathers, the tobacco dust.

16

Captain Souris was running, running for his life, his stone-heavy boots stumbling through the rubble. His legs ached, his heart pounded, his lungs were ready to burst. All around him blasted trees, blackened and broken walls, gaping windows where the snipers hid. In the darkness he could see their rifles gleaming, aimed at him. He saw lightning flashes of gunfire, heard the crack and whistle of bullets, felt the air part as they passed his ears. He must keep on running. If he stopped, even for a moment, to gulp for air, to ease his splitting chest, he knew for certain that he would be dead.

Someone, something was running behind him, crunching the broken cobbles, approaching nearer, nearer. He felt hot breath on his neck, a clutching at his shoulder, tighter, tighter. Turn around! it ordered. Turn and look me in the face! Then he heard a scream of such utter terror, so loud and despairing, so annihilating, so near to him, that he sat up suddenly, panting and wild-eyed. Had the scream been his own? The dream switched itself off. Mathieu lay down again, exhausted. Cold rivulets of perspiration trickled down his ribs. It had a life of its own, this nightmare. He knew it would return. It always did.

Captain Souris opened his eyes again and looked around, bewildered. Where was he? He was not in his big fancy bed at the gilded Hôtel Meurice. But recognition quickly washed over him, cleansing and comforting, like sinking into warm bathwater. This was Marina's apartment. The room was dim and peaceful. Soft shafts of light filtered between the slats of the tall shutters closed across the open window. The old Moroccan carpet glowed like stained glass. He closed his eyes again. Muffled noises drifted in from the street below, wooden soles clattering on the cobbles, the happy chatter of passers-by, the raucous trumpet of a rooster, and, quite close, the nervous cluck-cluck of chickens. Mathieu opened his eyes abruptly. Chickens. Is that where the shriek came from? Something had frightened Marina's chickens, that was all. The concierge's cat. Or maybe Marina herself. He smiled. He could hear her moving about in the next room.

He threw back the cover, got up from the bed, opened the shutters and frowned. Just a few feet away, the twisted faces of the gargoyles glared at him. They leaned out between the carved gables and pinnacles of the church opposite, their mouths wide open with shock or delight, stretching across the narrow gap of the street, bright-eyed, alert, precocious, taking far too much interest in him and what he did there. It made him uneasy. Whenever he looked out of Marina's windows those horrible stone demons were there, peering accusingly at him, threatening him with he didn't know what eternal torments. He returned to bed, curling up under the blanket, and stared back at them. When he first walked Marina home he had looked up at the grey dawn sky and was surprised to see how far, how precariously, they jutted out from the top of the church wall, reaching nearly halfway across the street, craning this way and that as if to get a better look. Their misshapen mouths dribbled in the drizzle. They no longer spewed stiff streams of water like they had for all the centuries of rain before the downpipes were installed, but they gaped wide as ever with anticipation and glee. When he ascended the whorls of stairs to her apartment he found himself on their level. Mathieu stood at the iron railing of Marina's small balcony and looked at them, at their evil, leering faces, so close he felt he could, if he tried, reach out and touch the curved beaks and thick lips, the scalloped feathers on their long outstretched necks, their tight little wings and great gnarled claws. The gargoyles' eyes stared stonily back at him. They were daring him, he knew, to do as he pleased, to follow his own inclination, his own will, at his peril. But with Marina by his side and a glass of wine in his hand, he'd looked straight back at them and wondered about taking up the challenge. What were they, after all? Outmoded and deactivated medieval rain gutters. Old, eroded stone carvings. Nothing more. And whenever he looked across at them after that, he felt a stubborn resistance to all those grotesquely grinning creatures, so vivid in his imagination, so eager to leap upon him, so certain of his impending doom. If he were to shake his head boldly, to snap his fingers dismissively, the whole regiment of soul-hungry stone demons, clustering so expectantly along the wall opposite, would fall from their perches and crumble into dust and rubble on the street below. If only he dared. Would he ever find that lonely confidence? Or would he always run away, go back to the predictability of the life already chosen for him? He sighed. What about all he had done in the meantime?

And then the bells began to ring, St-Germain-des-Prés, Notre-Dame, St-Phillipe-du-Roule, St-Sulpice, St-Séverin, all the bells of the city, filling the Sunday morning air with the clamour of a thousand years of certainties and obligations, resonating in his brain, sending his thoughts and doubts and naive challenges back into oblivion, where they belonged. He felt disloyal, a little ashamed at his arrogance. Who was he, just a soldier from Québec, to call Divine Authority to account?

*

The smoke, the music, the noise swallowed him up the moment he walked through the door of the Café Serac. His nose twitched at the unmistakeable smell of places like this, cigarettes and garlic, unwashed bodies and stale perfume, urine and red wine, all compounded and heated up in the packed, airless spaces that were Paris's cafés and bars on Saturday nights. He squeezed into a corner, ordered a pitcher of wine, and prepared to remain there, smoking and drinking, exchanging pleasantries, watching Marina to and fro, smile and joke, between the tables, her tray held high, until the early hours, when it was time to take her home. Moody, smoky jazz from a guitar and a clarinet wove through the conversations and laughter. The black musicians wore American army shirts, unbuttoned at the neck, loose at the cuffs. He listened for a while, sipping wine, inhaling deeply on his cigarettes, caught up in the slow, measured syncopations, until voices at the nearby tables began to intrude. Reluctantly he found himself eavesdropping on a conversation between several young men. Some wore dark-rimmed spectacles, one smoked a pipe, and their animated talk was accompanied by the lighting up of Caporals and Lucky Strikes, one after another, and lubricated with glasses of rough red wine. Other conversations paused to listen or stopped altogether as an audience of young people grew. Soon there was quite a crowd listening to the discussion, the rise and fall in its volume mirroring the clarinet and guitar.

Mathieu sighed impatiently. He didn't want to listen. He was tired, not in the mood for the current brand of abstract talk common in the left-bank cafés. He filled his glass again and tried to concentrate on the music. It was really quite good, he thought, better than the usual weekend entertainment at the Serac. But he found himself drawn back to the group of young men. They wore chequered flannel shirts, the kind sent over by American charities and picked up in the city's flea markets. Probably, if he looked under the tables, he would see they all wore tennis shoes as well. It seemed to be their required dress, like the uniform was his. Did any of them have regular jobs, he wondered. In his mellowing state he found himself paying attention, curious despite himself to know just what they found to be so passionate about this late on Saturday night.

Mathieu listened with a sinking heart. With great authority it seemed, these young barflies were discussing responsibility and anguish. What did any of them know about those things? He could certainly tell them a thing or two. But even in his hazy condition he did not want to think or hear or talk about any of that. At the moment life looked as though it might soon be safe and reliable again.

At last. Just as soon as he could, although he hadn't yet worked out how, he was going to marry Marina and take her back home to Trois Rivières. All the mess, all the chaos would be left behind forever. They would be very happy leading responsible, ordinary, quiet and long lives together. Anguish and the past would be banished from their thoughts. However, try as he might, he could not shut out the young men's discussion.

'Every person should act as though the whole world is looking at him, and the world is guiding itself by what he does,' one of the group said. Mathieu recognized him as Pierre Jaccard, who was often in the café. 'We all bear this great responsibility when we decide how we are going to act, because the choices we make show the world what we believe is the best way to live.'

'I wouldn't be so presumptuous,' replied another.

'It isn't presumption at all,' said Pierre. 'When you have to make a decision it causes you to be anxious, don't you agree?'

'Big decisions, maybe,' offered a third.

'No, all decisions to some degree,' Pierre said. 'It's because when a man makes a choice he isn't the only person involved. It's not good enough for him to say, "It's okay if I do this or that because not everyone acts in this way." On the contrary, he should always think, "Suppose everyone acted this way?" when he makes a choice. Otherwise he is not being honest with himself. He is trying to hide from his guilty conscience. He feels guilty because he has not acted responsibly. So before making a choice about how to act, everyone should ask himself, "Am I acting in such a way that the world can guide itself by my actions?"'

'Bah! No one asks himself that,' said another. 'If we did, we would never get round to doing anything. Nothing would ever get done.'

'It doesn't work like that,' countered Pierre. 'This is something that anyone who takes any kind of responsibility is already familiar with.' He looked at Mathieu in his captain's uniform, and continued, 'When an army officer takes responsibility for an attack and sends a number of men to their death, he decides, he chooses, to do this. Only he makes that choice. It's no good him saying he's only obeying orders from above because the orders to him aren't detailed. The officer has to interpret them, and the lives of the men under his command depend on his interpretation of those orders. He can't help feeling anguish when he makes his choice. But it doesn't stop him from acting. On the contrary, without feeling that anxiety, that anguish, he would not be able to act for the best.'

Mathieu was irritated. What did this barroom intellectual who had never even been a soldier, let alone an officer, know about taking decisions and obeying orders? Pierre was married, or nearly so depending on his philosophy, to Thérèse, Marina's sister or cousin or something. She hadn't yet explained her complicated family relationships to him and he hesitated to ask her.

Pierre continued, 'His anguish shows that he has a number of possibilities, and when he chooses one of them it becomes the important one. But it's only important because he has chosen it. The officer has a direct responsibility to those men under his command. He is anxious. He asks himself if, in making this particular choice, choosing this possibility over the others, he is meeting that responsibility. So, you see, his anxiety, his anguish does not stop him from taking action. Quite the opposite, in fact. The anguish is part of the action itself. Were you not anxious, Captain, when the orders to attack came and you had to decide how best to obey?'

Mathieu did not realize immediately that the question was addressed to him. He did not want to get involved in any arid discussions. 'I just did my job,' he replied reluctantly.

Pierre persisted. 'But there was always more than one way to do it? You made a choice. No one else. You.'

Mathieu's throat tightened. He swallowed. 'The choices were limited. And time was always short.'

'Of course. But you had to make up your mind and be responsible for your men. You must have felt some anxiety at least?'

He did not want to reply. He wanted to punch this cocksure windbag in the face. Instead he shrugged his shoulders. The clarinet player came to the end of his solo and they both joined in the lengthy applause. Damn that Pierre, thought Mathieu. He and his half-baked, newfangled left-bank theories and irritatingly penetrating insights. It really got under his skin. Where did he pick up all that stuff? He was supposedly writing a novel based on his experiences with the maquis, where, to listen to him, he had done everything, from carrying messages and writing pamphlets to assassinating Nazis. But after the liberation, every other person, it seemed, was claiming Resistance membership, often as not to cover up or excuse anything that might be interpreted as collaboration. And, as far as he could tell, all of these café communists were writing novels based on real or imagined experiences of the Resistance or the FFI or whatever, these young men in their charity shirts who'd never felt the fear, the horror, the glory of a real battlefield, where a bit of anxiety about complying with orders from above was so far down in the scale of things that needed to be done it was not even noticed. He, Mathieu, never had the luxury or the time to sit down and mull over whether this selection or that one from all the possibilities available to him was the best way to show the rest of mankind how he thought they ought to live their lives. No. He'd considered how a given objective could best be achieved with the minimum of loss, not that he ever had much room to manoeuvre.

For a while he concentrated on the music, draining another glass to the improvisations of the guitar. The conversation became heated again. God does not exist, Pierre was saying, with such grotesque finality that Mathieu was taken aback. There is no divine plan, no determinism. There is only the individual free will. There are no values other than the ones we choose. A person is ultimately responsible for everything he does.

Mathieu had had enough. 'No, you're wrong,' he intervened, annoyed to hear himself slurring the words, 'God does exist. We are here to do His will.'

Pierre grinned. 'That view is your choice, Mathieu. In the end it is you who decides what it is God wants. What you will do. There is no one else.'

'You're wrong. Just because it isn't easy to know what it is God wants doesn't mean He does not want it. We are imperfect beings and struggle to understand His divinity. We don't always succeed. Because we may get it wrong does not mean we should stop our struggle to fulfil His purpose. He will forgive us our wrongs.' Mathieu faltered. His words sounded straight from the catechism, but he continued nevertheless. 'Really, Pierre, I don't know how you can look at the world as it has been these past years and say God does not exist. Have we not overcome the greatest evil with His aid?'

None of the young men spoke. Had he touched a raw nerve, one that had survived the brave new intellectual order being advocated by the likes of Pierre? Had he plucked at strings of inbred belief? Or did they simply regard him as a coward and a fool? 'Ask Marina,' Mathieu added recklessly. She stood at a table nearby and turned at the sound of her name. 'Ask her about overcoming evil.'

There was a pause, a silence. The clarinet began another number. The young men looked away to listen and Marina continued with her task. The moment passed. Conversations were taken up again. Pierre leaned across the table towards Mathieu and hissed sharply, 'Do not involve Marina!' Mathieu looked stubbornly back at him. Pierre sighed, and then smiled sadly adding, 'Look, Marina is . . . It will be a long time before she is herself again. Remember she knows more than we can ever imagine about overcoming evil, as you put it. Please, it is better you do not ask her such things. I do not think she would say she has been helped by God.'

*

The bells of Paris were fading. The gargoyles leaned closer to watch him through the window. And then he realized he was becoming tired of it all, and that it was not the first time. He never found any answers. Or maybe they were always the same. He just went round and round in the same repetitive, irresolvable circles. Yes, thought

Mathieu, there was a tempting logic in what Pierre had said the previous night. Everything would be possible if it wasn't for God. There might be nothing to cling to, no divine commandments to guide his actions, no divine rule books at all. Everything would be for him to decide, and the heady freedom of that seemed suddenly as compelling as fresh air. He considered for a moment the idea that his existence in the world might be arbitrary, that now, here, this brief instant in time, with the sun shining brightly through the window, only this was real. It could be so exhilarating, if only he dared to believe, to really believe, that everything, his presence here on this Sunday morning, in Paris, on the left bank, in Marina's bed, resulted from his own random choices. All those unanswered questions, all his uncertainties, seemed not to matter so very much. Yet here he still lay, cowering under the blankets from medieval carvings. Was that his choice too? He heaved a long, deep, desperate sigh. The idea had to be wrong, he decided. The gargoyles looked so alert, so ready to spring, to tear him to pieces and hurl him down into hell.

Another unholy shriek split the air. Something was disturbing the chickens.

17

The room had been elegant once with its panelled walls and garlanded plasterwork but now it seemed irretrievably dilapidated. Thick grey cobwebs draped the corners. A dusty, pocked mirror in a tarnished frame stood over the smoke-stained fireplace filled with ash and cinders from fires long gone cold. Rags and bits of newspaper stopped up gaps in the windows. Fat brown chickens clucked and scratched between the carved, gilded legs of a rickety antique bureau with a drawer missing, a couple of armchairs with stuffing oozing through the torn pink satin and a small spindly table. Straw, feathers and bird droppings covered the furniture and parquet floor. In a corner, two brown rabbits hopped nervously about and raised their heads when Mathieu entered. Marina, still in her pink chemise, perched on the edge of a pink and gold chair, pulling the feathers from a dead chicken spread across her knees. Pale naked corpses sprawled over the intricate marquetry of the table top.

She looked up briefly. Curled feathers clung to her and when she brushed them away he saw streaks of dirt and blood on her hand. 'Did they wake you? I'm sorry,' she said. 'You can use the bath now. I've taken the rabbits out and cleaned it up. There is some hot water. Save a little for me.'

He watched her quickly, expertly pluck the chicken propped between her thighs, the head with its dead eyes and bright red comb dangling between her bare legs. The row of numbers was dark on her pale arm as she raised one of the bird's legs and then the other to remove the feathers. The thin chemise and boyish hair made her seem very young, very fragile. He felt an overpowering urge to enfold her in his arms and keep her there until everything was safe once more. He started towards her.

'I've nearly finished this one,' she said briskly. 'It's enough for today's plat du jour, I think.'

He stopped. So practical. So methodical. So matter of fact. While he agonized in bed over the state of his soul she was wringing the necks of her chickens, dealing with the daily imperative of making a living in the café. Food was still in short supply in the city. She was by no means the only Parisienne who kept poultry in her apartment and rabbits in her bathtub. He felt ashamed.

Marina noticed his sigh. 'What new idea from the Deux Magots has Pierre been recommending to you? I saw you talking together last night. The music was good, don't you think?'

He ignored her question and asked her instead, 'Do you still believe in God, Marina?' He did not miss the sudden, quickly suppressed, flash of feeling. Was it anger?

She shrugged. 'Pierre is all right. And Thérèse is mad about him.'

'You don't look like your sister.'

Marina hesitated. 'She is not my sister,' she said looking down, continuing to pull feathers from the bird. 'Emile is her father, not mine. We are not related at all.'

'But you have the same name.'

'Yes,' she replied and was silent.

'Marina?'

She paused in her task and sat back in the chair. The nearly naked chicken with its limp neck and closed eyes and slack beak and scaly yellow feet shifted in her lap. 'Emile has been a good friend since my family came here from Poland, before the war. Things were very bad for Jews in Warsaw. Thérèse and I, we grew up together. My father was a dealer in antiquities. He lent Emile money, the kind that doesn't have to be repaid. When the Nazis came he took me to live with them, and I became Marina Serac, false papers, baptism certificate, everything, just like one of the family. I had to learn quickly all I needed to forget. My mother and father, my whole family, are gone.'

She was speaking calmly and recommenced plucking the bird. She seemed so composed, almost as though she was not involved. 'What the Seracs have done for me is much more than you can expect even from your own family. And for a few years we got away with the deception. But people knew. It is surprising it lasted so long. Eventually someone with a grudge told the Gestapo about us. The Seracs were arrested and nearly deported, but Emile had his contacts and his explanations and my father's money to bargain with. So it was just me. Like the rest of my family before. Then the war ended and I came back. Thérèse went every day to the Lutetia to try to find me. She did not recognize me. Now I live here and help Emile in the café, and Thérèse is with Pierre, and thinks of nothing else but having a child. We were going to be teachers when we grew up, Thérèse and I. But the Nazis came. Everything is different now.' She looked at him and smiled a little. 'I am learning how to forget the past.'

Marina placed the plucked chicken with the others on the table and continued. 'I heard what you said to Pierre. It seems to be important to you to know how I feel about God. For me it is like this. When I remember the goodness of the Seracs I sometimes think there might be a God. But even so, it had its price. My father lent him a great deal of money. He lent him the antiques to look after when things became bad here. But there was no obligation. That kind of exceptional goodness, though, I think it must come from something more perfect. But I have been with Pierre and Thérèse to the Deux Magots and listened to the existentialists there. These new ideas Pierre and his friends are so fond of do appeal, don't you think? It is easier for me to think that what happened to me and to my family, to so many, was arbitrary. Yes, it was a great evil and must be punished but it was not part of some divine purpose or a trial like Job's to see if we are worthy in the eyes of God. I like to think we are free from all that now. So the answer to your question is no, I do not believe there is a God. I like to think there is no judge, just ourselves.'

Mathieu was surprised. Marina rarely spoke at length. Usually he did most of the talking, and it had not occurred to him that she was a thoughtful person. She had never told him so much about herself. He felt confused, a little diminished. He liked to think of her as compliant, quiet, ready to be guided and protected by him. Now he suspected this might not be so easy. She apparently had views of her own, had worked out meanings for herself, all very different from his. This morning, he had seen a glint of something hard and cold. Maybe she was stronger than he knew, maybe she was much braver than himself. Maybe she had an interior life he knew nothing about. Did he love her enough? His certainties about Marina wobbled briefly. Was she after all a part of his temptation, as his confessor had suggested, part of his own ordeal to prove himself worthy? The idea illuminated briefly in his brain. But just as suddenly it vanished. Here she was, alive, close to him, real, his lovely, melancholy Marina, in her grubby nightdress, with her lap full of feathers.

*

Captain Souris was alone in his big comfortable room at the Hôtel Meurice. Rosy light filtered through the brocade curtains. A sunbeam slanted across the parquet floor and onto the panelled wall. He got up and opened the window. Clean fresh air rushed around him, rising up from the lush trees in the Tuileries Gardens below. In the distance the Eiffel Tower pointed skywards. He walked onto the balcony and inhaled deeply, the cold air filling his lungs, clearing his brain. He looked across the rooftops of Paris, across the broad River Seine, to the left bank where Marina lived, somewhere in that maze of buildings, that maze of humanity. It was simpler, more coherent here at the Meurice, in the SHAEF officers' mess. He knew his role. Everyone did. Questions were easy to answer. Life could be this simple.

*

Yesterday he'd left Marina, the chickens, the gargoyles and hurried to say his confession. After Mass and communion he felt cleansed, absolved. He'd walked back to the Meurice, ambling along the quais at a Sunday morning pace, looking in the stalls at books, at pictures, crossing the turbulent river to the Île St Louis, pausing to inhale the heady mingled fragrances of the flower market, on past the Palais de Justice, all the complications, the doubts evaporating as he strolled, the weight on his shoulders lighter with every step. By lunchtime his feet echoed on the marble floor of the hotel lobby. He passed the brightly gilded candelabra as tall as men. He passed the potted palms of the plush, gilded Jardin d'Hiver and fell thankfully into the snug embrace of a leather chair in the bar. Classical murals, polished brass and mellow wood gleamed in the dim light. He ordered an aperitif.

'Well, if it isn't Frenchie, back at last,' said one of a group of officers. It was Rawlston, an American. 'Looks like you've had one hell of a night. Wanna tell us who she is?'

'Jesus, Matt, you do look completely shagged,' said another. 'Christ, it makes a difference when you can sweet-talk in the lingo. We've all been back for hours. By the way, the CO is looking for you.'

Mathieu yawned and winked at them.

'Did you know,' said a third, 'this randy Canuck was all lined up to go into the seminary before he joined up? Can you imagine Frenchie here a priest?'

'Don't believe it,' replied Rawlston, 'you gotta be celibate for that. He doesn't know what celibate means. You know what it means, Frenchie? No fucking. Ever.'

'Doesn't sound like it's for you, Matt.'

'He's just getting all his fucking in while he can. Hope

you've got a good supply of those little packages in your rations, Matt.'

'Is that right, Matt? You going to be a padre?'

'No,' Matt replied firmly, 'I'm getting married like everybody else.'

'Hope it's to some hometown sweetheart,' said Rawlston, 'they're not for marrying, you know, the lovely ladies of this city. They wouldn't fit in back home. Your mom wouldn't like it at all.'

*

'At ease, Souris,' said the colonel. 'It's like this. You're being shipped back to England before returning to your Canadian regiment. It could be as early as the end of the month. You might be home by Christmas. Your replacement is arriving shortly and I know you'll make sure he knows the ropes. If there's anything you need to finish before you leave you'd better see to it.'

'Thank you, sir . . . There is something.'

'What is it, Souris?'

'I'd like permission to get married, sir.'

The colonel looked up from his desk. There was no indication of interest on his face. 'I'm not sure that's such a good idea, Souris. Who is she?'

'Marina Serac, sir. Lives in the Latin Quarter, sir.'

'Parents?'

'Dead, sir. Auschwitz.'

A flicker of surprise passed quickly. 'Hmm. Doesn't sound like a good idea at all, Souris, but I'll look into it. Let you know. Dismissed.'

*

Mathieu leaned back on one of the gilt and satin chaises scattered about the hotel's salon. His fingers laced behind his head, he looked along his khaki-clad legs, across the carpet's worn expanse of roses, to the brass screen in front of the grate. The dusty mirrored walls reflected the gold and crystal chandeliers, the dull gold of the ceiling and walls, the tables and chairs, all glowing like embers. His eyes continued upwards above the marble fireplace, to where Madame de Pompadour simpered down from her own gilded seat in the painting high above the ornate mantle mirror. Madame de Pompadour, her ankles demurely crossed, idly leafing through some papers and looking somewhere else, at him perhaps? Unlikely, he thought. She'd been the king's mistress in her day. A pretty mistress too with her translucent white skin and her blue and gold dress and her uncanny resemblance to Marina Serac. Mathieu gazed at Madame and she gazed into space. Dazzling in the sumptuous room, in her sumptuous gown, with her pale unblemished skin, this mistress had no need for ornament. Not for her a showy necklace of diamonds or sapphires, or big amber beads like Marina wore. Madame de Pompadour, unadorned, smiling enigmatically at something or someone in the distance. Like the Virgin in the little gilt frame hanging on the wall at home in Trois Rivières with last Palm Sunday's leaves propped behind it. No, she wasn't looking at him. He was well below her sights.

There'd be big logs crackling in the fireplace at home right now. Papa would stir them with the poker and send flurries of sparks soaring up the chimney. Then he would turn his head and smile at Maman. And on the wall above the mantle the Virgin, demure in her white veil and blue dress, smiling the same mysterious smile as Madame de Pompadour. Who did they see? What did they share, the Virgin with her uniquely privileged knowledge and this mistress with her closely guarded secrets? Would Marina with her blemished arm and amber beads and unimaginable past ever look at him like that? It was Baltic amber, she told him once, from mines by the frozen Polish sea. He said the colour looked like maple syrup. She had never heard of maple syrup.

Mathieu sighed. He could not imagine Marina in the simple living room in Trois Rivières, with Papa poking the logs and Maman knitting by the fire and the Virgin gazing out at something they could never comprehend. Rawlston was right. She would not fit in there and Maman wouldn't like it. But they were resilient. They'd come to terms with it somehow.

*

Captain Souris stood on the balcony and surveyed the silvery rooftops of Paris, the golden dome of the Invalides, the Gothic steeples of the churches, the chimneys and statues of the Louvre and the Hôtel-de-Ville. The city seemed to draw itself away from him. He was taking his leave of it, he realized. A chilly wind stirred the trees in the Tuileries Gardens. In his mind he saw the trees of Trois Rivières, already tinted red and gold beneath the clear blue sky. In his mind he smelled the hints of wood smoke and burning leaves on the crisp autumn air. He could almost hear the voices of his friends, the barking of his dog. He turned back towards the room, and saw the chipped mouldings on the walls and doors, the stained plaster of the ceiling, the cracked mirror, the tarnished gilt, the abused furniture. He caught an echo of the smell that came strongly whenever he opened a drawer or a cupboard. It came from jackboot grease, he'd been told. Life was not simple after all. But soon he would go home. Somehow he would take Marina with him, take her away from all this, before it really was too late.

*

They sat under the awning of a bistro on the Boulevard St-Germain. In the light autumn breeze, leaves from the plane trees, edged brown, drifted to the pavement like torn rags. Mathieu leaned his elbows on the table and looked at Marina. She had become so quiet, so introspective lately. It was a sudden change, occurring only a week or so ago. Now she was leaning back in the chair, her legs crossed, rotating her foot slightly, smoking one cigarette after another, her coffee untouched. It was a while before she noticed he was watching her.

She made an effort to smile. 'I'm sorry, Mathieu,' she said, 'I'm a little tired.' Then she added, disarming him, 'I don't sleep so well when you're not there.'

That's probably all there was to it, he thought. He'd noticed her growing pallor, and now saw the dark circles under her eyes. But he wasn't entirely convinced. Marina seemed distracted as she scanned the crowds of passers-by. It had been like this for some time. 'What are you looking for?' he asked her again. But as usual she denied she was looking for anything.

Then suddenly she stiffened, her eyes wide. She sat up and stubbed out a half-smoked cigarette. As though she had forgotten all about him she rose quickly from her chair, placed her leather bag over her shoulder and walked away, hurrying through the crowd. Mathieu left a few francs on the table and went after her. She was obviously following someone, weaving in and out through the people moving along the sidewalk, now lost to him, now reappearing, on and on, eventually turning down the quieter side streets. He kept a little distance between them. There were fewer people here and finally there was only Marina and two others walking in front of her. They stopped outside a grand porte cochère, an older couple, he dapper in a suit and hat and she wrapped in a long fur coat. As they turned to open the door, to go inside, Marina reached into her bag. She walked up to them. They turned. A gold chain gleamed on his waistcoat, gold discs glimmered in her ears. They looked at her, enquiringly.

'Remember me? Marina Serac,' she said as their expressions froze. She was holding a pistol. It looked like a Luger. Where had she got hold of that? 'You betrayed me to the Gestapo. And Abraham Grochowski, the antiquarian. My family. They are all dead. But I survived. For this.'

She squeezed the trigger as she spoke, shooting bullet after bullet after bullet, pausing slightly between each one. The man fell first, and then the woman. They lay still in a spreading pool of blood on the narrow sidewalk outside the entrance to a sunny courtyard lined with pots of red geraniums. The wind rustled the leaves overhead. Marina crumpled like a rag beside the couple, her head bent, her eyes closed, her face white as death. Mathieu rushed towards her. She looked up into his face but did not see it was him. She did not move. Then she raised the gun and fired the last bullet into herself.

18

Time passes. The snow is falling again. You can hear it outside the window, like breathing. When I'm alone in the woods with the waking trees and the drip drip drip of the sap, I feel the breath of time on my face. Some here can measure time with their breath. They don't require clocks to tell them where a moment fits in. They sleep and measure time and wake up when they need to. Time breathes, even in dreams. You look at your watch, mon amie. Yes, it is late, but are you seeing the picture yet? Is it all beginning to make sense?

Zack Guillem was one who tracked time with his breathing, if he kept track of it at all. There were no numbered hours and minutes to his reckoning, just moments chasing moments either side of sunrise and moonset. I asked him once if he thought time stood still and he moved through it, meeting one thing after another on the way. Or did it flow like the river, carrying things along that became 'now' when they reached him and 'then' after they'd gone by. He said it didn't matter so long as you weren't late, and Zack was always punctual. He said mostly it seemed to be one or the other, but there were occasions when it was both together and he felt like he was falling headlong into space. That's when he knew it was time to lay off the liquor for a while. But, he said, there had been a time or two when he felt like that without a drop passing his lips. It was when he was with Marina Grochowska.

You sigh and look at your watch again. You think all this talk is going nowhere and time is running out. You ask us questions and wonder if we are listening. This James Levine from the city, you say, he was only the lawyer. He was just a bad poker player who had good reason to keep his mouth shut tight. But he wasn't the only one involved. What about the others, you ask, the ones who staked the claims? The prospector and the geologist, they must have come from somewhere. How did they get here? Where did they go? They can't have just disappeared. Somebody must have paid for it all. How come no one ever followed it up? They're good questions. And that's the queer thing about it. After the lawyer left we held our breath for quite a time but there was no more prospecting. No one took any interest. Nothing. We prayed that was the end of it and for a while it seemed our prayers were answered.

You seem mighty interested in those claim-stakers, my friend. Like I said, there was nothing more for a long time. The only unanswered question, if there was a question at all, was about the Braemar Lodge. Why did it burn down when it did? According to Frank Martello it was a terrible accident. He investigated, found nothing suspicious. Mind you, there wasn't much left to investigate there. But Henri Osweken wouldn't let it rest. He said the fire was deliberate. The door had been jammed shut. He only just got out of there himself. The Braemar was torched and someone was responsible. But he would say that, wouldn't he? He had a stack of blame to lay down after what happened to Flora. Anyway, that's what most everyone thought.

Zack wasn't convinced either. It was too much of a coincidence for him. There was nothing he could put his finger on, just a hunch there was more to it than an accident, there was something in what Henri said. But Henri took to drinking and like I told you, we heard no more about it. Everybody got to know about the staking claims and how Grand'mère had won them from a city lawyer in a poker game. Everybody assumed they'd gone up in Braemar smoke. It meant anyone interested now in mining explorations of the Sugarmilk country would have to start again from scratch. It's what we all wanted to think, and it was a big relief for us here, I can tell you. I guess it was a big relief for that lawyer fellow too. Things carried on as they always had, hunting, fishing, lumbering, sugaring off. Now and again Zack headed into the rough country beyond Roseau Lake, as a guide or a fire ranger, or just to have a mosey round to see what he might turn up. It would be a chance in a million if he did find anything in the endless empty bush.

It must have been a few years later when he took a couple of Yankee sportsmen up that way for a fall still-hunt. The short days were bright and crisp, the nights cold enough for shards of ice to form at the edges of the streams. Freeze-up was not far away. The game was as good as he'd hoped but so far the hunters' aims had been unsteady. Only one deer shot out of three stalked and a big-antlered moose, in full view, standing in a shallow pool surrounded by dense scrub, a target if there ever was, somehow missed. The marksmen slumped with disappointment as the animal vanished into the trees. Zack was sure he could have hit it easily, but it wasn't his hunt. He shrugged. There'd be more days and more moose, he told them; things'd get better now the whiskey was running low. That's often the problem with businessmen up for a week or two's sport. They want a lot of lubrication for the rigours of the trip. But there'd been no twisted ankles or broken bones or serious arguments so far and no one had gotten shot by mistake. Despite the misses they were all having a good time, including Zack who generally liked to pitch his wits against these city sangfroids.

Though Zack himself could stalk the fleas off a dog, he wouldn't hesitate to say the best he ever came across were the Indians from whom he'd learned not only the skill but also the patience. Joe Naiscoot had been good. Around here it was Oswekens, he said, especially old Jacques in his day, and Louis. Grand'mère too, when she was younger, had been known to drop a stag after a day's stalking. But Indians can be unsociable as hunting guides. Except Henri who liked his talk, they often tend to silence, watching and listening all the time, speaking only to answer a question, or not at all, seeing and hearing things our untrained senses do not notice, all essential to tracking an animal down but disconcerting to a vacationing sportsman out for some fun as well as a trophy. And Zack could be a lot like an Indian when he was concentrating on the hunt. That's how he located game and took it cleanly. Some say that's how he cornered the schoolteacher, Miss Grochowska, though others thought she cornered him.

I have hunted with Zack. In the woods he is quiet and moves like a shadow. He spoke only to say, 'You make too much noise, Lucien.' We didn't hurry, we didn't get breathless; we stood around for long spells, looking everywhere, listening for movement in the branches overhead, inspecting the ground for signs of disturbance. I heard no wind, saw no tracks. He crouched here and there to slowly crumble a handful of dry leaves, watching for a drift in the falling dust. From where I stood the dust fell straight down. But usually he saw something and was satisfied. He pointed, and in that direction we went, seeming to wander at random through the trees, listening for the breathing of the wind, holding up a wetted finger to feel what we could not hear. Eventually we came back again to a place where he'd listened long. I had seen nothing more than a few old tracks on our stealthy circular progress but he smiled knowingly and nodded at me. And then he became a predator himself, his eyes narrow, his ears even more alert.

One time Zack told me an experienced Indian hunter will focus his mind only lightly on the animal he's picked out for the kill, as too much concentration alerts it to the danger. Now he moved silently, almost invisibly, keeping to the shadows, back-tracking in places, circling and half-circling. By then I'd seen fresh moose tracks myself. He motioned for me to keep still. He tested the air currents, crept forward, moved backward, circled again, always keeping his target upwind. Cautiously, now retreating, now feeling for a shift in the breeze, now advancing from a different direction, he closed in on a dense growth of small trees. Suddenly he raised his rifle and fired. The charge exploded through the silence. A big brown moose materialized in the thicket not thirty feet away. It crashed forward, and dropped down dead. Zack blew the smoke from his rifle, lowered it and took a deep breath. For a moment he stood motionless, his senses all but drained, his head raised like a victor. Then he turned to me, grinning like a kid.

*

It's been said of Zack that he never brought anyone out of the bush without his quarry. There was a high demand for his services in the hunting season, and the money was good. Now it was nearly time to bring out the Yanks but so far they hadn't much to show and he felt all their reputations were at stake. Early on a bright afternoon the three men were spread out, advancing slowly in the cover around the edge of a clearing on rising land. Sunlight slanted through the coloured trees, flickering and hovering in the gentle breeze, filling the more open spaces with golden light. Red and yellow leaves drifted down and rustled on the forest floor. The hunters were in luck. Some distance back they had heard the hollow thunder of antlers clashing in combat.

At this time of year stags and bulls engage in vicious fights, sometimes to the death. The men moved silently towards the noise. It was nearer now; they could hear the grunts as the animals struggled together in a clearing between the trees. Above a rocky ledge two big moose lowered their heads and charged each other, locked antlers, strained ferociously for a time and disengaged. They paused, panting, foaming, then circled threateningly, upper teeth bared, eyes rolling, and charged again. The battle had nearly run its course by the time the men were within range. The bulls were tired, the pauses longer. During a halt in the fight a twig snapped beneath someone's feet. The animals turned towards the noise. The hunters were ready with their rifles. They fired, again and again. One bull buckled on the spot, tried to rise and fell down again. The other ran straight towards them, bleeding from the neck and shoulder. Zack took aim and squeezed the trigger. The moose dropped. The men moved cautiously towards the steaming carcasses as big as cattle lying on the ground, the huge panned antlers rising into the air like sumac boughs. The sportsmen claimed their trophies. One let out a long shrill whoop of glee. The other lit a cigarette with shaking fingers, inhaled deeply, then reached for his pocket flask. He handed it first to Zack, who glanced at him with grim satisfaction.

The combat had churned up the thin soil of the rocky clearing. Zack sniffed. He caught again a slight smell, like sulphur. Looking around he noticed, several yards away, a straight pole a few feet tall placed upright in the ground. He walked over to it. The metal tag was still attached; it was a prospector's stake. Zack searched around, more carefully. In one place light undergrowth gave way to what looked like charred wood, the remains of an old campfire. The moose battleground appeared to be on an old campsite, almost invisible now except where the fire had scorched the ground. And some claim-staking seemed to have taken place though he could only see one post. Zack had come across abandoned campsites before. He'd encountered forgotten claims a time or two, even found a decomposed and partly eaten body of a trapper once. What caught his eye here were the bones. There were several large ones scattered about on the ground. He picked one up. It was long and heavy, and he saw abrasions on it, as though from a knife, or teeth. The prospector's dinner, he thought. Or a bear's, maybe. He continued his inspection of the area. There was not much else to see, just a few mildewed bits of cloth on a heap of what might once have been spruce bedding, and at the bottom of the stake a small pile of rocks. A collection of mineral samples? A marker for a hiding place, maybe? Zack decided to take a closer look and dismantled the pile. Underneath the stones lay a man's wallet, the leather swollen from the rain and snow. He pocketed it. He pushed a low clump of blueberry bushes aside with his foot. More bones, the shrubs growing up through them, but here they lay together, limbs, ribs, a skull. His stomach tightened. It was a human skull, maybe that of the prospector himself. Zack turned quickly towards the hunters but they were too engrossed in dealing with their kill to notice anything else. The prospector, if it was he, could keep his secrets a while longer, thought Zack. He covered the bones again.

'I'm going to have a quick look round,' he called out to the others, 'I won't be long.'

Zack half-circled the clearing at a little distance and came to a small river, which he followed. Soon he was on a rocky outcrop where a wild panorama opened out. The sky was now overcast and the land was more rugged here. Water cascaded over a sheer cliff into a grey lake, clear as glass. He stood on the flat grey rocks by the edge of the narrow falls and looked around. The lake was deep and lay at the base of a steep-sided valley. Bare grey rock faces loomed on three sides, high above the tall, green-black pines and yellow birches along the shore. He scanned the shoreline, from the white turbulence at the foot of the falls to the mountains reflected in the glassy depths beyond. In one place not far from where he stood the trees leaned. Some were bent, splintered, snapped in two as though they were no more than matchwood. The ground rose steeply here. Zack went to investigate. He looked carefully to the left of the broken pines, behind them and to the right. He could see no trace of rock falls. A winter avalanche would cause more widespread destruction. He found nothing that might explain this localized damage and climbed back to the higher ground. He looked across the water. A wisp of wind rippled the surface momentarily, then all was still again. Something about the lake, no more than an irregularity in its smooth deep greyness, like a slub in the otherwise regular weave of a blanket, caught his eye. And then he saw it. There was something in the water, a little distance from the shore, something large, angular, rusty brown with traces of red and white, submerged in the crystal lake. Zack blinked. If he was not mistaken it was an airplane.

*

Constable Martello pushed a fresh log into his big office stove, though it was already late in the afternoon. He lifted the battered percolator gurgling on top and pulled a face. This time of day the coffee would be as bitter as it was thick, and the sugar was nearly all gone. Maple sugar for his coffee. With a good splash of Hudson's Bay rum, since it was nearly time to call it a day. He shivered as he drank. There was snow in the air; he could always tell.

A shadow crossed on the sidewalk outside the station window. He heard the door handle turn and looked up in surprise when, with a rush of bitter air, Zack Guillem walked in. 'Hello, Zack! Haven't seen you come through this door more than once in ten years. Is it snowing yet?'

'Won't be long now, Frank.' Zack accepted a mug of coffee and sat down by the stove.

Constable Martello grinned, rather pleased with himself that the woodsman had seen fit to call on him. He considered Zack to be a man of integrity but for some unaccountable reason thought of him as outside, even above, his own sphere of operation. And he couldn't help feeling this was okay because Zack's world turned according to a different set of rules, rules that had little to do with Sugarmilk Falls law enforcement. So he knew Zack would need a very good reason before he sought out the police.

Constable Martello waited a while for the man to speak and when he didn't asked, 'Is there a problem, Zack?'

'No, not really. Just that something you might be interested in has turned up, that's all.'

'How do you mean, interested?'

'Some things I came across when I was out in the bush last week. An old campsite. An old prospecting stake. That kind of thing.'

The policeman shook his head. 'Doesn't sound all that interesting, Zack.'

'There's more. A few bones. North of Roseau Lake, up beyond the Sugarmilk.'

'Bones, huh.' Frank sipped his coffee. 'What kind of bones?'

'Old bones. Might be some missing prospector.'

Constable Martello paused. 'Far as I officially know no

prospectors have been in the region for years. And I don't know of anyone gone missing.'

'Hmm,' Zack mused carefully. 'Wasn't there some business up at the Braemar before it burned down?'

Constable Martello smiled irritably. 'That file's been closed a long time, Zack. Don't want to open it up again.'

'It might be worth a look sometime, Frank. People might still ask questions.'

The policeman drummed his fingers on the desk and gazed out of the window. The sky had the raw greyness of imminent winter. 'Very few, Zack. In fact, hardly any at all. It's much better not to bother these sleeping dogs, just so long as they keep on sleeping.' He paused and sighed. 'But you're right. You never can tell what'll turn up, and it's as well to be prepared. We can't get there now before break-up, I suppose, even if I thought it was worth the trouble?' Zack shook his head. 'What I'll do is make a note of what you've told me and put it in the file. Think you'll be able to find the place again if I ever need you to?' Zack gave him a disdainful look. 'Okay, okay, I didn't ask you that.'

PART TWO

I

Mon amie, it is time now to tell you the truth about Miss Grochowska, Lucien said. Immediately the stranger looked up. She put down her whittling knife and listened intently.

*

The afternoon sun sparked pink and gold on the dazzling snow. It bronzed the bare maples stretching their branches beside the frozen river and up the hillsides that circled the town. It etched long blue shadows between the trees, across the snowy rooftops and onto the road. Wisps of wood smoke rose vertically from the chimneys. Marina inhaled the icy air and held her breath. This little place so snug under its thick glittering comforter seemed to her on this March day the perfection of winter. Nothing that she could remember was equal to this. What could possibly follow? Yet she felt as though the moment was a threshold, the beginning of something more sublime. It might be no more than the first subtle stirring of spring which always made her restless and nostalgic, like emerging from a deeply satisfying dream. She slowed her pace along the shovelled sidewalk to prolong the experience.

A sepia-coloured mongrel dawdled along the opposite side of Main Street. It cocked its leg against a telephone pole, sniffed and ambled on. The muffled rumble of a car approached, the chained tyres clinking and churning up the shiny packed snow between the bulldozed mounds by the roadside. The car slowed down almost to a stop as it drew level with a tall man walking with long strides a little way ahead of her. A blast of the horn, louder and clearer in the frozen air, made her jump. The driver rolled down the window and whistled loudly. 'Hey, you old reprobate! How ya doin'?' The tall man raised a brown-mittened hand in greeting and walked on.

Marina quickened her pace. The man had the sure, measured stride of someone used to walking long distances. Despite his heavy boots he seemed light-footed and secure on the ice and snow. Everything that she could see about him was brown. The long fringes on his coat sleeves and down the side of his breeches, made from some sort of hide – was it moose hide? – danced in step with his steady lope, as did the brown braids hanging below his wide-brimmed leather hat. His other arm steadied a bulky brown sack on his shoulder. At the entrance to the store he stopped and placed the sack under his arm. He stamped the snow from his boots and went inside. Marina followed him.

Phil Tronquet was behind the counter and looked up when the man entered. His face broke into a broad grin. 'Why, Zack, you son of a bitch! When did you get back?'

'Just a little while ago, Phil. Ain't had time yet to get cleaned up or start thawing out the old place. Thought I'd bring you these first and settle up what I owe.' He dropped the sack on the counter and took off his mittens and hat.

'Where did you get to?' asked Phil.

'Crowberry River, edge of the Barren Lands. It was quite a trip, I can tell you.' The storekeeper was clearly impressed. 'But I'm getting too soft for this, Phil. Maybe this was the last time for me. It felt a damned sight colder than I remember. I really coulda done with a body to warm my feet on at night.'

The men laughed under their breath. Marina looked around the store, trying to remember if there was anything she needed to buy. Shafts of sunlight streamed through the large front window, past the items displayed there, catching the motes of dust hovering in the warmth, and glancing across the floor onto the walls lined to the ceiling with shelves. These were stuffed with bags of flour and sugar, boxes of cereal, dried fruit and spices, and row upon row of cans of everything imaginable, from potatoes and corned beef, pineapple rings and condensed milk, to asparagus spears and whole chickens. There were bottles of ketchup and maple syrup, bars of soap, boxes of detergent, bottles of bleach. Behind the counter the wall held the drawers of nuts and bolts, nails, screws, hooks, and the oddly shaped objects she had been told on a previous visit were sap spiles. Along the opposite wall boxes of blankets, piles of work shirts and jeans were crammed into the spaces between the shelves and above them were skeins of knitting wool. Rolls of brightly coloured fabric, one decorated with an inverted rainbow of sewing thread strung on a piece of twine, sat upright in a barrel on the floor. Beside this, a rack of coats and a line of boots and shoes stood in front of another stack of boxes, next to the pickaxes and shovels, snowshoes, galvanized tubs and high towers of pails. Knives with varying grades of threat gleamed in a glass case near the packages of cartridges. Clusters of kerosene lamps hung at angles from a ceiling beam, alongside snares, jaw-toothed traps, fishing lines and nets, coils of rope and wire. Near the counter a revolving stand held a few magazines, greeting cards, well-thumbed comic books near the bottom where the children could reach them, and the latest edition of the *Sugarmilk Gazette*. On the long wooden counter, by the shiny brass cash register, was a small display of bright red nail polish at a reduced price. A soda-water cooler stood near the door – in the summer it would be moved outside – and on the cast-iron stove bubbled a battered and stained aluminum percolator. The profusion of items for sale, the richly muddled smells of wood smoke, spices, tar paper and coffee, such a contrast to the clean icy air outside, belied the orderliness of the store. Whatever Marina asked for, Phil and Sophie would know exactly where to find it if they had it in stock and they usually did, or how long it would take to order in if they didn't. Now, what was it she wanted? Surely she had not come in merely to look at this tall apparition?

'I can see you haven't lost your touch, though,' Phil said to him, running his hand over the sack. 'Let's have a look at what you got.'

'It's not like it used to be, Phil. I guess nothing is these days.'

Marina now stood near the counter, trying not to stare too obviously. So this was Zack Guillem. She had heard a great deal, since she arrived, about the legendary coureur de bois, forest ranger, deer hunter, wilderness guide. This shaggy and rather gamy relic from a bygone age did indeed look like the solitary kind of man she could imagine exploring the wild frontier, the kind of man she told her pupils about in social studies lessons, the kind of man who surely no longer existed in these days of indoor bathrooms a hundred years after Confederation. She sniffed and looked at his profile, the large hooked nose, the deeply tanned and furrowed cheek, the short brindled beard. He lifted the brown sack and with surprising gentleness slid the contents onto the counter, the raw feral smell heightening with the movement. Dust rose, like a swarm of black flies, as the bundles emerged from the sack and unrolled over the counter. With a frisson she realized these were wild animal skins. In the glow of the afternoon sun they had an almost metallic sheen, the lush golden, silvery, amber and deep brown furs with their little black and pink noses. Was this a fox, with its fine, thick tail? It seemed so small. That one with the tawny striations, was it a lynx? And could those be mink? So voluptuous, so irresistible, shimmering like still water in the moonlight.

Marina removed a glove and tentatively reached out a white manicured hand towards the inert wildness spread out over the counter. Her rings glittered as slowly, carefully, she dropped her fingers one by one onto and into the topmost fur and felt its seductive softness. The two men watched her intently.

'It's a mink,' Zack said.

'I have never seen one before. Not like this.' Cautiously, as if it might suddenly wake up and bite her, she stroked the animal, 'It's beautiful. They are all so beautiful. But very savage, and very sad.'

'Yes, it is,' he replied.

She looked up at him. From the aquiline brownness of his face bright blue eyes shone out. What did she see in them? Something like recognition or was he just laughing at her?

'I'll work you out a price,' said Phil. 'But I'm forgetting my manners. This is Marina Grochowska, our schoolteacher. And this trail-filthy trapper here is Zack Guillem.'

'I know,' she replied, reluctantly lifting her hand from the warm, silky softness and holding it out towards him. She braced herself for a rough engagement with a bear paw. Instead he lifted her hand to his lips. 'Enchanté, mademoiselle,' he said with a smile.

Marina felt a rush of icy air. The door opened and, silhouetted against the setting sun, a straight-backed woman with long grizzled hair falling over her animal skin coat entered the store. Past her rushed a small boy of about five or six.

'It's Zack! Zack!' he shouted. 'I told you it was Zack!'

The trapper crouched down and lifted the squealing child high into the air. 'If it ain't young Bobby. Hardly recognize you, boy, you've grown so big.'

'Where have you been, Zack? Did you see any bears?'

'One or two.'

'Were they big and mean?'

'They sure were.'

'Really? What did they do?'

'They ate me for their breakfast. Two mouthfuls and I was gone.'

For a moment the boy's face fell in horror, but just as quickly he laughed and hit Zack in the chest. 'No, they didn't!' he cried. 'You're making it all up.'

As she watched them, Marina could feel the eyes of the woman on her. She was old, thin and shrivelled, but held herself erect and she moved with grace. It was impossible to say how old she was. She seemed both aged and ageless. But it was her penetrating eyes that made Marina shudder. Her face was blank, indecipherable, her eyes dark and deep, yet at the same time bright like coals. They set her apart.

Marina turned to go. Glancing back by the door she saw Phil and Zack with his back to her, discussing the price for the furs. The old woman stood to one side observing them. Only the boy, an arm wrapped around one of Zack's long legs, watched her leave.

2

At first it was only whispers, little more than tremors in the air, absorbed without needing to be heard so when the gossip began in earnest it came as no surprise. 'The new schoolteacher, well, well . . . Sinking so low, and so soon too . . . But then she isn't the kind of woman you'd expect a grade-school teacher to be . . . Not when you remember where she'd been, the sort of things that happened in those places . . . To come out of it at all makes you wonder . . . Don't call them DPs for nothing . . . Guess she's no better than a bushwhacker herself . . . Such people oughtn't to be allowed in a nice town like this . . . Time she went back where she came from . . . High time he moved on too . . .' And so the party lines went on.

Miss Grochowska raised a lot of eyebrows when she came to teach in Sugarmilk Falls, and Zack seemed struck by her right away, more so than by anyone I can remember. What was the attraction? They were two such very different souls – she with her educated city ways and he a free spirit from the woods. I don't know what it was that made him pick her out like she was some exotic quarry he thought he'd try to bring down. I told him Claudine was concerned by what she was hearing. 'Pas grande chose, Lucien. Nothing to worry about. Another still-hunt, that's all,' he said. Mind your own business Lucien, is what he meant. It was not like him to dissemble. Zack must have reckoned he had enough patience and the skill to succeed. He had done it before, decided on a pursuit, gone about it, never letting up until he got his way, and then lost interest. But this was different from the start. It was not just a game for him this time and she was not one to be so easily fooled. Maybe it was the other way around all along, and Miss Grochowska had her eye on him. Suzanne used to say this was the real thing for both of them. They sometimes went out to the North Star and when you saw them together like that you felt she was right. Father Souris used to watch them like a hawk. That was strange too.

*

Zack lived at the edges, just this side of the wilderness, just beyond where people begin to leave their mark. Of course there are others, ourselves, the Perriaults, who like to think we are as close as we can be to the savage give and take of rock and water, forest and ice. But deep down we know our comfortable and civilized kind of living here is discord, not symmetry. This place, where we all sit tonight, talking, whittling spiles, though it's built of trees and backs right up to the foot of the maple hills, is a trespass on them. We take. At heart we remain aloof, at odds. That's been the way since Étienne Armand explored the haute terre in what was then New France and stayed on to trade for furs with Chief Osweken's band. We have kept his journals, and that Osweken chief made it clear to the first Armand that all the Sugarmilk lands belonged to his people and he traded here for furs entirely at their discretion.

But Zack was always more in harmony. He wanted only his self-reliance. He lived by the rock flats and the jack pines on the shore of a sky-blue lake which empties into the Sugarmilk River below the falls, a good canoe or dog-sled trip or snowshoe walk away from the town. Most everybody knew him but kept at arm's length, admiring and envying his hunting and trapping, his knowledge of the ways of the bush, and just as readily denigrating his easiness with Indians and half-breeds, not to mention the rough wandering woodsmen and shady women who found their way to his place now and then. This suited Zack, who liked silence and solitude. There was a feeling too that the civilized veneer he normally showed was easily cracked, that it masked a wild heart, that he could and wouldn't hesitate to do whatever he thought necessary if the last resort kind of necessity arose. And that suspicion wasn't groundless. I have seen him cut a man's throat as easily as a stag's and with as little conscience. But that was in the war. Some thought him unpredictable and dangerous, though I have known few men as disciplined as Zack could be, or as dependable and generous. And he was very charming with the ladies, eh, Claudine? You still miss Zack, I know. You cared for him. We both did.

*

The wood-lined walls inside the Armands' large sugar shack were warm and welcoming, the air rich with the aromas of food and boiling maple syrup. The sap run was nearly over, and the last batches had been brought inside for the final stages of reduction. Marina sat with the others around the long wooden trestle. She watched Lucien and Ed Perriault hold sample jars of syrup up to the light. The colour and translucency were like fine amber. She watched them taste and retaste, and when the long mouth feel was judged to be exactly right they smiled and held up their thumbs. The assembled company cheered and raised their glasses.

Claudine stoked up the wood stove. 'And here is Zack. Now we can eat,' she said. He came in with a gust of wet snowflakes and kissed her on the cheek. She pushed his cold wet face away with a laugh. 'Find somewhere to sit down.'

Zack took off his coat and squeezed himself in beside Marina. 'Any more trouble?' he asked her.

After their encounter in the store she saw him once and no more than a friendly greeting passed between them. Then early one morning, as she was about to leave for the school, he was outside her blue front door. 'Phil tells me you got noises in your attic,' he said.

She did not expect to see him there, especially at that hour. 'Yes . . . They keep me from sleeping. I asked him what to do about them. It sounds like the bears are waking up.'

He was looking at her intently. 'If it was bears you'd think there was a locomotive up there. Raccoon, probably. Happens sometimes. I'll set for it, if you like. Keep an eye on them for you.'

Marina stared back at him for a moment, trying to work out what he meant. 'Set for it?'

The corners of his eyes creased with amusement. 'Traps,' he explained.

'I see. That's very kind of you.' Marina hesitated. 'Would it be possible for you to do it when I'm not here?'

The request seemed to amuse him even more. 'Yes, if you don't mind me coming into your house.'

'That's okay. Thanks . . . It's just that I don't want to see what it is or what you're going to do to it.' She showed him the way into the roof space. 'I'm not really squeamish,' she explained, 'but I am the new tenant here. The animal was already in occupation when I arrived.' She departed.

He was as good as his word. She did not see him at all, or what it was he caught. A pencilled note lay on the kitchen table when she returned late one afternoon. 'Coon gone', she read. It was signed simply 'Zack'. That was all.

*

'No more trouble, thank you, Zack,' Marina replied to his question. 'You didn't leave a bill.'

'It's prime raccoon. By rights you should take a cut, but I expect you'd refuse as you didn't like to evict it. Do you want to see it?'

Marina shook her head. He grinned. 'Didn't think so.'

Claudine served up thick pea soup with haricot beans and maple syrup, to be followed by maple-cured ham, fried eggs and potatoes and more maple syrup to pour over them, and to finish, raft upon raft of syrupy pancakes.

'So,' he began after a while, 'where did you come to these parts from?'

'South Porcupine,' she replied.

'South Porcupine?' Zack said with amused disbelief.

She did not reply.

'Hmm.' He looked Marina over carefully, objectively, appreciatively, as though she was a new innovation in trapping or hunting equipment and he was minded to buy. Then he shook his head and said quietly, 'You're not like any South Porcupine girls I ever came across. You sure we're talking about the same South Porcupine?'

'I think there's only one,' replied Marina with a smile.

'So if I set about some serious backward tracking I'd come to South Porcupine?'

'You would indeed.'

'I would indeed.' Was he mimicking her intonation? 'What if I didn't stop there?'

'Then you'd be in France. Paris.'

'Ah.' Zack returned to eating pancakes. 'Claudine certainly knows how to feed a body,' he said when he'd nearly finished. 'You must be pretty good at this sort of thing.'

Marina chuckled. 'I manage.'

'Glad to hear it.' He paused, and mused between mouthfuls. 'Grochowska. That's not very French. What if I carried on back-tracking some more?'

'Warsaw. And that's all there is.'

Zack put down his knife and fork and lifted Marina's arm, indicating the row of tattooed numbers.

She stiffened and looked at him abruptly. Hardly anyone raised the question straight out.

Then Zack pulled her arm through his. Marina was taken aback. The action seemed so natural. Was it an apology? Some kind of recognition? To reassure her he intended no harm? It was not unpleasant. She must be crazy not to be offended by his impertinence. She bit her lip to suppress a smile.

'I was in France during the war,' he said.

Good, thought Marina with relief, he is going to talk about himself now. She felt exposed. He'd interrogated her too much already during this very brief acquaintance and she had the feeling he heard more in her replies than she intended to put there. Her hand rested on his soft buckskin sleeve, trapped there by his other hand. It felt warm and comfortable. Rather reluctantly she pulled it away, then she relaxed a little and prepared to listen politely to the litany of his French adventures.

But instead he continued, 'You don't hide it. That's nice.'

'Or discuss it, Zack,' she replied rather sharply.

'Of course you don't. It's nobody's business. But they talk about it here. Probably did back in South Porcupine as well. It bothers people.'

'Not you, it seems.'

He shook his head. 'Oh, I wouldn't go as far as that.'

She liked this man, despite herself. He seemed straightforward, yet subtle underneath, and surprisingly considerate for all his effrontery, not at all what she expected. 'And what about you, Zack? Where would backward tracking lead me?'

He grinned. 'I don't think you'd be good enough at it. I don't leave much of a trail.'

'Everyone leaves a trail,' she replied, feeling as though she had gained the upper hand sufficiently to head him off. 'And what were you doing in France?' she asked him.

'Hiding from Germans, mostly.'

Marina waited for him to continue.

His voice was serious but his eyes twinkled. 'My plane was shot down. I was trying to get back to England in one piece, but I get the impression you don't really want to hear about that right now.'

She smiled. 'No. We can each keep our secrets.'

'Maybe. For now,' replied Zack.

Marina looked at him, but his face revealed nothing. Was he just teasing her, having a bit of fun? Perhaps he did intend to provoke her. Well, he'd failed, hadn't he? Or was it something else altogether? She couldn't be certain what it was he meant and she was surprised at herself for even wanting to know.

Claudine placed another heaped plate of pancakes on the table in front of him. 'Here, Zack. This will give you something else to do besides monopolize our guest. You have to be careful around him, Marina. He's a tricky one if you're not used to him.'

Lucien chuckled. Ed Perriault laughed loudly. Zack grinned and looked up at Claudine. 'Delicieuse, merci,' he said, holding up a piece of pancake on his fork. She nodded knowingly and looked away, and he turned again to Marina. 'Quite a shock for you,' he said to her, 'South Porcupine. After Paris.'

It was a statement of fact, an observation he knew to be correct. She did not need to answer and helped herself to another pancake.

'Zack!' insisted Claudine. 'It's time to bring in the snow.'

'What? More to eat?' he asked her.

'The syrup's ready.'

Zack prepared to leave the table. 'Have you seen the falls at this time of year?' he asked Marina suddenly.

'No, I haven't yet been up that way.'

'They're a sight worth seeing.' He hesitated, looking at her carefully, and continued. 'The best time is when the sun is on them. We could walk up there. Take a look. Tomorrow afternoon, if you like.'

Marina was not prepared for such a suggestion. She looked into his face, level with hers, at the deep furrows in his cheeks and forehead, the crows' feet etched at the corners of his eyes, deep blue eyes that seemed honest and open. She frowned. Could she be honest with this man? she wondered. If so, it would be the first time. 'Oh, I don't know, Zack,' she replied, at a loss.

'They're quite a sight during break-up,' he explained, 'I thought you might like to see that.' There was no disappointment in his voice, just a recognition that perhaps he had miscalculated after all.

'Don't get me wrong. You just took me by surprise.' Marina paused, annoyed at her own confusion. 'Yes, I would like that,' she heard herself say.

Zack brought in the bucket of snow, which Claudine scooped out onto small plates. She poured maple syrup over the snow and instantly it became smooth and waxy. Marina tasted it. The sharp, fresh sweetness had all the clarity and restlessness of a northern spring.

*

Hadn't it been possible for her to say no, to put him off gently, or even rudely if necessary, she asked herself later, lying awake, berating herself for not having more sense at her age. He obviously had none. Couldn't she have made it plain he was wasting his time? Which indeed he was, she told herself firmly. Or was he? What was it about this man that had made her acquiesce? Perhaps she was reluctant to go out walking alone? No, she was quite used to doing that. Perhaps she wanted very much to see the falls? She knew it was not that either. Whether she wanted to see the falls at break-up was irrelevant. If he had suggested they take a walk along Main Street to go look at the gasoline pump she would not have declined. So what was it about this outlandish man that made her want to spend time with him? Curiosity? Certainly she was curious about him, but she knew it was more than that. She simply could not stop herself.

So what did he want from her, she wondered. He didn't seem to want anything except maybe a little company. But that idea was ridiculous. Of course he wanted something. In her experience everyone wants something sooner or later. For the moment anyway, all she could say for certain was he wanted to show her the falls at break-up. Well, she was curious. She would like to see them. She would like to go there with this Zack Guillem. But that still left open the question that had been pushed to the back of her mind, one that ideally should have been confronted before all this arose, a question barely admitted so far and one not easily answered. Marina yawned. It would have to wait. She was tired. And anyway, it was much too soon to consider what it was she wanted from him, other than that he might be able to shed a little light on her search.

*

He suggested they keep to the portage side of the river, then have an easy descent back to town along the ancient carrying trail. The bright spring sunshine seemed to magnify the roughness of the brown trunks of the trees and the swelling buds on the branches. Meltwater gurgled everywhere, creeping between the slush and the frozen ground, forming quick-flowing rivulets, gathering into pools in the hollows and streaming onto the path. The retreating snow was grey, grainy, dirty with the debris of winter. In more open places patches of ground were visible, littered with fallen branches, last year's leaves slimy and flattened by the winter's weight. Black granite and white quartz boulders gleamed in the clear yellow light. A whippoorwill called intermittently between the seismic booms of breaking ice.

'Why here?' Marina asked Zack as they walked towards the river. 'Did you just happen across it?'

'I'd heard of it from Lucien in the war. We were in the same air-force squadron based on the flat lands of eastern England. In the same ill-fated Lancaster bomber, as it turned out. In the barracks he used to talk and talk about this place until he had everyone nearly crying with homesickness. I guess I sort of got to know it without ever being here.'

'So you came here after the war?'

He did not answer for a moment. 'No, I went back to my old way of life.' He paused again.

'Nothing is the same after something like that,' Marina said, almost to herself.

'No,' he agreed. He turned to look at her. Marina glanced briefly at him, then looked straight ahead. For a while neither spoke.

The river was in flood, half thawed, filled with great boulders of broken ice that had tumbled over the falls. Ice, dripping and sparkling in the sunlight, encased the branches overhanging the water. Mounds of melting snow

now covered the path and impeded their progress. They sat down on exposed rocks to rest.

'It wasn't so easy to be alone out in the bush again,' Zack continued. 'Seemed like a lot more slaughter and not much else. One Christmas time I'd had enough. Took me three days through the fiercest blizzard I can remember to get to Senneterre, where I knew sooner or later there'd be a train. Didn't think I'd make it alive. I went straight to the hotel and there I met this old Indian guy name of Jacques Osweken. We had a few drinks, talked trapping, then had a few drinks more. He asked me where I was thinking of taking my furs. I told him I was getting out and catching the next train to Québec City. "Naw, you won't. You get a good price for them furs in Sugarmilk Falls," he said. We had a few more drinks, talked some more. "You'll get over it," he told me, "I've seen it before, this bush fever. If you don't, go see Grand'mère when you get to Sugarmilk Falls." In the new year I went back to my traplines. The spring hunt was good and I brought my furs here. It was the beginning of the sap run. I sold my furs and stayed on.' Zack paused.

'And did you get over it?' asked Marina.

'I reckon so,' he replied. 'I got to know Grand'mère. But this place draws you like a magnet once you've found it. After everything it seemed like heaven. Still does.' He grinned and turned to her. 'Now, tell me how somebody like you ends up in South Porcupine.'

Marina smiled briefly. 'It's very simple, Zack. All my family died in the camps. I am the only one left. But my mother had an older brother, Benjamin. When he was a young man he heard about the silver finds in Cobalt and he left Poland to make his fortune in Canada. He did.

They kept in touch, he and my mother. After the war I wrote to him so he would know what had happened to everyone. I was his only living relation. He persuaded me to join him and he was in Porcupine by then, gold-mining. At the time I was easily persuaded.'

'Why come here?

'He died a while ago.' She sighed. 'I wanted a change. I saw the job in *The Globe and Mail*. The name caught my eye. So I applied.'

Zack raised an eyebrow. 'Why would it catch your eye?'

Marina hesitated, about to dismiss the question with a shrug. 'I'd heard my uncle mention it a few times . . . I thought it was a pretty name.'

They were standing on the riverbank near the bottom of the falls. The low sun glowed golden on the side of the craggy gorge carved out over aeons by the fierce Sugarmilk River. The water rushed and tumbled between great cornices of snow and ice hanging from pinnacles of rock jutting through the foam and the mist. Gnarled icicles the size of trees hung at the edges of the cataract. Where the sun did not reach, the waterfall was still frozen, a solid white turbulence mirroring the thundering cascade. Sections of broken ice from the river and lake above the falls hurtled over the precipice, crashing into clouds of white spray on the boulders at the base. The sun retreated behind the trees, turning the sky green and gold, the rushing ice flow pink and gold and blue. The black rocks gleamed and the icy trees glittered like prisms in the reddening light. The waters roared, the ice falls thundered.

Marina shuddered. 'So much ice,' she said. There was a tremor in her voice.

*

'Have a care, Zack,' said Grand'mère. 'She's not what she seems.' They were sitting in her kitchen, a whiskey bottle and coffee mugs between them on the worn oilcloth.

'Naw. She's just a schoolteacher. They're like that – act like they know everything.'

'She is a cold one.'

Zack looked up in surprise. Grand'mère was watching him intently. Her sun and wind and life etched face was impenetrable.

He shook his head. 'No, Maggie. You're wrong,' he said decisively.

'Your eyes are full of dust,' she said sadly. 'There's ice in her heart. Believe me, I know.'

3

On a bright spring day hovering near the edge of summer Marina's car bumped along a rough road cut between the trees. After a few miles the road degenerated to a rutted track, and a short distance later it all but disappeared. When it seemed she could not go much further she stopped the car, and after a moment's hesitation decided to walk the rest of the way. Birdsong and the light sweet scent of maple blossom filled the air. The path meandered under the trees and around large grey boulders where flies buzzed on the sunny stone. Sunlight flickered through the perfect miniature bronze or pale green leaves and the clusters of small yellow flowers covering the branches. In the woods white trilliums pushed up through the dead leaves. Remains of snowdrifts survived in the deep shadows behind the rocks and here and there meltwater trickled. The path descended. Below her a lake glittered in the breeze like a cut sapphire and in a clearing between the jack pines on the shore she saw the rough cabin.

Marina stopped. What do you think you're doing? she asked herself again. She looked along the path towards the building. This was her last opportunity to go back to the car unseen and drive home. Another step and it would be too late. She heard the sound of hammering. He was busy. He wasn't expecting her. She had no business just dropping in out of the blue like this, although he'd suggested it. What did she actually want, anyway? Better turn around right now. Retreat.

A dog began to bark. It was already too late. A gruff voice ordered it to silence. Marina knew she had no choice now but to go on. She moved towards the sounds. Zack was bending over an upturned canoe and looked up as she approached. The last time she saw him they'd walked together to the spectacularly icy waterfalls and in the weeks that followed he was often on her mind. Now he stood up and took a step towards her and he seemed taller, leaner, finer-featured than she remembered. A large brown dog stood next to him, vigorously wagging its tail. His face creased with pleasure at the sight of her but she had the feeling he was not altogether surprised. Had he been waiting for her to make the next move, knowing she would? Was his pleasure as much at being proved right as at seeing her there?

'Hello, Zack,' she said.

His blue eyes danced merrily. Was he playing a game? She held his gaze for a moment. He did seem genuinely pleased. And there was something about the way he was looking at her too, a kind open look that concealed nothing. There were no hidden agendas here, she decided, and she couldn't remember the last time anyone had looked at her like that. Maybe Matt did once. He certainly didn't nowadays. Marina felt a little ashamed at her cynicism. But she thought Zack probably saw right through her in any event and he didn't seem to mind about what he saw.

There wouldn't be any point in cleverness and artifice and prevarication when dealing with him.

She looked away. Was she imagining it all? 'It's such a fine day,' she said, 'Saturday too. I was curious to see where you live.'

He was repairing the canoe, he explained. 'Winter damage. Nearly done.' He invited her to take a look round. 'Don't worry about the dog.'

The dog licked her hand and Marina began to relax. Zack's cabin was built on a point of land where the lake breeze could blow away the mosquitoes and blackflies. It was a simple rectangle built of logs, with a veranda overlooking the water. A few birch trees grew between it and the flat rocky outcrops surmounted by pines. The path continued down to the lake shore where a couple of boats were hauled up. On the veranda snowshoes and fishing tackle leaned against the cabin wall. Traps and a beaver pelt stretched over a frame hung from hooks. She sat down on the rough step and watched him work.

'It's a bit late for trapping, isn't it?' she asked him when he'd finished.

'Yes, but sometimes I get lucky, like with your raccoon. And now,' he replied wiping his hands on his shirt. 'To what do I owe this pleasure, Marina?'

The sudden formality in Zack's speech amused her. She smiled at him. 'I'm not sure. I felt like exploring.' She looked around. 'It's beautiful here. No wonder you stayed.'

'Let's have some coffee and you can tell me what you mean to explore.'

*

The inside of the cabin seemed dim after the bright sunshine. The wooden walls were bare, the furnishings sparse, nothing more than was needed. She had an idea that he wanted to be able to pack up in a hurry if ever the need arose. He poured out two tin mugs of coffee from the percolator on the stove. 'It's like the old schoolhouse,' she said, sitting down beside him at the table. 'Have you always lived alone?'

'No,' he replied, but he did not explain further. She felt him scrutinizing her again. 'Sorry. Didn't mean to stare,' Zack said, noticing her discomfort. 'You look like someone.' He got up and rummaged through a wooden chest in the corner. 'This might help your exploration too.' He handed her an old photograph. 'It is you, isn't it?' he asked.

Marina took the picture and stared at it in amazement. It was crumpled and damaged, as though it had been wet and dried out again. She nodded. 'Where on earth did you get this?'

'Hunting trip a few years back. Happened on it by chance. Miles from anywhere, deep in the bush. Found it in this.' He showed her a man's wallet.

The leather was brittle and cracked as though from exposure to the weather. She inspected it for a moment and then pulled out two stained, yellowed sheets of paper folded together. They were badly faded, torn along the creases and discoloured from the rain and snow. The outside sheet was an old prospecting licence but the licensee's name, the date and the stamp of the issuing office had all but disappeared. The second sheet was covered on both sides with small close writing. Again the ink had run badly so that parts of it were illegible. 'Have you tried to read it?' she asked him.

'Didn't get very far.'

'Was it just lying on the ground?'

'It was hidden under some rocks. Whoever put it there marked the place with a prospecting stake. That's the only reason I found it.'

'Is this all there was?'

'No, but you'd better read what you can.'

'What else was there?'

'Read it out.'

'I'll try, it's not very clear.' Marina began, 'I think it says it's August, I can't make out the date. There is a name too but it's very faint. It says: "When you find this even my bones will be gone."' She stopped. Her face was white. 'Oh, this is awful.' She continued reading. '"We've been up this way most of the summer staking claims, making good progress as the lawyer will confirm. The country round here is fair busting with potential but I guess it won't be realized now. Could be as much as two weeks since . . . " I can't quite make out the words but I think it says "two weeks since the plane crashed."' She paused. 'So that's what happened . . . I think I know who wrote this, Zack.'

Marina did not look up from the paper, and it was a moment before she proceeded. 'It goes on: "Mike was piloting and I was looking out of the window for colours. Saw heavy reddish staining on the rock outcrops, pinks, blues and greens too, in particular the purplish cobalt bloom, indicating nickel and silver ores, also lots of black pitchblende that could be high-grade uranium ore the way the Geiger counter was ticking like a time bomb."'

Marina stopped. There were tears in her eyes. 'It's Tom's. It's his writing. I knew him.'

'Thought maybe you did.'

She turned back to the paper. '"We were flying low, way beyond any flight plan we'd lodged and were about to turn back. This was a new lake to us with a very steep descent between the cliffs but the land around was looking likely." Then there's something about it being mid-morning and the bad glare off the water. He goes on, "That must've confused Mike. One minute he said he couldn't see properly and the next we were crashing through tall timber. I don't remember much after that. It must have damaged the Beaver's floats. I came to under water. There was still some air in the cockpit. I looked at Mike and he seemed to be dead. I tried to move but my legs weren't working too well. I thought they were broken. The plane began to shift and somehow I got out, I don't know how but soon as I did the whole thing tipped forward and sank to the bottom of the lake." There are some words I can hardly read, something about it being on a ledge or the trapped air keeping it up and then it says, "I guess Mike is down there."'

Marina stopped reading again. 'Mike,' she said softly, and after a moment continued, 'The writing is clearer just here. Tom says: "I remember floating to the surface and somehow made it to the shore. Bad pain in my legs, one definitely broken and my foot smashed up. I took my clothes off to dry them in the sun and must have passed out from the pain. When I came to it was dark and very cold. I was shivering. I knew I had a chocolate bar in my pocket and some cigarettes and my lighter. That's all there was, except for my wallet, a pen and a piece of paper to make navigation notes as we flew along. I ate some chocolate and drank water from the lake. I didn't feel too good. I couldn't light a fire or have a smoke. I splinted up my leg as best I could. The chocolate kept me going but it didn't last long. I thought it unlikely anyone would come looking for me soon. Next day or so I took a look round as well as I could manage. There's nothing except wilderness."'

Marina paused again. 'The next bit is quite faded,' she said. 'It could say it's two or three days later, but I'm not sure. I think he says he found blueberries nearby. I can read the rest. He says, "No one has come and I'm getting desperate. Crawled back to the lakeside where I'd be easier to spot. Got a fire going on the shore and tried sending some smoke signals using my shirt as a blanket. Don't hold out much hope. Come down with a bad fever or something. Pain in legs very bad. I'll mark out a place in the blueberry patch where I'll leave this account, in case I'm ever found. I don't want to disappear without trace."

'The writing becomes much scratchier. "Lost all track of the time. No strength to do anything much. Don't know how I'll get back to the lake. No sign of search plane even if I did. Wolves or something waiting around for me to give up. This place is going to be my grave. I feel delirious a lot of the time. Animals come to me in nightmares."' Marina's voice cracked. She wiped her cheek and after a moment continued to read. '"All hope gone. God rest my soul."'

Marina bent her head and heaved a long sigh. 'His name was Tom Gordon,' she said tearfully. 'You'd think a geologist would be better prepared.'

'All his gear was at the bottom of the lake.'

She nodded and closed her eyes. 'I hadn't known him very long.' She swallowed and after a while continued, 'They were working for my uncle. He was a mining promoter and lost most of his money on this enterprise. We never found out what happened to Tom and Mike. Everybody just came to the conclusion they disappeared somewhere in the bush. The lawyer told him nobody ever showed up at the rendezvous.' Marina paused. 'My uncle died. Then the job came up here. He'd talked about this place. Why didn't you hand the wallet over to the police?'

'Don't have a lot of dealings with the police. Do you remember the lawyer's name?'

'Oh, I don't recall. He was just another city lawyer. Does anyone around here remember him?'

'Maybe. One was staying up at the Braemar Lodge about the time it burned down. He lost a bunch of mining claims in a poker game.'

'What happened to them?'

'Story is, they all went up in smoke.'

Marina looked sad and thoughtful. Her eyes wandered around Zack's cabin, through the open door to the trees and the lake. 'Do you own this bit of land here, Zack?' she asked.

He seemed somewhat surprised by the question. 'Not sure anybody owns it. It's mostly Ojibwa land round here.'

'My uncle owned the exploration rights.' He shrugged his shoulders. 'What else did you find?'

'I could just about make out something at the bottom of a lake. It was big. Could be the Beaver.' He hesitated. 'And I came across a few bones scattered around.'

'Presumably you reported this.'

'Frank wrote down the details. Don't think he ever did much about it. Nobody reported missing round here. People disappear into the bush. Happens now and then. I reckon your geologist's remains are still out there.'

'Did you tell anyone else?'

'Lucien. He knows about the plane too.'

'Is that all?'

Zack shrugged. 'I guess Ed knows most things.'

'Would you be able to find the place again?'

'Not easy.' They sat for a moment in silence. Then Zack asked her, 'Was this geologist the only one for you? Nobody else?'

She looked at him, wondering whether to reply or tell him to mind his own business. 'You mean how have I got this far along the road without finding myself attached to a man?' He gave her a nod. She looked at him and decided he liked things to be out in the open. 'There was someone, a long time ago, after the war. It was the kind of thing that completely alters your life. But other things got in the way. Afterwards I concentrated on my work. Then Tom Gordon came along. That might have worked out too in different circumstances.' Marina shook her head and wiped her eyes again. 'I don't know why I'm telling you all this, Zack, when you haven't even told me your war stories.'

'Don't think you want to listen to war stories.'

'That doesn't usually make any difference to an old soldier,' she replied. He laughed and Marina smiled. She put the papers and the photograph back inside the wallet and handed it to him. 'Enough exploration for one day. Was there anything else in it?'

'Couple of fifty-dollar bills.'

It was Marina's turn to laugh. 'Finders keepers, eh?' She leaned forward and kissed him lightly on the cheek. 'Thanks for showing me this. I'd better go now before you know all my secrets.'

He grinned and shook his head and walked with her back to her car. When she was seated behind the wheel and about to turn the key in the ignition he leant over the open window of the car door and said, 'I still got them fifties.'

'Those fifties.'

'The very same.' He was smiling broadly.

What was amusing him now, she wondered? He always seemed amused by something. Did she mind this? Not really, but not knowing what it was could be a little exasperating. She tried to look at him severely but there was mirth in her eyes too. 'What do you always find so entertaining, Mr Guillem?'

'Entertaining? Nothing especially. I'm just glad you called by. I'd like it very much if you came again. Maybe just go fishing next time.'

She searched his face. His deep blue eyes looked back into hers with such warmth, such friendliness that she was a little taken aback. But there was no threat there. She felt she would be safe. She was curious about him and the more she saw of him, the more she liked him. She nodded. 'Yes, I'd like it too.'

'When?' he asked.

Tomorrow, she wanted to say. 'Next Saturday?'

*

They went fishing, often. He showed her how to bait the lines and how to paddle the canoe. In the late afternoons they cooked their catches over a fire on the shore. The hot wind sighed through the dark pine trees and the cicada flies droned. Fish leapt in the bright clear water. The summer sun crossed over the lake and dipped behind the treetops. The fire died to a red glow in the dusk. Sometimes Marina would lie very still on one of the wide flat sun-warmed rocks overhanging the shoreline and listen to the ripples lapping under the edge. She wondered why she always found contentment in this place, with this unusual man. They seemed so different, it seemed so unlikely. True, he made no demands on her. He was generous. Unlike Matt, he seemed happy to take her as she really was, whatever might turn up. There was more to it, though, than his easy-going ways. It was in that look of recognition he sometimes gave her. At first she thought it had to do with the photograph he'd found in Tom Gordon's wallet. Her natural suspicion made her mistrust his motives. But when he looked into her eyes and she looked into his, right away at some level there had been a sense of communion on equal terms, a recognition that everything in the past, in the present, simply was, like the hills and the icy waterfall. Quite soon she realized that he understood, and he didn't judge.

'Another Saturday nearly over,' she sighed regretfully one evening, 'and soon you'll be away on the fire watch.'

Zack was sitting beside her, his arms folded across his knees, squinting across the shadowy lake. After a while he said, 'You could stay. Try Sunday as well. Maybe you go to church on Sunday.'

Marina said, 'I stopped pretending during the war.'

'There's things you keep close.'

'You would know about keeping things close.'

He smiled. 'There's Matt.'

Marina opened her eyes and frowned, 'Yes, I suppose I should tell you about him, though you've probably worked it out anyway. It was in Paris after the war. I knew him there. He wanted me to marry him and then things happened. That was the end of it. But I didn't know he was here. When I came, there he was. The priest. It was quite a shock.' She stopped speaking.

'That's it?'

'Hardly, Zack.' He waited, but she did not go into detail. 'It was over for me long ago, though there's still something. Affection? I don't know. And there's some unfinished business too.' She paused. 'He has those mining claims, you know, the ones that were supposed to have been burned. I saw them.'

Zack grinned. 'I guess he got them from Grand'mère.'

'Yes, how did you know?'

'Figures.' Then he said, 'You know what happened to the prospectors and you've seen the claims. What are you going to do?'

'It could all have been mine by now.'

'That's why you got a job here.'

'Yes. To see if I could find out what happened and take back what I own. Things have always been taken away from me.'

'What about your unfinished business with Matt?'

'That too.' There was sadness in her eyes but she would not explain. 'I don't know if it can ever be finished. It's something I can't speak about, even to Matt, and that's a problem for you. For us. I will tell you about it, of course I will tell you, but not now.'

'There's no hurry, Marina. Just so long as we keep things straight between us.'

'I don't want to lose this too, Zack.'

*

On an Indian-summer morning Marina strolled down the track to Zack's cabin. The crisp air tasted of autumn. Dewy painted leaves shimmered in the cool sunlight. The silvery lake, smooth as glass, mirrored the hazy contours of the red and gold hills. Zack sat on the veranda step, absorbed in cleaning his rifle. A second larger rifle leaned against the cabin wall. The dog ran towards Marina and Zack looked up to watch her approach.

'Would you leave without saying goodbye?' she asked, sitting down beside him and kissing his cheek.

He grinned. 'Of course not.'

The tang of wood smoke tainted the chilly breeze. Marina looked around, at the thick red and ochre Hudson's Bay blankets airing in the sun, at the cleaned traps stacked by the door. She frowned. 'A lot of traps, Zack? How far are you going?'

He hesitated. 'Crowberry River. Other side of the haute terre.'

'How long for?'

'I'll come back when the hunting's done, before I set off. Day or two, to pick up supplies from Phil. Not sure when that'll be exactly but I'll let you know soon as I can. Then I'll be gone a while. Back before sugaring at the latest.'

'That's months away!' she said with surprise. 'I thought it was just the moose hunts. A few weeks at most. I didn't realize you'll be away all winter.'

He put the gun to one side and gazed into the distance. 'To be honest, I thought maybe I'd quit the trapline for good. But come this time of year, I have to be up and doing. Can't help it. It's in the air, in the blood. By the end of January it'll feel like a curse, always does. But on days like this, seems I just have to get back on the trail.' He looked at her hopefully. 'If you came with me you'd see what I mean.'

She shook her head. 'You know I can't.' Marina leaned her head on his shoulder and sighed. 'I'll miss you.'

'Good.' He put his arm around her and asked, 'What are you going to do?'

Marina shook her head. 'I don't know. What I usually do. Teach.' She smiled knowingly at him. 'Probably nothing else, Zack.'

He glanced knowingly back at her but remained silent. Marina closed her eyes for a long moment. 'Whatever I did or said, it wouldn't surprise you, would it? Very little seems to escape your notice. I can feel you reading the signs, you know, even when you touch me. I'll bet there isn't anything you haven't already worked out for yourself. You have no questions left. I have no secrets left.' She paused, and looked at him. 'Is that why you're going away?'

'No. Don't think that. But what would I do holed up here all winter when I could be in the bush earning money doing what I'm good at.' He looked at her seriously. 'Maybe you're right, Marina. Maybe I make my guesses, but it doesn't make for explanations.' Then he grinned affectionately at her. 'You don't seem to have a lot of questions left yourself.'

*

The first raucous ranks of Canada geese headed north across the cobalt sky. The spring sun grew stronger, warming the snow-bright days. The nights were clear but still bitterly cold. Imperceptibly, the snow began to crystallize. The sap run was imminent.

Zack stared at Marina with disbelief. 'I went over to see Grand'mère and Bobby like I always do when I get back. Did it have to happen, Marina? Bobby's just a little kid. He was a happy kid too.'

'He's in Penetanguishene, with a good foster family,' she replied. 'He's better off there. Bobby was making a lot of trouble here. You should have seen what he did to my house.'

'I heard about that. Doesn't seem likely for a six-year-old kid.'

'He wasn't going to school. He wasn't learning, Zack. Now he will.'

Zack shook his head. 'It won't work out. Hardly ever does. Seen it plenty of times. Grand'mère's real mad about it.'

'I know. She came here.'

'She can be dangerous, you know.'

'Dangerous? Why? This is normal procedure. She knows that.'

'She's a medicine woman. I've seen what they can do. It doesn't make sense but I've seen things with my own eyes you wouldn't believe if I told you. You don't want to antagonize them.'

'That's what Matt said. And I don't believe it. All the more reason to send Bobby away.' She looked at him anxiously. 'I'm responsible for making sure the children are educated. In the situation we had here it had to be done.'

He looked at her angrily, his loyalties torn. 'It would be much better for everybody if you'd let things be.'

'I couldn't, Zack. It was too serious.'

'Doesn't make it right.' He sighed in frustration. 'Grand'mère won't do nothing. And I can't say I'd blame her.' Then he added with deep concern, 'Please be careful, Marina.'

4

It was one of Ed Perriault's regular jokes, that a place with a thousand miles of rivers and three hundred and eighty named lakes could still be dry as far as the law was concerned. Not that he was especially in favour of change. Ed liked to watch the parade and see which way it was moving, then walk out in front. But it wasn't so easy with that particular question. Before long it had turned into anything but a carnival.

It was after the new schoolteacher arrived that Hugo Jansen began to drop hints he was thinking of taking steps to open up a licensed bar. Whiffs of change were in the air, unsettling a lot of people who believed change could only ever be for the worse, some influential ones as well. Anyway, that's how they saw this notion of Hugo's. The Falls Hotel was not much more than a rooming house till the Braemar burned down, but afterwards it began to see a steady rise in business. Birgit was all for expansion and came up with the bar idea. There was a big demand, she pointed out. You only needed to be in town on a Saturday night to see that. There was lots of money to be made in setting up the first and only legal outlet for what had traditionally been illegal across the entire Sugarmilk country.

So Hugo began to get his list of names together. He wasn't all that enthusiastic, but Birgit always got her way. And although it caused a deal of muttering, in truth nobody expected anything to come of it. Just hot air, people said, another pipe dream. But when the municipality meeting voted to support the petition the No Committee hurried to get itself organized. 'NO' posters appeared around the town. Several mornings Hugo found one pasted on the front door of the Falls Hotel itself. 'NO' flyers were handed out in the street, and Reverend Byers began to preach, calling down the wrath of God on the perpetrators and supporters of so unholy a proposition.

Roy Byers had been greatly affected by the petition. He didn't expect it to get much support. He thought he knew his congregation and was convinced the population as a whole would never tolerate such a development. The realization that there was actually going to be a vote on changing the status quo hit him like a bolt of lightning. He stormed in his pulpit about the evils of the demon drink, how it undermined the nation's moral fibre, how it led to destitution in this life and eternal damnation in the next. People were struck by the unusual heat of his oratory and the cold zeal in his eyes. Outside church he could not let the matter rest. He exhorted visitors to his manse into praying with him for the defeat of this evil aberration. He persuaded his wife to have the Presbyterian ladies' quilting circle prepare a banner for the No Committee and its supporters to march behind in the run-up to voting day. 'The devil has been let loose among us here, Lydia,' he remarked to her often, 'I feel another sick headache coming on.' Increasingly she had to put him to bed in the afternoons.

People in favour of changing the status quo weren't impressed or affected one way or the other. However, there were quite a few, enough to swing the outcome of the vote, who remained undecided. They wanted to think about it coolly, at their own pace, to consider the advantages, weigh them up against the disadvantages, and arrive at a reasoned view of what was suitable for a modern municipality in the modern world. Things were different nowadays. A Chinese restaurant had opened up in Sugarmilk Falls. There were human footprints on the moon, for Heaven's sake. Maybe this was a good moment to reconsider the status quo. They were all old and sensible enough to listen to persuasive arguments on both sides and then make up their minds. But this continual bombardment with NO felt like harassment. The old-fashioned threats of moral decline and damnation got under their skins. After all, most of them had a drink or two now and again, however obtained. What they wanted from the No Committee were sound social reasons for keeping things as they were. All they got were Roy Byers' wagging finger and warnings of doom, as though they were wicked children who had to be frightened into good behaviour. It drove more than a few, like Dave and Elaine Shaw, to support Hugo's plan.

*

Father Souris spread the *Sugarmilk Gazette* on the table in front of him. He continued to eat his cornflakes while he glanced through the pages. What a field day the newspaper is having over this business of the vote, he thought.

The letters section had doubled in size. He knew from the editor, Tim Buszek, that the print run had to be increased twice. His eyes landed on an advertisement. The No Committee must be worried. It seemed to be spending a bit of money. The piece was headed THE EVILS OF DRINK, in bold capitals. Below the words was a photograph of a man slumped beside the road. An empty bottle lay beside him, a half-full one leaned in his hand. He was rough, unkempt, his clothes were torn. His head lolled to one side, his eyes were glazed. The words DON'T LET THIS HAPPEN HERE. VOTE NO! were printed in large black letters underneath the picture. An article followed, no doubt another one of Roy's Armageddon tirades, thought Father Souris acidly and he began to turn over the page. But his eyes were drawn back to the newspaper photograph. He looked more carefully at the vacant eyes, the drooping mouth, the stringy unwashed hair. The photo was grainy, but something about the figure seemed dimly familiar. The angle of his position too, almost a squat, tapped at his memory. He raised his head trying to remember, then studied the man again, and slowly, piece by piece, a picture illuminated in his brain, a man squatting by a lakeside in the twilight, tossing stones into the water, a man overwhelmed by grief. Father Souris was appalled. He was looking at a photograph of Henri Osweken.

*

Arnie Anstalt replaced the telephone receiver without waiting to hear the telltale clicks as the listeners-in put down theirs. He reached for his copy of the *Gazette* and quickly paged though it until he came to the No

Committee's piece. Matt Souris was right. It did look like Henri. He closed his eyes and rubbed his forehead in dismay. One of these days he really was going to strangle Charlie once and for all, never mind the fact he was his brother. This sort of thing made the No Committee look so bad. It did nothing to promote their chances of bringing off a strong vote against abandoning the dry status quo. And there was always the chance it might resurrect questions far better left buried.

Arnie took the newspaper through to the workshop, where Charlie was engrossed in his latest project, not a car this time – he'd finished working on the convertible – but an airplane, of all things. After Charlie and Suzanne Armand tied the knot they were somehow going to fly off together high into the wide blue yonder. What romantic hogwash, thought Arnie. Probably it'd turn out to be nothing more exciting than a honeymoon in a Niagara Falls motel. Charlie's problem was that when he thought big it was in a vague sort of way, and when it came down to working out the detail he couldn't think big at all. Even with Suzanne his brother had mundane aspirations. Arnie told himself if it were him, he would whisk her off somewhere fine, New York, maybe even Paris. Extravagant, but it would pay dividends in the long run. Of course he'd only been able to whisk Irene away for a week in her father's summer cottage, no more than a shack really, on the Rideau Canal, but that was long before he became principal partner in Anstalt Motors. Anyway it was more like Irene whisked him in those days . . .

Also Charlie didn't think things through. Look at that Braemar business, for example. That might have turned out real bad if Arnie hadn't intervened. And now there was this cockamamie airplane idea. Probably a complete aerial enterprise of one sort or another already flew fully fledged in his brother's head, but all Arnie could see were a few engine components and a mail-order outline drawing of a small aircraft. Charlie had dropped hints about having more big plans for the plane but either he hadn't worked out what they were or he was keeping them close to his chest. He wondered if even Suzanne knew about those. Mind you, her own vagueness could make Charlie's flights of fancy seem like pieces of precision planning. But all that was still a long time off, considering Suzanne was only just out of university, the Armands weren't too thrilled with Charlie, and only a collection of engine parts was so far in evidence.

'Charlie,' shouted Arnie. His brother noticed the irritation in his voice and grinned. 'Charlie, that picture you took for the committee, did you know who it is?'

'Does it matter? You wanted a picture of a drunk. I got you one.'

Arnie pushed the newspaper under his brother's nose. 'It looks like Henri Osweken, doesn't it?'

Charlie looked at the picture. 'So?'

Arnie sighed deeply. 'You can be so stupid! Hasn't Henri been through enough? First the Braemar. And Flora. Then Rachelle. Now this. People used to like Henri. They still sympathize with him. They'll think the No Committee is hitting him too hard when he's down. He's got good reason to be down.'

'It's still a good picture of a drunk,' replied Charlie defensively.

'It's a picture of a drunken Indian, you saphead! You know people think Indians aren't like the rest of us. It's the rest of us the No Committee is aiming at, not the Indians. They're a lost cause as far as the No vote is concerned.'

Arnie paused, looking at his brother and shaking his head. 'You really fucked up good here, Charlie!'

Charlie was taken aback. Arnie almost never swore. 'If it's so important why didn't you check it out before you sent it off to the *Gazette*?' he asked.

Arnie sighed in exasperation. 'I did,' he said, 'I thought it was just another drunk.'

'Then I guess most people will too.'

'Matt Souris didn't. He's just been giving me the third degree down the phone. He wants a printed apology.'

'The third degree? Doesn't sound like Matt. Anyway, he's not like us either, is he, Arnie? Even though he's got something going with the grade-school teacher.'

Arnie shook his head. 'You're full of shit.'

His brother did not respond but turned his attention back to the engine on the work bench.

'Charlie,' said Arnie coldly, 'we don't want to give people an excuse to start talking about the Braemar fire, do we? You've got to be more careful. Okay?'

*

Father Souris sat behind the wheel of his car in the presbytery driveway and wondered what to do next. The automatic garage doors refused to open again. This began to happen at the beginning of the summer and was becoming more and more frequent. He'd checked over the mechanism but hadn't been able to locate a fault. He'd looked inside the fuse box but there was no sign of a problem there. He had Charlie Anstalt give the installation a thorough inspection but he couldn't find anything either. It's that Grand'mère, Father Souris thought angrily. She's gone and put a curse on the garage.

He rested his forehead on the rim of the steering wheel and closed his eyes. He must be losing his mind. A curse on the garage? What was the matter with him these days? Well, he knew the answer to that all right. He knew why he'd become so impatient, so unreasonable, so ready to fly off the handle and hurl blame everywhere and on everyone. Except himself. He might as well face up to it. Marina was what was the matter with him. Or to be absolutely accurate, Zack Guillem. His forehead began to hurt where the steering wheel pressed into it. He opened his eyes, and looked directly at the plastic Virgin mounted on the dashboard. Funny, he'd never noticed she had blue eyes, blue painted ones. They were not like Marina's at all. Another current of anger charged through Father Souris. He aimed a swipe at the little statue. The Virgin rocked forwards and backwards in ever decreasing arcs until she vibrated to a standstill. And there she stood, just as before, on the dashboard in front of him, her immaculate hands folded together, her smug blue eyes raised to heaven.

Father Souris leaned back on the seat, feeling very ashamed. He began to interrogate himself again. What really was the matter? Who really was to blame? He began to pray. Hail Mary, full of grace, the Lord is with thee. Blessed art thou among women and blessed is the fruit of thy womb . . . He could not continue. The routine words meant nothing anymore. Of course he knew what the answers would be if he was honest. He knew exactly what the problem was. Sin. His sins, to be precise. Not just the little everyday kind of sinning that everyone was susceptible to but prolonged big mortal sinning that surely placed him well beyond redemption's pale. He'd broken commandments. He'd committed all seven deadly sins except gluttony and maybe sloth. He'd broken his vows to God. He more than anyone knew it was wrong. But he hadn't been overly concerned. He had not made excuses for himself, but somehow the sinfulness of what he was doing seemed remote and unimportant. The way he saw it, his love for Marina easily outweighed everything in the balance of good and evil. And he was completely, utterly, blindly in love with Marina. Sins, certainly. Big sins, too. But he was not in control, not responsible for his actions. There was no cold calculation here. His were sins of passion, he told himself, understandable and ultimately forgivable, like crimes passionnels.

Unfortunately it did not end there. Marina had turned her back on him and gone to someone else. She was now with that Zack Guillem, of all people. A man without any sense of obligation, moral or otherwise. A man at ease with his choices. A man totally free. Father Souris was surprised by the strength of his reaction. Is this what it feels like to be insanely jealous? he wondered. This agonizing debilitating emotion was a new experience for him, far more painful, he thought, than all the guilt and remorse he ought to be feeling if he was a better person. No doubt he deserved it. He did not know how to deal with it. Marina was his. Of that much he was certain. He couldn't reason himself out of it. He couldn't pray himself out of it. The more he tried the more intense this jealousy became. It was as physiological as his breathing, as autonomous as the beating of his heart. All he could do was endure it and hope that it would begin to ease away soon, before he did something reckless because of it.

Father Souris tried the garage doors again. This time they began to move but just as he put the car into gear and started to creep forward, they stopped. The doors would not open fully. They would not close. This was far worse than before, he thought. 'Damn that Grand'mère and her curses!' he shouted. The doors opened.

*

The No Committee's lambasting woke the Yes Committee from its petition-induced slumber. Because enough names had come forward to trigger a vote it was natural for the Yes supporters to consider success almost a foregone conclusion. Even though a big majority was required, biding their time was all that was needed and come voting day the Jansens had only to fill in the application form for a liquor licence. Maybe there'd be a bar open in town in time for Christmas. So the summer was well advanced before the Yes campaign began in earnest. Its organization was somewhat haphazard. The supporters were inclined to leave everything to Birgit because they felt it was her petition after all. Birgit was sensitive to her conflict of interests. As the main beneficiary once the vote went her way, she didn't want to be seen to be taking over the committee. Although these wrinkles were never completely straightened out the Yes Committee produced enough posters and handbills, and did enough by way of a couple of coffee mornings and a jumble sale, to show they were serious and active contenders for the minds of the voters.

Their most effective weapon, however, turned out to be the *Sugarmilk Gazette*. The Yes Committee became adept at manipulating the letters section. It began with a couple of straightforward paragraphs in support of a change to the status quo and when Reverend Byers replied in his usual style, the Yes Committee went on the offensive. Members wrote to the newspaper, putting forward their reasonable arguments in favour of change. It got so they were making all the points and the No Committee could only respond. But the No's worst tactic was the EVILS OF DRINK piece. Instead of the apology he'd requested, Father Souris's complaint triggered a detailed explanation in the following edition of the newspaper, pointing out how the pitiable state of the person depicted was an example of the consequences of alcohol addiction. This brought in quite a few more letters. Yes it was due to drunkenness, they agreed, but that had nothing to do with the question of licensing. It was unlicensed, illegal, unregulated alcohol that caused the dire condition of the man in the picture. Rather than act as a warning against disastrous future consequences should the Yes vote prevail, it graphically illustrated what was happening at this very moment on the streets of a DRY Sugarmilk Falls. One letter stated, 'For those so far gone in their addiction, the legality or otherwise of the provision of alcohol is not a consideration. These unfortunates need assistance from a different quarter, which is a subject for a different debate altogether. The No Committee, Reverend Byers in particular, cannot see the nose on its face.'

*

Early on a dull damp summer morning Father Souris got out of his car at the old Braemar site, where Henri still lived in a cabin that had survived the fire. It was the first time in years, since the night of their vigil for Flora in fact, that he'd come back here. He looked around. The whole place was depressingly desolate now, the charred ruins collapsed and overgrown except where the stone chimney rose out of the tangle. A fine rain fell straight down. The warm windless air smelled of wet vegetation. The trees dripped noisily, the rocks glistened, the undergrowth and long grass were covered with silvery beads of water. Henri's cabin was dilapidated. The porch leaned, a window was broken and there was a large tear in the screen door. Father Souris knocked. Silence. He knocked again and went inside. As his eyes became used to the dimness he saw half-empty cans of food, dirty plates and forks, empty bottles, dead and dying flies. An unmade bed stood against one wall, the mattress bare, the pillow stained, the blanket frayed.

'Henri?' he called softly.

There was no reply. He went outside. 'Henri?' Still nothing.

Father Souris walked down to the lake. The trees along the near shore faded into the thick drizzle. The jetty, wet and slippery, was mostly intact. He could not see far across the flat grey dimpled water before it merged into the general greyness. 'Henri?' he called again. His voice seemed too loud in the close damp air.

'He's not here, Matt.'

Father Souris turned around. Squatting under a birch tree, her back against the white trunk, he saw Grand'mère. 'Where is he?'

'Gone.'

He looked at her, trying to work out what she meant. 'Gone? Where?'

She sighed deeply before she spoke. When she did her voice was flat, exhausted. She sounded barely able to order the words. 'I haven't seen him for a while. He's gone for good now. He said he would go last time I talked with him.'

'Grand'mère?'

She shook her head but said nothing. Father Souris waited and after a while she continued, 'He said he'd failed.'

'Failed? Why?'

'He never squared things up for Flora, never got the guy who burned this place down,' she replied.

'Guy?'

'He thought he knew who did it, but was never sure enough to deal with him.' She laughed without mirth. 'Henri was more careful to get it right than I would have been. But he knew Flora would want him to be absolutely sure.'

Father Souris shuddered. 'Where's he gone? He might still come back.'

'No. You're too late. I don't think you could've done anything for him. I couldn't. Zack couldn't.'

Zack again.

He looked at her, and saw she was dressed in finely beaded buckskins. Around her neck hung a string of animal teeth and claws. Gradually understanding began to dawn. 'Have you been here all night, Grand'mère?' he asked her.

She nodded once. The realization dropped like a stone in his heart, and he knew then that Henri was dead. 'When did it happen?'

'Oh, maybe a couple of weeks ago.' She sighed again,

a long drawn-out sigh, 'He's in there somewhere, in the lake.'

'Did he drown himself?'

'I don't know. He said it was time for him to leave, to go to Flora and explain, ask her to forgive him. Maybe he just knew he was going. It sometimes happens like that.'

Father Souris was shocked. He squatted down beside her, his throat tight and with tears in his eyes. 'I'm sorry, Grand'mère . . .' For a moment he was unable to continue. 'I should have realized . . . I've failed too.'

She looked at him with her dark inscrutable eyes. She touched his arm. 'You're very troubled lately, Matt.'

He wiped his cheek. 'Forgive me.' He could not contain himself. He broke down. Suddenly everything seemed utterly pointless.

'I can try to make things easier for you? Or would that be too compromising?' She placed her gnarled hand over his.

He stared at her, not knowing what to say. He saw what he thought was compassion in her black eyes, but he couldn't be sure. Again he felt a sense of connection. And he knew the stories, how a medicine man could keep someone's life in suspension as long as he wished, how only when the payment stopped the shaman stopped and the sick one either died or recovered. Were they true? He pulled his hand away. 'You know I can't do that. It goes against everything I believe.'

After a moment she said, 'There are more things in heaven and earth, Father Souris, than are dreamed of in your philosophy.'

Where had he heard those words before? His look of

confusion seemed to amuse her. He paused, wondering what he should say.

'*Hamlet*, Matt. The residential school was a terrible place. We didn't have names, just numbers. Like your schoolteacher, but not marked on us. We were beaten for speaking Ojibwa, but there was sometimes magic in the white man's language too.'

'It's different now, Grand'mère,' he assured her.

She spat.

'Anyway, it's more than my philosophy that's preventing me. It's your sorcery. You see so much. You are better at what you do than I am at what I do.' He hesitated. He tried to sound flippant and added, 'I guess you frighten me a little, Maggie.' There. He'd admitted it. It was out in the open. Let her do her worst with that knowledge.

'I'm old, that's all,' she replied, but he heard the note of satisfaction in her voice. 'Then we shall pray together for Henri's soul,' she suggested.

As always, he thought, she was the one in control.

Father Souris crossed himself and they prayed. After a time he said to her, 'Is there anything I can do for him? For you?'

Grand'mère looked past him to the lake. 'He wants to find Rachelle. He had things that are hers now.'

'I'll make some enquiries. It won't be easy after so long. Maybe she doesn't want to be found.' Then Father Souris asked her, half serious, half joking, 'You haven't put a curse on my garage, have you?'

Grand'mère continued to look straight ahead. 'Good curses are not that easy to manage, Matt. So why would I stop at the garage?'

Her words, her matter of fact tone made him uncomfortable. Was it as he sometimes feared? he wondered. Had she put a curse on him? Then she opened her medicine bundle and gave him a loop of braided sweetgrass. 'What's this for?' he asked her. 'Another payment?'

She shrugged. 'Keep it.'

5

You've been busy prodding under stones, Lucien said to the stranger. You say you're familiar with the police files too. The open-and-shut record of what happened here. Mon amie, you must have influence somewhere. As far as we know those files have never been released.

We'll stick with that version for now. As Arnie says, the town was running a high fever but this cut right across the No–Yes divide. It's the story we agreed on at the time, not that we got as far as actually agreeing. It was more the one we ended up with, all of us, the Jansens, the Shaws, the Tronquets, the Anstalts, especially them, right on up to the reeve, Ed Perriault. Roy Byers too. And Father Souris. Even Frank Martello himself. Every one of us, that is, except Zack Guillem, who disappeared. Nobody could ever be certain just how much he knew, but he didn't miss much as a rule.

Alors. The official story, then. It all began when Grand'mère Osweken lost the maple forest in a crap game. So she did, and a great deal more besides. As I said, it happened like they say. You've read the files, you know that's what's supposed to be at the bottom of it all, that's what provided the motive. How she lost everything she had. How she took her terrible revenge. And afterwards people said they were not surprised it turned out the way it did. What really lay behind it was never talked about.

After the Braemar burned down the gambling didn't stop. It went further underground so to speak, a poker game here, another one there. Players seemed to know where to find them and Frank Martello made sure he was always a step or two behind. It wasn't only poker. The crap games began to get a reputation. Arbitrageurs used to drive in from all over the place during the summer, park up behind Anstalt Motors and be there all night sometimes, at a table specially set up in the back of the repair shop. Not as salubrious as the Braemar but it was the size of the money changing hands that was the big attraction. Arnie swears he never knew and when he did find out he put an end to it. And we still believe you, Arnie, that it was Charlie's doing. Eventually the crap games relocated to St Augustine's Church basement, after the bingo suppers, and you can't go much more underground than that. Father Souris always claims he was completely in the dark about what was going on. We believe him too. He would not lie, though it's been said he exorcized the room after every session. And it was in the basement under the church, they said the table was right below the altar, that Grand'mère's long winning streak ended. Strange how she almost never lost. We used to wonder if her dice were shapes, or maybe loaded on occasion, but she was never found out to be a cheater and her luck was just as good whatever the dice. Most put it down to her spells. It got so the challenge was to try to outwit her gambling magic, and many of us failed at that, I can tell you.

Lucien grinned at the stranger and continued.

*

The darkness was dense, bitter and moonless. Swirling leaves rattled along the sidewalk in the gusty wind. Father Souris and Miss Grochowska left the presbytery, their way lit only by a shaft of light slanting across the frosty lawn.

'What's going on over there, Matt?' asked Marina suddenly. There was a glow in the row of windows at the bottom of the wall of the church.

'Where? I don't see anything.'

She looked at him, bemused by his question, but could not make out his face. 'Come on. You can see the light.'

'Probably somebody forgot to turn it off.'

'I can hear noises too. There's something going on in the church basement. And at this time of night it won't be bingo. I'm going over to take a look.'

Father Souris pulled her back. 'Marina. There's nothing there . . . only a few old people maybe . . . playing canasta.'

'Canasta? After midnight? I don't believe you.'

'Well, I really can't see anything with my blind eye.'

'You sound like Constable Martello,' she laughed. 'What about your other eye?'

He sighed. 'I suppose it might see a poker game or something just as awful that I'm not aware of because I've got my blind eye turned to it.'

She shook her head and laughed again. 'Does Frank know?'

'I'm not sure . . . he might . . . I honestly don't know. He's got that blind eye when it suits him. You're not going to report it, are you? He'll have to do something about it if you do, and the canasta players always leave a nice donation in the collection box.'

She did not answer his question but asked, 'How long has this been going on?'

'A while. Ever since Charlie Anstalt's sessions in the back of the repair shop had to move, I guess. Maybe Frank's good eye eventually landed there. Or maybe Arnie found out.' He paused, then began to explain the unusual situation. 'Look, Marina, after the Braemar Lodge burned down . . . you know, Henri Osweken's place . . .'

'Those Oswekens again!' interrupted Marina irritably. 'That horrible Grand'mère is behind it, I suppose. I just do not understand how she can twist you around her finger like she does, Matt. What has that old witch got on you?'

'Don't be ridiculous.'

Miss Grochowska hesitated, and in the darkness a knowing smile crossed her face. 'She's down there, isn't she?' She laughed. 'Is Grand'mère running a gambling den underneath your church?' His silence gave her all the answers she needed. 'This beats everything. You are such a fool! Gambling in the Catholic church basement, whatever next? This I've got to see for myself.'

'Don't, Marina,' he pleaded. 'Officially I don't know anything about it. Better to keep it that way.'

'Well, you don't have to come with me. Good night, Matt,' she said brightly and walked briskly away.

*

Marina entered the church and paused at the top of the stairs. A harsh neon tube lit the far end of the basement room where the youth club's pool table was pushed against the wall, and the men wedged in tightly, crammed up against the table. Others a row or two back tried to get fistfuls of dollars between the players to place bets. The air in the long low room was thick with cigarette smoke, the clatter of dice thrown against the wall and a medley of voices shouting words Marina did not understand.

'Who wants a hard raise ten?' she heard, followed by, 'You want a hard way raise?' and, 'Two to one the hard way,' and then another clatter of the dice.

'Money! You got it!' shouted another. It was Charlie Anstalt.

'I got five open . . .'

'Two sevens . . .'

'Winner! Winner!' It was Charlie again. He looked up when she began to descend the stairs. So did Freddy Chen and Sammy Dutoit. The room fell silent. Hugo Jansen and a couple of Oswekens, Louis she thought and his cousin Ovide whose family lived with Grand'mère, had their backs to her but turned their heads to watch her. Zack Guillem too, with a look of surprise to see her there. At the centre Grand'mère herself, her eyes wide with concentration, swaying slightly, paused in the middle of a roll. Under the garish light of the neon tube she looked as gnarled and ageless as a tree. Around her neck hung a string of animal teeth and claws and as she raised her head and recognized the newcomer a look of such menace crossed her face that Zack who was standing near her frowned.

'This doesn't look like canasta to me,' Miss Grochowska

said, moving down the steps. She walked up to the table into the space that opened up for her between Charlie and Hugo.

'Evening, ma'am,' said Charlie with a sly grin. 'Come to join in or just watch the action?'

'I'll just watch for now, Charlie. It isn't bingo either, is it?'

'Ah . . . no. In fact, we're shooting craps,' he explained.

'So this is a crap game. I've never seen one before.'

Charlie exchanged quick looks with Sammy, then Hugo, Freddy, and Louis. 'You've never rolled the dice before?' he asked her.

'Only in Monopoly. I've played quite a bit of Monopoly.'

'So, you've never rolled the dice in a crap game,' he repeated with satisfaction. 'Stick around, lady. You might find you're in luck tonight.'

The game continued. Grand'mère placed a bet and rolled the dice again.

'If you want to play, you'll need to lay a bet,' explained Charlie.

'I've only got about five dollars with me,' replied Marina, 'Anyway, I don't gamble.'

'I don't believe it. You've never bought a sweepstake ticket?'

'Never.'

'How about a raffle ticket or a bingo card?'

She nodded. 'True, I have.'

'You see, everybody gambles one way or another,' Charlie said. 'C'mon. Try it. You might go home a few bucks the richer.'

'I'll lay a bet for you,' put in Freddy Chen quickly.

'And me,' said Hugo Jansen.

'What about you, Zack? You gonna lay a bet for the lady?' There was an edge of sarcasm to his voice.

Zack inclined his head towards Grand'mère, and then shook his head. 'I'm not superstitious like you all.'

'What superstition is this?' asked Marina. 'Beginners' luck?'

'It's a great deal more scientific than beginners' luck,' said Charlie. 'Some bettors have a high regard for certain doctrines.'

'Oh? What sort of doctrines?'

'Well . . . for example, there's the one that says chances like to take it in turn so you lay your bet according to when you calculate a particular number's turn is expected.'

'It doesn't sound like a very reliable doctrine, Charlie.'

'Maybe not. Then there's the virgin principle. It's probably the most reliable one of all.' He winked at her. 'Don't often come across it so we're all real keen to make the most of it when it does. Except Zack here, who doesn't think doctrines make any difference to the way dice want to roll.'

'How does this principle work?' asked Marina.

'It's really very simple. It says a woman who's never rolled the dice before in a game of craps always has a hot roll the first time,' Charlie explained innocently.

Marina ignored the sniggers. 'All right,' she said, 'I don't want to deny you the opportunity to put this rare doctrine to the test here under the church. Do I have to do anything in a particular way?'

'No,' said Charlie, 'you just need to get into the game, place a bet with your five dollars. Do you want to bet now on Grand'mère making her point? She's trying to throw an eight.'

Marina watched Grand'mère empty her glass of whiskey. 'Is it a good idea?' she asked.

'A lot of people think that when Grand'mère starts rolling points you'd be crazy not to bet along with her. An eight is an easy number for her to make especially when she's hot. But Hugo over there has decided to bet against. So if you take the odds and bet against Hugo, and Grand'mère gets her eight, you'd have fifteen dollars in your pocket. What do you say?'

'Why not? I'll bet my five dollars against Hugo.' She took a bill from her purse and handed the money to Charlie.

Grand'mère put down her glass and threw the dice. They flew against the wall and rolled onto the table, a five and a three.

Before long Miss Grochowska had won over a hundred dollars. Then Charlie said to her, 'Right, now it's your turn with the dice, ma'am, and the dice are nice and warm. Take your time so we can get the betting sorted out.'

Marina tested the feel of the dice in her hand. She shook them in her fist and threw them onto the table. It was a six and a one.

'Wow! Money!' called Charlie. 'You got it! You've already won with your first throw. See what I mean about the virgin principle being reliable. You're certainly in the money now and so are a few of us. Now, you can either keep the dice and lay another bet, or pass them on.'

'I'll try again.' She rolled the dice in her hand and threw a four.

'Four isn't so easy to make,' Charlie said.

Grand'mère looked at Miss Grochowska. 'I will take the odds off you, mamselle. I will lay a hundred dollars you do not make your four.'

Marina rolled the dice in her fist and threw. It was a three and a one. Next she threw a nine, and another hundred dollars left Grand'mère. The excitement mounted. The noise of bets being laid rose. The dice smacked against the wall until all Grand'mère's money had gone. 'I think it's time I went home now,' said Marina.

'Oh no,' Grand'mère said thickly, picking up the dice, 'I will win it back. Next throw I bet the land against you.' She swayed as she spoke. Louis and Ovide looked at her in alarm. 'I know why you have come here, schoolteacher. It is because of our land. Well, maybe you think now you will get it. I bet all the land against you. It is yours if you win, but if you lose you must leave this place. Go back to South Porcupine or anywhere you like. But never come here again. Will you bet with me on these terms, mamselle?'

Marina looked intently at the old woman. 'Do you mean it?' she asked her. 'If I win I get the land and if I lose I have to leave Sugarmilk Falls?'

'Oh, yes. I mean it. You are the sickness here. Maybe it will end if you get what you want. But if you lose, you must leave this place for good. These are my terms.'

'Don't do it, Marina,' warned Zack. 'It's dangerous.'

Marina paused, looking at Zack. 'Dangerous? How can it be dangerous?'

'It is, that's all.'

'But you know she's right, Zack. That's why I came here, to take back what's mine.' She hesitated for a moment only. 'Yes, Grand'mère, I will bet with you on your terms.'

Grand'mère nodded once and handed the dice to Marina. 'Louis will get the papers. He will not take long. Would you like a drink while we wait?'

Marina shook her head. Grand'mère refilled her own glass.

*

Father Souris returned home and reluctantly went to bed. He lay awake, too tired, too anxious to sleep. Most nights were like this. Urgent questions presented themselves in the darkness. What did he think he was doing? Going to do? What had gotten into Marina lately? Or rather, what had been the matter all along? He would fall asleep at last and then the nightmares began.

When she first came to Sugarmilk Falls, she did not make herself known to him, though she'd known him immediately. It was only after he recognized her on that summer morning she began to take any notice of him. She had never tried to avoid him, true, and right away she'd been the one in control. Increasingly he got the feeling there was something she was waiting to tell him, as though the right moment had yet to arrive. It seemed to be always there, on the tip of her tongue, the words already arranged for maximum impact. And accompanying this growing feeling that some enormous revelation was imminent was his own growing reluctance to know what it was. It was something cataclysmic, he was certain, or else why would she play with him like this? Why would the exact right moment be so essential unless it was something so explosive that its detonation had to be perfectly timed, the range of its devastation perfectly calculated?

For a while they'd come together again in secret. Initially he was as captivated as he'd been in the Café Serac. She was maturely beautiful now, no longer a girl, but confident, self-possessed, and, he had to admit, even intimidating. When they talked she would sometimes look at him affectionately and at the same time shatter his convictions as easily as if she blew on a house of cards. He kissed her, and it was as he remembered it, intense, ecstatic, like balancing on the edge of a new universe. He tried to recapture the free fall of their passion but very soon realized that she remained perfectly balanced on the edge. And an old repressed question bubbled again to the surface of his consciousness, had the love he believed they shared always been in his mind only? Had she merely gone along with it for convenience, for a distraction, before emptying a pistol into herself? But then he would look at Marina and quickly bury the thought again.

Sometimes he woke suddenly in the darkness, and in the passing minutes and hours of his clock radio's green glow watch her sleeping beside him in his presbytery bed. He would think that it was all as before, that only their youth had gone and what they had now was far richer, deeper, more intense. But in the pale grey dawn light he would hurry her awake and dressed and back to her house before anyone was around to draw inferences about what was going on between the schoolteacher and the Catholic priest. Then he would kick himself for his delusions. What on earth did he think he was doing? And always, the growing feeling that there was something important he didn't know yet, but was on the verge of finding out. What could it be?

It was no better when he stayed at her house. In fact it was worse. He'd hoped it would be like her apartment had been all those years ago. Once he joked about where she kept her chickens now, and though she'd smiled a little he could tell she did not relish the memory. 'It was a lifetime ago,' she said, 'in another world. They were a necessity to survive.' Did that apply to him as well, he wondered? He never mentioned the chickens again. He did not like to spend the night in Marina's bed. He couldn't relax. He'd wake up often and try to read the time on his watch in the dark. She would mutter something, turn over and go back to sleep, while he lay awake, trying to keep still, waiting for the first dawn opportunity to creep back behind his celibate facade. Once, after they made love, when he lay beside her, replete, exhausted, momentarily at peace in a golden cosmos, he broached the possibility of leaving the Church, marrying her as he should have done all those years ago. She was taken unawares. He saw her old vulnerability exposed, like a desperate grasping for handholds in a storm. But it was a brief moment only. She had years of experience of storm defences. 'What would you do outside the Church, Matt? You were always its prisoner, even before the war. Anyway, it's too late now.' He could feel the pull of her retreat from him, like the moon on the sea. It left him floundering against its current and his whole existence seemed to him a travesty.

Afterwards their lovemaking became more and more of an ordeal, initiated because that's what they did rather than out of desire. But he had to admit he still enjoyed the feeling of rebellion it gave him. These were the only times he could still kid himself he was making choices.

'Do you love me, Marina?' he asked her once in desperation.

She looked at him, a little amused, a little detached. 'I never loved anyone else,' she replied. He had to be content with that, although he guessed she referred to the past only. He did not pursue the question further and then he heard the gossip that Zack Guillem had caught her eye. He determined not to believe it, but he was devastated.

They sometimes met by the river, in the clearing above the falls. Once on a summer's day they'd made love there, but only once. Mostly it was just to talk. She'd sometimes visit him at the presbytery, sitting in the corner of his study, near the window. Even after his desperate pleadings on her doorstep she still came now and then. He'd gone round to try to talk her out of this madness. Useless. And tonight she'd told him she thought she might marry Zack. He ought to know what was going on, she said, after all they'd been to each other in the past. And again the sense that there were words tumbling over themselves to be spoken out loud, words she fought to keep unsaid for the time being.

Yes, she was always the one in control. He should have resisted her over sending Bobby Osweken to a Catholic foster home. It was education policy, she said. It irked, but of course she was right, though the procedure had not been implemented in Sugarmilk Falls until she came. And now Bobby was in jail. A child of seven, or maybe he'd be eight by now. In jail.

Grand'mère told him Miss Grochowska was possessed. 'There is a madness in her, Matt,' she'd said. 'She is a destroyer.'

A destroyer? Marina? He remembered her sitting in the pink satin chair, looking so vulnerable while she plucked feathers from chickens. He hadn't seen her wring their necks. He remembered red geraniums, blood spreading on the Paris sidewalk. He remembered taking the gun from her hand and secreting it in his pocket. Quelle horreur. The ambulancemen shook their heads. 'C'est désespéré,' one said to him before they rushed her away and he hurried from the scene as soon as he could. Snipers, he'd told the military police. They nodded. Just another shooting. It often happened. So many scores to settle in the months and years after the liberation.

He remembered her stubborn determination to remove Bobby from her class. 'Bobby is almost uncontrollable. He needs to be removed from Grand'mère's influence,' she said.

'You're taking him away from the only family he's got?'

'It's education policy for Indian children,' she replied coldly. 'You know that as well as I do. Besides, he's a troublemaker. He needs a firm hand before he becomes an incurable troublemaker.'

'He's so little, Marina. He's only six.'

'He's a six-year-old monster,' she said. 'Look what he did to my house. He needs proper parents in a foster home. The younger the better, in the long run. I can vouch for that.'

She seemed so hard, so cold, so inflexible, so right once she made up her mind. He didn't remember her like that at all. Had he been blind, or had she become that way with the passing of the years? 'Can you?' he replied.

The sarcasm in his voice was not lost on her. 'It's normal procedure, Matt. It's for the best reasons.' She looked at him with such coldness but spoke so calmly, so reasonably. 'He needs to be taken away from all the native influence he's getting. Bobby is not stupid. Quite the opposite, but at his age he doesn't know what's real and what's make-believe. No child does. That takes time to learn. In a civilized community a child gets clear-cut experience of what is and what isn't real. In the primitive world there is no clear distinction. Grand'mère tells him stones can sometimes be alive. They all think that way. They're not so interested in what's real and what isn't. They're still like children themselves. We have to give Bobby the chance to grow up.'

He'd tried to argue against her. 'You're looking at it through your European eyes, Marina. Indians have their own view of how their world works going back thousands of years. That's how they have survived. You'd be like a child in that one.'

'You know that's not true, Matt,' she replied.

He tried again. 'When the man in the moon looks down at you and the rationality of your world and at Grand'mère and the intuitive logic of hers, he sees two different approaches, that's all, each one complete and distinct and successful on its own terms. But if you ask him which one is better, even the man in the moon can only make that judgement using his own set of principles, the ones that are important on the moon.'

'The rational world has taken over. It's not a question of whether it's better. It's a question of how to best get along with what is. Bobby has to live in the modern world, Matt. That's the whole point. And you don't need to lecture me about how difficult it will be.'

Father Souris sighed sadly. Marina looked at him and he sensed again that she had something to tell him. Would she tell him now? Did he want to hear it? 'The last time I saw my father,' she began, her voice quiet, 'it was the last time he took me to the Seracs. I have never forgotten that day. My mother was completely distraught. He took my hand and we walked and then sat down for a long time under the chestnut trees in the Luxembourg Gardens. It was summer. Children were playing by the pool, sailing their boats like they always did. I remember looking up at the leaves. They looked like big green hands. I was twelve. I knew what I would have to do. My father told me that I would have to forget many things and learn lots of new ones, even new ways to think. All he asked was that I never forgot what he was about to tell me. I never have, Matt.

'My father said, "Never forget that it has broken my heart and your mother's also to do this to you. You must never think we do not love you anymore. It is our love for you that makes us do this painful thing. We love you, Marina, and we want you to survive. Because we love you, we will do anything so that you will stay alive." He told me I was old enough to know what was happening in the world, how our friends and neighbours were being deported. There were terrible rumours about where they were sent. My mother and he would not escape, he said, but if they did and it was safe again he promised they would find me. In the meantime I had to forget everything I needed to forget and not try to find them. If I saw them in the street I had to walk on past. "You must be a little French girl like Thérèse so that you can live as happily as possible in this new strange Aryan world."

'I asked him, "Can't you and Maman do that too?"'

Marina hesitated a moment. 'My father said no. They were marked out as not fit for this new world. It was too late for them, he said. But not for me if I was careful. I had everything I needed, papers, new identification. I was young and could adapt. If I had to forget almost everything about them, I must not feel sad or guilty. I was to do all that was necessary to survive. That was what they wanted most, that I would be safe, even if it meant I had to forget even their broken hearts. "Don't be ashamed when the memory of us fades, and it will as the years go by. We know this is not because you do not love us and respect us. What we do now is the best thing we can do for you at this terrible time. It is necessary to do it now, before it is too late for you as well. When you are grown up you will understand better how extremely painful it is for us to do this. There are no words big enough to tell you all that we feel. But you must look ahead. Look to the future. Do whatever you think is necessary to survive. Always remember that. The important thing is to survive. You must promise me that you will do this. It's the most important thing we ever have or ever will ask you to do, Marina. Our love and your life walk hand in hand." That's what he said to me.' She paused and looked away. 'I have never forgotten what he told me, Matt.'

Father Souris was watching Marina's face while she told him this story but it told him nothing. Is that it? he wondered at the time. Is that what she had wanted to tell him but could never find the words? And now was she telling him in this roundabout way about her pain when he abandoned her in Paris? How he broke her heart? How she needed to forget everything about him just to be able to survive? And was there an indication here of what attracted her to Zack? He was someone on the outside of any world. He was completely self-sufficient. He had his own logic, his own disciplines. Nobody's world caused him pain or grief. He wouldn't hurt her.

Or maybe it was just as Grand'mère said and she was possessed. What madness possessed her? he wondered. And then she was in his arms again, stirring up echoes of a time when the world beckoned to him and tempted him with all its possibilities and he still believed there were choices, though none ever amounted to much.

Father Souris sighed with weariness. He never found any solutions, only more questions to worry about, the latest one being what Marina might have to tell him. He was so exhausted, so worn out by never knowing anything for certain. He turned his face to the wall and tried to sleep.

*

Mathieu Souris opened the shutters and quickly closed the window. They were there again, the gargoyles, nearer this time, almost touching the glass. Every time he looked they were closer, craning forward, leaning farther out from their perches in the intricate coils of carved stone, their mouths and beaks wide, grinning, hooting, screaming, all the misshapen heads clustered together, the beady eyes glaring at him through the glass, and in their midst, Marina, perched on the wall, stretching her long, thin, scaly body to peer at him, her cold, hard eyes watching him, her lips parting to say his name. Mathieu. She called his name, over and over. Mathieu. Her face, no longer beautiful, pressed closer and closer to the glass. All the stone gargoyles crowded round. He saw the catch on the window move. They were opening it. He saw Marina's thin hands working the catch, pushing the window inwards. Soon it would open wide. They would all burst in, all the demons who had waited and waited so long for this, watching and licking their lips in anticipation. And Marina, his Marina, was letting them in to seize him, to devour him. She was one of them. What a fool he had been. What an utter, utter fool. And with a scream of despair he saw the window fly open and the demons rush towards him.

*

He woke suddenly to the sound of heavy pounding on the presbytery door. Father Souris staggered out of bed and down the stairs. At the door was Louis Osweken holding some sort of pouch. 'What's the matter, Louis?'

'Grand'mère is betting the land in a crap game. She's had a lot to drink. You have to stop her before she loses it all.'

*

'What is going on here?' The priest spoke loudly from the top of the basement steps. No one answered as he descended and walked up to the table. Louis followed him and handed the bundle to Grand'mère.

Father Souris looked at the dice, the money on the table and each person's face in turn. For a stony moment his eyes rested on Marina. 'This is an abomination,' he heard himself say. 'It stops now, this minute. All of you, get out of here and don't come back.'

'Sorry, Matt,' replied Charlie. 'This is one we gotta see to the finish.'

Marina picked up the dice.

'Don't do this, Marina,' warned Father Souris.

'Go home, priest,' spat Grand'mère, laying the leather pouch on the side of the table. 'This is no place for you.'

'Do you remember Pierre Jaccard, Matt?' Marina said. 'Thérèse's Pierre, who used to come to the café? He thought life is like a game of chance where you gamble on the possibilities that turn up. Now I am about to throw the dice. Grand'mère has bet the land that I will lose. This could be the throw of a lifetime. Do you want to place a bet?'

'I said it's over.'

Marina threw the dice. They bounced hard on the church basement wall and clattered onto the youth club's pool table. They lay still, a five and a six.

'I'll be damned,' said Charlie.

Grand'mère stared at Marina. In the flickering glare of the neon tube she seemed suddenly wizened and stooped. She tore the string of animal teeth from her neck and threw them down on the table. 'This is not finished.' She spoke huskily and walked away.

'I said it was over when I came in,' said Father Souris angrily. He picked up the bundle, the necklace and the dice. 'Now, all of you, get out of here, or I call the police.'

6

The seamless minutes passed, then an hour, perfectly measured out on the atomic clock. Father Souris pressed down the lid of the black tin box. It resisted. A little rust probably, after all this time. He pressed harder but it refused to shut. 'Close, damn it!' he muttered. With trembling hands he raised the lid again and saw the edge of one of the documents had caught between it and the side of the box. Those damned papers, he thought. The trouble they'd caused, might still cause. Most of them probably weren't worth a hoot anymore. Except as evidence, maybe. Why didn't he just burn them? He'd been sorely tempted more than once. Well, the answer to that was simple enough. They weren't his to burn.

He picked up the documents again. No, he never felt they were truly his, even the ones Grand'mère had given him to keep. He was their custodian, that's all. Like a museum curator, he kept them safe, undamaged, ready for the time, which would surely come, when they'd be at the top of somebody's agenda. They remained here ready to shed light on the past, explain events and motives, show what was so important back then, important enough to kill for. Under the floorboards of his study he dutifully preserved this particular piece of history. He thought of the box and its contents as a small time capsule, a string of moments caught like the flies in Marina's amber beads. Even now most of them were little more than curiosities, yesterday's detritus to be perused and commented on in the context of a past that was already becoming difficult to visualize.

Father Souris could imagine a time in the future when curious men or women might open up the box. They would wear latex gloves to avoid damaging these relics with contaminants that did not yet exist while they fingered them with the excitement of schoolchildren inspecting an arrowhead. Look at all this, those incisive detached professional people would say, smell it, feel it, it's the real stuff behind the legend. Inhale slowly enough and you may still catch a whiff of tobacco. Grand'mère's tobacco. These are the actual dice they used. This string of teeth was worn by the medicine woman who lived around here all those years ago, and these were the schoolteacher's amber beads. The braid of sweetgrass too, still intact, and here, here are the papers that were at the bottom of it all. The grisly murder. The horrible revenge. This is one of the staking claims. See the name crossed out, hers put in. Time-expired long, long ago. Worthless now in mining terms, but as a piece of history, quite valuable. But now look at these. Here is a loyalist occupation permit, very old, look at the date. A couple of Crown land grants to war veterans too, not that unusual long ago to give an ex-soldier a few hundred acres, or even a few thousand, to farm, even as far north and unfarmable as this. And how about this one? There's no record of it in any copy book. We've checked them all. No mention of this anywhere, a full patent of all the land from here to Roseau Lake to beyond the Sugarmilk. All the surface rights, timber, fish, game, and all the mineral rights, in perpetuity. That's some grant. Originally bought for a couple of cents an acre by – can't make out the name – a gift even then, and probably traded for furs or lost at cards to one or other of those Ojibwa Indians whose amazing luck held out all down the years. That could be worth a bit nowadays, if the land claims are ever settled.

Father Souris sighed and straightened the bundle of papers. It was quite a collection. And all the land was Ojibwa land if you believed Grand'mère Osweken, who'd been the last keeper of their oral history. No conquest or charter or treaty covered it, she once told him. Look in any official record you like, she'd said, you'll never find a signature or mark or agreement by or on behalf of an Osweken Ojibwa. They were not named in any treaty-payment list, nor is there any mention of the Sugarmilk country, even by inclusion in any treaty-map land coordinates. And there was plenty of evidence to the contrary, she said, letters, records of meetings down the years.

She'd kept the papers well out of sight, adding to them now and again if an opportunity arose, never depleting their number. But people guessed she had them though they didn't know the details. So what, people scoffed, the Indians lost out years and years ago. But it stoked up hatred and rumours and worries and unsettling tales of dispossession and retribution told by the fire on winter nights while wolves or blizzards howled in the frozen wilderness just the other side of the windowpanes. And then the bundle appeared, thrown down on the youth club's pool table, a wager in a game of chance, a desperate wager to rid the Sugarmilk country of Marina's troubling presence, and the long run of Osweken luck finally ran out. There was blood on these papers, though you couldn't see it. There was blood on his hands, on all their hands. He'd gone along with the rest. Gratefully. He'd hidden the truth. He'd hidden from the truth. He was good at that.

*

'Go home, all of you,' he'd said, his heart pounding in his throat, as he picked up the dice, the necklace of teeth, the leather pouch containing the papers. 'Go home and never come back. Or do I call the police?'

Charlie challenged him. 'What's in there, Matt? Let's have a look at what's in the school bag. We want to see what the teacher's won.'

'Nobody's won or lost anything here, Charlie. The game was over before the dice were thrown. Now get out of here.'

He glared at Charlie with what he hoped looked like righteous anger, but Charlie did not move. Then Father Souris took hold of one edge of the pool table with both his hands. 'This is an abomination!' he said loudly. Fortunately the table was as light as it had been cheap. He overturned it, dropping the bundle as he did so. Papers, money, dice, animal teeth clattered to the floor. The players scrambled for the cash and Charlie reached for the leather pouch. Matt got to it before him. 'Out!' he shouted. 'This is the house of God!'

That stopped Charlie. The others slunk away and he followed them.

Marina watched them go. 'Matt?' she began.

'Go home,' he said to her.

They filed out slowly, some muttering, others looking back over their shoulders. At last he was alone in the basement. His heart pounded in his chest, in his ears, his throat was dry, his hands shook. Had he always been such a coward? he wondered. How had he gotten through the war? Dieppe. Normandy. He'd come through it all with medals. Along with a few hundred other Canadians he'd volunteered to serve in the British army after too many of their own officers were killed in action. He'd dealt with far more sinister situations than this in lawless liberated Paris. Lately he'd been reading about split personalities. He'd seen the movie too, the one about the faces of Eve. Maybe he was really two people himself, maybe even more. He smiled nervously at the thought. Father Souris found the dice and the necklace on the floor and picked them up. He found a few stray coins but nothing else. There wouldn't be any more of those big anonymous donations in the collection box now, he thought regretfully. Tant pis, it had been good while it lasted and St Augustine's could always do with more money. He righted the pool table, put the coins in the collection box and turned to go.

He went outside cautiously, half expecting Marina to be there demanding her winnings. Or Charlie, waiting in the dark to grab the papers and run away. Why was he so interested in them? Father Souris wondered in passing. But there was no one. Marina was not in the presbytery either, though he knew it was not the end of the matter. Grand'mère had said as much. Marina would be back. She believed she had a right to it all anyway, had been cheated out of it. He took the black tin box from its position in his bookcase, separating Jung from Freud, and removed the documents from the leather pouch. He'd look through them another time, he thought, when the heat surrounding them died down. He placed the papers, the necklace, the dice, on top of the assigned mining claims inside the box. He closed the lid, and hesitated. It could not go back on the shelf. Where could he hide it safely, for good?

There was a place between the floor joists, a place already made, where his wandering attention had once landed on a few screw heads caught in a passing shaft of sunlight. The housekeeper had taken the rugs outside to beat. The screws seemed too close together here, at odds with the rest of the floor, which was nailed. The sermon he was writing did not engage him, and the out-of-sequence screws in the short length of board intrigued him irresistibly. Was it merely a repair? Could it be something more interesting? He'd taken his letter opener out of the drawer, cleared the floor wax from the grooves and twisted them out of the floor. He'd lifted the cut length of board and put his hand into the space between the joists. There, among the cobwebs, he felt books. Dusty books. He pulled one out and opened it. *The Opinions of Mr. Jerome Coignard*, by Anatole France. He picked another. *Monsieur Bergeret in Paris*, by the same hand. Hadn't that writer won a Nobel Prize in literature once? And been put on the Church's Index of Forbidden Books? Father Souris looked through the hidden collection. Nostradamus' *Centuries* was there. And *Studies in the Gospels*, by Alfred Loisy. Father Souris smiled. He remembered that name well from his seminary days, Loisy the modernist who'd lost his job by upsetting the Bishop of Paris little more than half a century ago, for teaching that the writers of the gospels had been products of the times in which they lived. Mathieu Souris, the soldier-turned-ordinand, had felt inclined to agree with him, and not only because he liked the Paris connection. That was a grave error, he was told. He was severely reprimanded. He'd nearly left the seminary in disgust but after much study, prayer and penance, Mathieu Souris was once again persuaded of the inherent frailty of his own judgement. And when he was ordained he dutifully took the oath denouncing modernism. He shook his head at the unpleasant memory. That's how things were done back then.

They were all books on the Index, books that if you dared to read them meant instant excommunication from the one and only true Church, and eternal damnation. Father Souris was excited by the discovery. It seemed his predecessor in the vast empty parish of Sugarmilk Falls, that quiet, gentle and by all accounts saintly old man, Father Tyrrell, had kept a secret collection of forbidden books underneath his study floorboards. At the time Father Souris laughed out loud. The presbytery, a secret store for forbidden books! All the sermons he'd written there. All the prayers he'd said. And all the time, right under his nose, his feet anyway, with nothing but a floorboard between him and them, was this little collection of Indexed books. The devil's works. He'd put them back in their hiding place and replaced the board and the screws. He did not want to be tempted to read them. But he did not want to dispose of them either. Although they stayed out of sight, they did not fade from his consciousness. He remained keenly aware of their presence, out of reach but temptingly only a turn of a screw away. Desperate to find a distraction to relieve his torment over Marina, it was all he could do not to delve under the floor and find out at last just what terrible things Mr Bergeret had done in Paris that the account of them should be forbidden by the Church.

Now he blew off the dust and distributed the volumes, except the Nostradamus, throughout his bookcase, pushing Jung and Freud together, and filling up the rest of the shelf with Indexed books. Their forbiddenness had been officially eased during the last couple of years and he was somewhat disappointed to see how innocuous they looked out in the open. In the void between the joists, alongside *Centuries*, he put the black tin box. He replaced the board, tightened the screws and covered up the place with the rug. The empty leather pouch lay on his desk. He folded the *Sugarmilk Gazette* to size, put it inside the pouch and hid it at the bottom of the bottom drawer, under the heap of old sermons. He placed his hands together and looked around the room. Everything seemed in order. Everything felt safe.

*

Marina did return to the presbytery. 'There are things you ought to know, Matt.'

Is this the moment? he wondered. What is she going to tell me at last? Did he want to hear?

'About those mining claims, the ones Grand'mère gave you.'

Did he feel relieved or disappointed? 'What about them?'

'There is a name crossed out on them.'

'Yes?'

'The name is Benjamin Rabinowicz. He was my uncle. He put most of his money on a mining venture. When it came to nothing he took it very hard. He died and left everything, what was left of it, to me. I own the exploration rights now.

'Zack found some things on a hunting trip once. It turns out they belonged to the geologist who was working for my uncle. I knew him. His name was Tom Gordon. Among the things was a record of what happened to the expedition. The plane crashed into a lake. He managed to get out but must have died from his injuries.'

'Did Zack inform the police?'

'He says he did, but I don't know how much he told Frank.' Marina continued, 'If the plane hadn't crashed Grand'mère never would have gotten away with keeping those claims, Matt. Now they belong to me and I want them.'

'They expired long ago. And they're Grand'mère's. They were assigned to her. She gave some of them to me to look after.'

'You know the story as well as anyone. She won them at cards,' said Marina. 'She would never have gotten away with it if Tom Gordon's plane hadn't crashed. I want them now.'

Father Souris did not reply at first. 'I don't know about that. They say the guy who assigned them to Grand'mère was a lawyer.'

Marina hesitated and her expression was cold. 'Okay,' she said, 'if you're going to take that line I'll make it clear. I want everything, the claim assignments and what I won the other night. Everybody knows there's a lot more in

Grand'mère's bundle than just the rest of those staking claims. And all those papers are now mine.'

'You didn't win anything. I stopped the game before your last throw.'

'You know you didn't, Matt. I won fair and square. Give me the papers.'

'Yes, I did stop it. I can stop an illegal crap game going on without my knowledge in the basement of my church. I can confiscate the bets.' Confiscate the bets. He liked the sound of that.

'Without your knowledge!' Marina sneered and went into his study. He followed her. 'Where are they, Matt?' She was looking at the bookcase and turned back to him, 'Where is the box you kept the claims in?'

'Gone.'

'And all the papers?'

'I told you. Confiscated. They've all gone.'

'Don't lie to me, Matt. There hasn't been time for you to do anything with them. What would you do with them anyway? They're here somewhere.'

He shook his head. 'Sorry, Marina, but that's the way it is. They're no longer here. I think you should leave now.'

She put her hands in her coat pockets. 'Not until I have those papers, Matt.'

He sighed, sat down in the chair by the window and closed his eyes. 'This is absurd. Go home, Marina.'

When he looked at her again, she was holding a revolver, pointing it at him. 'I didn't want to do this,' she said icily, 'but I will use it if you don't give them to me.'

It had been a long time since he had looked down the barrel of a gun, and though he felt a chill on the back of his neck and down his spine, he remained calm and even unsurprised that Marina should be pointing one at him. He sighed wearily and held out his hand. 'Put down the gun. Give it to me.'

'The papers, Matt.'

'I've already told you, they're not here anymore.'

'I can see that! But you know where they are. They're mine! Now get them!' Her finger tightened on the trigger. 'I will use this. You know I can.'

'What would be the use? They're gone.' He remained seated, looking at her, looking at the woman who had twice now been at the centre of his universe. For half his lifetime he had loved her, to the point of obsession, been willing to betray himself, his God, everything he valued in this world and the next, for her. And yet what did he know about her, about what really drove her? But even now, even when she seemed to him more like a stranger, so distant, so very, very cold, standing only a few feet away pointing the revolver at him, he could easily persuade himself it was not his Marina who was doing this. His Marina was someone else. As always he'd do everything he could to help her out of her distress. His Marina only needed to put down the gun, ask his indulgence, give him the smallest bit of encouragement and he would be helpless to resist her once more.

She said, 'You know I only ever loved you, Matt. All my life there has never been anyone else. You are my life. You and I . . . How can you make me do this now?'

It was as though she was reading his mind. And again he had the feeling that she had something important to tell him. He felt his resolve begin to waver. 'Put down the gun. Please.'

Her hand was trembling. 'Give them to me!' she screamed.

He stood up quickly and pushed her hand away. An explosion echoed in the presbytery silence. He struggled briefly, viciously to take the pistol from her and it fired again.

*

With shaking hands Father Souris placed the bundle of papers inside the tin box and tried again to close the lid. It fitted easily. No, this wasn't the right time to tell Frank Martello he still had everything here. He should never have told him about them in the first place. It was the home-made wine and the friendly warmth of Frank's basement that had loosened up his tongue, and maybe his need to tell the awful truth to someone made him almost forget his friend was a policeman. Almost, but not quite. He hadn't gone so far as to tell him everything that happened. Now he put the black box back into the space between the joists, bleakly amused to see the volume of Nostradamus' prophecies still there too. He replaced the length of floorboard, tightened up the screws, and covered the place with the rug. Everything was as before. He looked at his watch, at the atomic clock. He picked up the telephone and dialled Sergeant Martello's number.

7

Why would his friend be lying? wondered Sergeant Martello as he put down the telephone. Of course Matt still had those documents. Why say he didn't? And he'd know exactly where to find them. The policeman drank another mouthful of wine from the side of the glass jug and rolled it around his teeth before swallowing. It was easier to lie on the phone. If they'd had the conversation face to face it would have been different. But would Matt have been truthful even then?

When exactly did Father Souris begin to lie? he asked himself. It was a long time ago, probably soon after that pretty schoolteacher arrived in Sugarmilk Falls, that he first detected a blatant bit of dishonesty. What it was about he couldn't now recall, but he'd been surprised, even a little shocked. Matt's honesty was something he'd taken for granted, relied on. Thinking about it at the time he realized that his friend had become increasingly evasive. He'd heard the gossip about her too. You can't be a policeman and not pick up on that. In the end he asked the priest outright, 'Have you and that schoolteacher got something going, Matt?' Father Souris appeared genuinely put out by the question. 'Of course not, Frank. Why do you ask me that?' He'd used those words, he could still hear them in his head: of course not, Frank. A categorical denial and to tell the truth the rumours had mainly concerned that woman and Zack Guillem. There were indications though that Father Souris was more than ordinarily affected by them. Apparently he'd been heard taking the schoolteacher to task in her own classroom after lessons were over and she'd told him in no uncertain terms to mind his own business. And there was that incident, around Halloween he thought, when her house was vandalized with paint. Why had she called Matt over? It was criminal damage, pure and simple. Police business. True, she was distressed. Understandable, in her case especially. But why think of the priest straight away? Why not Zack? It was Matt who eventually persuaded her to report the matter.

Sergeant Martello took another sip. He'd never gotten to the bottom of that one although he had a suspicion that spiteful Grand'mère was behind it, no doubt annoyed over something to do with Bobby. He shook his head. Kids. The trouble they caused. And there were some real sickos around too. Even in a backwoods hole-in-the-ground like Sugarmilk Falls, they can go unnoticed, get away with it for years, maybe even for good. Fortunately his own files were all nice and tidy; he'd always made sure of that. Nothing much was still unsolved. There were no cracks as far as he could see where even the most determined probing could break open the big embarrassing void.

It was Elviana who first alerted him. 'I think Father Souris is in love with the new schoolteacher,' she said to him one morning at breakfast.

He'd nearly choked on his coffee. 'You're crazy. He's the priest.'

'Oh, I'm not saying he's doing anything about it. But the feelings are there all right. It must be very difficult for him, poor man.'

'How do you know all this?'

'You just need to look at him when he's with her. You can tell.'

That was all she was able to explain. Frank watched Father Souris. He watched Miss Grochowska. He watched his friend and the schoolteacher together. He saw nothing concrete, detected nothing in the air. But he did not dismiss Elviana's observation. Women were sensitive to this kind of thing. He'd wait and see, not that it mattered to him one way or the other, he told himself. But afterwards he began to notice Matt's evasions and increasingly it bothered him. He felt let down, he supposed, nothing more. It wasn't easy being the only police officer around for hundreds of miles. People were friendly but they always kept a little distance between them, because he was the police. It was the same for the priest, he knew. Both dealt in law and order of one sort or another. Rules. Father Souris told you how to stay out of hell in the next life, and Senior Constable Martello told you how to stay out of jail in this one. They were custodians of the peace, in the soul and on the street. So when he realized Matt was not being honest with him any more, he was disappointed. No, it was more than disappointment. He felt taken for a fool. And he suddenly felt very lonely.

'We always used to talk about everything. No holds barred, that's what I thought,' he complained to his wife.

'Why doesn't he talk to me about whatever his problem is?'

'It's hard for him to do,' replied Elviana. 'This has hit him right out of the blue. It's not something he ever dreamed would happen and he doesn't know how to handle it. It'll pass. He'll get over it. You'll see. God will help him.'

But it didn't pass, and even now Matt was still lying to him. Tonight he seemed more worried than he'd been in a long time. What could Lucien Armand and the others say that hadn't been said already? What was it about that nosy parker who'd been hanging around for weeks that seemed so dangerous to Matt? Did his friend know something the others didn't? Did this snooper know something nobody else did? Not even himself? He was the policeman round here and it was his business to be informed. The last thing he wanted now was to have his neatly closed files opened up again, his tidy bows untied. Not before he left for Florida, anyway, and the new constable was installed to deal with any new fallout. But, he thought, there was little likelihood of that. Everything had been taken care of.

He remembered it like yesterday, and it still made him shudder to think of it. It was very nasty, very bizarre. Father Souris telephoned to say what he'd found along the old portage trail, in a clearing beside the river above the falls. Damn those party lines. Matt should have had a lot more sense than to use the phone for something like that. By the time Senior Constable Martello arrived at the scene, quite a little crowd had already gathered. He remembered seeing Charlie Anstalt, and Ricky Shaw with a couple of other boys including Arnie Jr. He'd gotten rid of the youngsters damn quick. Angela Norton was there too, of course. She told him she'd sent for a doctor before leaving the station but she needn't have bothered. And Tim and Jenny Buszek who ran the *Gazette*, him with his big press camera flashing and her busy scribbling in her notebook. Everyone was ogling, gaping, muttering quietly to one another. And no doubt disturbing what evidence there might still be. He'd put on his sombre policeman-on-duty air and pushed his way through, moving the people away from what they were all so intently looking at as he went. And then it was right there in front of him, on the ground. He caught his breath. His stomach lurched. He could feel everyone's eyes boring into his back.

Senior Constable Martello turned around. 'Go home,' he shouted, 'go back to your homes. This is a police investigation now.'

It was as bad as anything he'd ever come across. A body, contorted and charred. Another suicide maybe? Some desperate Indian who'd poured gas all over himself before lighting a match? It happened. Or maybe deliberately set alight and burned to death? Dead it most certainly was. He looked around but saw no sign of a gasoline can. An accident? Seemed unlikely. And if it was murder, cold-blooded and calculated, did it happen here or was the already dead corpse brought here and burned? Either way it must have been a hell of a fire to get the body into this state. Didn't anyone see the smoke? He began to look at it more closely, crouching down to study it from different angles. It was grisly, nauseating. Questions and rusty procedures raced around in his head. He looked up. Jenny Buszek was still standing there, her ballpoint poised to write. 'Clear off, Jenny,' he said, 'I'll talk to you later on, after I've had a chance to get a good look and maybe got something worthwhile to tell you.'

She nodded. 'Have you seen that, Frank?' she asked him, pointing at the corpse with her pen.

He followed the line of her hand and swallowed. 'Of course I have. Talk to you later.'

'Got anything to say about it?'

'Not at the moment. Later, I said. Now get out of here.'

She moved back a few steps and stopped again. Senior Constable Martello looked at Angela Norton. Neither spoke. What Jenny had pointed to was the gaping hole in the centre of the corpse's chest about where the heart would be, a hole crudely hacked, its outline hardened, exaggerated by the effects of the fire. It seemed to be almost in the shape of a cross.

'Would you say this looks like some kind of ceremonial killing, Frank?' Jenny spoke loudly enough for the retreating onlookers to hear. A few of them stopped and looked back towards the policeman.

He stood up and faced her angrily. 'No, I wouldn't say that at all at this point. Have you got a hearing problem, Jenny? Get the hell out of here. Now.'

'You'll have to talk to me before the deadline, Frank. You know I've got a duty to report on something as big as this.'

He glared at her, biting his tongue, and waited for her to leave. 'You might as well go too, Angela,' he said to the nurse with a sigh.

The policeman was alone with the body. It lay on its back, turned slightly over onto its right side. The corpse wasn't large. It could be a youngster, or more probably a woman. Judging by the size and shape of the skull it was a woman. The facial features had gone. What remained were the empty eye sockets and two rows of scorched yellow teeth in a horrible grimace. The hair was gone too, just the bare bony dome remained, still pale, shattered by a blow maybe, or burst by the heat. The arms were bent rigid as if to shield the face, the hands clenched almost into fists. Caused by the fire contracting the muscles, or was it from the pain of the fire? he wondered. Had the person still been alive when she was put on the fire and burned to death, like some medieval witch? He already thought of the remains as female. Most of the fingers were there. And the toes on the left foot. No apparent indication that the body had been tied up, but rope and clothing could have burned away almost as quickly as the hair. Here and there the flesh was completely gone, consumed in its own ignited layers of fat, leaving the charred skeleton visible. The fire would have needed to be very hot and kept going for quite a time for it to do that, mused Senior Constable Martello, especially out in the open. On the abdomen and left thigh the flesh had burned away and split to reveal the yellow curdled fatty tissue underneath. The blackened end of a large thigh bone protruded from what remained of the right knee. Between the hacked open ribs on the right side and through the abdomen, a little blood still oozed.

He walked around the body again, bending down to look at it closely, carefully studying the orientation, trying to find something that might help him in this most unusual and grotesque situation, something that might point him in a direction, any direction at all. He studied the hole in its chest. Did it look like a cross? Or was there something else, almost obliterated by the fire? The remains of the incision on what had been the left breast, suggested not a cross but a swastika. Probably just the effects of the fire or his imagination. He looked at the arms again. In the sharp angle by the elbow where the inside of the forearm almost touched the upper arm a little flesh remained, nearly intact. Were there some marks on the scorched skin? He couldn't be sure. What he knew he had on his hands was an incinerated body with a hole gashed into its chest, all its clothing, all immediate means of identification burned to ashes. Judging by the amount of ash and charcoal and the gaping hole, suicide was out of the question. More like the person had been put on a pile of wood and set alight. It must've been one hell of a fire too. A regular inferno. It certainly looked to him like a very brutal murder, well beyond his own resources to deal with. He'd need to call in assistance for this one.

Who would want to do such a thing to a woman? Of course there was somebody out there who knew who it was, who'd done this terrible thing. Maybe even one of the sightseers he'd had to get rid of. He sniffed the air. Not much there either other than wet ash on a damp fall afternoon full of the smell of rotting leaves. Hardly anything lingered on the light breeze to suggest burned flesh. The corpse was stone cold too, what had been skin and muscle seemed brittle, a little moist. Possibly it had been lying here for days. With wood smoke and leaf-burning tainting the air at this time of year another fire could easily go unnoticed. Besides, nobody much came up this way these days, except Father Souris. And Zack Guillem. And occasionally that schoolteacher Miss Grochowska who'd also had a bit of trouble a while back with swastikas.

*

Sergeant Martello drained the last of the wine from the jug. He sighed deeply. That was a nasty business, all right. And the consequences had been worse, if that was possible. That file, however, was closed too, had been for years, although it never was as completely cut and dried as the record of the investigation made out. Afterwards he'd gone over it several times to make sure he'd covered everything, to see if he could put his finger on where problems for the future might lie. But he always found copper-bottomed answers to any of the likely or unlikely questions he dreamed up. It held together, so long as everybody remembered what the story was back then, or some completely new piece of evidence turned up. Even if it did he'd be in the clear, anyway. It didn't exactly keep him awake at night, but over the years he'd felt a tremor of unease now and then. No one talked about it much but he knew he was not the only one to feel this way. It was as though something subterranean was restless in its sleep, something everybody hoped would never wake up and rise to the surface.

Is that what Matt thinks might be happening tonight over at the Armand place? he wondered. A new story, or maybe the whole story is coming out? If that's it, why would his friend be so deeply worried. Unless he knew more than he ever let on.

8

So you see, my friend, they were not wrong to say it all began when the maple woods were lost in a crap game. I'm just an old sugar-maker but I know that nowhere in the records is there any mention of what happened to the deeds, or where they could be now. Nobody thought about what it was made Grand'mère risk the land in a game of chance. A lot more than too much moonshine, that's for sure. Nobody thought about what it could mean for the Oswekens if she lost.

Mon Dieu, it was a terrible business. You've seen the photographs, you say. You'll have a good idea just how bad it was. Frank Martello and that detective from Wawa asked us all lots of questions. Everyone. Where we were, what we might have seen or heard or knew. Long before the time they concluded it was indeed Miss Grochowska who'd been killed, the talk was underway: 'the schoolteacher murdered . . . burned . . . her heart cut out . . . some sort of execution . . . sacrifice . . . some evil son of a bitch gone loco . . . get him quick before it happens again . . .' And so it went on.

There'd been an incident a few months back, in the

dead heart of winter, Grand'mère Osweken, on a drinking binge, shooting her rifle off in all directions on Main Street. 'You'll regret it! You'll pay!' she shouted. 'The windigo will kill you all! All of you!' Constable Martello arrested her before she shot anyone. 'Go after the windigo, Frank!' she screamed at him. 'It's here! It'll get you too!'

'What are you talking about? Where?' he asked, trying to calm her down.

'That schoolteacher. She's possessed. She'll eat us all.'

'Miss Grochowska? You're drunk, Grand'mère.'

In her delirium she cowered all night in the corner of the cell. The following day the magistrate released her. So the story went round.

*

Father Souris heard about it listening in on the party line. 'That crazy old woman's got herself arrested . . . Drunk again . . . Disgusting . . . Told Frank Martello the school-teacher is a windigo . . . Ha! Ha! Ha! . . . Could be she's right . . . Miss stuck-up Grochowska, an ice monster . . . Ha! Ha! . . . Maybe she's gonna eat all the kids in her class . . . Maybe she's already eaten young Bobby Osweken they say's been sent away . . . Ha! Ha! Ha! . . . Maybe the windigo's gonna eat us all . . .'

He was alarmed. 'Has Grand'mère been to see you?' he asked Marina. 'Has she threatened you?'

She sighed. 'She was upset about Bobby, that's all.'

'What happened? What did she say?'

'It was a few nights ago. There was a knock on the door and she walked straight in, quite a bit the worse for drink. She said she knew what I really was. She was going to use all her magic against me to send me back to the spirit world.'

'Is that it?'

'She had a rifle with her. In case I attacked her then and there, I suppose.'

'It's not funny, Marina. Was this the only time?'

'No. She came to see me about the time Bobby was placed. She was sober then and told me not to do it or I'd be really sorry. I explained the situation to her, told her what Bobby had done, how sending him away was for the best, but she wouldn't be reasonable. Matt, she actually spat at me. And she said I was possessed.'

'Did she do anything?'

'Just talked. She said I must have done something wicked and offended powerful spirits. It was making me very sick. Unless I was healed I would become an ice monster, a windigo. She offered to help me, to cure me. She was a strong healer, she said, but I needed to confess to her how I'd offended the spirits.'

'Did she say how you might have done that?'

'Not really. It was a bit strange, though. She stared at me with those bright black eyes of hers. "It concerns Matt Souris," she said.'

'What did she mean?'

Marina shrugged her shoulders and shook her head. 'How do I know what goes on inside her primitive brain. She doesn't function like the rest of us. Has she tried to heal you too?'

He ignored the question. 'Did she take anything?'

'Take anything? I don't think so. I don't know. What difference does it make.'

'She can use it against you. She's a sorcerer, Marina. A necromancer. She can make you do things.'

'Matt! You believe in all that stuff! How has that ridiculous old woman mesmerized you like this?'

'No, of course I don't believe it. It's more subtle than that. You must have heard stories about what Indian medicine men can do? There's quite a lot of evidence, from white witnesses too, of the effect they can have. Don't underestimate her.'

'Don't be so absurd.'

'She's a shaman. You've angered her by sending Bobby away. There will be some kind of retaliation, believe me. She'll get her revenge.'

'Oh, I don't think so Matt. After all, if I'm supposed to be possessed by some kind of ice monster, don't I stand a pretty good chance of winning here?' Marina laughed and added, 'She makes my skin crawl.'

But Father Souris felt that something was different. Marina seemed to recede from him while he became more helplessly obsessed. Was it really happening, he wondered, or was this Grand'mère's magic at work? Which was worse? 'Are you sure she didn't take anything that was yours, Marina?' he asked her more than once.

His questions annoyed her. 'What is the matter with you, Matt? Where is your common sense? She has really got inside your head, hasn't she.' A statement, not a question.

*

'It's true!' the party lines screamed. 'The body. It's the schoolteacher! Miss Grochowska! Some sort of ritual murder, a big hole cut into her chest, the body burned! Isn't that what the savages used to do? Isn't that the way they went about getting rid of a windigo? They burn the body to melt the ice in its heart. Whoever did this, they're nothing but savages.

'Our schoolteacher too. A bit stuck-up but that's not surprising. She was a very smart woman and a brilliant teacher. So dedicated too. We were really lucky to get her to come to an out-of-the-way place like this. We trusted her with our little children's education. Now she's been murdered. Horrible. By those savages. We can't let them get away with it. Which one did it? Grand'mère? It looks like the old witch doctor's doing. But no way she could have done it by herself. It must have been all of them. They were all in on it. They're all savages. All murderers.'

9

During the run-up to voting day Arnie Anstalt took to making speeches, which was something new for him to do, for although he'd long been a lay preacher he never spoke in public about things he felt were not his territory. To Arnie's way of thinking Ed Perriault did the speaking on political matters in Sugarmilk Falls. But as the summer passed he became more and more concerned about the effect the No campaign seemed to be having. He sensed it was shutting a lot of people out, and he decided to have a talk with Reverend Byers about its general direction. 'Roy, I'll come right to the point,' he said to him one Sunday morning after church. 'The No campaign isn't going down so well with the undecided voters. We need to give them more to think about.' More than threats, he wanted to add but didn't.

The minister was nonplussed. 'I'm doing my best, Arnie,' he said defensively.

'I know you are, but what about the people who aren't churchgoers or too interested in why things have always been the way they have here. What good reasons can we give them for voting No?'

'I see what you mean.' Reverend Byers thought for a moment then shook his head. 'I think you'd better take that one on. They're more likely to listen to you than me.'

Arnie thought it only proper to run the idea past Ed Perriault. 'Ed, I want to do some speaking for the No campaign,' he said to him. 'See if maybe we can get some kind of public discussion going.'

Ed laughed. 'Nothing to stop you, Arnie. Could even be a real good move. The Yes people might have a problem coming up with a speaker of their own, though. There's Birgit, of course, but she's trying to stay in the background a bit. Who are you planning to talk to?'

'Not sure yet. Any suggestions?'

Ed thought for a moment, then grinned broadly. 'Can't go far wrong for openers with the WI. Real nice ladies. Fill you full of real nice homemade cake and stuff too. And they're pretty influential people, if I'm not mistaken.' Ed chuckled as the idea took hold. 'Yes, they're ladies with a lot of influence when it comes to voting matters, Arnie. "The hand that rocks the cradle rules the world." Don't ever forget that.' He paused and grinned some more, then he added with a loud laugh, 'You persuade the WI to vote No, the Yes campaign won't stand a chance in hell.'

Arnie composed a speech along the lines that just because the dry status quo didn't always succeed as well as it ought at keeping Sugarmilk Falls temperate, that was no reason for abandoning it. Yes, there was too much moonshining and bootlegging going on. Yes, there were sometimes drunks on the street, and the public nuisance caused by their disorderly behaviour was the inevitable and regrettable result. But these problems were due not so much to the status quo itself, as to the poor enforcement of the status quo. If the liquor ban was being properly enforced, the moonshiners, the bootleggers, the drunks, the nuisance wouldn't be there. Senior Constable Martello needed to take a much firmer hand. Maybe these problems even showed there was a need for another police officer to assist him, but that was a question for another day.

No. The lack of enforcement of the dry status quo was not a good reason to vote Yes. In fact the exact opposite was true. Voting Yes would mean the opportunity to enforce the dry status would be lost for good. Voting Yes would mean that drink and all its associated problems would be with them for good.

Arnie tried his speech out loud one evening after supper. When he got to the end Arnie Jr. sniggered but apart from that there was complete silence in the kitchen. 'What do you think of it?' he asked Irene.

She hadn't interrupted him once during the delivery, and even when he'd finished she still could think of nothing to say.

'Well?' he insisted.

'I don't know, Arnie. Maybe people don't want to think about problems. Maybe they want to think about having fun.'

'I can't make speeches about having fun, Irene. This is a real serious thing, this vote. It could change everything about the place we live in and work in and call our home.'

*

The members of the Sugarmilk Falls Women's Institute began fussing over Arnie as soon as he arrived at the old schoolhouse. They listened attentively to his speech and applauded it politely. Sophie Tronquet raised her hand and asked whether it was likely that Sugarmilk Falls would get an extra policeman in the near future. Arnie had to admit he didn't really know a great deal about that. When there were no more questions Sylvie Perriault gave a generous vote of thanks and the ladies pressed cups of tea and maple-sugar cake and gingerbread on him until he felt as though he wouldn't need to eat again for a week. Then Sylvie asked him to judge the floral displays.

Arnie wasn't prepared for anything like this to happen. Why didn't Irene warn me beforehand? he wondered. She must have known. He didn't like the idea at all but couldn't see a way out of it. Slowly he realized Elaine Shaw was busy talking to him, explaining how the arrangements were all based around the same theme, and the theme was 'Spring is the mischief in me'. Arnie swallowed.

'We think it's from a Robert Frost poem,' she told him.

He didn't read much, mostly workshop manuals and motor-trade magazines. Certainly not poetry, though Irene said the Bible was poetic in places. Elaine continued, 'We all loved it when Sylvie first suggested it but we couldn't do it till now because there aren't hardly any flowers hereabouts in the spring.'

'We have daffodils in our yard,' he said, baring his yellow teeth in a smile.

Arnie hovered over the flower arrangements lined up on a table pushed against the rough mellow wooden wall of the old school room, and the air around him was dense with their fresh fragrance. He gazed at all the vibrant summer blooms, red and purple petunias, pink carnations, blue delphiniums, yellow marigolds, and quite a few things he didn't recognize. He turned around to see the members of the Women's Institute watching him expectantly, ladies with grey and brown curls, wearing earrings and red lipstick and flowery summer dresses, ladies with bare brown legs and brown sandalled feet. There they stood, patiently waiting for Arnold Anstalt of Anstalt Motors, who was here to talk to them on behalf of the Vote No Committee, to make up his mind, for Arnie Anstalt, who knew hardly anything about flowers and even less about poetry, to evaluate their efforts, to pass judgement, to have the final say and award the prize to one or other of these flowery takes on a line by some poet he'd never heard of. 'Spring is the mischief in me'. What was that supposed to mean? 'The hand that rocks the cradle rules the world' he could understand, but 'spring is the mischief in me'? And here he was now, being closely observed by the women he'd known most of his life and he felt nearly as uncomfortable as he ever had. Was there mischief in these gals? he wondered, looking at each of them in turn, at Sylvie and Elaine and Sophie and Claudine and Irene. In springtime or any other time, like now? What was this mischief anyway? Just playfulness, like a child's? Or something more sinister, like making trouble or doing harm? The members of the WI looked back at him, smiling demurely or talking to each other about their children or their baking. They were not at all easy to reconcile with the spiteful gossips on the party lines.

Arnie felt at a complete loss. Then he saw Irene's look of encouragement. He blinked and turned again to the flowers, surveying them from left to right and back again.

Something now caught his attention. With a rush of relief he knew. The arrangement was not immediately eye-catching, but he thought it had a look of spring and of mischief about it. Yellow daisy-like things and bits of greenery and coiled bits of metal. Springs. Arnie felt himself relax and he pointed to it. The women applauded and Claudine gushed with pleasure as he congratulated her and gave her a box of candy. She beamed. She didn't really deserve to get the prize, she said with a little apologetic smile. Suzanne had told her not to be too arty-farty. And Lucien had put in the springs.

It had been a difficult evening, more difficult than he expected. He sincerely hoped the Sugarmilk Falls branch of the Canadian Legion would be an easier audience. He hoped his speech had made enough of an impression on the ladies of the WI to increase the number of No's on voting day. He hoped he'd been right not to award the prize to Irene's wild free bouquet of blue chicory flowers and goldenrod they'd picked together in the rough open ground behind the second-hand car lot, even though it was the one he'd liked most.

*

On the morning of voting day it rained, sharp slanting fall rain that tugged the tinted leaves down from the branches and matted them into a wet mosaic on the ground. Streams of water poured from the roof corners onto the sidewalk and ran in rivers down Main Street. It soaked into the summer-dry wooden houses. It seeped into hats, coats and shoes, and ached in the bones.

At the Falls Hotel, Hugo Janssen peered out through the rain-streaked window of the dining room and groaned.

'How are we gonna get a big enough Yes vote if nobody bothers to turn out?'

Birgit too was concerned. 'They've got all day,' she said encouragingly. 'You never know, it might clear up. Besides, this could be a good omen.'

Hugo thought for a moment. 'A wet vote on a wet day, you mean?'

Birgit nodded, smiling at him affectionately. Hugo might be a little slow, but he was always behind her somewhere, caught up in the slipstream of her wavelength.

'I hope you're right,' he said, 'I'd take it kinda hard if we lost this now. I've sort of got used to the idea.'

She put her arm through his. 'Me too, Hugo. We'll know one way or the other later on today.'

10

Sergeant Martello emptied the jug of wine in two large mouthfuls. He tapped his fingers on the bureau and listened to the snowflakes tapping on the window. It had been a strange and dreadful affair, he remembered, as easy to solve as it was difficult to rationalize. In fact it had almost solved itself. Everything tied up, but it never felt right. Even taking into account what'd needed to be done to keep the awful reality out of the picture. Maybe that was something that still had to be dealt with. At the time he just wanted to wrap the whole gruesome thing up as quickly as he could.

The body wasn't easy to identify other than it was a female; about twenty-five to thirty-five was his first impression, but it could have been much older. It was hard to tell. Nothing else, except in the pile of ashes a couple of pieces of thick cloth, like the stuff used to make coats out of, cut and folded over tightly as though it had been part of something else. Something used to wrap the body in maybe, to take it to the place where it was burned? A braided rag rug, perhaps? It was the only clue, not much to go on and it never led to anything.

Almost everybody had at least one braided rug around the house.

It had seemed so eerily straightforward at the time, deciding who was the last one to see the corpse alive, the first to see her dead. That detective who flew in from Wawa to give him a hand with the investigation, Neil Reilly, whose wife was due to have a baby anytime, what he wanted most too was to clear this up just as fast as possible and go home. Together they sifted through the lumber camp and interviewed just about the whole population of Sugarmilk Falls, which didn't really amount to a lot of people. The policemen asked them all the obvious questions: where they'd been between this date and that date. Whether they'd heard or seen anything suspicious. Anything unusual. Anything at all. What about the rumours going round? Did anyone in particular have a grudge? Against whom? About what? When was the last time they'd seen Miss Grochowska? Zack Guillem? Grand'mère Osweken? Louis? Ovide? A few they talked to more than once. Charlie Anstalt, about the crap game. Zack Guillem, about his relationship with the deceased, with the Oswekens. And Matt Souris, who'd found the body.

*

'Sorry to trouble you, Matt,' said Senior Constable Martello, 'we just want to go over a few things with you again. Maybe you've remembered something since the last time we talked with you.'

'That's all right, Frank. Anything to help.' Father Souris led them into his study.

'Tell us again about the last time you saw Marina Grochowska.'

'It was on the night I threw the crap game out of the church basement. She was there. She left with the others.'

'You didn't know she'd be there?'

'No. I didn't know about the game.'

'How did you find out about it?'

'I was asleep, like I told you. Louis Osweken woke me up. He said Grand'mère was about to bet everything she owned in a crap game going on in the church basement. He wanted me to stop it pretty quick.'

'That was the first time you knew anything about it?'

'Yes.'

'We talked to some people who were at the game and they all say Miss Grochowska turned up real late. Any idea where she'd been before she went over to the church?'

Father Souris hesitated. 'I'm not sure. She was here earlier that evening.'

'Oh? Any reason in particular?'

'She wanted to discuss a personal matter.'

'What was it about?'

'It was something private.'

'We're investigating a murder, Matt. You're the one who found the body. You say you talked with her the night of the game and she hasn't been seen since.'

'I just can't believe she was murdered, Frank.'

'It sure looks like it could be her. What did she want?'

'She came to talk. She wanted some advice.' He paused, reluctant to say more. The policemen waited, looking sternly at him. 'She said she was thinking about getting married.'

'Why would she want your advice about that, do you think?' asked Detective Sergeant Reilly.

Father Souris looked at him squarely. 'Maybe because I'm the priest?'

'But she wasn't Catholic, was she?'

'Does that matter?'

'Did she often ask you for advice?'

'Now and then, yes.'

'Why you? She was an educated woman. Old enough, too. I'd say she was probably the sort who knew her own mind. Why would she need advice from you? About getting married?'

'She said she valued my opinion. We talked for a while and then she left. I don't know where she went after that.'

'Who was she going to get married to?'

Father Souris hesitated momentarily. 'Zack Guillem.'

'No wonder she needed advice,' muttered Senior Constable Martello. 'And you saw him down there in the basement too, you said.'

'Yes.'

Frank Martello continued the questioning. 'So what happened when Louis woke you up and you went into the church basement?'

'I found a crap game going on. I stopped it right away. I told them all to leave. They went, including Marina.'

'What about the money?'

'They took it with them.'

'And what about the land papers. They took those too?'

'What papers? I don't recall there being any papers.'

'That's not what we're being told, Matt. We keep being told there was a bag or something containing lots of land documents and you kept them.'

Father Souris hesitated again, looking puzzled. Then he reached into the drawer of his desk and pulled out a leather pouch. 'I guess you mean this. Louis brought it with him that night. Look inside.'

Neil Reilly opened it and took out the folded copy of the *Sugarmilk Gazette*.

'The Oswekens aren't stupid,' said Father Souris.

'They don't usually cheat either, from what I know,' said the senior constable. 'Somehow everybody seems to think Grand'mère lost the land in the crap game, Matt. Why do you suppose that is?'

'It's pretty obvious, isn't it? None of them have seen inside the bag.'

'Charlie Anstalt, even Zack believe Grand'mère lost the land. They were there.'

'I suppose they reckon she lost the bet.'

'But you're saying you stopped the game before Miss Grochowska threw the dice?'

'Yes. I most certainly did stop it. She threw them anyway. As far as I'm concerned nobody lost or won anything.'

'Where are the papers now?'

Father Souris shrugged. 'I guess Grand'mère must still have them. If there ever were any. Nobody has ever seen them, as far as I know.'

'And that was the last time you saw Miss Grochowska alive, Matt? When she left the church basement?'

'Yes, Frank. It was.'

'Now, tell us again about finding the body. What were you doing up there by the river?'

'You know I go up that way now and then. To think things over, to pray.'

'And that's what you were doing when you found her?'

'Yes. It was a nice fall morning. I was walking along and there it was. It was just awful, terrible. All I could think of was to pray. I prayed and then went back to call you. You know the rest.'

Detective Reilly asked, 'We've been told a gun was fired in this direction a couple of days before you found the body. Did you hear anything like a gun being fired round here?'

Father Souris thought for a moment. 'Could have been, I suppose. It's the time of year for it. But no, I don't recall anything.'

Senior Constable Martello looked at Matt. The priest seemed genuine, composed, greatly moved by the tragedy, as everyone was. 'Why didn't you come straight to me?' he asked him. 'Why go home first and then use the phone?'

'I . . .' Father Souris stumbled. 'I don't know, Frank. I guess I should have. I was pretty shocked by what I found up there.'

The policemen looked around the study, into the corners, at the walls, along the floor but they saw nothing unusual. It was clean, sparsely furnished, just a bookcase, a desk, a couple of chairs and a braided rug. 'Have you read all these, Matt?' asked Frank Martello, peering at the books, his hand poised to pull out a volume.

'Most of them.' The priest was watching him intently. 'How did she die?' he quickly added.

The senior constable turned back to him. 'We're not sure yet.'

'They're saying her heart was cut out.'

'There was a hole in her chest. You saw it. Maybe she was hacked to death.'

'Who'd want to do that to her?'

'The last person to see her alive.'

Father Souris's face was white.

The policemen thanked him and left the presbytery. 'Well, it certainly wasn't the priest,' said Neil Reilly. 'That's one name we can safely take off the list.'

'He could be right about those land papers too,' suggested Frank Martello. 'Maybe there never were any. Maybe those stories are just something the old witch conjured up. The only ones anyone ever laid eyes on were those mining claims Charlie Anstalt saw her win off some lawyer fellow way back before the Braemar burned down and they wouldn't be any use now even if they hadn't gone up in smoke.'

*

And then one night, it was a long time afterwards, Matt told him right out of the blue he'd had some papers since long before that crap game. Grand'mère had given them to him as some kind of payment, he said. It was soon after the Braemar fire, when she asked him to pray for Flora Osweken.

Frank Martello was annoyed. 'Why didn't you say so when we were investigating the murder?'

'I'd never really looked them over and I just didn't think of it. Honestly, I'd forgotten I even had them. It never occurred to me they could have anything to do with that horrible business,' he said defensively. Then he added, 'Do you want to see them now? I only came across them again the other day.'

'No, I don't. Not now. That case is gathering dust nicely. You keep them.'

'Okay.'

He thought the priest was going to say something else, but nothing came.

And now Father Souris was denying all knowledge of them again. Surprising how his memory came and went. Snowflakes tapped on the window. Something wasn't right, thought Sergeant Martello again. Something didn't fit.

11

The policemen drove along the rough track that led up to Zack Guillem's cabin. 'What's your take on all this, Neil?' Frank Martello asked.

The detective from Wawa had already made up his mind. 'It's the schoolteacher's body, you'll see, and I'm pretty sure the rumours are right,' he said confidently. 'That old woman they all call Grand'mère is behind it. She's the only one with a real motive. And then there's the way the body was mutilated and burned. Looks like the work of some madman but I heard of a similar case once, happened quite a while back now, somewhere north of Lake Winnipeg. Two Indian guys killed and burned their mother. They were done for murder, but they could never see it. They thought it was the right thing to do, the only thing they could do in fact, seeing she'd turned into a windigo. Apparently it was their custom.'

'The Oswekens aren't some isolated wilderness band, Neil. But you might be right. Grand'mère had the motive, though she couldn't have done it by herself.'

'You know what they say. You can take an Indian out

of the wilderness, but you'll never take the wilderness out of an Indian.'

Senior Constable Martello thought about this for a moment. 'Hmm. Not sure about that. Anyway, let's hope we wrap it up soon. Your wife, is she still hanging in there?'

'Far as I know but I need to get back home, Frank. She's already overdue.'

*

They found Zack inside his cabin, sitting at a bare wooden table, a bottle of pale moonshine and a nearly full glass in front of him. His head slumped on his chest. A dead fly floated in the glass. The whiskey seemed untouched. Zack looked up when they entered but did not speak. His face was pale and drawn, his eyes were sunken and bloodshot, he had not shaved for days.

'You okay to answer a couple of questions, Zack?' Senior Constable Martello asked.

Zack nodded, and motioned for them to sit down.

'About Marina Grochowska?'

'Yeah.'

Zack's eyes glistened and when he spoke, his voice was lifeless. He had little to tell them.

'Did she stay here with you?'

'Sometimes.'

'Do you know why she was so interested in the land?'

'Wouldn't you be?' Zack said. He sighed. 'She was interested in everything. It was a bet, that's all.'

'What exactly was she to you, Zack?'

He looked at the two policemen, then looked down at the table. 'A friend. A very close friend,' he said thickly.

'We've heard the two of you were going to get married?'

He could barely speak. 'We'd talked about it.'

'I'm sorry about this, but we have to find who did it.' Zack nodded again. 'When was the last time you saw her?'

'It was after Matt threw us out of the church basement. I drove her home.'

'And?'

'That's all. I came back here.'

'How did she seem when you left her?'

'Tired. It was late. Elated.'

'Elated?'

'Well, she'd just won all the maple bush off Grand'-mère.'

'I thought Matt stopped the game before anything like that happened.'

'That's maybe what he thinks. But she won it all fair and square. If you want to know for sure just ask Grand'-mère.'

'And you didn't see her again?' Zack shook his head. 'Do you have any idea who might have wanted to kill her?' Zack continued shaking his head. 'Who might have held such a big grudge against the schoolteacher to want to hack her to death?'

'I don't know.'

Detective Sergeant Reilly asked, 'Who could have been so afraid of her that they hacked open her body and burned it to make sure she was dead?'

Zack could not reply.

'I've heard that's what sometimes happens though, with the Indians. You know about this sort of stuff, don't you? Don't they believe sometimes a person can become possessed by an evil spirit and has to be killed like this? That's right, isn't it? Isn't that what they do to get rid of windigos? Kill them and burn them? You don't think that yourself, by any chance?'

Zack remained silent. Frank said to him, 'Sorry, Zack, but we're trying to find out who did this terrible thing. We were hoping maybe you could shed a little light on it.'

'I'm not an Indian,' Zack replied. 'And I've never known it happen. They wouldn't hack the body up like that before they burned it.'

'Are you telling us you don't think Miss Grochowska's murderer was an Indian?'

'No. I'm just saying that whoever did it probably had other reasons.'

'Like what?'

'How the hell would I know? If I did . . .'

'If you did you'd what?' asked Frank Martello.

Zack shook his head and swallowed. 'I don't know, Frank.'

*

Senior Constable Martello left the questioning of Grand'-mère to the detective.

'When was the last time you saw Miss Grochowska, the schoolteacher?'

'At the crap game in the church basement. She won.'

'And you lost. You have not seen her since?'

'No.'

'How did you feel when you lost.'

Grand'mère shrugged. 'Pretty pissed off. But you win, you lose. That's gambling.'

'Did you like Miss Grochowska?'

'Not much.'

'Any reason?'

'She does not listen. She can only see one way to do things, her way.'

'Did you dislike her enough to want to do her harm?'

'Harm?' She turned to the senior constable. 'Frank, tell this man I'm a healer. Tell him to go to Father Souris if he wants a character reference.'

'Someone has harmed her, though, Grand'mère,' he replied. 'She recently arranged to have your grandson Bobby sent to live with foster-parents. Did that upset you?'

'Of course it upset me. What a stupid question, even for you. She had them take him away. That weak-willed priest was no use. And now Bobby's in jail.' The old woman sighed. 'He's seven years old.'

'Did that upset you enough to hurt Miss Grochowska?'

'I'm not responsible for what has happened to the schoolteacher, Frank. I did not wish her well, but killing her is not something I would do. A lot of things have upset me down the years, Frank. You know that well enough.'

'What about the way she was killed?'

'What about it?'

'The body was mutilated, you know, cut up, and burned. Isn't that the way you'd get rid of a windigo? You told me she was possessed, remember.'

Grand'mère looked at him and shook her head in disgust. 'You've been reading too many comic books.'

It did sound far-fetched, he thought. And she had alibis for her whereabouts at all the relevant times. Osweken alibis.

*

Then there had been Suzanne Armand's lurid story, how she'd seen it all as it happened. No mention of Grand'-mère in that. The policemen felt they were on to something there until they began to realize she'd dreamed it all up.

*

Charlie Anstalt seemed shifty during the whole interview, but then Charlie often seemed that way, like he was up to something that was not quite as it should be.

'When was the last time you saw Miss Grochowska?'

'At the crap game.'

'After that?'

'Don't think so. Not sure. She went round to Matt's.'

'Before or after?'

'Not sure. Afterwards, I think. Or it might have been before. Couple of days, maybe.'

'How do you know this, Charlie?'

'I saw her with my own eyes.'

'You saw her?'

'Yeah. She walked to his front door and went in.'

'Did you see her come out again?'

'Nope.'

'What were you doing there anyway?'

'Just walking past.'

'Did you see or hear anything else?'

'Nope. Maybe a gun went off. Can't really remember.'

'A gun went off?'

'Dunno. Maybe I heard a bang. Coulda been a car back-firing. It sounds pretty much the same.'

'Did you ever see her go there before?'

'Plenty of times. They were, like, you know.'

'Like what, Charlie?'

'Dunno. Just a hunch, I guess.'

Frank and the detective shook their heads. 'We need a lot more than your hunches here, Charlie.'

*

'Come in, Frank. Come in, Detective Sergeant.' Ed Perriault looked drawn and concerned when he opened his front door to the policemen. 'Terrible thing, this murder. Don't recall anything this bad ever happening here in Sugarmilk Falls.'

'We need to ask you some questions. Just routine, you understand. We're asking everybody.'

'Of course, of course, anything to help.'

But Ed hadn't seen or heard anything, and no, he'd no idea why something so awful could have happened. 'Before you go, Frank, I feel I ought to mention this. I'm more than a little alarmed by all the wild talk I've been hearing around the place. The party lines are jammed full of it. I'm worried there could be some sort of reprisal brewing if it isn't sorted out damn quick.'

'Thanks, Ed, I'm aware of it too. We'll try to keep the lid on it. Keep it to yourself for the time being, but we might be making an arrest real soon.'

*

'What do you want this time, Jenny? . . . No, there aren't any new developments . . . You'll be the first to know, just as soon as I've got something to tell . . . Now don't go putting anything silly in the *Gazette* . . . Yes, of course I've heard all that crazy talk . . . No, of course I don't give any credence to it . . . I'm a policeman, Jenny, I look for real evidence.' He put down the telephone.

*

SLAYER STILL AT LARGE: NO ARREST YET IN FALLS MURDER CASE. Father Souris's hands trembled as he read. Marina's death had been the lead story for a couple of weeks now. Today the headline filled nearly half the front page of the *Sugarmilk Gazette*. Under it, next to the now familiar picture of a smiling Marina standing with her pupils in front of the school, another long article told readers nothing new. 'Police admit they are no nearer to finding the murderer of Sugarmilk Falls grade-school teacher Marina Grochowska, whose cremated body was discovered on the portage trail near the top of the falls . . .'

He listened in on the shrieking party line and detected an increasingly sinister, more imperative note in the ranting. 'Our schoolteacher! Those savages! Something shoulda been done long ago . . . Nobody's safe . . . Something's gotta be done before it happens again . . .'

He tried to write a sermon that would put a stop once and for all to this unholy ferment, but the only words that he allowed seemed so thin, so fragile, so worn out, nowhere near robust enough to stand up to the cold blast of vengeance now howling through the valley.

12

Ed Perriault laughed a long low rumbling laugh that heightened the hum of expectation inside the old school-house. 'Well, I'll be darned,' he muttered. He read the numbers again. 'And I'll be damned darned too!' He turned to Jerry Sinclair, who had handed him the sheet of paper. 'Seems the law is about to catch up with the way things really are round here,' he said and chuckled under his breath. 'I have to admit I didn't think it would happen but hell, the people have spoken their mind. They have spoken out indeed!' He waved the piece of paper in the air. 'Everybody,' he called out, 'I can now tell you the result of the vote. The people have decided it's time for change. Sugarmilk Falls will no longer be dry.'

There was a general intake of breath. Hugo Jansen could not believe his ears. 'No kidding?' he asked Ed.

'Here. Take a look for yourself.' Ed handed him the piece of paper and laughed again. 'You look as if you could use a drink right now.'

'We'll all live to regret this day. Mark my words,' intoned Reverend Byers gloomily. 'Lydia, I feel a sick headache coming on. It's time we went home. Come, my dear.'

'Sorry, Arnie,' said Hugo, 'I know you were against this. No hard feelings, I hope.' He held out his hand but Arnie turned and walked away.

Instead Ed Perriault shook Hugo's hand. 'Congratulations are still premature and don't go wild with the celebrations yet. The municipality is still officially dry until we get all the paperwork sorted out and then there'll still be the question of if and where to have a bar. Now I gotta get home before Sylvie feeds my supper to the dogs.'

Jenny Buszek approached Hugo, her ballpoint poised above her notebook. 'What do you think this vote will mean for Sugarmilk Falls?' she asked him. 'Would you say it's the beginning of a new era?'

'Yeah,' he replied, 'something like that.'

Jenny wrote it down. Then she asked him, 'How do you think it will change the place? Do you think it will help to make Sugarmilk Falls more modern and maybe more welcoming and accessible to outsiders?'

'Yeah, I guess it might do that.'

Jenny scribbled. 'What about the Falls Hotel? Will you have to expand?'

'Ummm . . . Birgit? Jenny wants to know if we're expanding the hotel.'

'Maybe we will. I'm not sure yet,' replied Birgit. 'We need to get a licence first. A couple more hurdles still have to be jumped.'

'A couple more hurdles still to jump,' repeated Jenny, scribbling in her notebook. 'But you agree that it could be good for the locality?'

'You never know.'

Jenny scribbled some more. 'Of course you're both really happy about the result?'

'Of course,' said Birgit.

'Yeah,' said Hugo.

'Did you ever think it would turn out this way?'

'We hoped it would, naturally,' said Birgit.

'Yeah. We kept our fingers crossed,' said Hugo.

The result of the vote took up the front page of the *Sugarmilk Gazette*, displacing the murder for the first time. Quite a few people commented that Hugo Jansen had a lot more to say for himself in print than anyone could remember from a face-to-face encounter.

*

The fall rain brought with it a wintry chill. Tentacles of ice began to stretch out from the edges of the lakes and streams and form hollow opaque layers along the shore-lines. In the morning stillness freezing mists spread over the water, catching in the vivid branches, veiling the white receding sun. The grunts of rutting deer echoed through the trees and the clash of big antlers rang between the hills. Ranks of geese and menacing snow-dark clouds crossed the cobalt sky and the wind hissed of ice storms and blizzards to come.

Zack walked along the path to Grand'mère's cabin on the edge of the muskeg, his head bent against the bright coldness, the brim of his hat low over his eyes. Red and yellow leaves fluttered from the maple trees and rustled on the ground. He stopped suddenly. In the tawny glow beneath the branches a pair of legs turned oddly, the moccasined feet nearly level with his face. He froze. He looked up, at the torso and the arms hanging straight down, at the head unnaturally on one side, at the blue swollen face and the bulging eyes of Grand'mère Osweken staring down at him. The rope around her neck had been pulled taught over the branch of a tree and tied around the trunk. He looked around quickly. A little way into the woods another body lay face down on the ground, its back red with blood. Zack went to it, turned it over. It was Ovide. Cautiously Zack entered the cabin. The silence here was thick, almost a presence. The air reeked of blood. The children, Ovide's little boy and girl, sprawled motionless on the floor. Near them lay Betty, his wife. Zack backed away to the wall and slid slowly to the floor. A sudden gust of wind keened through the gaps in the window until the silence closed it out again and all was still, only the distant rush of the waterfalls.

*

SUGARBUSH MASSACRE, screamed the *Gazette*. Father Souris stared in disbelief at the headline. What on earth did Tim Buszek think he was doing? Things were bad enough without this sort of thing fuelling the already overheated party lines. He looked at the photograph and recognized Grand'mère's cabin. He read Jenny's graphic account of what had happened there. He hung his head, sickened by the nightmare that had been set in motion. Who had done this terrible thing? Who was responsible? Where would it end?

*

The *Gazette*'s sensational story caught the attention of newspapermen from further afield. Radio reporters, even a TV crew turned up in Sugarmilk Falls. For a few days the Jansens' hotel didn't have a room to spare.

*

Senior Constable Martello shook his head. 'It doesn't add up, Neil. I can't see him killing the Oswekens like that. Where was the gun?'

'Got rid of it, of course. It's straightforward enough. They killed his girlfriend. That's his motive and he had plenty of opportunity. Nobody to bother him out there. What was he doing over there anyway if he wasn't taking his revenge? He's a wild man from the woods.'

'I just don't believe he'd go out there deliberately to kill the Oswekens. Doesn't sound like Zack. I know him better than you do. He's not the homicidal head-case kind.'

'Look, Frank. Which one of us is the detective here? We've got newspaper reporters crawling all over the place wanting to know all about the massacre. We need to wrap this thing up damn quick. Soon as we make an arrest they'll all go home. I want to go home too.'

The senior constable did not argue further. Instead he shrugged his shoulders with annoyance and asked, 'How's your wife? She still holding on?'

'They're worried about her, Frank. She's more than ten days overdue and says she can't feel the baby moving any-more. She may have to be induced, before she starts hav-ing fits. I really need to get back to Wawa soon as I can.' He paused a moment, then continued, 'Look. This Zack Guillem. We found him with the bodies. And anyway we need to keep him locked up or he'll disappear into the bush. I wouldn't be surprised if he was involved in the murder of Miss Grochowska too. You remember how unhelpful he was when we talked with him.'

'He was pretty upset, Neil.'

'Not surprising in the circumstances. But why was he upset? That's the crucial question. I think you'll see I'm right about him.' He tapped his nose. 'I'm the detective, remember. I have an instinct about this.'

More like roulette than police work, thought Frank Martello. However, Neil is the detective here, even though he has to tap his nose to prove it. Better leave the detecting to him. But Zack? It just didn't feel right. 'I don't know,' he said, 'it doesn't fit. Even if it was a lynching, and I'm not so sure it was, it was too frenzied, for God's sake. Zack isn't the frenzied kind.'

'If it's not him, who is it, then? Not some lumber guy?'

'No, the lumber crews are working too far away. And if it isn't Zack, that seems to leave a whole lot of decent people in the frame. Arnie and Charlie Anstalt, for example. And Dave Shaw. And Phil Tronquet. And Sammy Dutoit and Jerry Sinclair. Even Ed Perriault and Lucien Armand. And not forgetting all those women yakking on the party lines. None of them fit either, of course. But Zack? Four shootings and a hanging? I can't see it.'

'Like I said, he's a wild man from the woods.'

For a while the policemen were silent. Then Senior Constable Martello cleared his throat. 'I have another suspect.'

'Oh? Who's that?'

'And she's already dead, Neil. It's Grand'mère herself.' The detective looked up sharply and began to grin as Frank continued, 'A while back she was shooting off her rifle and screaming the place down about the windigo. If anyone was possessed it was her, but it was moonshine that got to her. She goes on these binges. She gets delirious. I'd say it was Grand'mère shot the others and then hanged herself.'

Neil Reilly considered the idea. 'Not a lynching but a suicide? She was on a binge, maybe they were celebrating what they'd done, and she killed her own flesh and blood in a shooting spree while she was plastered out of her mind. Not the first time that's happened, either. Then she hanged herself. Indians do it all the time, don't they? Kill themselves.' He was now grinning broadly. 'And I could get back to Wawa.' He hesitated. 'If we're talking Indians, what about that other one? Louis?'

'He was miles away, up near the Barrens. He split before anybody was killed.'

'Okay. And what about the gun? Grand'mère could still have got rid of it first. There's one problem though with your solution, Frank. Her feet were nearly five feet off the ground. How did she hang herself?'

Senior Constable Martello thought for a moment. 'Jumped off something, of course. I thought you were the detective here, Neil.'

*

'Zack's been arrested,' Charlie Anstalt said to Arnie. 'He's in Frank Martello's cell.'

'What for? The Oswekens?'

'You got it.'

'Zack? I thought it was Grand'mère herself did it.'

'They're holding Zack on suspicion.'

Arnie looked concerned. He puffed his cheeks and blew the air out slowly. 'Maybe he wasn't even there,' he said.

'Who's ever going to know who was there?'

'Why do they think Zack had anything to do with it?' Arnie asked.

'He was nuts about the schoolteacher. The Oswekens killed her and now they're dead too. Two plus two equals Zack, I guess. That Wawa detective sure likes his arithmetic,' Charlie replied. The brothers sat in silence. After a while Charlie asked, 'What are we gonna do about it?'

Arnie looked down at his fingers and then straight into his brother's face. 'Nothing, Charlie. Except keep our mouths shut.'

'What about the others?'

'Don't worry. They'll do the same.'

*

It was after midnight when Senior Constable Martello walked silently towards the cell. Zack was crouched in a corner, asleep, but he looked up quickly as the policeman approached. 'Zack, I want to have a little off-the-record talk.'

Zack did not reply.

'This isn't easy.' He rubbed his face with his hand and took a deep breath before continuing. 'Okay, it's like this. I have some serious concerns about what's been happening here but to try to settle it in my mind I'll ask you again. Did you have anything to do with these murders?'

'No, I did not. That's what I keep telling you, Frank.'

The policeman paused, biting his lip. 'What's your hunch about who killed Miss Grochowska?'

'I just don't know. It could have something to do with the land she'd won, but Grand'mère wouldn't do that.

Charlie was mighty interested in the land but he didn't kill her.'

'What about who killed Grand'mère and the others?'

'It'd be kind of hard to do all that by yourself.'

'Sure. But not impossible?'

'No. Not impossible.'

The policeman thought for a while. 'At the moment it looks like this, Zack. It seems maybe, and it's by no means certain, Grand'mère shot the others when she was drunk and then hanged herself. That's the preferred outcome, so to speak.' He paused, peering at the woodsman. 'Your face tells me you don't hold with that explanation, and to be honest, neither do I, but it's the one where nobody's got anything to lose.' He paused again. 'You were there at the scene with the bodies. Nobody else had any reason to do it if it wasn't Grand'mère herself. At the moment we're keeping you in jail just so you don't run off on us while we do our job. But the more we have to look into this terrible business the worse it's gonna look for you. It could get about as bad as it can for you, Zack.' He hesitated again as though he'd finished saying what he'd come for, but after a moment he said, 'Do you reckon you could get away from here by morning and disappear for good? We'll come looking for you, no mistake.'

Zack stared at him in amazement. 'How am I going to get out of here?'

'That's the easy part. But you'll have to disappear off the planet. I mean it.'

'Why are you doing this, Frank? How're you going to explain it?'

'Let me worry about that. With all the tall tales that go

round about you, jail-breaking won't seem out of place. I reckon there never was a better lock-picker than you.'

Senior Constable Martello unlocked the cell door. Zack stood up and looked him in the eye for a moment. 'Goodbye, Frank,' he said and walked out into the night.

*

It hadn't been quite so easy to explain away but the disappearance of their prisoner in no way undermined Detective Sergeant Neil Reilly's conviction that they'd satisfactorily solved the case. He hurried back to Wawa, to his wife and day-old daughter. A pickup truck loaded down with Niagara grapes arrived in Sugarmilk Falls before the first heavy snow. The coroner left an open verdict as to what caused the death of Grand'mère Osweken.

*

The snow began to fall, gentle bright flurries at first but soon growing to howling whiteouts that buried the frozen lakes and rivers and cut off the roads. The narrow channel along Main Street was re-ploughed almost daily. Hard snow drifted against the walls of the houses. It covered the bottoms of doors and windows and piled up high on the rooftops. A hungry wolf crept out of the forest to scavenge in the yards on the edge of town. Father Souris said daily Mass to an empty church. The party lines fell silent. Under the thick hard winter crust people turned inwards and kept to themselves.

One morning in March a large crow landed on the wind-exposed top of the presbytery sundial. It cawed in the cold still air and hopped once or twice to investigate the white glittering world. In the clear sky the sun shone brightly, sparking red and blue and gold on the hard-packed snow. The frozen air seemed restless. Father Souris picked up the telephone to hear a voice say, 'Sap's starting to run.' He heard the words repeated and before long the refrain 'Sap's running . . . Sap's running strong . . .' crackled along the wires. Soon the woods began to thrum with the drip drip drip of the sap buckets, like the tick tick tick of a million clocks.

13

Suzanne inhaled deeply on a hand-rolled cigarette. The smoke filled her lungs and accelerated her brain. She heard a voice very close to her ear, 'Put it out. This ain't no opium den.' She looked up. Freddy Chen stared hard at her until she stubbed it in the tin ashtray and placed the unsmoked portion back inside her purse. 'That's better. What do you want to eat?'

She shuffled in her chair and gave him a challenging look. 'I'll wait till Charlie gets here.'

'Fine. Just remember you're not at home but in my restaurant, okay?' Freddy turned and walked back to the kitchen.

Stupid Chink, she thought angrily. As if she could smoke pot at home. Suzanne opened her purse, gave a little sigh of defeat, and closed it again. Damn this stick-in-the-mud hole-in-the-ground Sugarmilk Falls. If it wasn't for Charlie she never would have come back here after getting her degree. She'd be in the city right now with a real job paying her real money, starting out on a real career. Instead she was pregnant, still waitressing in Hugo and Birgit's shitty place and no better off than she'd been during the high-school summer holidays. Suzanne shook her head and sighed again. But she had Charlie. Gorgeous, wonderful, talented, romantic Charlie. If only she could imagine life without him. 'Hey, soon we'll be able to drink and dine at the Falls Hotel,' he said to her the other day. Sometimes he could be nearly as bad as the rest of the people in this hick town, getting all excited about some crummy bar. If only she didn't need him so much. She was working on him, though. Sooner or later he'd get out from under the thumb of that weirdo brother of his. Charlie had big plans of his own, especially since he found his grandfather's old prospecting map. As soon as they made a bit of money they'd high-tail it back to the city and have some real fun. Charlie's singing would get noticed at last. They wouldn't be stuck in this hole forever, not if she could help it.

And there'd been all those gruesome murders here. She kept on having the most horrible nightmares. She'd even been asked to help out with the teaching until they could sort it out. In Miss Grochowska's own classroom! She couldn't bear the thought. Everything was just too awful for words, except Charlie was surely going to marry her now. He'd have to when she told him about the baby. He could be a little bit rough sometimes but it was exciting. Afterwards he'd be really sorry, and so nice. Then he'd turn the charm back on and she'd be helpless again. If only she could make herself dump him like her parents were always trying to persuade her to do, but he was like an addiction, damn him. Anyway it was too late now. Damn everything. If he didn't get here this minute she'd leave and finish smoking her joint outside. And if stupid old Frank Martello saw her he could go jump in the lake even though he'd just been made sergeant.

'Hiya, honey. What's the matter?' Charlie stood by the table, looking down at her.

Suzanne's face lit up immediately. 'Only that you're late. You're always late. But you're here now.'

'Sorry. Lost track of time.' He sat down opposite her and got out a cigarette.

'I hope you never have to choose between me and some stupid old motor, Charlie. You came pretty close to it tonight.'

He grinned at her and the cigarette drooped from the side of his mouth. 'So do I. It wouldn't be an easy decision to have to make. Here comes Shanghai Lil.' Lily Chen, dressed in red silk, approached the table. 'What's real tasty tonight, Lily, other than yourself?' he asked her.

She gave him a bored look and handed each of them a menu. 'It's all good. Today's special is sweet and sour meatballs with noodles. You'll like it.'

'That sounds nice,' said Suzanne. 'Freddy puts maple syrup in the sweet and sour sauce.'

'What kind of meat is it?' asked Charlie.

'Good meat. Delicious.'

'What? Regular meat? Like beef?'

Lily paused. 'Today it's moose.'

'Sort of regular, I guess. You've dished up raccoon meatballs in here before.'

'Well, we like to use fresh local ingredients as much as possible, you know. Whatever we can get hold of,' explained Lily with a weary sigh. 'This time of year it's not so bad but come January, February, that's when we have to be a little more creative with the food.'

They looked at the menu. 'I'll have the meatballs,' said Charlie.

'Me too, with lots of sauce.'

Lily took away the menus and went back to the kitchen.

Suzanne looked at Charlie to see if this was the right moment to tell him the news. She decided to introduce the subject gently. 'You look very satisfied about something. Is it a secret or will you let me in on it?'

'Sure. You remember that lost airplane a while back, ended up in a lake somewhere . . .'

'Shush! I overheard Zack telling Dad about it. You're not supposed to know, Charlie.'

'Yeah, yeah, that was a long time ago. Anyway I found something that could really mess things up around here.'

'What do you mean?'

'Remember you said Zack found some other stuff as well, the prospector's wallet or something? Well, I got it.'

'Where?'

Charlie grinned and shook his head. 'Just got it, okay.'

'Tell me where you found it.'

'Zack's place. He's disappeared so I thought I'd take a look round.'

'I wish you wouldn't do that. One of these days you're going to get into trouble. Why did you want to go there, anyway?'

'On the off chance those land deeds might be there. He was awful friendly with the Oswekens, and they weren't at Grand'mère's. I looked.' Suzanne stared at him disapprovingly. 'Look, this could mean a lot for us.'

'What did you find out?'

'There's a letter or something written by one of those prospector buddies of that lawyer who lost all the claims.'

'So what's new?'

'It was in his wallet, along with a picture of you'll never guess who?'

'Come on. Who?'

'The dead schoolteacher.'

'Charlie! You'd better tell Frank about this right away.'

'Don't think so. Remember I wasn't supposed to be there. Anyway it proves everything can't have gone up in smoke or why would she come here?'

'Just coincidence. Got herself a job here, that's all. It doesn't prove a thing. Anyway even if you discovered where they were staking out you'd have to re-stake it all.'

'Maybe not. Not if we owned the land.'

'But you don't.'

'Who says?'

'Well there's no proof.'

'Look Suzanne. I'm nearly there. All I need now is those papers and I'd be willing to put money on Matt still having them.'

She frowned. 'Don't you dare go poking round his place. Promise me you won't.' He grinned at her. 'There's something I have to tell you, Charlie. We're going to have to get married like yesterday. There's a little Anstalt on the way.'

He looked triumphant. 'So Lucien and Claudine are going to be grandparents. I told you they'd have to come round sooner or later.'

*

Father Souris woke up with a start and immediately realized he had been aware of the noise for some time. He quietly got out of bed and crept slowly, stealthily through the midnight presbytery and into the study. His fingers reached towards the wall switch. He turned on the light. Someone was seated at his desk shining a flashlight into a drawer. 'What are you doing here, Charlie?'

'Shit.' Charlie looked rapidly towards the open window, then leaned back in the chair. 'Well, actually, Matt, I'm looking for something.'

'What's that?'

'Those deeds of Grand'mère's. I reckon they're here somewhere. They're nowhere else.'

'I told you back then they're not here, Charlie.'

'Yeah, guess you did. But I didn't think you were telling the truth, Matt.'

'You haven't found them, have you.'

'No, but I reckon I haven't finished looking.'

'You won't find anything. But as you're here, do you mind telling me why you're still so interested in them? You've pretty well turned the place inside out.'

'No, I guess I don't mind, Matt, since you've caught me in suspicious circumstances as Frank would say. It's like this. Our grandfather, Arnie's and mine, he always used to say he'd be a rich man if it wasn't for those damned Oswekens. He was a war veteran, fought in the Boer War or something, and it seems they cheated him out of the land he got when he came out of the army.'

'Cheated?'

'Yeah. Gramps liked to gamble though he wasn't so good at it. But till he died he swore he lost his land to the Oswekens in a dishonest game. Anyway, I want to get it back.'

'Why now, after so long?'

'Gramps always said it was shit land for farming anything on other than mink but it'd be worth your while digging down deeper. He had this old survey map. Arnie and me, we used to play with it when we were kids. And now things are settling down about, you know, the Oswekens and everything, I thought I'd have a good look for the papers.'

'Did he try to get it back himself?'

'Dunno. He wasn't the farming sort. He thought engines were the up and coming thing.'

'Well, there's nothing here that would interest you. You'd better go home, Charlie, while the going's good. I don't want to have to report this break-in to our new police sergeant, Frank Martello.'

Charlie grinned at him. 'No, I'll bet you don't, Matt, not with what you were up to with that schoolteacher. Now, what did you do with those papers?'

'What papers?'

'Don't be dense. The ones Louis brought along to that crap game. In some sort of a bag. Remember?'

'You must mean this.' Father Souris reached into the bottom drawer of his desk and pulled out the leather pouch. 'Open it,' he said, handing it to Charlie. Charlie reached inside and brought out the yellowing *Sugarmilk Gazette*. 'What was that you were saying about dishonest games? Were there ever any papers? Who's ever seen them?'

'I saw the claim assignments sure enough.'

'And weren't they destroyed a long time ago in the fire?'

Charlie gave him a knowing look. 'Is that what you

told Miss Grochowska? And what about the night she came here?'

'I don't know what you mean.'

'She was here. I saw her. Then a couple of days later you found the body.'

'What has that got to do with what you're looking for?'

'You know the answer to that better than me. But I saw her come here. I figured she was after her winnings.'

'There were no winnings, Charlie.'

'So you say, but there's a lot of people think she won the land off Grand'mère and that's why the Oswekens killed her. Then Grand'mère went crazy and hanged herself. Why would they do that if they still thought they owned the land? So I reckon those papers have to be here somewhere, Matt.'

Father Souris paused. 'You've been after those papers a long time, haven't you?'

'You bet.'

'You used to pester Flora Osweken about them, didn't you?'

'She was a good-looking woman.'

'From what Henri said, about the time of the fire somebody turned over the Braemar office. Henri had an idea it might be you trying to take back your family's losses, especially now the prospecting work had been done.'

'Did he tell you this?'

'Who started the fire at the Braemar Lodge, Charlie? Henri said someone torched it. Was it you?'

Charlie grinned nervously. 'It was an accident. Like Frank Martello said.'

'Someone lost their life. Are you responsible for that?'

'No. It was an accident.'

'Henri said the door was jammed. He was sure the fire was deliberate. Were you hoping to get away with the papers before it took hold?'

'I couldn't ever find them. Hell, why would I start the fire if I was inside?'

'If it wasn't you, who was it?'

Charlie shrugged. 'I guess Frank was right. It was an accident. Or it might've been that lawyer, Levine or whatever his name was.'

'Oh, I don't think so. He'd gone back to the city by then.'

Charlie looked straight at Father Souris and grinned again. 'Well, Matt, here we are and I guess we can call it quits. Maybe you had a visit from the murder victim you'd rather nobody delved in to. And maybe I had a considerable interest in what Henri kept in the Braemar office I'd rather nobody knew about. So where does that leave us? I'd be willing to put money on you not telling Frank about my little visit here tonight.'

Father Souris smiled back at him. 'Maybe I will, maybe not. It all depends on what you're going to do now.'

Charlie got up from the chair. 'For now I'll say goodnight. I was hoping to leave here with the bundle of papers but I guess they'll keep. They're safe enough with you for the time being. You're not likely to bring them out into the open, are you, Matt. Not for a long time yet at any rate.'

The priest shook his head. 'And I never will, Charlie. Because they don't exist.'

*

Ed Perriault leaned back in the chair and put his glass down on the table with a thump. 'Didn't think I'd ever see you walk into Hugo's bar, Arnie,' he said with a laugh. 'Do you want a beer?'

'Well, even an old cuss like myself has to move with the times eventually.' Arnie bared his yellow teeth in a smile and sat down. 'I'll even go as far as a beer, thanks Ed.'

Ed signalled Hugo to bring another glass and looked at the other man with pleasant surprise. 'I'm real glad you feel that way about things. Doesn't do to let what's happened in the past fester. Can't go back and do it over again differently.'

'True, true. You're right enough there. Nothing stays the same forever, does it? No matter how hard we try to keep it that way.' There was a note of regret in his sigh, but he shook his head and looked around the simple bar. 'It's not so bad, either.' He cautiously sipped his beer and continued talking casually, as though the thoughts were just forming in his mind, 'I guess things all round are getting back to normal now too.'

Ed looked rather solemn and twirled the glass in his hand. 'I don't know if they are, Arnie. I'm not sure they ever will. Just too many terrible things have happened here. Things like that take an awful long time to heal up. They leave scars. Big deep scars. And with Grand'mère gone it's like the spirit of the place has gone too. I'm not sure it will ever be normal again.'

Arnie did not reply immediately. After a while he said, 'Hope you're wrong. Seems a shame if it keeps everybody from moving on. Looking ahead.'

Ed ruminated. 'I didn't mean it'll do that exactly. It's just that it'll always be there. Something like that keeps you looking over your shoulder. It keeps you from being optimistic about the future. Makes you think twice about trying something new.'

Arnie nodded sagely. 'I just hope things aren't going to stagnate, Ed. We got a real nice little community here. I'd like to think we were still up for the occasional challenge.'

'Me too, Arnie. Me too.' Ed Perriault narrowed his eyes. 'Got anything in mind?'

'No, no. Nothing in particular,' he replied dismissively. Then he added, 'But I have been wondering a bit about what might be some sort of a step forward. Any suggestions?'

'No, Arnie. It's not something I've thought about yet. But maybe you'll come up with one or two ideas?'

Arnie shook his head. The men sat quietly contemplating their drinks. After a while he said innocently, 'Any idea who owns the land now?'

Ed grinned broadly. 'Not sure anything's changed. What are you getting at?'

Arnie smiled again. 'Maybe we own it now.'

Ed Perriault was rather surprised by this suggestion. He looked closely at Arnie. 'What do you mean?'

'You know the stories. How the Oswekens won it all off people like my grandfather through gambling. Maybe they aren't true. Maybe the Oswekens never did own it. Anyway I just wondered who owns it now the Oswekens are gone, where it goes from here.'

Ed laughed. 'You can always try to claim it back, I suppose. Land gets recorded. If I were you I'd check the land records to see if there ever was anything made out to your grandfather. That'd be a good place to start wondering from, Arnie. Or you could try just appropriating it back, if you know where it's supposed to be.' He shook his head and drained his glass. 'I gotta get home or Sylvie will begin to think I'm turning into a regular alcoholic.'

*

Arnie began a lengthy correspondence that started at the Land Registry Office and moved on to the National Archives themselves. He never found a record of any veteran's grant to anyone by the name of Anstalt. Furthermore he found very little relating to the Sugarmilk country. He began to wonder if the stories could be true, if it might really be unsurrendered land.

Charlie was sceptical. 'If there's no record of it, who did Gramps get it from?'

'Government, of course.' Arnie thought for a moment. 'I reckon the records must be incomplete.' He paused again. 'What would we do with it if we did own it?'

'Mine it, I guess. Make our fortune at last.'

'How are we going to do that? We haven't got the money to finance even the exploration work ourselves. We can't borrow it using the land as collateral because we can't show it's ours. We could borrow money on the garage but we don't want to put that at risk for something so speculative. So how are we going to finance this getting rich?'

Charlie looked blankly back at his brother. He shrugged his shoulders angrily. 'Matt's got those papers hidden somewhere. I just know he has.'

'Well, you're not about to get them back from him. You haven't got anything on him to persuade him to part with them, and he might just have something on you, don't forget.' Arnie looked stern as he continued, 'But how about this for an idea. Let's just assume for a minute we could prove the land was ours and we didn't want to borrow money on it. Suppose then we sold some of it off to finance the exploration, a few bits that didn't look so valuable in mining terms but might be real interesting to hunting and fishing types. Now suppose for a minute those papers really are gone. We have other stuff of Gramps' to show he got a land grant of some sort here, his war medals and letters and so on.'

Charlie stared at Arnie. 'Which bits are we thinking about selling off?'

'Roseau Lake, up around where the Braemar Lodge used to be.'

'Isn't that awful risky?'

'Even if we can't prove we own it, it might be worth trying just to see what happens. You never know, we might even get away with it.'

14

'Dear Mr. Levine,' he read. 'You probably don't remember me but I can remember you. You are the only real lawyer I ever met so that's why I decided to contact you first. I hope you don't mind and I wonder if you can help me?'

The letter was dated 12 May 1975, and had been written with a green ballpoint pen at the top of a sheet of lined foolscap ripped from a spiral-back notebook, the kind he'd liked to use when he was in law school. He smiled to himself. It was nice to think they were still around all these years later. The paper was torn along the left-hand edge and the ink had smudged – another southpaw, he thought and the notion pleased him. The handwriting itself was firm and neat.

He read on. 'My father died a few years back but I didn't know about it until now. He used to have the hotel on Roseau Lake where you stayed once. It got burned down. My mother died in the fire and I don't know if anyone is still up there. I moved away a long time ago and now live in the city too. What I want to know is how do I find out if my father left me anything when he died? I could sure do with some money at the present time.

Yours sincerely, Rachelle Macleod.' There was a P.S. 'I still owe you a quarter.' It was a carefully considered letter, he thought, worried over for a long time and then written down in a hurry and mailed before her nerve failed.

He read it again. Rachelle Macleod? No, he couldn't remember anyone by that name. Roseau Lake? That didn't ring any bells either. An old twenty-five-cent debt? Intriguing, but he was no wiser. However, lakeside hotel, even a burned-out one, plus the death of the owner might add up to a sizeable legacy. And the work involved could mean a nice fee for him. He'd check it out when he had an hour to spare. You never could tell what might come up in these situations. He looked again at the address and grimaced. It was in a rough part of the city. Unlikely there'd be anything worthwhile in it, he decided, but he hadn't been over that way for a long time. He'd go incognito to avoid the chance of being noticed, or even worse, confronted, by some dissatisfied old client. Maybe he'd have a bit of fun like he used to over on the wild side of the tracks.

*

James Levine paid the taxi driver and crossed the dusty run-down street. He checked the number painted on the door of a ramshackle wooden house and rang the bell. A man's head appeared out of an upstairs window. 'What do ya want?' he shouted irritably.

'Rachelle Macleod?'

'Not here.'

'Where can I find her?'

'She's gone to work. You can try the men's room at the Cabaret, a couple of blocks away.' The man pointed vaguely and closed the window. James Levine smiled to himself. The Cabaret Bar. He hadn't had a drink in the Cabaret for years.

The sidewalk felt hard through the soles of his shoes as he walked along. In the unfamiliar warmth of the spring afternoon his jacket soon grew heavy and he took it off. He saw a bar and went inside for a drink. He entered a second bar and downed another, a snow-capped, golden, throat-freezing, brain-soothing Labatts. Fantastic. He hadn't bar-crawled like this in the middle part of the day since he was a student, when he and his friends would come into this part of town to raise hell, to drown for a time in drink and women, to release the pressure of learning his way round all those endless, intricate and seemingly useless details of the law. At last he arrived at the Cabaret Bar. It probably looked much the same as he would remember it if it had been more memorable. Beige plastic tables and chairs, brown linoleum, a bit of wrought iron scrolling under the bar, a few coloured lights and a mirror ball on the ceiling. He remembered the mirror ball, and it was turning now. And the little stage was still there, across the far corner. The dark blinds were down too. It seemed he was on time for the show.

The bar buzzed with afternoon drinkers all gazing around expectantly. Now, as then, the others looked him over without looking straight at him, drawing away slightly, surreptitiously feeling for their flick-knives. He ordered a draught beer, feeling his knuckles begin to tighten. He grinned. Nothing much had changed. The years dropped away and he was young again. Suddenly the balding man with the rolled-up shirt-sleeves struck a chord on the electric organ. Glasses were slowly raised to lips and all eyes slowly turned to the stage. 'Et maintenant . . .' the organist said, the tattoos bright on his forearms. He began a vague, gurgling tune. 'Et maintenant, gentlemen . . . Rachelle does une foxtrot.'

She strutted onto the stage and struck a pose. Then moving more or less in time to the music she began to remove her clothes. The balding man played loudly. Rachelle twirled and swayed and littered the stage with her clothing to shouts and whistles and rhythmic clapping from the men. 'Rachelle!' they called. 'Rachelle! How's chances?' The nickels, dimes and quarters rained down. She danced towards them, turned and backed away, smiling over her shoulder, and each one felt it was meant for him. 'How's chances, Rachelle?' The melody meandered. She was all but naked now. Under the whirling stained-glass lights her ochre skin gleamed like summer sunshine on granite, her crow-black hair shimmered like moonlight on deep water.

Of course, thought James Levine, Roseau Lake, far away, up in the Sugarmilk country, wasn't it? That out-of-the-way hotel with the Scottish name where he stayed the time he was doing a job for old Ben Rabinowicz. Funny he remembered that name. It was run by a nosy woman and a big Indian, a gambling den as it happened. And that creepy old lady who'd cleaned him out. He cringed at the recollection. The place had burned down since, the letter said. Sugarmilk Falls. Never heard of it before or since, except once when it was briefly all over the news a few years back on account of some murders. Nothing to do with him, of course, but in a place like that . . . ? He'd gnawed more than a little at his fingers. He'd been awfully lucky to get away with it all as easily as he had. Better just enjoy the show, finish his beer and leave.

But this magical creature so tangible before his eyes, was this that talkative little girl they had? Not so little any more. No, sir. Was it so distant, so long ago? Even back then she was a pretty kid you couldn't easily take your eyes off. She already had this natural grace. And now looks aplenty too for everyone to ogle at. No wonder the Cabaret was packed out on a fine weekday afternoon in springtime. Up on the little stage she looked so beautiful, so imposing, so inaccessible, and maybe even a little intimidating. As he watched Rachelle perform her artless foxtrot, half-forgotten pictures of tiered green-grey hills and formations of wild geese above a silvery lake flitted through his mind. It felt like a rush of mountain air in the stale closed barroom. What was she doing in a dive like this? Strapped for cash, she said in her letter. Careful here, Levine, he warned himself. He knew he would not heed the warning.

*

He hesitated, but only momentarily, then knocked. 'Miss Macleod?'

'Who wants to know?'

'James Levine.'

She quickly opened the door to the dressing room, inspected him for a moment, and smiled broadly with undisguised pleasure. 'Gosh. You'd better come in. It's not much of a room but there's somewhere to sit down. It's so nice of you to visit me. You could've just written a letter back, but I really didn't think I'd hear from you at all. You don't really mean to say you remembered me, do you?'

'Not at first, no. But I think it's come back to me. I didn't recognize your name. Macleod.'

'It was my mother's name. It's mine now.'

'And your father's was . . . ?'

She hesitated. 'Osweken.'

Of course. Henri Osweken, wasn't it. 'And he has died?'

'Quite a time ago. But I lost touch with everybody up there so I didn't find out until recently.'

'And how did you get my address?'

'That was easy. I recognized your name in the yellow pages.'

'Well, Rachelle, why didn't you just write to the police up there, or the priest, or the municipality? They'd be able to tell you a lot more than I can and for free. Or why don't you go back for a visit?'

'I can't do any of that.'

'May I ask why not?'

'No. But I have good reasons. Mr Levine, I never want to see that place again.' Something to do with the murders? he wondered. He waited for her to continue. 'Some land at Roseau Lake is for sale. I saw it advertised in the newspaper. I got someone to ask about it for me and the realtor told him the previous owner died. That's how I found out. But I don't want anyone up there to know I've been asking about it.'

'I see. Who is the realtor?'

She named a well-known city real-estate company and added, 'But it's Arnie Anstalt who's selling the land.'

Anstalt? The name struck a faint chord. 'You say you need money. You're not being blackmailed or threatened or anything, are you?'

She was taken aback by the question and frowned. 'You think because I take my clothes off in a dump like this I must be into all kinds of trash? It's not like it seems, Mr Levine. I know a few girls that do this too and some of them are happily married, just having trouble making ends meet like I am.' She paused and added emphatically, 'Stripping is where it ends.'

'I'm sorry. I didn't mean to offend you.'

She smiled again and continued, 'The pay isn't great but I can keep the money they throw on the stage. It gives me enough to live on and plenty of time off. But I'm still building up a lot of debts. If there is any money from my father, I could maybe stop doing this.'

'What sort of debts are they?'

'My student loans.'

'Student loans?'

'I dropped out of school when I was fifteen, but later on I went back.'

'And now you're at university?'

Rachelle nodded. 'Art school. Finals pretty soon. I'd like to study in Europe. If I could afford it or get a scholarship or something. But I want to get rid of the debt first.'

'Well, Rachelle,' he began, then hesitated. Hold on there, Levine, he thought, trying to stop himself and failing again. 'Well, Rachelle, how would it be if I had a quick look to see what I can find out for you? Just a couple of simple enquiries ought to clear it up one way or the other. If there is anything though, getting hold of it might be more complicated and time-consuming. And there'll be a charge for any work I do for you. I have to make ends meet too.'

'I thought there would be. But no charge if there's nothing there? I really can't afford it.'

He was about to say there'd be a charge either way. Then, damn it, he thought to himself, once a sucker . . . 'Okay.'

She looked at him with astonishment. 'Thank you, Mr Levine.'

* * *

Claudine strolled briskly through the woods carrying a basket on her arm. The sap run was coming to an end. On the rising slopes where the sugar sunshine was strongest, the old snow had melted enough for brown patches of earth to appear between the trees. The yellow morning light glared on the undersides of the branches and on the straight brown trunks of the maples. Sparkling droplets quivered briefly on the ends of the spiles before falling into the collecting buckets. There was no path but she followed the lines of slushy tracks made by the big sled. She knew Lucien would be tired. He still liked to sit all night among the silent trees to boil the sap, tending it carefully with a branch so it didn't bubble over. In the beginning she often kept him company. Now the long cold nights were too much for her, though each day of the brief season she cooked breakfast for him in the sugar shack. Lucien nodded sleepily beside the big cauldron and woke up when Claudine kissed the top of his hat. The fire was low and she saw the sap was nicely reduced. She went on a few yards further towards the shack. Stamping her feet to remove the snow before going in, she was aware of a shuffling noise inside. She looked down. There was a small footprint, like a child's, in the snow by the door.

Claudine entered cautiously, leaving the door open. When her eyes adjusted to the dimness she saw that the items of food she kept there during the sugar off, butter and bread and the ketchup bottle and the cookie jar, had been disturbed. She looked into the corners of the room. There, crouching in the shadows on the other side of the table, she saw a figure. She moved towards it. It drew back. In the corner was a boy of about eleven or twelve with dark hair and dark eyes. Claudine was struck by the look in those eyes, a look of wild terror and fury and desperation and pain. It reminded her of a lynx she'd once seen, its leg caught in the jaws of Zack's trap, struggling to pull itself free. The boy's hand was bloody. Instinctively Claudine began to move towards the child. Immediately he brandished a knife. She stopped. The angry frightened eyes of the boy looked back at her. The cookie jar was open beside him on the floor. There were crumbs on his face, and there was something familiar about that face. More in the hope of calming him than in the expectation of being right she smiled at him. 'Bobby?' she said gently.

A hint of curiosity flickered through the fear. Yes. It was him.

'It's me, Claudine. You remember? I used to visit Grand'-mère when you were little.'

The fear seemed to abate slightly.

'Are you hungry?' she asked. He continued to stare silently at her. 'Would you like some breakfast?' He did not respond. 'Stay and eat with me. You'll be safe here.'

The boy seemed to calm a little. 'You've hurt your hand,' she said. 'Can I take a look at it?' Claudine dared not move closer, and the boy simply stared.

'Will you come out of the corner, Bobby? Come and sit

on a chair by the table here and I'll fix you some breakfast. I promise no one will hurt you.'

He stayed where he was, holding the knife ready between them. Claudine moved slowly towards the stove. Always moving deliberately she stoked it up and put the bacon on to fry. She added slices of bread to the pan and made coffee. Out of the corner of her eye she watched Bobby carefully. He was thin and dirty. He seemed flushed, with dark shadows under his eyes, and once he seemed to drift off to sleep. She moved slightly nearer, hoping to take away the weapon, but he woke immediately and brandished the knife at her again.

She tried to calm him by talking as she worked. 'We haven't seen you for a long time, Bobby. When did you get back here?' He was silent. 'Does anyone know you're here?' Again, nothing but silence. Claudine began to feel more and more alarmed. 'Where are you staying, Bobby?' No reply. She looked at him and asked, 'Grand'mère's place?' He stared back and the look of desperation in his face gave it away. He'd been living for who knows how long in Grand'mère's derelict cabin. What had he been living on? To look at him, nothing. Bobby must have run away from wherever he was supposed to be. He would not speak. She remembered him as a lively engaging child, difficult to control but not at all difficult to talk to. Claudine turned the eggs over once and put them onto a plate. 'Here you are, young man,' she said as though nothing at all was unusual, 'I'll put it on the table here for you. Would you like a glass of milk?'

Bobby looked at the food and slowly came out of the corner. Suddenly he dashed past her and straight into Lucien who filled the open doorway.

'What's this, Claudine?' he said grabbing the boy and taking the knife from him.

Claudine gave a long sigh of relief. 'It's Bobby Osweken, Lucien.' She still tried to sound as though everything was as it should be. 'The clever boy has found his way back to Sugarmilk Falls. I promised him he'd be safe here with us.'

Lucien relaxed his hold on the boy. Bobby stood between them, eyeing them suspiciously. His breathing was shallow, his face feverish. Cautiously, gently Claudine placed her hand on his forehead. 'I think he's quite sick, Lucien. He's hurt his hand too.' She bent down so her face was level with the child's. 'Don't worry, Bobby. We'll get you well again.'

*

Father Souris looked at the silent listless child who sat in Claudine's kitchen darting wild looks at everything and everyone. He was clean and pale and seemed less weak.

'He's a little better today, Matt. His hand has healed up nicely too.' Claudine smiled encouragingly at the boy and turned back to the priest. 'He's said hardly a word since we found him, but he's stopped running away.'

'Hello, Bobby. Remember me? Matt Souris?' He said this whenever he came to see the boy, who always stared back at him suspiciously but gave no sign of recognition. He sighed. 'Today I've brought some people with me who'd like to meet you.'

The boy did not respond. Outside the open window the sun shone brightly. Birds sang in the budding treetops and Lucien's dog barked and rolled over on the grass. Once Bobby told Marina even the stones were alive. Now he sat in the corner by the stove as though his spirit was dead. Father Souris sighed sadly. 'Bobby,' he said indicating a girl and an older man, 'I'd like you to meet Donna here, and this is Karl. He's a kind of doctor. He thinks you might like to hear what we've got in mind for you.'

'Hi, young man,' said Karl gently. 'We've come a long way to see you.'

The boy looked suspiciously at him.

'Hello, Bobby,' said Donna. She was a girl of about fifteen with long black hair and dark eyes and high cheekbones. The child stared at her without a flicker of interest.

'Let's have some milk,' said Claudine. 'I've just baked some maple-sugar cookies. They're his favourite.'

Donna sat down next to the child and poured out a glass of milk for him. She passed the plate of cookies. Mechanically he reached for one. Karl observed them closely.

When Father Souris heard that Bobby was back his immediate thought was to hand him over to Frank Martello. But Lucien said no, he and Claudine could have done that themselves. The boy wasn't well. They thought the priest might be able to come up with a better idea. He'd gone along to see Bobby for himself and what he saw worried him. The child seemed to be deeply disturbed.

Now he listened as Donna talked gently. After a while Bobby's attention seemed to engage and he looked up at her. Donna paused for a moment to let his eyes wander over her face. 'I'm a Mohawk,' she said, 'but there are one or two Ojibwa where I live. There's lots of children there, not just Indians. It's a really great place and we thought maybe you'd like to come and live with us for a while, Bobby. It's a place that will make you better. It's in the city but all summer we camp out in the bush. Would you like that? I was sick too when I went to live there. It has people who can heal you.'

The boy watched her resentfully while she spoke and continued to gaze at her when she stopped. 'Fuck off, cunt,' he said suddenly. Then his eyes glazed again and he stared past Donna into nothing.

Karl nodded. 'That's just fine, Bobby,' he said as though nothing unusual had occurred, 'you don't need to worry about anything anymore. You can come and stay with us just as long as you want. You can take all the time you need.' He turned to the priest. 'Bobby can join us as soon as you like.'

*

Shortly after the arrangements were put into place, Bobby took Claudine's largest kitchen knife and ran away. Claudine was in tears. 'We are responsible for this, Lucien. All of us. That disaster called Bobby Osweken is our fault. We have to find him. We have to sort this out.' Lucien tried to calm her down. 'Tell Matt to try Grand'mère's place,' she wept.

Father Souris walked along the path to the derelict cabin. Sunlight flooded the woods and chipmunks scuttled among the dry leaves on the ground. The door stood ajar and he entered. The boy sat quietly on a bunk by the wall, as though he was waiting. 'Grand'mère's gone,' the priest said. 'She can't come back.'

Bobby stared blankly, a damaged child, alone in a decaying cabin in the vast maple wilderness that he supposed the old medicine woman would say was all his.

The priest held out his hand. 'Come with me back to the Armands. We're all looking after you now.'

* * *

'Rachelle.' James Levine motioned her into the chair on the other side of his desk. 'I've been able to find out a few things you might be interested in,' he said.

A new buff-coloured folder labelled 'Macleod, Rachelle' lay on the desk between them. She looked at him expectantly. 'Does that mean there is something for me?' she asked.

'Not exactly. Not yet at any rate.' He opened the folder. There was not much in it, a few letters only. 'First of all, your father, Henri Osweken, doesn't appear to have made a will, not one that can be traced, anyway.' Her smile faded. 'And from what I can discover, he was in a pretty destitute condition by the time he died.'

'How did you find this out, Mr Levine?'

'Enquiries were made. The reeve, a man called Edouard Perriault, was very helpful.' The lawyer paused and looked at her. 'He filled me in on a lot of the background too, Rachelle.' She stared back and he saw the hurt in her eyes. 'There's no need to be concerned. He doesn't know who my client is. Nobody needs to know that for the time being.' He waited for her to recover her composure before adding, 'And people call me Jim.'

She smiled a little and he continued, 'So although it looks as though there isn't anything, there is the question of your father's hotel. Do you know if he owned that piece of land?'

Rachelle shrugged. 'I guess so. There were papers about land.'

'Did you ever see any?'

She nodded. 'Sure, when I was small I saw them once or twice. My mother saved them from the fire but she wanted to save their money.'

Jim Levine hesitated. He looked at her intently and asked, 'When did you first see them, Rachelle?'

'I don't know. I think they were always around somewhere. Grand'mère always had them. Henri looked after them for her.'

'Your grandmother always had them,' he repeated, 'and you saw them with your own eyes.'

'She wasn't my grandmother really.' Rachelle sighed sadly. 'Grand'mère was everybody's grandmother. Even Jacques, he was really old too, he used to call her Grand'mère. Yeah, I remember there were some old papers.'

'Did anyone ever say who owned the land?'

'It wasn't talked about much, not an issue, I guess. Dad once told me it was all Ojibwa land and the papers were just to make sure it stayed that way. That was after Mom died.'

He hesitated again before asking her, 'Do you have any idea where the papers might be now?'

'Mr Levine, Jim, I know what happened up there. It was on TV. And no, I don't know where those papers could be. Why? Are they valuable?'

'Maybe. It depends on what kind of papers they are. Now, the land at Roseau Lake. I've checked it out, not that there is much to find, but Arnold Anstalt's entitlement to sell it seems questionable at least.'

Rachelle looked confused. 'Do you mean it isn't his to sell?'

'Not quite. I think he might have trouble proving it was, that's all. But that doesn't necessarily mean it was your father's and now it's yours. All I'm saying is you could challenge his right to sell it. I could handle all that sort of thing for you, Rachelle.'

'I already told you I can only pay you if I get something out of this.'

'I know. And that's what we agreed. I would only send you a bill when you had enough money to be able to pay it.'

Rachelle looked at him quizzically. 'Why are you so interested in all this, Mr. Levine . . . Jim?'

He closed the folder and looked out of the window. 'I'm what you might call a jobbing kind of lawyer, Rachelle. Land claims are something I'm not too familiar with at the present time, but it's an area I'd like to get into. I'll have to do quite a bit of homework on this myself.' He paused. 'From what I've been able to find out, and as I told you it isn't nearly enough to go on, the land around Roseau Lake could still be Crown land. That means only the government is entitled to sell it or any rights over it. Maybe that's already happened in the past. Sometimes the records can be difficult to trace.

'Or just maybe the land wasn't included as part of any treaty settlement at all. If it is still unsurrendered, then title to it could still be with the relevant First Nation. Either way it could be the subject of a sizeable land-claim action. There could be some hefty compensation payments at the end if it, and that's when I'd send you my hefty account.' He looked a little sheepishly at Rachelle.

'And I lost a very expensive watch in a poker game at your father's hotel. That still rankles.'

He became businesslike again. 'We can start by entering cautions on the Land Register – that's a bit of legal formality whereby you indicate you are claiming rights in the land. It would mean the land can't be sold or mined or de-timbered, no dealings in it at all while the cautions are in place. It should bring Mr Anstalt's scheme to at least a temporary halt. It will give us, give me, time to look into it more thoroughly.'

'Who is going to pay you while you do all this homework, Jim?'

He smiled encouragingly. 'This is a long-term thing, Rachelle. There might be others who have rights, other Oswekens for example. Land claims are complicated. They can take years to settle. But I have plenty of other clients who'll keep me fed and watered along the way. Now, what do you say?'

She thought for a moment and gave a little sigh of disappointment. 'I hoped there might be some better news so I could maybe go to Europe. Something worth panning through the past for.'

Rachelle hesitated again and then smiled back at him. 'Okay. I guess I'm a real client now. We ought to shake hands. And I owe you this.' She handed him a quarter. 'That's one debt paid. Maybe you threw it at me on the stage.'

15

Sergeant Martello laced his fingers behind his head and leaned back in the chair. The wine had warmed and relaxed him. He gazed at the ceiling, along the parallel joins in the planking, and then out of the window where the bright blue moonlight cast tangled tree shadows across the snow. What was Matt so worried about? he asked himself again. And what had he himself not thought of that didn't line up? The schoolteacher had been brutally murdered and it looked like the Oswekens did it. They were shot by Grand'mère, who then hanged herself. That had been the all too easy conclusion. Or, far less likely though still plausible, they were killed out of revenge by Zack Guillem. Senior Constable Martello had intervened on the quiet, a fact which nobody, not even Elviana, knew anything about, and Zack got away. Case solved, if not resolved. The coroner left an open verdict, but it all held together, just so long as nobody came up with anything new. So far nobody had.

In the dead of night he'd let Zack go. He'd been a little surprised at himself, but only a little. Looking back, it still seemed the right thing to do even if it was totally out of line with the operation of the law in a murder investigation. Sergeant Martello sighed. If he'd been a city cop it would never have occurred to him to release Zack. But he was a solitary law enforcer isolated in the wilderness and it had made him independent. He'd gotten used to handling things by himself. He found the law could sometimes be inconvenient and when it was he didn't always go by the book.

So why had he let Zack go? For a start that Wawa detective got up his nose. He wasn't really interested in the truth, just went for the quickest result and headed back to his wife and fellow officers. That was bad police work, thought Frank Martello, though it had its upside. Neil Reilly put a good word for him in the report and soon afterwards Senior Constable Martello was made Sergeant.

But the real reason he'd intervened was because he had principles. Looking back he realized he'd always had them; that's why he joined the force in the first place. Not that they stood out or in the way on a regular basis. Day to day he decided things by himself and he guessed the principles were just below the surface, an unconscious part of making decisions. On his own, he wasn't even aware of them. But when he and that Wawa detective locked Zack up for no better reason than he seemed an obvious suspect and Neil Reilly wanted to be sure of a quick result, the principles suddenly got in the way. Sergeant Martello had to admit, even now, that Zack did fit the arithmetic. But at the time it felt all wrong.

What exactly hadn't felt right? he asked himself. It was not that he was particularly fond of Zack. He'd never had much to do with him. He supposed he liked him but it was in the same way as he liked the trees and the lakes and the hills. He still couldn't put his finger on anything except instinct: murdering the Oswekens like that was just not something Zack would do.

When Frank Martello was a young police recruit he'd heard a lot about natural justice. Fairness. The idea that there is a natural sense of what is right and what is wrong common to all mankind. Anything against common right and reason was against natural justice, he was told. A bit romantic maybe, though Elviana had given him such a smile when he tried to explain it to her. After a few years in the wild Sugarmilk country he began to think that the savage balancing of the natural world is also just. It hinted at a sublime kind of justice he could barely imagine. Natural justice, natural law, the balance of nature, common right and reason were all connected in his head with an ideal of fairness, and putting Zack in the cell had seemed to him about as unfair and unnatural as it could be. So he let him go. Letting a murder suspect go might look like a very odd thing for a policeman to do, but he'd been true to his principles.

Sergeant Martello went over the events again in his mind, working backwards this time and looking at them from the angle of who might have wanted what kept quiet, back then and since. He started with himself. After all he certainly didn't want the fact that he'd expedited Zack's disappearance to come out. His reputation, his career, and especially his imminent pension would be in ruins if it did. Nobody knew about it though, except Zack and he wasn't likely to run at the mouth. But if Zack didn't have anything to do with the killings, who was responsible for the Osweken massacre? There was Grand'mère herself, of course. Gone crazy on one of her binges. Even at the time he thought it looked more like some sort of vendetta, but he hadn't wanted to believe that what he was hearing on the party lines could lead to anything like that. All that talk about doing something about it before it happened again had been quite alarming, though. So who might have taken the law into their own hands if it wasn't Zack? Afterwards Sugarmilk Falls seemed to close ranks and closed they stayed ever since. It reminded him of stories his father told him about life back in the old country. What about Father Souris, then? He seemed so worried tonight and he had found the schoolteacher's body. But Matt couldn't be involved. No way. Though there had been an air of everyone's nerves stretched to breaking point, including Matt's, around the time Bobby Osweken turned up again.

*

It was one night during a run of break-ins, where money, liquor and gasoline went missing, that the policeman woke to the sound of a window, this very window, being smashed. He grabbed his gun, hurried downstairs and fired at a movement in the shadows. He heard a gasp of pain but by the time he switched on the light there was nothing, just a little blood on the windowledge. He rushed outside. The midnight street was dark, empty and silent.

A few days later a very concerned Father Souris came to see him. 'It's Bobby,' he said. 'He's with the Armands. They found him in a real bad way hiding in their sugar shack.' The priest's face was troubled. 'It seems the boy's been living up at Grand'mère's old place. He isn't well. They've asked me to do what I can for him.' He hesitated. 'This is a bad situation, Frank.'

When he did not say more Sergeant Martello asked, 'How unwell is he, exactly?'

'He's hurt his hand, but Claudine is seeing to that.' He paused again and shook his head in dismay. 'I'm no expert as you know, but I've done a bit of reading on the subject and from what I've seen of the boy I'd say he is very disturbed, clinically disturbed.'

The policeman waited for him to explain. Matt continued, 'He won't talk. He can be quite violent. He steals from Claudine. He tried to set fire to his room. The Armands are doing their best but it needs a more permanent solution, and soon, too, or he'll end up in trouble again and it'll be too late.'

'It might be too late already. There's been a bit of trouble.' He indicated the boarded-up window. 'What have you got in mind?'

'I guessed as much.' Father Souris sighed. 'However, there's a place I know about that treats emotionally disturbed kids. I'd like to see if they'll take him. It would be a lot better for everybody in the long run.'

Sergeant Martello drummed his fingers on the desk while he considered the situation. 'Well, Matt, it's like this, but only for the time being. So far as my blind eye can see, I don't know that it's Bobby himself who's done anything to warrant me picking him up. How's his hand? Grazed by a bullet, wasn't it, trying to break in? Good thing it wasn't reported.'

'A bullet?' Matt asked. 'It was just a bad graze, far as I know.'

The policeman smiled. 'So long as he doesn't make trouble, you do what you think is best. My deaf ear hasn't heard any reports yet that he's missing.'

'Thanks, Frank. I'll get onto it right away.'

'Just make sure he stays out of mischief in the meantime. Remember I can't stay deaf and blind indefinitely.'

*

The wine made Sergeant Martello's mouth feel dry. He remembered the way they all fell over themselves to help, even to the point of paying for years of treatment in a psychiatric clinic for kids. Not just Matt, but the Anstalts, the Jansens, Sammy Dutoit, the Perriaults of course to give it credibility, and the Armands, especially Claudine. You'd think Bobby was her own flesh and blood the way that woman carried on at the time. 'It's our fault,' she was heard to say more than once. 'We are responsible for this. We have to fix it somehow.' No one argued with her. Father Souris was the one who sorted it out. Why? Was it no more than priestly duty on his part? Or might he have had his own reasons? Why might he be concerned to keep the Osweken file closed? What could he be afraid of there? If who really did it came to light how could that affect him?

Sergeant Martello went over the interviews again in his mind. He recalled that at one point the Wawa detective said in passing maybe the Oswekens didn't kill the schoolteacher and maybe Zack had something to do with it. Unlikely, he'd said. A wild man from the woods, the detective countered. Yes, but not a brutal killer, he'd replied. How about jealous rage, then? Neil Reilly suggested, but he was grasping at straws in the wind. It seemed too improbable at the time, especially with the party lines and the *Gazette* blasting down their ears.

Now Sergeant Martello lined them up again. Miss

Grochowska. Jealous rage. Zack Guillem. It still didn't fit. Who was there to be jealous of? Who else had his eye on that pretty schoolteacher? Plenty in a casual sort of way, and there had been a little rumour about Matt Souris. Elviana noticed something too. After Miss Grochowska was dead Zack seemed just a deeply bereaved man, no more, no less. Jealous rage and Zack. It didn't fit.

Who, then? For the sake of completeness, he told himself though the idea was absurd, he tried Matt in the role of the murderer. They had questioned him several times about the schoolteacher. Always helpful, always calm, sympathetic, like you'd expect a Catholic priest to be. He was always her first port of call, too. Was there something going on between them after all? And when Zack stepped in, was the priest jealous? With an unbearable jealousy he couldn't talk to anyone about, because he was who he was? Did Matt kill her while the balance of his mind was disturbed? And then stand by and let the Oswekens take the blame? And the consequences? Could that be the reason for his deep concern to do something for Bobby? The possibility seemed altogether far-fetched.

He remembered the interviews clearly. The priest was utterly shocked. He said, 'I can't believe she was murdered, Frank.' Maybe she wasn't, the policeman thought again. They had a burned corpse on their hands, but how the corpse had died was never proved. But then there was the way the body was mutilated. The idea that Mathieu Souris could have anything to do with that was grotesque. And ridiculous.

Was all this wine-induced contemplation of a dead file leading anywhere? Sergeant Martello wondered. He looked out at the tangled shadows of the maple branches on the moonlit snow and yawned. There were those papers too, he thought. Why would Matt lie about those? Maybe it wasn't a lie. Maybe he had got rid of them long ago. Maybe it just seemed like a lie because Matt seemed so unaccountably nervous. Why would he be so nervous, then? What did he think Lucien and the others could say? The names of who really killed the Oswekens if it wasn't Grand'mère? When they'd never done that in twenty years? And to a complete stranger too? It seemed so unlikely as to be preposterous. Still, the policeman reckoned there'd be one or two who had a desperate need to get it off their chest. Claudine, maybe? Mostly, though, they wanted to keep it under wraps. If someone did break ranks and talk it could destroy everything they had. It would bring the whole matter out into the open again. He thought about what that could mean for a moment. Maybe Matt was right to be worried. There would be questions asked about how Miss Grochowska died and who was responsible. There would also be questions about whether the police investigation had been as thorough as it should have been. Questions too about how Zack got away so easily.

Of course Matt still had those papers, Sergeant Martello told himself again. And for some reason he was scared. Maybe there was a lot more to them than a few expired claim assignments. Maybe there had been a load of land papers in that leather pouch Matt dug out of his desk drawer. Maybe Matt himself put the *Gazette* in there. Maybe Miss Grochowska really had won all the land. And if Matt had kept those papers hidden away it meant he could well be involved in the death of the schoolteacher.

Sergeant Martello sat up. Suddenly his retirement, his pension, his hard-worked-for carefree future with Elviana on the Florida beach felt threatened. Maybe he should drive over to the Armand place to see what exactly was going on there. He looked at his watch. It was too late. Anything that was going to be said would have been aired by the time he made his way over there through the snow. He thought he could rely on them all sticking to the story. They had far too much to lose to start naming names, especially to someone they hardly knew. Interesting, the policeman thought, how this likeable stranger had managed to worm her way so far into everyone's confidence that they were prepared to talk about it at all. Of course Lucien liked to sit around the fire on a winter's night telling tales to anyone who'd listen. But unguarded talk can be dangerous. If this persistent newcomer turned out to be more than she appeared, she might hear things that weren't intended and make some very unwelcome connections. She has to be encouraged to leave here as soon as possible, Sergeant Martello decided, before she can make trouble. He would have another word with Father Souris. The last thing he wanted was for the stranger to worm her way into getting a look at those papers.

16

Father Souris shivered and looked at the clock again. Ten minutes to midnight, perfectly synchronized with atomic vibrations. He watched the snowflakes swirl in the blackness outside the window and thought about all the words set loose over at the Armand place. Revelations? Confessions? Accusations? Explanations? Lies? He hadn't wanted to join in what he privately called their damned group-therapy session. Maybe that was a mistake, he thought now. He knew he'd have to do something at last, whatever came out of it, and what came out of it was beyond his control. For now he would have to bide his time. Kill time. Can time be killed? he asked himself in passing. He knew he wouldn't be able to sleep. He'd wait here in the quiet of his study, chewing his fingers. It was the best place to keep himself together while a million snowflakes pressed against the windowpanes and a million atoms whirled in the void. He could almost feel the world around him shifting on its axis. All because of words and what were they except vibrations in the air?

So why had he never spoken out? Father Souris had asked himself this question a million times and he gave himself the usual reply. No one ever talked about those things. Until tonight, that is. Why, though, had he never admitted to himself his part in the truth? He never had to. And first you had to decide what the truth was. That seemed reasonable enough, he thought, or was it only another way of evading the question? It wasn't that difficult to find an answer, and it certainly wasn't silence. He wondered, as he sometimes did, what or who had possessed him to keep his lips so tightly sealed? That's too easy, he reminded himself again. It was easier at the time, almost impossible not to be swept along on the whirlwind, to let the blame fall where it did and leave it lying there. It was easier still to offload the blame onto someone who was dead and convince himself he wasn't responsible for his omissions to speak. He was in far too deep for anything else now. But he'd never yet found an answer acceptable to his secret self, an answer that would justify what he'd done. Anyway, he wasn't the only one involved.

At first he did not have to try very hard to make himself believe it was not his fault. It was just like making any act of faith, he told himself, and repeated over and over he was not to blame. Marina came to him. She had a gun. She was unreasonable. Later he would tell himself she was deranged. There'd been an argument, a struggle. The gun fired. She was dead. It was a terrible, terrible accident. No, it was not his fault. He had not killed her. Not his fault, not his fault, not his most grievous fault, but entirely hers for being so reckless. She might have killed him. It was an act of self-defence.

So far, so good, he thought. But more questions scuffled to be asked. Why hadn't he immediately picked up the telephone and asked Frank Martello or even Angela Norton to come over? Maybe because he'd panicked? Father Souris went over the scene again. Marina was pointing a gun at him. He recognized the Smith & Wesson revolver. The barrel was no more than three feet away from his heart. Her hand trembled. He saw his opportunity and tried to knock it from her hand. A shot rang out. He remembered how strong she seemed as he struggled to take it from her. Another shot, then suddenly no more resistance. She slumped forward into his arms and slid down onto the rug. Gently he helped her down. 'Marina?' he whispered hoarsely. Nothing, only reverberations from the bullets in his brain. He felt for the pulse in her neck. There was none. Had he panicked then? Perhaps. He had not behaved normally, but it wasn't a normal situation. How are you supposed to act in a situation like that?

Marina lay absolutely still at his feet. She was dead. Really dead this time. What should he do next? Call Frank, of course. Or maybe not, it could be awkward. How would he explain this away convincingly? Frank had asked him once if there was anything going on between himself and the schoolteacher. He'd probably heard that bit of gossip too. The policeman in him might suspect this was the result of a jealous rage. Better to get her out of here, get rid of her altogether, give himself time to think of an explanation or just give himself time. And he'd better do it right away before the blood went everywhere. Thankfully she'd kept her coat on – well, she had to with his gun in her pocket. Funny how he never noticed it was missing. She must have taken it some time ago, before she stopped seeing him. Father Souris brought towels to absorb the bleeding and wrapped her in the rug. He lifted her. She seemed so light, so insubstantial for one who weighed so heavily on his mind and heart.

What should he do now? He'd have to make her disappear, for now or for good. But how? And what about the bullet, his towels, his rug? What else might she have with her that would point at him? And that was when it came over him; sparks flashed in his brain. He could pinpoint it almost exactly. He recognized it immediately from long, long ago, from the chaos of the Normandy beach, from the lawlessness of the Paris street. All these years it had lain dormant, all but forgotten like his army revolver, and suddenly it was here, clear, cold, calculating, decisive. When he first met it he was obeying orders on a battlefield, true, but there are all kinds of chaos to survive, all kinds of orders to interpret. Hurry now, it's time to make up your mind, to act.

The fingers moved on the atomic clock. He always needed to give himself more time. Particles of time colliding in space. Once it was believed the only real things in the universe are the eternal atoms and the empty space in which they move. Everything is nothing but effect as the atoms whirl and collide in the emptiness and come together in an infinity of combinations and configurations. Life and death and time itself are no more than this. Eternity is nothing but the atoms of the soul sparking in the void. Marina hadn't agreed, of course. She'd pointed out that there are other forces at work, like gravity and electromagnetism. There was space-time too. And don't forget your free will, Matt, she added with a little laugh. But he was explaining an ancient theory that constructed the soul out of smooth round delicate atoms, a little like caesium atoms he thought now, and as material as any others in the universe. According to St Augustine himself, who was an authority on souls, it is where the true person resides. So what chance configuration of soul atoms moved Father Souris to do what he did? Did he have any choice at all? At the time it felt almost mechanical.

*

In the dawn greyness he looked at what he'd done and was appalled. The mutilated corpse still smouldered on the dying embers. Nearby the river rushed towards the falls. It had been a very difficult thing to do, a great deal harder than he expected. What now? Another imperative glowed in the exhausted blackness of his brain. Yes, it was his turn. He went to the edge of the river. In the half light the water raced past, black, shiny, foaming, rearing over the rocks, roaring towards the precipice. He threw the gun and the knife far into the river and waited. Go on, he told himself. After what he'd just done it was the only way left. Only annihilation remained. But what had he done that required his own annihilation? He turned around and looked back at what was left of Marina, what was left of her funeral pyre. He remembered only fragments. He had killed her, but wasn't that an accident? He must have brought her here, after Mass he thought though he couldn't recall it clearly. Did anyone see him? Was he in a state of panic? He must have got together enough wood, damp wood too. How had he done that? How did he get the fire going? Oh, yes, the can of gasoline. How had he kept it burning so long? He'd seen his hands covered with blood. He'd only wanted to remove all evidence of the shooting. Maybe the bullet could be traced back to him. Get rid of the bullet. Destroy the body. The first bullet penetrated his bookcase. Get rid of the damaged books. He'd rearranged them on the shelf to cover up the splintered wood behind them. It was soft, the hole small. He smoothed it with his letter opener. You wouldn't see it now unless you were looking for that kind of a hole. The second bullet . . . His mind refused to go there again but he'd gotten rid of that one too.

Father Souris bent over by the side of the river and retched. It was the only way left, he could see the logic of that. He looked into the black water rushing past the rocks, at the yellow leaves swirling and tumbling on the vortices, at the mercy of the turbulence, as he was. He stood up. Go on, it won't take long, the water will sweep you over the falls and that will be it. Oblivion. He stepped into the icy river. It was waist-deep, even by the shore, and the current immediately caught hold of him. He slipped. Coldness clamped his heart and his lungs. He could not breathe. His feet slid on the rocky bottom, the racing water pulled his head into its cold suffocating blackness. He struggled, resisted, came up for air. Frantically he fought the current and tried and failed and tried again to clamber up the bank. At last he lay by the river's edge, panting, shaking uncontrollably, as cold as stone. He wasn't able to drown himself. Maybe he was already dead. After a while he got up. Disgusted at his own cowardice he turned away from what he'd done. He picked up the empty gasoline can and went home, determined to exorcize everything from his mind.

*

The morning sunlight flickered through the yellow leaves still clinging to the maple trees as Father Souris returned from Mass. It filled his study with a bright golden glow. He inspected the room carefully again. Everything was in its place, books on the shelves, arranged a little differently but who was going to notice that? Rugs on the floor, a different one, not that different, but who was going to notice if even the housekeeper hadn't? He sat down behind his desk and placed the tips of his fingers together. It's been a few days so how do you feel now? he dared to ask himself. He didn't feel anything today except surprisingly calm. And more surprising still, his head was clearer. Everything seemed so much less messy. The confusion, the frustration, the anger and that horrible debilitating jealousy were gone. She was gone too and it was not his fault. He had loved her. Everything that happened to her was her own doing. Now it looked as though his life might be about to resume its tranquil path at last. Life would be like it was before she came to Sugarmilk Falls.

The golden glow in the study began to dim. He had loved her, done his best for her, but she turned on him. He threw the gun into the river. He disposed of the body as well as he could. It would be unrecognizable. Everything was burned, destroyed. There was nothing left up there or in his car or here at the presbytery that might point the finger at him. He sighed. But what about Zack Guillem? Zack was clever. Would he work it out? And now Miss Grochowska had been reported missing. That would get a lot of police attention. Maybe he should check things over again, just to make absolutely sure? Father Souris looked out through the window. The sky was becoming overcast. It might rain, but he'd take a walk along the old portage.

*

Tall trees grew thickly on either side of the rising trail. The path was gloomy and narrow, scarcely wide enough in places for two to walk abreast. A light drizzle began to fall, so fine it seemed to hover in the air. Several days had passed and much to his surprise nothing had happened yet. What had he done since? The first thing he did on his return was have a hot bath. Then he said morning Mass, as he did every day. He'd observed his daily offices, gone to bed early and slept, long, deep, dreamlessly. Was it the sleep of the damned? he'd wondered when he awoke. Was he damned? he wondered now as he walked along. Did he still believe in all that stuff? How could he do what he had if he did? How could he continue with his daily routines as though nothing had happened if he did? But a fragment of memory switched itself on in his brain and for a moment he felt himself fighting fiercely to escape from the clutches of the river. Maybe it was because he wasn't yet ready to face eternal damnation, he thought. If so, he must still believe.

But maybe he was wrong. What if all that Paris café talk after the war was right? Life is random. A man has choices. A man is the only judge of his actions. A man is responsible only to himself. Through the trees Father Souris caught occasional silver flashes of the river. Maybe that's why he fought so hard to get out of it, because deep down he believed this life is all there is and he'd take his chances in it while he could. There was nothing else in the universe for the random transient configuration of atoms that made up Mathieu Souris, only the void.

He walked on, alone among the dark looming trees. The farther he went, the louder the roar of the waterfalls became. The rush of the river, the roar of the falls, like the rush and roar of the Paris traffic after he'd given his explanation to the military police and rushed away, his legs trembling, his heart racing. He'd needed desperately to sit down, to let the surging wave crash over him. At the church of St-Germain-des-Prés he had stopped, unable to go on.

Inside, the abbey was dim and still. Candles flickered in front of the stony saints, the smell of incense and beeswax lingered on the stony air. He sat down and let the wave submerge him. Drown him. When it passed he knelt and tried to pray. Abruptly he left, his footsteps echoing through the painted pillars, golds, crimsons, dull dark greens and blues, like gloomy autumn woods he remembered thinking at the time. He threw the gun into the Seine. He threw off a great weight with it, and back in his room at the Hôtel Meurice he was overwhelmed by a sense of relief. Would he feel as relieved now?

She was still there. Had he imagined that somehow she wouldn't be? The fire was cold. The body lying there, contorted, blackened, seemed hardly human at all. Leaves fell all around it. A few brown leaves had drifted onto it. He stared at it and was surprised that already he felt as though it had nothing to do with him. He looked around carefully, once, twice, three times. No, there was nothing there that could implicate him in any way. He scrambled along the riverbank and came to the top of the falls. Dark water swirled and raced between the black boulders and dropped suddenly in a storm of glittering spray. How had he managed to escape? He felt the cataract draw him towards the edge, like a magnet on his will. He stepped back, as though another force pulled him. This was not the time, it seemed to say. The falls would be there when he needed them. He would go back now and telephone Senior Constable Martello about the awful discovery he'd made on his morning walk. And strolling home between the gloomy painted trees like he'd once strolled between the painted pillars inside St-Germain-des-Prés, Father Souris felt something like relief.

It was after this that Marina began to interrupt his thoughts, as if she had strolled back with him from that place beside the river above the falls.

I thought you had forgotten all about me, Matt.

He'd looked up from what he was doing to see her sitting in the chair in the corner by the window, like she used to. I'll never forget you, he replied, but she was gone. What did she want to say to him?

Is it so difficult for you, Matt?

Yes, Marina, just tell me what it is.

*

Father Souris listened to the whispering of the snow outside the window. He never could decipher what it was Marina had to tell him and long ago he tried to persuade himself there probably was nothing. It was in his imagination only, due no doubt to his heightened psychological condition at the time which was understandable in the circumstances. Perhaps he'd only ever wanted her forgiveness. He remembered the shrieks for vengeance on the party lines. That should have alerted him. But Marina was mistrusted, a stranger, an outsider here. He thought she was unlikely to inspire a need to avenge her death. Nevertheless he'd preached a sermon on the subject of revenge but said nothing much of any consequence. Marina was dead and it was not his fault. That was enough for him. But then Grand'mère was found hanged, the others shot, and suddenly it was not so easy to avoid the blame. Could he truthfully say to himself he was blameless there? What should he have done? Yes, he should have spoken out but that was insignificant compared to what had happened up at Grand'mère's cabin. The weight of his indecision kept him too impotent to speak, or walk to the top of the falls.

It hadn't stopped there. Father Souris remembered how his hand shook as he held the receiver to his ear. Was it with relief? Or shock? The party line was in full flow. 'He's in jail . . . That no-good bushwhacker . . . Did everyone a favour if you ask me . . . The newspapers are calling it a massacre . . . There's a guy from the *Toronto Star* . . . Wants to know all about the crap game . . .'

He couldn't listen in any longer. He replaced the telephone and tried to write, another feeble attempt to trace Rachelle, but his hands trembled. He couldn't sit still. He began to pace the study, back and forth, back and forth, looking out through the window each time he passed. The sky was low and grey. Minute snow crystals hovered in the air. There has been an arrest, he mused. An arrest. The furore could now die down. And winter was coming. Very soon the portage trail would be hidden under deep white snow. Snow would muffle the accusations, snow would hide the truth. And by the time spring stripped everything bare again, that place would look like it always did after the winter's weight of snow melted away, only the thick sodden layer of last year's matted leaves and broken twigs. The charred ends of the branches would barely catch your eye, unless you were looking for them, and the grass and weeds would soon hide these too. Everything would be as though it had never happened. Like things used to be, before Marina came.

Father Souris passed the window again. A thin layer of white crystals now covered the top of the garden sundial, gathering in the grooves that marked out the hours. The newspapermen would be hurrying to leave now, before they were stranded here by the snow. The TV crew had already gone. They'd all talked to him, asked him a lot of questions, about Marina, about Grand'mère, about everything. He'd been helpful, collected, he'd toned down their more sensational angles on what had taken place. They'd already spoken to anyone who'd talk about this terrible aberration. And now that an arrest had been made they lost no time in hurrying away to chase after the next piece of news.

It was just as Grand'mère had said, he thought. It was as though that crazed man-eating monster, the windigo, was here. It had brought this madness and destruction. He had been possessed by it himself. Snow crystals tinkled against the window, like seeds.

'See, Mathieu, I have a galaxy in my hand.'

The words whispered in his mind. The picture lit up in his brain: a day like this one and Marina stretching her hand out towards him, her glove covered in crystals of snow, each one a tiny star, each one unique, each one quickly dying on the warm black universe of her leather glove and instantly replaced.

'They were like this in Ravensbrück too.'

He'd seen the ice form behind her eyes to freeze out the past again. She quickly brushed it from her hands. It was the only time he ever heard her say the name.

*

Father Souris watched the thick snowflakes whirl and eddy in the blackness outside the window. Now he raised his own hands and inspected them again, a little afraid of what he might see there. But as usual they lied. He saw only hands, the soft scrubbed impotent hands of a man of the cloth. Would she always be with him? he wondered. Would she follow him around forever, whispering things in the reccsses of his brain? If he knew what she had to tell him would she leave him alone? He certainly should have spoken out at the time or since. How had he been able to live with this for so many, many years? Could anyone ever rid him of her now?

The continuum of time had tamed his nightmares and sometimes he even began to see where Marina's place might eventually be in his mental gallery of past loves and acquaintances. But then she would wreck everything with another whisper in his brain and echoes of words he never understood. And the horror of it all would return.

He knew it was the same for everyone. Over the years words that should have been said remained buried under the hardening crust of guilt, but now and then excuses breathed desperately in the darkness of the confessional. 'We had to do something, Father. She was our schoolteacher, after all. We gave our children into her charge. Our anger at what had been done was so unbearably intense. It was righteous anger, too. We took matters into our hands.' The rapid whispers from the other side of the grille stopped. He waited and felt the rapid beating of his own heart.

And another time, 'We did it, Father. Then we simply covered it up. All of us are responsible for what happened up at Grand'mère's cabin. And all of us colluded in what

I suppose is called a conspiracy of silence. It seems such a criminal-sounding phrase for what we did. We are not criminals. It was not some great deliberate deception carefully worked out in every detail to protect one or two or a few. It was a gradual thing, a joining up of seemingly unconnected links, one onto the next, until we found ourselves bound up in a chain of silence. But the effect was the same as if we'd planned it. Guilty ones were never named. We don't even know for certain who they are. Only they themselves know that. We decided not to allocate the guilt but spread it thinly over ourselves. We all took our helping of the blame, all of us together, not one or a few of us in particular. That's how we have tried to live with it, Father. But I can't anymore.'

A gasp. A hesitation. A palpable fear. 'When it was finished, we were stunned by what had been done. It was like waking from a hideous nightmare. We tried to hold on to our righteousness but it seemed a sham. Not one of us would dream of doing such a thing, yet together . . . ? We asked ourselves who was responsible. The hooded ones who put the rope around her neck? Those who pulled it tight? Fired a gun at Ovide? At Betty? Even at the children? We refused to answer the question. We wouldn't be able to bear the awful knowledge that a friend, a neighbour, a husband, ordinary nice people, good people, loved ones, were capable of these atrocities. But that left us with a difficult problem. Blame needs a home, but who could take the blame when we had so diluted it? There was talk that Grand'mère did it and hanged herself. Zack was arrested. We held our breath. And then he dis-appeared. That was a stroke of luck. It was convenient for everyone. It lightened the load on our conscience. And conveniently, thankfully, he has never been found. The story is still that Grand'mère herself was to blame for everything. So you see, Father, it was done out of con-venience, before any real intentions had been formed. We are not evil people. At bottom, we are cowards, no more. But it has to be said there was a feeling no one dared put into words that somehow the Sugarmilk air was cleaner once the likes of Miss Grochowska and the Oswekens and Zack Guillem had gone. It is a terrible thing to confess.'

Another pause, another sharp intake of breath. 'But time does not make it easier. We did it for the best reasons but it weighs on my conscience. Should I tell the police, Father? Please help me. I don't know what to do. I don't know how I can go on. Is it worse to betray a loved one than to cover up the truth? I don't know what the truth is anymore, Father. Is it a mortal sin to protect the one to whom I have been joined by God?'

The whispered words oscillated in the blackness of the confessional. You have confessed your sins to God, Father Souris had said. And for that you are forgiven. Now you must do your penance.

17

Look, said Lucien. Outside the windows the maples stir and begin to stretch across the snow. Wahpun, the east wind, is bringing in the day. Soon the sap will start to rise and the restless sweet-water weather will send our winter stories back to sleep. In the corners of the room the dreamed ones rise and prepare to depart. They grin and they nod. They are content with what has been told.

My friend, it is late. I would say more if I could. I'm just an old sugar-maker but I'm as involved in this as everyone. Now the time has come for you to tell us what really brought you to Sugarmilk Falls. You've said it was the yearly leases you bought to a few of our maple trees. You wanted to see them and touch them, to smell the earth that gives them life, but we guessed it was more than that. You spend so much time here. You try to gain our confidence. And tonight we have told you a lot about the things that happened here. But there are questions you need to answer, such as why, after so long, you are probing so deep. It isn't just for your amusement.

You look at us with your sincere honest face. You are trying to clear up a mystery, you tell us now, an unexplained episode in the affairs of a company you are connected with. A mining expedition that disappeared without trace some thirty years ago. You tried to track down the lawyer but didn't get anywhere, you say. That's all very well, but you must know something else to make you think that we are able to help you. You seem interested in more than just the smell of the land, mon amie. You ask about the documents too. Were they ever found? Charlie Anstalt for one is still looking for them. They are at the bottom of all the problems between him and Suzanne. Were there any to find? You aren't the only one who would like to know.

You have heard enough from us now to know what happened here. We kept it quiet. The best we can say is we did it to keep our close community intact. It was a few years after the Braemar Lodge burned down. Ed and I and others, we persuaded Zack not to tell Frank Martello or anyone else about what he stumbled over on a hunting trip. After all, it was a chance in a million that he did. We put two and two together, as you have. We believed the mining claims were all destroyed in the fire. We counted on the lawyer wanting to keep it quiet too and from what you say he did. And with the plane and the prospectors at the bottom of some inaccessible lake we thought we were safe from any mining boom. No one would ever know what they were doing round here or even that they'd been. Henri never mentioned it, nor did Grand'mère. As far as we were concerned the matter was closed. And then you come here, and ask us too many questions about the schoolteacher. Forgive us if we offend you by suspecting your motives.

It is late. We have told enough of our stories. Indeed,

no one could tell you much more, except Father Souris, though you won't make much progress there. I fear nobody is going to complete the picture for you. You have done well with the spile whittling too, but there are never enough as you'd see if you stayed to lend a hand. It's up to you now. Nothing is ever simple, is it, my friend?

EPILOGUE

Sugarmilk Falls, le 15 février 1993

Father Souris stares at me when I tell him my name. His face is grey, like ash. He is much older, frailer than I imagined.

I make my demand.

He sits down heavily when I tell him Pierre Jaccard is not my father and Thérèse was not my mother. He shakes his head in disbelief and holds his hands out in front of him, to push me away or to cover his face. 'It's not true,' he says over and over. 'It can't be true. Marina would have told me about this.' But he remembers how she always seemed to leave something important unsaid. 'Can it really be true?' he asks.

It's true, I say. I have her letters, the letters she sent year after year from Sugarmilk Falls. I tell him the things she told Thérèse about herself and the priest. How she really felt. How she could never bring herself to talk to him about me. How it wouldn't be or couldn't be punishment enough to tell. Or not to tell. How she never loved anyone as much. Or hated. How she won the land.

'Did she write anything about Zack Guillem?' he asks.

No, I reply.

I didn't know it myself, I tell him. I saw the letters for the first time recently, after Thérèse died. I always thought Marina Grochowska was an old friend of my mother who lived in another country far away. And it was only after Thérèse's death that Pierre, the great respecter of the truth, chose to acquaint me with the facts. Was I as appalled as Father Souris is now? Was the sudden revelation about a father and a mother as big a shock as my sudden appearance as his grown-up child?

And now I'm here, I say, to take possession of what is mine.

I speak. I explain. But the words are Pierre's.

'He had no right!' Father Souris exclaims in anger.

No, I agree, but Pierre did what he decided was right at the time. Marina had all but died. The captain had abandoned her; he didn't know about me. She had no other realistic choice. And it was what her friend Thérèse desperately wanted. Marina could not bear the deception. She could not bear to stay in Paris. She studied and worked and sent money. It was the best thing they could do for me in the circumstances. And I tell him my life has been happy and good.

But, I say, now I have come to find answers, to collect what's due. Marina's letters stopped long ago. I came to find my mother; instead I came across her murder. I learned she left everything to me.

We talk together long into the night.

Come tomorrow and we'll talk some more, Father Souris says at last. He needs time to get used to the idea, he says. Time to pray. Time to remember. Time to regret.

After all, it isn't often you are faced with something like this.

I am beginning to like him. He can tell me all about Marina. Okay, Matt, I say. I already feel I can call him that and I take my leave. I look forward to getting to know him.

*

Father Souris meets me at the presbytery door. He stands determined, ready to face the challenge I have brought. He welcomes me inside. He begins to speak. 'Yes, I have what you want. They have been in my keeping for a very long time. Some were payments made to me, placed here on trust, and some just came my way. One way and another I have ended up with them all in my care. And yes, some came by way of Marina, but not everything.

'I have spent an anxious time praying for guidance. None came. It never does for me. I also received a warning not to let you see them, to do what I can to make sure you leave this place. It could lead to disaster, I was told. Would you do that to us?

'But this morning I decided to open the box where I keep everything. Here it all is. You can still smell the tobacco. These are Grand'mère's things, the sweetgrass, the medicine pouch, the amulets. Here is Marina's amber necklace, Baltic amber she said. It has the look and colour of unfiltered Sugarmilk syrup. Take it. This, at least, belongs to you.

'And these are the papers you've come for. But I am not sure they too are yours. You have listened to Lucien Armand and the others, and I'll bet he kept you at it, making spiles. You'll have some idea how they came to me.

But I have to tell you they are not mine, though they are for me to dispose of, and the time for that seems to have arrived. Grand'mère said it would. But where to place them? Who has the best claim? Rachelle? A long time ago Grand'mère asked me to find her so that Henri's things could be passed on to her. She couldn't be traced, though I suppose I should have tried harder. Bobby, then? Or Louis, maybe? They have at least as much right to them as you. A better one, if you take the view there is nothing here that Marina won. She died for nothing. If it were up to me I would burn them all. They were meant to be burned but a life was lost to save them from the flames. I should hand them over to the archbishop but the Church has too much mammon as it is. Or I could give them to Ed Perriault and they would be exploited wisely to benefit us all. And what the Anstalts and others wouldn't give to have them, with these land claims pending.

'So how do I choose among the alternatives? How do I act wisely? Pierre Jaccard, who was a true father to you, once told me I should always act in such a way that it demonstrates to the world what I believe is the best way to live your life. But how do I decide which is best? There is no way to choose. There is no single set of criteria by which to decide which option is to have a greater value than the rest. Each one is best in its own way. Everything is subjective. What then is the way to be wise now?

'This is what I'll do instead. I'll be wise in another way, in the way of someone Marina used to scoff at. She was a little afraid, as I was, of the one she used to call a primitive tribal witch doctor, but she wouldn't admit it. Your mother was well educated but her imagination could be narrow. What I'll do is follow Grand'mère's intuitive wisdom. We'll leave everything to chance. You put what you want most up against what we in Sugarmilk Falls want most, and we'll play for it. If you win, everything here is yours. If you lose you must leave this place and never return. I'll see to it the papers are put back in Osweken hands. If you lose, maybe you know enough to have the case re-opened, to implicate us all, to point the finger at this one and that one, at me your father? So you could say you win even if you lose, but I'll take that risk. You know enough to devastate this whole community but for what they're worth the documents will be safe.'

Father Souris smiles. He reaches into the black tin box and hands me Grand'mère's dice.

I was not expecting it to be easy. It's a bet, I say.

ACKNOWLEDGEMENTS

The characters and events in *Sugarmilk Falls* are all fictitious, as is the vast region in which they live. Although they reflect some of my own experience, I have also drawn from others' encounters with the Canadian wilderness. Among these, the publications of Professor A. Irving Hallowell, who studied the Ojibwa people of eastern Manitoba during the early to mid-twentieth century, have been particularly inspirational. *Culture and Experience* is a collection of his papers.

Many publications were important in my research, including *The Shaman* by John A. Grim. His discussion of the shamanic trance experience is the basis for Grand'mère's chant. Henri's farewell to Flora follows similar prayers recorded by the anthropologist Ruth Landes in *Ojibwa Religion and the Midewiwin*. Charlie's version of the traditional blues ballad 'Saint James Infirmary' is similar to one performed by Louis Armstrong in 1928. Grey Owl's *Men of the Last Frontier* influences Zack's moose hunt. M. W. Von Bernewitz's *Handbook for Prospectors* and Alice Payne's *Quin Kola* cover aspects of mining exploration in northern Canada. *The Dispossessed* by Geoffrey York gives a troubling overview of contemporary Canadian First Nation conditions. Fifty years were lifted from the face of the Paris I am familiar with by A. Beevor and A. Cooper's *Paris After the Liberation 1944–1949*. Mathieu and Pierre's café discussion is based on the philosophical ideas Sartre set out in his public lecture of October 1945, as published in *Existentialism and Human Emotions* by Jean-Paul Sartre.

Several legal decisions have provided valuable insights into the background to competing land rights. Examples are the Canadian Federal Court's reasoning in *Hamlet of Baker Lake* v. *Ministry of Indian Affairs and Northern Development*, which concerns Inuit title to a remote area far north and west of where Sugarmilk Falls would be if it existed, and the Ontario High Court's judgment in *Attorney-General for Ontario* v. *Bear Island Foundation*, which involves a four thousand square mile Indian land claim in the north of the province.

Many people have been generous with their help and encouragement, especially Ian Mills, David Greenacre, Jim Sutton, Valerie Foster, Elizabeth Taylor, Rosemary Smith, Jane and Sophie Hughes, Rowan Routh, Roman Zenzer and the staff at my local branch of the Essex Library Service. The Crime Writers' Association must be mentioned; without them this book might never have been written. Thanks also to Peter Straus and Maria Rejt for their ever positive comments and suggestions, and for taking the risk.

Finally, a special heartfelt thank you to Harvey Perkins.